FRANCES F
THALI,

FRANCES FAVIELL (1905-1959) was the pen name of Olivia Faviell Lucas, painter and author. She studied at the Slade School of Art in London under the aegis of Leon Underwood. In 1930 she married a Hungarian academic and travelled with him to India where she lived for some time at the ashram of Rabindranath Tagore, and visiting Nagaland. She then lived in Japan and China until having to flee from Shanghai during the Japanese invasion. She met her second husband Richard Parker in 1939 and married him in 1940.

She became a Red Cross volunteer in Chelsea during the Phoney War. Due to its proximity to the Royal Hospital and major bridges over the Thames Chelsea was one of the most heavily bombed areas of London. She and other members of the Chelsea artists' community were often in the heart of the action, witnessing or involved in fascinating and horrific events throughout the Blitz. Her experiences of the time were later recounted in the memoir *A Chelsea Concerto* (1959).

After the war, in 1946, she went with her son, John, to Berlin where Richard had been posted as a senior civil servant in the post-war British Administration (the CCG). It was here that she befriended the Altmann Family, which prompted her first book *The Dancing Bear* (1954), a memoir of the Occupation seen through the eyes of both occupier and occupied. She later wrote three novels, *A House on the Rhine* (1955), *Thalia* (1957), and *The Fledgeling* (1958). These are now all available as Furrowed Middlebrow books.

BY FRANCES FAVIELL

FICTION

A House on the Rhine (1955)
Thalia (1957)
The Fledgeling (1958)

MEMOIR

The Dancing Bear (1954)
A Chelsea Concerto (1959)

FRANCES FAVIELL

THALIA

With an Afterword
by John Parker

DEAN STREET PRESS
A Furrowed Middlebrow Book

A Furrowed Middlebrow Book
FM7

Published by Dean Street Press 2016

Copyright © 1957 Frances Faviell
Afterword copyright © 2016 John Parker

All Rights Reserved

The right of Frances Faviell to be identified as the Author
of the Work has been asserted by her estate in accordance
with the Copyright, Designs and Patents Act 1988.

Cover by DSP

First published in 1957 by Cassell & Co. Ltd.

ISBN 978 1 911413 83 7

www.deanstreetpress.co.uk

For

Sir Ernest Rock Carling

But when, unmasked, gay Comedy appears,
How wan her cheeks are, what heavy tears.

> from *Thalia*, THOMAS BAILEY ALDRICH

AUTHOR'S NOTE

THE DINARD of *Thalia* is the Dinard of almost twenty years ago when the little seaside town had a flourishing colony of Anglo-American residents. Although I have used the names of the streets and local places which to-day are almost unchanged, the names and characters in this novel are fictitious, and do not refer to any living persons.

PART I

CHAPTER I

WHEN THE CAR was approaching the docks I looked at my aunt and it seemed to me that this—a profile—was all we ever knew of anyone. We can never know all the aspects but merely those which are shown to us. Was she as lonely as I was? She appeared suddenly such a small person and one at whom I had never really looked.

Taking a packet from her handbag she said crisply, 'This is for emergencies. You never know in a foreign country. I remember being in France when we went off the Gold Standard. It was chaotic! Now where are you going to keep this? You lose everything.' Her voice and manner were matter-of-fact, devoid of any feeling, but to my own astonishment I was flooded with some violent emotion and couldn't speak.

She watched me struggling with tears. 'There are five-pound notes in this packet, Rachel. Here's the address of my London bank. They'll always know where I am. You can write to me at Cairo, Alexandria, and Luxor. A letter to Port Said should reach me on the journey.'

I took the packet reluctantly. My aunt never gave anything graciously. Perhaps that was why I found it difficult to feel gratitude. 'You're too good to me. I don't deserve it.' She looked surprised and gratified. 'No, I don't think you do. But it would be a poor world if we only got what we deserved.'

I said I was sorry—sorry about everything.

'If you were really sorry you'd have apologized and come with us to Egypt.'

Her acid tone dried my tears, scorching them as if with a hot wind. Why couldn't she see that it was possible to be sorry without the formality of expressing it all in speech? That there were degrees in remorse I had already learned.

I watched her figure recede as the boat drew away from the quay. She didn't look back once, and for one split second the strangest feeling of sudden terror overwhelmed me; then I thrust it away, and went up on to the top deck where I sat up in the bows on a coil of rope. The boat was the *St. Briac*. It was a fine clear night and sheltered here from the wind. A large party of hikers were discussing plans. The craze for walking about with a rucksack, clad in the strangest if most utilitarian of garments, had spread from Germany. The men in this party wore shorts—the girls shorts or slacks. A number of large young women were leaning over the rails, their rear views presenting a solid challenge. I reflected that whereas nude their buttocks could have been beautiful, compressed thus into tight material they were hideous.

A tall, attractive man who had been looking at me for some time suddenly threw away his cigarette and came over to me. 'Mind if I sit down there too? Those enthusiasts are making me footsore with their indefatigable journeys on their maps.'

I said I didn't mind.

'You're alone, aren't you?' he went on. 'I saw you being seen off.'

It was as light as day but with the milky elusiveness of moonlight. I saw that his hair, which I had thought dark, was red, and that the backs of his hands were covered with fine red hairs. I thought it a pity—I don't like red-haired men.

'Cigarette?'

I said I didn't smoke. After the usual exchange of platitudes on the night and the stars he asked me bluntly where I was going. He was clever at putting me quickly at ease, and I began telling him of the recent illness which had interrupted my art training at the Slade and which necessitated my being out of London for the forthcoming winter.

'I shouldn't have thought Brittany would be exactly the place for you,' he said, when I told him I was to spend the winter in Dinard. 'You should be going with the lady who saw you off. I heard her talking to you about Egypt.'

And then I began telling him about the disastrous portrait of our vicar, the Reverend Cookson-Cander. I told him how I hadn't wanted to do it but that my aunt had insisted—of how I disliked the pompous little man—and of how the painting in spite of my efforts grew with each sitting more and more like a disagreeable egg. I could still feel the smart of the furious criticism which had been hurled at me by the admiring ladies of the 'Friends of the Past' circle who had commissioned the portrait from me.

I could still hear my aunt's 'It's outrageous!' when I had reluctantly pulled the coverings off the canvas and displayed it in the scented luxury of her crowded drawing-room.

My companion was much amused at my description of my sitter.

'I gather that you didn't like him?' he said laughing.

'No,' I admitted. 'But he's a wonderful lecturer. I enjoyed his lectures on the Valley of the Nile because we did Egyptian Art at the Slade last winter. He was very enthusiastic about the Amarna period and the Amarna theory—the "Living in Truth"—but when I embodied those ideals in my portrait of him—he just couldn't accept it.'

'"Living in Truth"!' exclaimed my fellow traveller, looking down at me as I huddled into my coat collar. 'How young you are if you can believe in such things. God, I remember having the same impossible ideas once.'

'Akhenaten didn't think them impossible!' I retorted. 'He achieved a tremendous amount. He built the Town of the Horizon.'

'And lost it all through his intolerance. Don't forget that!'

'I like his ideals,' I insisted. 'And I intend to try to follow them.'

'Akhenaten was himself deformed. You'll become one of those wretched salt-of-the-earth women who tell everyone their faults from a distorted idea of truth.'

I was angry and pulled away my hand which he had been lightly holding.

Go on. Tell me some more,' he said teasingly.

'More what?' I was offended.

'*Why* are you going to Dinard? Is your aunt a follower of the "Living in Truth"?'

'No, she isn't,' I said, thinking of her anger over my explanation of the failure of the portrait, and of her ultimatum to me. 'Do another portrait—a conventional one—if you want to join the party to the Nile Valley.' I had refused.

'You live with your aunt?'

'She gives me a home while I'm at the Slade.'

'But you still haven't told me why you're going to Dinard.'

'My aunt wouldn't take me with her to Egypt unless I apologized to the vicar and did another portrait so I'm going to a family in Dinard.'

'An English family or a French one?'

'English.'

'You don't sound very enthusiastic.'

'I hate having to interrupt my studies. I want to be a painter. It takes years. I'm not experienced enough to accept portrait commissions. I should never have accepted the one of the vicar—but my aunt insisted.'

'You're going to young people?'

'I'm going as companion to the daughter of a friend of my aunt's. I've only met her once at a club in London.'

'You're very courageous,' he said, taking my hand again. 'Suppose you don't get on with them?'

'I shall run away.'

'But your aunt's going to Egypt.'

'I shall go to my father in Devonshire.'

'Tell me about *him*.'

I told him how disappointed I had been in Father. How he hadn't understood any more than my aunt had. He said I had been silly to tell the vicar that I had painted him as I saw him—like a pompous egg. He had urged me to apologize. My father, in order to indulge his love of fishing, lived on the wilds of Dartmoor. Fish and their elusive habits were far more real to him than people.

'So this family you're going to are really strangers to you?'

'My aunt knows them quite well,' I said shortly. I was remembering the woman to whom I was now going as I had seen her in the ladies' annexe of a famous military club in London. The memory was not reassuring. Superbly dressed in tweeds, her hands busy with the tea cups, her eyes had been at once watchful, aware and appraising as I answered her many questions.

There had been no mirror in the falsely cosy drawing-room but I had been as aware of my badly hung skirt, my untidy hair and unsuitable borrowed hat as if I could see my own reflection in her beautiful guarded eyes. I was being appraised and weighed as a possible companion for her young daughter Thalia.

'Thalia's a difficult girl,' she had said doubtfully. 'And you look terribly young.'

'Thalia... Thalia.... What a lovely, lovely name!' I had rolled it on my tongue. She had said indifferently that the choice had been her husband's, not hers.

Thalia was fifteen—three years younger than I. There was a little boy aged six and a half. When his mother mentioned him her face had come alive and into her cold, clipped voice there had come a sudden warmth and colour.

When I had asked my aunt about this friend Mrs. Pemberton all she had said was, 'Her father was a very famous general. She's been brought up in the tradition of a great military family. She's a woman who would never fail in her duty—something you'd do well to emulate, Rachel.'

I was suddenly embarrassed at talking so freely to a stranger. My aunt had warned me not to talk to foreigners. Would she have included Irishmen in this category? On whom did she think I should use the French and German I had learned in the expensive finishing school she'd sent me to in Switzerland?

The stewardess coming up looking for me prevented any further talk. She was determined on doing her duty by me. I said good night.

'I know that gentleman. He's often on the boat. He lives in Dinard. You'll see plenty of him. He's Captain the Hon. Terence Mourne,' she said as she hustled me below.

'The Hon. Terence Mourne.' I liked the name.

'He's a good-looking man. I'll grant you that. And he's kept his figure. But he's old enough to be your father. He'll risk lumbago to sit up all night with a young thing. Your aunt didn't tip me for nothing. You'd best get to bed, Miss.'

I was somewhat abashed at her information. I had thought he had found me intelligent. If it was merely youth which attracted him I couldn't claim credit for that.

'I'd like some brandy, please,' I said.

'You're not ill, are you?' she asked in astonishment. 'It's as calm as a mill pond.'

My aunt never allowed me to drink spirits. It always fell to me to offer brandy and liqueurs to guests after Janet the parlourmaid had withdrawn. I was already an expert at savouring their perfume without having sampled their flavour.

'What kind will you have?'

'Courvoisier'—I asked her to have one with me.

She departed, amused, to get them.

Before I climbed into my bunk I untied the flat parcel my aunt had thrust into my hands just as she was leaving. It proved to be a sampler which I had admired in an antique shop we'd visited in Southampton. Worked in fine cross-stitch bordered with a faded design of flowers and animals were these words:

> How pleasant it is at the end of the day
> No folly to have to repent.
> To reflect on the past and be able to say,
> This day has been properly spent.
>
> Elizabeth Jane Walker,
> aged 8 years and 3 months.

The date was 1782.

As I sipped the Courvoisier I did some reflecting. Had she really wished to give me pleasure by giving me the sampler? Or had she intended it to serve a double purpose? Thinking again of the appalling scene over that disastrous portrait it seemed that the latter was the more likely.

We were already in the bay of St. Malo when I woke on the Sunday morning. Through the porthole the great ramparts of the walled city of the old corsairs rose out of the mist like some lovely and impossible mirage. An elusive quality in the light—a cobwebby shimmering veil—made it appear to be suspended in the vastness of the sea and sky like a fairy city. I had never seen anything so beautiful.

When I went on deck the *St. Briac* lay beside the quay, which was crowded with people waiting for the arrival of the boat. The babel of excitement between those on the quay and those waiting to disembark, their interchange of chaff and greetings in both French and English, fascinated me. I had hitherto only passed through France on my way to school in Switzerland. Now I was actually going to live in it.

Terence Mourne, who was standing near me, inquired after my night's rest, and whether I was to be met. He looked fresh and alert in spite of his lazy manner. I was searching the crowd on the quay for Mrs. Pemberton. Suddenly I saw her waving to me. She was standing a little apart from the crowd with a tall man, a little boy and a tall girl.

'They've come to meet me. Look!' I cried, waving back.

He gave a start of surprise, and muttered something which sounded like 'impossible'. 'Is *that* the family to whom you are going?' he asked harshly.

'Yes.'

'Does your aunt know Cynthia Pemberton well?'

'*You* know them?' I said, surprised. I hadn't mentioned the name Pemberton to him.

'Does your aunt know Cynthia well?' he repeated.

'I don't know.' I was nettled at his insistence.

'Damn!' he said. 'Oh, *damn!*' and then apologized.

'*You* know them then?'

He didn't answer and from his sudden peculiar change of attitude I didn't like to pursue the question. A closed, watchful look had taken the place of the former nonchalant one on his face. I was intrigued—but at the same time apprehensive. What was this? What was the matter? He had been so attentive and anxious to see that I was being safely met, and now when he knew by whom he had completely changed. I was upset at his strangeness.

We were preparing to disembark, crowded together waiting for the gangway to go down. He was smoking rapidly—one cigarette after another—and I saw that one of his long, sensitive hands was shaking a little.

'How long have the Pembertons been here?' he asked.

'Only a week.'

'Which villa have they taken?'

I told him the name of the villa.

'We'll be meeting again. Dinard society is very limited—as you'll discover—and you may need a friend.'

He put so much emphasis on this last remark that I was very uneasy. What did he mean? I thanked him perfunctorily, resenting his desire to detract from my pleasure in the first exciting impressions of the place. What was he trying to do? To put me off the family or the place?

I turned resolutely away. It *was* exciting. Wonderfully alive and different with the grey forbidding ramparts with their towers and spires, the masts of the idle fishing boats, the funnels of the ships and *vedettes* and small steamers, the gulls swooping and screaming above the shouting porters. The swarthy fishermen standing about with their wives in their Sunday clothes had a dignity which was enchanting; and above all the light in the sky—something which was to delight me during my whole stay here.

A sudden surge of excitement so great that it threatened to burst my lungs assailed me. I turned back to Terence Mourne.

'Isn't it *wonderful*?'

'Think so?' he said dryly. 'Wait until you live here—it's pretty dull.'

Dull? I thought he must be a very stupid person to find this place dull.

'Why d'you live here then?' I asked tartly.

'For the same reason that the Pembertons and the rest of the Anglo-American colony do—because it's cheap.'

The gangway was now in position and we were being pushed down it by the surge of passengers. An enormous sailor hoisted my trunk and suitcases on to his back and was bawling something to me from the quay.

Come along. He's telling you he'll see you in the Customs shed. I'll see you through.'

I didn't think that Mrs. Pemberton was very pleased at finding that I had already made a friend on the journey. She greeted me warmly enough, introducing me to her husband and the children, then turning to my companion she paused, held out her hand and said formally, 'My brother wrote me that you are living here now. I've already met several friends who were in India. Tom, isn't this a surprise? Who would have expected to meet Terence here?'

To me she said: 'We were once all stationed in the same place in India.'

The two men, both very tall, shook hands stiffly. They were eyeing each other as my aunt's spaniels eyed strange canines. I sensed immediately that whereas to Colonel Pemberton this meeting with Terence Mourne was completely unexpected, to his wife it was, in spite of her words, no surprise. And yet she was momentarily disconcerted. I was intrigued that this woman who, in London, had been so cool, poised and distant that she had put me at an immediate disadvantage was now herself uncertain and at a loss. But it was only for a moment. She recovered herself quickly and thanked Terence Mourne for having looked after me on the boat. He looked at her with the same suppressed cynical amusement with which he regarded me—but said nothing.

Colonel Pemberton said stiffly: 'It'll be nice for Cynthia to have you here, Terence. I'm off in a few days—back to the regiment. My leave's almost up.'

'Thank God I've finished with all that,' Terence Mourne said lightly, and he and Colonel Pemberton busied themselves with the baggage.

I had turned to the two children, who were staring at me with unabashed interest. Thalia shook hands formally. She was, as my aunt had said, a very plain girl, and at the worst age. She had dull mousy hair worn in two thin, untidy tails, eyes which didn't stay quiet, a long but straight nose and a sulky mouth. She was covered in freckles—not the pretty powdery kind but ugly brown patchy ones, and was all arms and legs like a spider, and had a stoop as if she were afraid of her height. But when, after studying me gravely, she suddenly smiled, her whole face changed as if a high-light had transformed a dull patch of colour.

The little boy, Claude, offered me a demure hand. He looked an angel with his mother's golden hair in tangled curls and her violet-blue eyes, but his chin and mouth were astonishingly firm, and the look with which he appraised me from under sweeping black lashes showed me that he was already a person with whom one would have to reckon. A disturbing child—and in spite of his striking beauty he sent a little shiver through me.

We stood on the quay waiting for the porters to bring the baggage. Before we turned to board the *vedette* which the children told me would take us to Dinard I saw as in one of those hyper-sharp silhouettes this family group. Lovely mother, lovely son, plain father and the still plainer daughter who was somehow out of focus. Against the grey ramparts and the swirling wings of the gulls they looked curiously out of place—even alien; whereas the tall lounging form and amused sardonic face of Terence Mourne fitted into this background quite perfectly.

When we were all piled in the *vedette* with the baggage, waiting to set off across the bay, I saw that Terence Mourne had been claimed by a gay party of French people and was in the other *vedette*.

'He's gone in the green one,' screamed Claude. 'I hope we'll race him! I hope we'll win.' He was jumping up and down with excitement. A strong wind was rising and the water was quite choppy. The little boat rocked like a cockleshell and Mrs. Pemberton looked pale and uneasy.

'She's going to be sick,' announced Claude hopefully. 'She *almost* was coming. Are you sick too, Rachel? I'm not, but when I see Mummy sick then it makes me sick and that makes Thalia sick . . .' He paused for breath and I said firmly that I was never sick.

'But you've never been on big boats to India, so you don't know.'

I said I'd been often on small yachts and Channel steamers and that as they didn't make me sick I saw no reason why big liners should.

Claude was unconvinced. 'Can you sail a boat?' he demanded.

'If it's a small one, yes.'

'All by yourself?'

'Yes.'

'Can you row?'

'I can get along.'

'And swim. Can you swim?'

I said I'd been able to swim since I was six.

'I'm six and a half and I can't swim,' he said resentfully. Can you teach me? Mummy can't swim and there were sharks and crocodiles in India so we couldn't learn. You've never seen sharks and crocodiles, have you?'

'Only in the Zoo,' I said mildly.

'If you were in India and you went swimming you'd soon be eaten up. They'd scrunch you up bones and all—nothing left but your wrist-watch which they couldn't digest!'

'Shut up, Claude, you're enough to make us sick. . . . Don't talk like that—it's babyish.' Thalia was looking determinedly away from her mother, who was holding smelling salts under her nose.

They pointed out the landmarks as we went across the bay. The sun was now out strongly and the water the clear, translucent green of my favourite colour, emerald oxide of chromium. Waves were splashing right over the small *vedette* as, rocking violently, she chugged her way through them.

'There's St. Servan! There's Paramé! There's the Rance up there on your left! Up there is La Vicomté. It's lovely. You'll see it to-morrow.' Thalia was pointing out the lovely wooded slopes of the Rance.

'Here's Dinard! Here's where we get off. See the lift up from the *vedettes*?' screamed Claude excitedly. 'Ooh! Look, we're racing the green *vedette*. Go it, white one! Come on, white one! Good! We've won.'

And so, with both children hanging on my arm, and the parents following slowly behind, we stepped on to the Bee at Dinard—one minute ahead of our green pursuer. From the gangway of the other *vedette* Terence Mourne waved good-bye.

CHAPTER II

THE VILLA was right above the sea on the St. Enogat side of the coast. Standing well back from the road it was almost hidden behind a great hedge of fuchsias and hydrangeas. Amongst the wealth of tamarisks, oleanders and mimosas in the garden I was surprised and enchanted to see palm trees. The house itself, of grey stone, was rather ugly, but mimosas climbed all over it and even now on September 1st were mingled with tea roses, both blooming as if it were early summer. The path to the front door was of white pebbles. At the back—the sea side of the house—were terraces of white pebbles with clumps of yuccas and more palms. The lowest terrace ended in a stone wall with an iron gate set in it. From this gate steps had been cut in the living rock down to the beach below.

It was to this last terrace that the children led me as soon as I'd been shown all over the villa.

'The steps are always slippery,' warned Thalia, holding on to Claude, who was struggling to free himself from her grip. 'At high tide the waves come right over them—and when there's a storm they dash right over this wall!'

'Thalia! Thalia!' called Cynthia's voice. 'How many times have I told you that you're not allowed on those steps?'

Thalia was holding the great iron key of the gate in her hand and Claude suddenly snatched it from her.

'Give it back. At once. Give it back.' Thalia launched herself upon Claude and they began struggling violently. I caught Thalia by the arm. 'Stop it. You'll both slip.' But as Colonel Pemberton had come to the gate I let her go.

'Claude, give me that key. At once!' His voice was stern. The child swallowed back something he was about to shout at his sister, and giving her a push ran up the steps to his father. Thalia staggered on the slippery step, recovered her balance and, very pale, with her freckles standing out like livid stains, clung to me. For one awful moment I felt myself swaying—then I recovered my balance too.

I expected to see Claude punished for this. Thalia had all but fallen below, taking me with her—and as I looked down at the savage rocks I felt sick and faint. It would have been an unpleasant introduction to the beach. I pulled her down on to a seat as we regained the terrace. She was still pale and upset. Colonel Pemberton was rebuking Claude sharply until the studiedly dulcet tones of his wife cut him short. 'He doesn't understand how dangerous it is—how can he? Don't say too much, Tom. He didn't mean to push her. He just wanted the key.'

'He did it on purpose. You saw him. So did Rachel.' Thalia's voice was shaky. 'You always defend him. Little beast.'

'Rachel, I'm sorry about this. I'm going to leave this key in your charge. Neither Thalia nor Claude is to touch it. If you use the steps—and at low tide you'll want to—I trust to your good sense to see that this gate is always kept locked.' He locked the gate and handed the great key to me. I didn't like being made responsible for it. 'I'll find somewhere where it shall be hung. Somewhere high and out of reach,' I said. 'It's too heavy to carry about—and I might lose it.'

We found an old hook in the hall so high up that I could only reach it standing on a chair.

'No one may take down this key except your mother and Rachel—d'you understand, Claude?'

'Yes.'

'Then give me your word that you'll never try and unlock this gate.'

'I won't.'

'You mean you won't promise?'

'No. It's silly to ask me. You know I can't reach that key—not even on two chairs one on top of th'other.'

Cynthia Pemberton laughed delightedly.

His father didn't look so pleased.

'Thalia,' he said, 'this applies to you too. You're not to use these steps to the beach unless Rachel is with you. Will you give me your word?'

Thalia hesitated, then she said slowly and pointedly, 'I'll give my word to *you*—but to no one else.'

Her mother merely shrugged her shoulders impatiently. 'If you've given your word to your father that's sufficient. There's no need to dramatize it.'

The gong sounded, and we all went in to lunch.

The *salon* and the *salle-à-manger* were on the ground floor, separated by sliding doors of glass. The *salon* was papered in hideous broad stripes of crimson and pale blue and had gilt furniture. The walls of the *salle-à-manger* were even uglier in bilious citrous yellow and purple, but its huge windows opened on to the lawn of the overgrown front garden. We sat around a heavy oak table and a bold-eyed young girl handed the plates and dishes. She had been introduced to me as Madeleine and was for the moment the '*bonne à tout faire*'.

'We shall have to teach her to do this properly,' Cynthia Pemberton said to me as Madeleine served us all familiarly with a nudge and giggle for Thalia and a pat on the head for Claude. I thought it charming after Janet's stiff prim service at my aunt's.

'It was very clever of you to find her, she does very well. It's no use your trying to get the same service here as you had in India,' said Colonel Pemberton.

The food seemed excellent to me, but Cynthia found fault with it—so did Claude.

'It's not cooked in the way he's accustomed to,' excused his mother. 'To-morrow I'll get you to have a talk with Madeleine for me, Rachel. It'll be such a help having you to speak the language for me. I don't know a word of French. Hindustani's quite another matter, I can get along in that.'

Madeleine came in at that moment to say that my baggage had arrived and Colonel Pemberton and I went into the hall. There stood the old man with the wide black hat I'd seen when we'd stepped from the *vedette*. He had a horse and cart and had offered to bring up my things. There were only two taxis on the quay and both had been taken. He immediately began a long conversation with me. Had we all the help we needed in the villa?

'No,' said Colonel Pemberton. 'Cynthia really needs a cook. Madeleine's only cooking to oblige.' He explained to me how difficult it was to get service in the villas. In addition to the large Anglo-American colony there were so many hotels and *pensions*.

'The best cook in Dinard is my sister Marie,' said the old man, 'but she'll only work for those she likes.'

'Where is she?' I asked.

'At home—where else would she be on a Sunday?' he said simply.

'Tell her to come up as soon as she can so that we can talk to her,' said the Colonel in his halting French.

He said he would tell his sister. His name was Yves Duro and his sister was Marie Duro.

'Is she old?' I asked.

'Compared with you, mademoiselle, she is old—but not too old to do a good day's cleaning and cook a perfect meal.'

'I want to see the horse, I want to see the horse,' shouted Claude, escaping from the dining table.

'I'm afraid his manners are pretty awful,' apologized his father. 'He's been brought up by an Indian ayah and Indian servants and he's very spoiled.'

I liked old Yves. He had a wrinkled face like a chimpanzee and spoke in a curious way, mixing some strange words with the French ones. I supposed they were Breton. He was devoted to his horse, Napoleon, who could count up to twelve and would knock with his hoof the correct number of times.

When we returned to the dining-room, Madeleine was placing cheese and fruit on the table.

'Ask her where Claude's milk pudding is,' said Cynthia. I asked. Madeleine looked astonished. 'I didn't know what she meant so I didn't do it,' she said. She went out and began shouting at Yves. Shrieks of laughter amidst loud bumps came from the hall as they carried my trunks up the stairs.

Just as we were emerging from the room to go into the garden we saw Yves kissing Madeleine most efficiently on the bend of the staircase.

'These French!' said Cynthia disgustedly. 'Rachel, tell her we'll have coffee on the terrace and I don't want to see that sort of behaviour in my house.'

I looked up at the laughing rosy face of Madeleine. She had a teasing, taunting look in her dark eyes. It seemed a pity to interrupt her flirtation.

'Please bring the coffee on the terrace—and Madeleine—Madame doesn't approve of what you are doing. . . .'

'No?' she called, still laughing. 'She needn't envy me. Yves is a dirty old man!'

His answer to this was to seize her again until he realized that we were all watching in the hall. Then, with a hurried apology, he came down the stairs. As he passed us he said to the Colonel, 'You must excuse me, Monsieur, but if you have a girl like that in the house you must expect it.'

'Like *what*?' I asked.

'Like *her*,' he said cryptically, and taking the money for the baggage he went out of the gate.

It was very hot and still in the September sun, and to sit on the stone terrace under the palm trees with white pebbles under our feet and drinking our coffee to the rhythmic sound of the waves beating against the steps below seemed unbelievable to me. I looked at the water—blue now—as blue as the Mediterranean was on postcards—as blue surely as the Nile to which I was *not* going because of my behaviour. Well, not only my aunt had palm trees! I had them too—and yuccas. It was glorious!

Claude came dashing on to the terrace. 'I don't want to rest on my bed. I want Rachel to tell me a story.'

'Rachel's tired. She's travelled all night.'

'I'm not tired, Mrs. Pemberton,' I said. 'I'll tell him a story.'

'And Rachel, I think you'd better call me Cynthia—after all, I'm not so much older than you!'

I looked at her in amazement. She was incredibly beautiful—but not old? Her daughter was over fifteen. I was only eighteen. She could easily be my mother.

'Very well,' I said. 'If you like it that way.'

'And my husband. Call him Tom.'

He looked at me whimsically: 'Rachel can address me as she likes.'

He looked much older than Cynthia—but his figure was spare and upright like my father's. They are the sort of men who have no age because they've never grown up.

On the afternoon of his last day in Dinard, Tom Pemberton asked me to go for a walk with him. When Thalia wanted to accompany us he refused her gently. 'I wanted to have a talk with Rachel.'

I wondered if all Englishmen found it necessary to take exercise while discussing serious or emotional matters. I remembered how my father invariably took us fishing whenever he had anything unpleasant to say to us. The last expedition after the affair of the portrait had been particularly memorable. He had been talking to me while leaping from rock to rock casting upstream. His eyes had been far out following his fly, his hands busy with his reel. In spite of the difficulty of hearing what he said I could recall every one of his biting remarks.

We went this afternoon along the cliff walk round the steep sheer cliffs and up to a wild piece of ground, where under pines the bracken was thick and harebells and wild cornflowers grew. Here the path wound round the rock face with a sheer drop of thirty or forty feet to the beach below.

It was difficult to talk against the wind and watch one's feet carefully on the rough path, and when at last we sat down on some rocks, looking straight out to sea, Tom Pemberton said: 'I hope you're going to be happy here, Rachel, and that you'll look after Cynthia for me. She's not very strong, you know. That's the reason why she's not coming back with me to India this year. And don't spoil Claude. He's a headstrong child and needs a firm rein.'

I had found to my dismay that my aunt had said that I could teach Claude to read and write. I already disliked Claude. But I said nothing. I wasn't at all sure that I liked Cynthia.

'But it's about Thalia that I want to talk to you,' he said, turning to me with that same disarming smile which saved Thalia from ugliness. 'It was I who insisted on your coming here, Rachel. Life hasn't been very kind to my poor Thalia. She has been in a lot of trouble. You'll find her affectionate and loyal—if you'll try and win her confidence. She's a darling—but she's at some disadvantage. She just can't compete with her mother . . . and it seems she's backward in her education, although I find her disconcertingly clever.'

'She should be at boarding school,' I said abruptly.

'She was,' he said quietly. 'We tried two. She couldn't settle down and was so unhappy that they asked us to remove her.'

'And now?'

'She'll learn French here, and she's to share your Italian lessons. She likes drawing. It seemed the perfect chance when your aunt wrote to Cynthia and said that you had to go abroad for the winter. We knew you were studying art. Thalia really has some idea of drawing. You *will* do all you can for her, won't you? You can help her as no one else can. You're young—but you're just that much older than she is. And you're so gay! She likes you. I've heard her laughing more this week than since we left India. Make her laugh, Rachel. She used to laugh so much but now she takes everything so hard. Try and give her more confidence in herself.'

I could tell how much he loved this daughter who was so like him. He adored his wife and his handsome little son but this fear, this anguished love for Thalia moved me.

I wasn't pleased at being expected to be a kind of wet-nurse to his family. I had come here to get well. Not that I felt ill. I was resentful of the stupidity of the doctors in having interrupted my life at the Slade. But I hadn't come here to look after a family. Or had I? My father had pointed out the fact that I was entering into a contract. The first one I had undertaken.

'People don't invite you for a whole year just for the pleasure of your company,' he had said. 'You'll be expected to pull your weight. To give something to that girl. To help with that small boy. To cosset the woman. You've got plenty to give—the question is whether or not you'll give it.'

'But they're not paying me a salary,' I had objected.

'They're feeding and housing you—and paying your expenses,' he retorted, 'and you have a healthy appetite.'

He said this as I was piling cream and jam on my bread at the water bailiff's cottage that afternoon when he'd last taken me fishing.

It seemed that he was right. Colonel Pemberton obviously thought that I had made a bargain and he expected me to keep it. Taking my hands he said gently, 'I like you, Rachel. I like you very much. You're so frank and open about things. Stay like that. It'll get you into trouble sometimes . . . but . . .'

'It already has,' I interrupted. 'I should be in Egypt now if I hadn't said what I thought about a certain person.'

'I think it'll all turn out for the best, certainly for Thalia. If you'd gone to Egypt with your aunt, you couldn't have come here. Thalia needs a friend very badly. She has no one. I *can* count on you, can't I, Rachel? If anything goes wrong you can telegraph my sister. Here's her address. But you'll write to me, won't you? Air-mail letters reach us quite quickly now. I'd like you to let me know how Thalia is getting on at the British school here. And how Cynthia's health is. You *will*, won't you?'

I hesitated. He pulled me round so that I was facing him. 'Of course I will,' I said, feeling suddenly deeply ashamed of myself for the hesitation.

'And you'll be good to my Thalia? You'll try and become real friends?'

'I promise to be *very* good to Thalia,' I said gravely—and I meant it.

The night her father left for Marseilles I heard Thalia weeping. Her room was next door to mine, above Cynthia's and Claude's. Thalia and I were on the top floor. Our rooms had sloping eaves and a magnificent view of the sea. A third room on our floor was for the maids.

I slept in a huge double bed carved in Breton style. The cupboards were old and carved in the same way. I loved my room. At night the many lighthouses flashed their revolving beacons on to my bed, and in the morning I could put my head out of the windows and smell the mimosa and the late jasmine on the walls of the villa.

I went to Thalia's door and knocked softly. A muffled 'Come in,' answered me. She was lying buried in the same kind of bed as mine, her face hidden in the great square pillows. 'Thalia . . . Thalia . . .' I whispered. She put out a hand but did not raise her face.

'Is it your father?' I asked gently.

'He's gone to that beastly place. And all alone,' she cried bitterly. 'I wanted so much to go with him . . . I can look after him better than anyone can. He oughtn't to go alone . . . I'll never see him again. *Never.*'

'Thalia!' I cried sharply. 'What nonsense. Supposing I cried like this because I've had to leave my father. Pull yourself together now!'

She sat up in bed. The shutters were open, and every twenty seconds or so the beacon of one of the many lighthouses on that lonely, treacherous coast flashed its light across her white face. I studied her curiously, her face half lost in shadow and its sharp outlines lit vividly by the flashing light, and I decided that the Old Masters would have made her quite beautiful in a painting. If you dissect most of the world-famous portraits the subjects are very ugly. It is the knowledge of the trick of lighting which creates beauty. I was so interested in my discovery that I found it difficult to concentrate on the shaking misery I was regarding. And then her voice intruded on my reflections. 'Rachel . . . Rachel. . . .' Just at that moment the lighthouse beacon caught her and showed me her long nose and the red blotchy eyes and cheeks. 'She's really ugly—like a mouse . . .' I thought disgustedly and I couldn't bear to touch her, so that when she suddenly clutched me and buried her wet face in my shoulder I felt a violent revulsion. But my promise to her father was still fresh with me and I patted her harsh mousy hair. She snuggled her face up against my neck and I could feel her whole body shaking with sobs.

The door opened suddenly and Cynthia was framed in the doorway. She wore a pale blue ruffled négligée and her golden hair hung down in two long plaits. Her blue eyes were dark now.

'Thalia!' she said harshly. 'What do you mean by this childish behaviour? You're a soldier's daughter. Get off her bed, Rachel, and leave her alone. If I hear you making any more noise, Thalia, I shall punish you. Go to sleep.'

'She's unhappy about her father going,' I said angrily. 'She can't help it.'

'There's no such word as "can't help it" for a soldier's daughter any more than there is for a soldier's wife,' she said sternly. 'Go back to bed, Rachel. Good night.'

I waited until she had closed her door, and then I stole back to Thalia. It was chilly with the night air coming in the wide open windows. She was crying silently with her face buried again, her shoulders shaking with her sobs. I climbed into the great bed and pulled her head on to my shoulder. I hated the touch of her body against mine but I felt a profound pity for her. I held her close until her sobs grew quieter and then I found to my amazement that I was crying too—and so we fell asleep.

CHAPTER III

SUDDENLY the season was ended. Gone were the visitors from the *plage*, the hotels, the *pensions*, the shops and the cafés. They seemed to have departed in one great flash. Overnight from the crowded noisy beaches and streets there was a silence, then a few days of furious activity everywhere. Chattering, singing young girls throwing blankets over the balconies and cleaning furniture on the terraces and in narrow streets behind hotels and *pensions*; older women grumbling as they scrubbed floors and tables and wiped out drawers and cupboards before shutting them away for the winter. Then overnight the whole great sweeping arc of hotels on the promenade of the Plage de l'Ecluse presented a dead, closed face. The heavily shuttered windows looking on to flowerless, flagless terraces stripped of tables, chairs and umbrellas gave a curious blind look to the great deserted *plage*. Only the residents themselves came now in the afternoon sun with their children, grandchildren and friends. The Casino and the Hotel Crystal remained open, and some of the smaller hotels and *pensions* which catered for the British and Americans—but they were few compared with the great mass of those closed for the winter.

'Now it's our own town. Now it's the Dinard we love,' said the residents. The shopkeepers were not so pleased. Many of them closed too. Life was settling to a routine for me. Cynthia wished me to take over the shopping. It was useless to explain to her that in a French household the *bonne* expected to do the shopping and got some small rake-off from the stall-holders, and that Madeleine would resent it. Cynthia was adamant. All French shopkeepers cheated —it was no use my telling her that she only thought so because she couldn't understand the language. 'It's the same as in India. I never allowed the cook to do the shopping,' she said firmly. 'Other women did so—they were abominably cheated.'

'No,' intervened Thalia suddenly. 'You were cheated, Mother, because you wouldn't let Ali go to the bazaar.' She explained to me in detail the system of marketing in India. 'The cook always does the shopping. He gets a *dasturi* from all the stall-holders—and if they don't get the custom he still has to pay them. It's a kind of blackmail.'

Yes, I thought, Cynthia must have been a very unpopular mem-sahib—and she was going to be an equally unpopular one here if she did not allow the *bonne* to do the marketing.

So I went every day with Madeleine to the market where the fish, the meat, the vegetables and the eggs were all mixed up with necklaces, brooches, materials, sabots, rosaries and crucifixes. Madeleine was treated with a curious familiarity of affectionate contempt by the men and with indifference by the women. They looked from her to me and laughed and sniggered. I wondered what was the matter but Madeleine seemed to me to be an excellent market woman. She bargained in a way I knew I could never copy and she invariably knocked off a few sous. She soon made it clear to me that almost the same system as that which Thalia had described in the Indian bazaars was also the custom here. The *bonne* or the cook got the equivalent of the *dasturi*, and there was great resentment if she wasn't allowed to do the marketing.

I liked Madeleine. She was pretty, gay and good-natured, and went out of her way to introduce me to all her acquaintances there.

'You are Madeleine's friend?' they would say, and laugh loudly when she said proudly that I was staying with her English Madame. One morning old Yves was outside the market with Napoleon and the cart. '*Hola!*' he called, 'wait a minute, mademoiselle.'

Madeleine was bargaining for a cabbage and I went up and patted Napoleon. 'You've still got her, then?'

'Who?'

'Madeleine.'

'You can see we've still got her.'

'My sister won't come until she's gone. She'll come then.'

'Madame won't get rid of Madeleine until she has seen Marie.'

'That's fair enough—but my sister Marie's a *good* woman.'

He put such an accent on the 'good' and gave such a leer at Madeleine as she came hurrying to me carrying a large cabbage triumphantly that for the first time I began to wonder about her. Cynthia—who had engaged her—was becoming every day more dissatisfied with the girl. She was untidy, she was dirty, she was unpunctual. According to Cynthia she had no good qualities at all, but I didn't tumble to Madeleine's profession until one morning when she had brought in my early-morning tea, an innovation which Cynthia had taught her. She looked at me in the great Breton bed, then flung back the shutters. 'Don't you ever sleep with a man?' she said casually. I was taken aback but did not show it.

'Not as yet,' I said, as casually.

'You are a virgin?'

'Yes.'

'How dull!' She used the word *ennuyeuse*. I hadn't considered the subject much but this aspect of it amused me.

'Why?' I asked.

'Because you're a woman. What's the use of being a woman if you're a virgin?'

'One has to begin sometime,' I agreed.

'There's some of the Navy putting into port at St. Malo next week. If you like to come over there with me I'll soon fix you up. I've plenty of friends in the Navy.'

And then I saw why the local people were so amused at Madeleine being in Cynthia's household—and at my being her constant companion in the market. I sat up in bed and laughed. The idea of Cynthia having found and chosen this particular girl amused me enormously. Madeleine was affronted at my laughter. She dumped my tea down and began a volley of angry French at me—she called me all kinds of unpleasant names ending up with accusing me of being an ungrateful fool. But it was no good—I couldn't stop laughing. The thought of my aunt's face if she could have heard that within two weeks of coming to France I was being offered an introduction to the unmentionable profession amused me even more than the vision of Cynthia's face when she discovered what she was harbouring.

At last I stopped, and asked her weakly why she should think that I would receive such suggestions with anything but anger.

'You draw pictures of naked men. You must be interested in their anatomy,' was her answer. This sent me off into fresh peals of laughter.

'You've been looking in my portfolio!' I accused her. 'It's tied up—you must have untied it.'

She reddened, then admitted it. 'It's because of Monsieur Xavier Tréfours,' she explained. 'He's a painter from Pont Aven, and he's always asking me to take my clothes off—not for any good purpose, you understand—just to draw pictures of me. I would never allow such a thing and I told him in no uncertain terms. I'm a modest girl.'

This upset me again and I laughed so much that Thalia came in. Madeleine whisked out, angrily slamming the door.

'What's the matter? *Do* tell me.'

'She's just suggested that she shall fix me up with a sailor next week,' I said weakly. 'She's what is known as a bad girl.'

Thalia's eyes flickered—then she broke into one of her smiles. 'I knew it! I knew it! And Mother's so proud of having engaged her herself.'

'How did you know?' I asked curiously—I hadn't known—and I was nearly three years older than Thalia.

'Ali had girls from the bazaar. They all walk, move and look at men in the same way—one gets to know them. And the little English she knows—it's all those sort of words.'

'What sort of words?'

'Oh, you know—they begin with f and b.'

But this sent me off into more laughter. Thalia lay down on the bed with me and, the tea forgotten by the bedside, we clung together laughing immoderately.

'Don't tell Mother—it's too lovely!'

Our laughter became an uncontrolled gale.

It was still warm enough to bathe, and every day we went down the steps from the villa in our bathing suits and, leaving our wraps there, ran across the hard firm sands. When I had first arrived, Tom Pemberton had come with us. He found the water cold after India, but he wanted to satisfy himself that Thalia would be safe with me. 'There are strong, treacherous currents all round most of this savage coast,' he said to me. 'I know you can swim—but even good swimmers are helpless against a relentless current.'

It was difficult to believe that this dreaming, hazy coast-line with its rose-tinted islands and its hard white sands was dangerous, but his statement was borne out by the notice-boards on every *plage* warning bathers of the dangerous currents.

'Wait until the weather changes,' said the fishermen. 'You'll see how cruel is our land of Armor.'

But now it was peaceful with the strange quality of a fairytale coast where any of the Cornish legends of the Arthurian kingdom could take place even now. I would lie after swimming on the sands with Thalia and tell her all the stories of the Knights of the Grail. She did not know any of them. As far as I could make out she had read almost nothing except Kipling and seen practically no films or plays, except *Tarzan of the Apes*, which she had seen seven times, and *The Lives of a Bengal Lancer* which she had seen almost as many. Tom Pemberton had told me that these two films ran permanently in the Indian cinemas. I was not only trying to teach her to swim but to get to know her. She was not an easy pupil as regards either. Both she and Cynthia had a quality of remoteness difficult to assess, but whereas with Cynthia it embodied coldness, in Thalia I sensed a repressed spontaneous warmth.

With swimming she was nervous and acutely self-conscious. She made excellent progress until Cynthia began watching us from the terrace.

'You can't drown if you keep your head,' I would reassure Thalia. 'It's easy to keep afloat even if you can't swim if you keep your arms down and your head up.'

But she would suddenly become conscious of her mother on the terrace, and immediately her arms would go up and her head under and she was hauled out spluttering and choking, red and blotchy.

'Why d'you look at your mother?' I demanded angrily one morning after several hopeless efforts. 'Look at me, swim to me, watch my arms and legs. Don't look at the shore at all.'

'Couldn't you ask Mother not to come out on the terrace?' she pleaded. 'I can't do anything when she's looking at me.'

I asked Cynthia at lunch that day. She only smiled in a remote irritating way and said that she didn't watch us just for pleasure, but for our safety.

'You couldn't do anything if we got into difficulties,' said Thalia. 'You can't swim.'

'In any case I think it's getting too cold for bathing now. Rachel can continue if she likes but it's too cold for someone who can't swim.'

'It's still very warm in the water,' I said, 'and really Thalia can almost swim—another week would make all the difference. *Do* let her go on for one more week.'

'I have said that it's too cold for Thalia. You may do as you like, Rachel, although I should have thought that after pleurisy you shouldn't swim at all.'

'The doctors said it was excellent for me,' I said, 'and in Devonshire I've swum in the sea at Christmas.'

'Mother, *do* let me have another week—really it's not cold,' Thalia begged.

'It's useless to argue, Thalia. I have said no.'

'Shall you go on swimming, Rachel?'

'Yes.'

'Until it's ice-cold and snow is on the ground?' asked Claude.

'They almost never have snow or ice here.'

'Shall you go in on Christmas Day like you did in Devonshire?'

'If it's good weather, yes.'

Cynthia looked at me as if I were a curious object. 'Rather you than me. Ugh! the very idea makes me shiver. I'm always cold after India.'

The next day I went alone to swim. Although she hadn't made much progress, Thalia had enjoyed her bathes with me, but Mademoiselle Caron had begun her duties and a sulky Thalia and Claude were closeted with her in the little room on the first floor which Cynthia had set aside as a schoolroom. It looked on to the garden and tall palms reached to its balcony.

Mademoiselle Julie Caron had been interviewed with me acting as interpreter. She had been sent by the agents for the villa. She was short, dark and plump, with lively eyes.

'Ask her how old she is,' said Cynthia after we had all shaken hands and the letters of introduction and references had been presented.

I didn't like asking her this. She seemed old to me—and I was not surprised when she replied that she was thirty-five.

'It's a very suitable age,' said Cynthia.

'Suitable for what?' I asked. It seemed to me that thirty-five couldn't be suitable for anything.

'For the post of governess to Claude, and for teaching French to Thalia.'

'She's not Mademoiselle. She's Madame,' I said. 'She's a widow. Her husband was killed in the war. If the war ended in 1918 she must have been married terribly young.'

'Seventeen,' said Cynthia, 'only a little older than Thalia is now. Tell her that I prefer to call her Mademoiselle.'

I thought this ridiculous of Cynthia—as I explained to Madame Caron. She looked at me with a smile, and then at Cynthia.

'As Madame wishes,' she said demurely, 'but as I have a son of sixteen—it isn't seemly that I am addressed as Mademoiselle.'

'If she has a son she will understand a little boy far better than if she were unmarried,' I said.

'Ask her where her son is,' said Cynthia.

'At sea with the French Navy,' said Madame Julie proudly, pulling a photograph of a tall lad from her hand-bag and showing it to Cynthia.

'Tell her I still prefer to call her Mademoiselle.'

'I don't like it—but I need the job,' said Julie Caron. 'What does it matter? Everyone here knows I was married in the St. Enogat church to my Jacques before he went back from his last leave.' Tears filled her eyes and suddenly I hated Cynthia.

'She married a soldier who was killed fighting for his country—she's proud of having been married to him. Why can't we call her Madame?' I asked angrily.

'I'm not asking your advice, Rachel. I'm asking you to translate for me. Ask Mademoiselle Caron when she is able to begin her duties here.'

'At once,' said the little widow simply.

'She can start next week,' said Cynthia, 'and I want her to be very strict with Claude's accent. I wish him to speak perfect French. Ask her if she's French or Breton.'

'French. We are all French. I am a Parisian—but my husband was Breton.'

'I'm not interested in the husband or the son. She's Claude's governess here, and we'll call her Mademoiselle.'

'I shall address her as Madame,' I said firmly.

'You will do nothing of the sort, Rachel. She will be Mademoiselle to us all, and if she doesn't like it she needn't take the post.'

'But I don't mind it at all,' cried Julie Caron, more tears brimming over. 'I need the money and I love children. I will do my best for Claude and for Thalia too. Please make that clear to Madame.'

Did I fancy it or did she put the faintest insolence into the word 'Madame' as she used it of Cynthia?

We started Italian lessons with Madame Valetta. She was fat and somnolent and smelt of sardine oil. I would look at her and think she was asleep; and she would suddenly snap a question at me as a crocodile will snap at its prey. She was a good teacher and I began to talk instead of merely reading Italian. Madame was impatient with Thalia, saying that she didn't try. But Thalia had a quick brain and an excellent ear, and she just didn't want to learn Italian.

She knew some French—one of her father's servants had come from Pondicherry, and from him she had picked up a little. But she had no intention of learning any more, she told me.

'Why not?' I asked.

'It's stupid. In India we speak Hindi or Urdu. What's the use of learning French? I like India—I don't like France.'

'You'd like to go back to India?'

She became intent, closed as in some inner dream, and I watched her curiously.

'Tell me about your life there—your home, what was it like?'

'We've had heaps of homes. We move a lot in the Army. But they are always bungalows—all on one floor and always heaps of room with big compounds so that we could keep animals. It's always hot and sunny, and everyone laughs a lot—except Mother.'

'And you want to go back? But you *are* going back. Your father said that I could come out with you next year if all goes well.'

She was delighted. 'Did he really say that? *Really?*'

'Yes,' I said regretfully, knowing that I wouldn't be able to go.

'I'm longing to go back. I love India, and I want to keep house for father. I did it when Mother was up in the hills last year.'

'If you were to learn French you could run the house here,' I said.

'I don't want to. I only want to do it for him—in India.'

'He's keen on your learning languages, he told me so. You must try more with them.'

'I don't want to. I like drawing and writing things.'

Cynthia had asked me to teach Claude the elements of reading and writing. He didn't want to learn either. It took all my powers of concentration, invention and patience. He was extremely intelligent, but, like Thalia, he didn't want to concentrate. After the first week I went to Cynthia in despair.

'I'm no good at teaching. Claude just won't learn. He'd be much better with other children.'

'He's getting on very nicely. You can't expect any progress in one week. I want him to learn to read and write in English, I don't care for my son to read French before he can read English—and I dislike their pointed writing.'

It was useless to argue. Claude and I sat opposite one another every morning in the little room with the balcony looking into the palm trees while Thalia and Mademoiselle Caron were in the *salon* below. The Reverend Cookson-Cander had sent me a set of readers for very young children. These, he said, were being used with great success in the church schools.

Claude would look at me with his great fringed blue eyes.

'R-A-N. Make the sound of R-A-N now. What is it, Claude?'

'Cow,' he would say gravely, his mouth set in a curiously firm line and his jaw jutting out.

'But if C-A-N is can, R-A-N isn't cow. Now think, Claude, make the sound of the letters. What is it?'

'Cow,' he would repeat firmly without taking his eyes from the window, 'and if we were in India now there'd be monkeys in that palm tree, lots and lots of them, and they'd come in here and pull your hair and scratch your face and smash up all the silly things in this silly room and tear up this silly reading book.'

And he would give me an angelic smile.

I was so entranced by this vision that I would listen to his description of the monkeys who had got into Cynthia's bedroom and upset and torn to pieces all the cosmetics on her dressing-table.

'There are s'posed to be wire nets to keep them out—but Thalia took them away—she let the monkeys come in.'

At the end of a month, Claude had learned practically no reading and writing but I had learned a great deal about his life in India and a smattering of Hindi. He was alarmingly observant; intelligent in the same curious way as his sister. They seemed to me to have been trained to see all those things which children shouldn't see—or rather which adults think that they shouldn't see. He not only knew all about monkeys but all about their mating habits, which he described at length and in detail.

'But don't tell Mother, she'd be cross with Ali for letting me see. When Ali let me see the little goat's throat cut in the Kali temple I woke up in the night and screamed. Mummy said Ali must be sent away. He's a Mohammedan and shouldn't go near the Temple—Kali's a Hindu goddess, you know. So when Mummy said he must go I screamed and screamed until they got him back.'

'You like Ali?'

His eyes went dark and his chin quivered a little: 'Better'n anyone in the world. I *love* Ali.'

I asked Thalia about Ali.

'He's Claude's personal bearer. His own servant. He's had him from a baby. Ali's a Mohammedan.'

'But I thought you both had an ayah?'

'Yes. We have. She's a Hindu. She's gone to her village until we get back. She still belongs to us. But boys have a bearer as well. He brings all the things for ayah—the meals and milk and things, and he carries Claude when he's tired.'

'Until we go back. When we go back. In India we did this or that. In India it was always sunny. In India people always laugh ..' These phrases were constantly on both children's lips. My own family had always been connected with India, and the family albums at home were full of photographs of cousins with ayahs and bearers in attendance. Claude was a maddening child—but the look of wistful misery on his face whenever he spoke of India moved me. Thalia said less, but when I asked her about India she had the same nostalgic tone when she spoke of the jungle and the wild life there. She was passionately fond of animals, and both children were missing their pets.

There was a British school in Dinard which Thalia was to attend for certain classes. But to comply with the French authorities' regulations almost all the teaching was in French. As her French was so poor it was arranged that she should attend for English subjects only until it was possible for her to follow the teaching in French. On the first day of her attendance I went with her to the school. As we approached the building she became very agitated.

'I feel sick. I can't go.'

'It's only nerves—you'll be all right. I know how you're feeling. It's only the first time. To-morrow'll be better.'

'You don't know. I *can't* go. There'll be heaps of girls all staring at me because I'm so ugly.'

We had reached the iron gates of the school. Thalia refused to go in. 'Why should they stare at you? They've other things to be interested in.' But how well I knew how she was feeling. So I had felt when I had grown so fat last year. Everyone was staring at me. Everyone was laughing. There is no agony like self-consciousness—I knew it; but to help Thalia over her form of it was beyond me.

'And I'm stupid—and backward—they'll all laugh at me—they did at the other school.'

She stood leaning against the railings and wouldn't open the gate. Her head poked forward on her lumpy chest—her arms and legs were too long and thin. Her suit had been made by Cynthia's Indian tailor who had certainly never studied the girl's figure. Her straggling hair escaped constantly from the thin plaits and hung in wisps over her freckled face. The freckles were the worst blemish—for whenever she was frightened or overcome with any form of emotion they stood out as livid stains when her skin paled.

'Thalia,' I said, 'you have one lovely thing which I envy you more than anything. I'd give you all my good points for it.'

She looked at me in sullen astonishment. 'What?'

'Your voice.'

She stared, puzzled.

'It's a very pretty voice—it will be a beautiful voice later on,' I said.

'What's the good of that? I want to *look* beautiful. I don't want to be clever. I want people to like me. Mother can't speak French and she never reads a book—but all the men look at her. In India she's surrounded as soon as she goes into a room.'

'You'll have another kind of beauty. There are lots of kinds. You must learn to be amusing and witty and then people will surround you even if you're not beautiful in actual features.'

'But that's the only kind I want. It's all very well for you. You're very pretty—even Mother says so.'

'Thalia,' I said impatiently, 'it's something I never bother about. There are so many other lovely and interesting things to do and see I don't think of my own looks.'

'You don't have to bother,' she said obstinately, 'it's all there for you.'

I opened the gate. 'You're already late for your lesson. Come on. I'll go in with you.'

But she hung back and her mouth was trembling, her eyes flickering wildly as they did when she was acutely nervous.

'I can't, Rachel. I *can't*.'

'All right. We'll go on the beach. But if you don't go to your classes to-morrow I won't take you sketching with me. I promised your father I'd get you here—'

'To-morrow I'll come alone. I promise you.'

We went on the Plage de l'Ecluse and looked for anemones and shells in the pools left in the hollows of the rocks by the tide. Here, leaning over the sea treasures with her hair hanging almost in the water, Thalia was absolutely happy. We bought a prawning net in the town and spent the morning trying to catch the darting brown shrimps hiding under the seaweeds. The sun was quite hot and we waded in the pools with our skirts tucked up. It was lovely.

'To-morrow I'll wear my shorts,' I said, 'and I'll lend you a pair, too.' But I had made a gaffe.

'But I shan't be here to-morrow,' she said shortly, 'I'll be at school.'

When we got back to the villa, Cynthia greeted us angrily. 'The school telephoned to ask where Thalia was. What on earth have you been doing, Rachel?'

'We went prawning. Thalia didn't feel well.'

'And Madeleine hasn't returned from the market this morning. There's no lunch. She just hasn't come back. I'll speak to you presently, Thalia. Rachel, go down to the market and see what's happened to Madeleine. Claude's hungry—he wants his lunch.'

Thalia and I were hungry, too, but to Cynthia only Claude mattered. It never occurred to her to do anything for herself when there was anyone else about. She had always had servants in India and simply expected whoever was about to wait on her. I went to the market and asked our usual stallholders whether they had seen Madeleine. They laughed and chuckled in a knowing way. Yes, she'd been there. 'But she's gone now—she'll be back soon and all the richer for it. Tell your Madame that!'

I bought a long roll of bread which they called a *baguette* and stuck a piece of chocolate in it and put it under my coat. Thalia and I would take it with us on our afternoon ramble round the coast.

When I got back Madeleine had returned. Cynthia was speaking to her in louder and louder English. Madeleine was slicing potatoes deftly, her head downbent over a piece of steak which she had covered with butter before putting it under the grill.

'I won't have all that butter on the meat! You know that,' Cynthia was saying furiously. 'And what were you doing all this time?'

'I had some important business,' said Madeleine without looking up from the food she was preparing.

Thalia and I exchanged glances, and went off into hopeless giggling. Madeleine looked up at our laughter, then she began laughing too.

'*Je m'excuse*, Madame, the lunch is ready immediately,' she said demurely.

Cynthia was very angry with all of us. Claude had been tiresome and Mademoiselle Caron had complained of his behaviour.

'I'm disappointed in you, Rachel,' she said to me when the children were washing for lunch. 'I thought you had enough sense to know that Thalia was playing up—she wasn't ill. She didn't want to go to school.'

'She was ill because she dreaded going to school. She looked terrible.'

'And Madeleine! She goes off like that and you just laugh. You must support me with the servants. I expect that, Rachel. You're always giggling with Thalia. I should have thought you were past that silly giggling stage.'

'Your husband asked me to make Thalia laugh as she used to do. He said she took things too seriously.'

'There isn't so much to laugh about if one does one's duty properly. Life isn't a joke. You should know that by the age of twenty.'

It was on the tip of my tongue to tell her that I was only eighteen and not twenty. But what did it matter? For after only four weeks in her house I knew that Cynthia and I would never understand each other.

CHAPTER IV

AFTER THE FIRST week when she came home tense and white and merely played with her food, Thalia began to settle down at school.

'It's not so bad as it was at that English boarding school, the girls here aren't so clever. Some of the Americans know less than I do. There's one girl I like very much. She's asked me there next Wednesday—and you, too, Rachel.'

Her face was radiant as she told me this. 'It's the first time anyone's ever asked me to tea themselves. They've always asked me because their mother made them,' she said.

'How d'you know that?'

'They told me,' she said simply. 'But this girl, Clodagh, doesn't even have to ask if she can have me—she can have anyone she likes.'

Cynthia wasn't enthusiastic about the invitation.

'The mother of this girl hasn't called on me,' she demurred. 'I don't know who she is. One can't be too careful in a place like this.'

She sounded exactly like my aunt. Wasn't it enough that Thalia, who had no friends, had been invited by the one girl she liked?

'I haven't met this Mrs. Tracey at any of the bridge parties yet,' she said. 'I must ask about her.'

She was lying in bed giving me the day's orders for Madeleine. Cynthia's bed was different to all the other carved Breton ones in the villa. It was painted in late Louis XIV style—with swans and cupids and lovers' knots. Above the head-piece two cupids held up a heart and from it fell small draped curtains forming a canopy. I don't know why Cynthia always looked out of place in this bed—but she did. She lay there in a pale blue bed-jacket, her lovely hair in plaits like a little girl. Her night-dresses were ruffled and of finest crêpe de Chine—sewed and embroidered by Indian *dirzis*. She was very beautiful—but it was a beauty which made me uncomfortable.

Every morning when Thalia had gone to school and Claude was with Mademoiselle Caron I went to her room. It never failed to give me a shock to see her lying there under those cupids holding up the heart. She would tap her teeth with a little gold pencil and write down the food and things to be bought for the day. I would then put it down in French on Madeleine's kitchen slate.

'Go with her to the market, Rachel, I'm tired of her saying that whatever I order wasn't there—and do the bargaining yourself. Your aunt told me you've been thoroughly trained by her in shopping and keeping accounts.'

It was useless to tell her that it didn't matter which of us did the shopping, the prices had already been arranged between Madeleine and the stall-holders.

I hadn't seen Captain Mourne since the day of our arrival—Cynthia told me that he had been ill. He was living in an hotel quite near us. When I had said that I would like to go and inquire after him she said that there were plenty of people ready to do that. She said it so bitterly that I asked her if she knew him well. 'Too well,' was the cryptic answer, and she had changed the subject. I asked Thalia about him. 'Didn't you know?' she said. 'He was in India—in the army—and something funny happened—and he left. He used to come a lot when we lived at Dehra Dun.'

'What d'you mean by something funny?'

'I don't know exactly what it was. I don't like him—but Mother does.'

'No. She doesn't. I think she dislikes him.'

'She dislikes him *because* she likes him. One day I'll tell you how I know. But not now. Don't let's talk about her.'

Just after this conversation I was going to the market with Madeleine and we encountered Captain Mourne in the rue de la Pionnière. We were swinging the large market basket between us and singing. Madeleine had taught me the song. It was not the sort which either Cynthia or my aunt would have appreciated—but it was good for my French to learn such things. I liked Madeleine more and more—she was so gay and made fun of everything. I hadn't laughed so much for years. After the earnestness of life at my aunt's I found it lovely. True, some of her language and swear words shocked me—but it was interesting to learn those. She wasn't much older than I was—but she knew the world very much better. She had been sent out to service at the age of twelve, and had worked in private houses until she was seventeen. She spoke very little of what she had been doing since then; but I gathered from Cynthia that she had been in an hotel in St. Malo for the last three years until she had quarrelled with the proprietress.

We were near the little cinema when we saw Terence Mourne.

'*C'est le beau Capitaine Mourne*,' said Madeleine, her face alight with interest. 'You know him, Mademoiselle?'

He looked from me to Madeleine, then said to me without any preamble, 'I want to speak to you.' To Madeleine he said quite roughly, 'Go on, wait down the road.'

Madeleine gave me a strange imploring look, then walked away and stood waiting outside the little cinema, staring at the posters on it.

'That girl. What are you doing with her?'

'She's the *bonne*. She was in the villa when I arrived. We're on our way to the market.' I was resentful of his strange interest.

'Good God! D'you mean to say she's living in the villa?'

'Yes. Cynthia engaged her before I came.'

'Tell Cynthia that I'm coming to call on her this afternoon. I'll come about four.'

'She's playing bridge this afternoon.'

'Where?'

'At Mrs. van Klaveren's.'

'What time does she get back?'

I remembered Cynthia's remark of the morning. Would she want to see him? I said I didn't know.

'I'll come about six—I'll take my chance of finding her in.'

'Why don't you telephone her?'

But he made some absurd excuse that the telephone was impossible in his hotel.

'And you? How d'you like Dinard?'

'Very much,' I said politely.

'What d'you do with yourself? Have you been round the coast at all?'

'We walk miles in the afternoon. We've been round the cliffs from Paramé to St. Servan and from St. Enogat to St. Lunaire, and we go to La Vicomté very often.'

'Who's we?'

'Thalia and I.'

'The freckled monstrosity. Poor Cynthia! Who'd have thought she'd produce that.'

At this vile description of Thalia I felt a violently protective anger. I choked back my words and turned to join Madeleine. I was astonished at my own fury.

'Rachel!'

I turned.

'You're angry! Like a little ruffled hen. Come back! I want to ask you something. I haven't seen you because I've been ill. Have you been to the Casino yet?'

'No,' I said shortly.

'I'll take you there on Saturday.'

'What for?'

'For your education. It'll amuse you. I'll tell Cynthia when I see her. That'll amuse *her*.'

'What will amuse her?'

'That I'm taking you.'

'I haven't said I'm coming.'

'But you will,' he laughed. And in spite of my anger I knew that I would go.

When I joined Madeleine she looked apprehensively at me. 'What did he say?'

'Nothing. He wants to see Madame.'

'He'll get me sent away, Mademoiselle Rachel, and I'm so happy with you. The Madame is mad—but she can't help that. She's kind to me and I'm so happy with you and Mademoiselle Thalia.'

'Why should he get you sent away? It's none of his business.'

'He's cruel—that one. Very cruel.'

'How d'you know?'

'He's well known here, Mademoiselle. Life has hurt him and he wants to hurt. You'll not let him get me sent away?'

'I'll do my best—but it's Madame's villa,' I said unhappily.

Did he intend to speak to Cynthia about Madeleine? He had looked so pointedly from her to me and told her so roughly to wait down the road. And yet there had been a look of amused tolerance in his face and a kind of secret delight when I had said that it was Cynthia who had engaged Madeleine.

At lunch I said that I'd met him and that he was coming to call at six.

'I won't be back,' Cynthia said. A colour had come into her cheeks at the mention of his name. She so seldom allowed any kind of emotion to show, that I was surprised. She had told me that laughter and any kind of strong emotion ruined one's looks. 'You'll have lines all round your eyes and mouth if you go on with this incessant laughing.'

I said that I didn't care because I was not beautiful.

'You've improved a lot since you've been here. You looked ill when you came and in one month you look quite different.' She said it grudgingly as if she would have preferred me to stay the way I had been.

'This is the afternoon that Thalia and I are invited to tea at the Traceys,' I reminded her. 'If it's all right with you Mademoiselle Caron will give Claude his tea.'

'Where do they live?'

'On the way to St. Brieuc. We can walk along the little railway track.'

'I wish they had invited Claude. I don't like him being left alone.'

'We're going to walk there. It's too far for Claude.'

'Don't be late back. You must start early if it's a long way.'

Madeleine served the lunch in an exemplary fashion that day. Cynthia was delighted. 'She's really learned to do it the way I showed her,' she said. 'Tell her the food was excellent, Rachel.' I told Madeleine.

'Ah, Mademoiselle, the food is horrible cooked in so much water and without any butter—but if Madame likes it that way I am glad she is pleased.'

In the afternoon Thalia and I set off. It was sunny and lovely but Cynthia insisted that we should carry mackintoshes.

'Say, yes; and we'll leave them in the bushes near the gate,' said Thalia. 'It saves a lot of bother. Ayah always did that, so did Ali. It's no use arguing with Mother.'

We hid the mackintoshes under a myrtle bush. Claude howled because he couldn't come with us.

'Let him howl,' said Thalia when I suggested that perhaps the Traceys wouldn't mind if we took him. 'We'd only have to carry him—he's used to Ali lugging him around.'

'He ought to be able to walk—he's almost seven.'

'No European born in India can walk.'

'In time they'll be born without legs—sort of tadpoles.'

'They couldn't drive a car—unless they used their tails—and tails fall off. Imagine Mother without legs! Imagine it!'

'And you. You were born there too.'

'No. No, I wasn't. I was born in Camberley. I *can* walk.'

We went along the railway track giggling at everything we talked about. It was the sort of day which was made for laughter.

'I mustn't laugh,' I said. 'Your mother says I'll get lines and wrinkles . . . lots of them . . . .'

'Bet I'll make you laugh . . . how much will you bet?'

'*A bouchée.*'

These were the most delectable, very large chocolates with all kinds of fillings—Thalia and I adored them. Claude liked *sucettes*.

'*A praline bouchée?*'

A *praline bouchée*. Go ahead . . .' and in less than a minute I was laughing and Thalia had won the *bouchée*. She was an incomparable mimic and had given a perfect imitation of Cynthia telling me that if I laughed so much I would get lines round my eyes. We giggled so much that we sat helplessly at the side of the railway track. An old peasant came along and stood looking at us.

'Better get up, there's a train coming!' he said. It was a little single track and no one would mind us walking along it, Clodagh had told us.

'How good it is to be young—one laughs at nothing—wait until you're old and you'll cry at nothing . . .' he said, wagging his head sagely. We got up, thanking him for telling us about the train. It came puffing by as we stood up on the bank—the driver in a blue shirt waving his bare brown arms and blowing us each a kiss . . . . We began laughing again . . . . *'Ah, c'est la jeunesse! C'est la jeunesse!'* sighed the old man, regarding us as if we were strange objects indeed.

As soon as he had gone, Thalia gave an imitation of him. She reproduced his Breton accent so perfectly that I stared.

'Thalia! You're a wonderful mimic. You could make a fortune. If you catch an accent so quickly and easily you could learn languages with no trouble at all. Why don't you learn French?'

'Why don't you learn French?' She mimicked me. Did my voice sound like that? It must. For she had caught the others marvellously. But what a voice *she* had! It could change from the old man's deep throaty one to Cynthia's clipped cold one and now to my own light, clear tones.

'Thalia, darling! You're wonderful! What a gift. When did you discover it?'

'In India. I amused Ali and all the servants imitating the silly memsahibs . . . I can do animals too. Listen . . . I'll do the hoolach monkeys in the jungle, they call like this. . . .'

Her voice began in a strange low key and rose and fell in an extraordinary call. 'And this is the hyena or jackal at night. And this is a tiger . . . and this is a rogue elephant trumpeting. . . .'

I was so enchanted that I could visualize the whole jungle as she made the sounds she had loved in the wild parts of India. Then she suddenly stopped. 'You called me *darling*. Did you mean it?'

Had I? It had slipped out unconsciously. It was an endearment I never used. We used none at home—and my aunt neither kissed, embraced, nor called me by any endearment at all.

'Yes. I meant it.'

'You like me then?'

I thought of that wild moment this morning when I'd wanted to smash Terence Mourne's face. 'Yes, I like you, Thalia.'

The face she turned to me for my answer was alight and eager. 'I'm glad,' she said. 'I'm glad, Rachel. You see I like you quite terribly. . . .'

A curious embarrassment fell over us both. I pulled out two *brioches* and some chocolate.

'Oh joy! Food, glorious food.'

We fell upon the rolls, which smelt of my jersey under which they had been hidden.

'We turn left here,' I said, looking at the piece of paper Clodagh had given Thalia. 'It says turn left by the first signal box and cut through the orchards down to the coast-line, then left again.'

The cider apples on the trees were ripening, they hung low over the track. We plunged into the thick, sweet grass, bending low to avoid the laden branches. The scent from the ripening fruit was strong as the sun caught the trees. Thalia seized my arm. 'Look, look, the sea! And that must be the house . . .'

Framed in apples the sea lay ahead, scintillating and unreal like scenery in a play, and to the left through more trees was cradled a low white house.

To say that I liked Catherine Tracey on sight was to put it mildly. I was absolutely fascinated by her. She lay, on that first visit, in a bed near the balcony of a room overlooking the sea. It was a perfectly plain iron bedstead and she wore a plain white wrap. She lay there not because she was lazy, but because she had been suffering from a migraine.

She had copper-coloured hair which grew in strong, shining waves from a high rounded forehead, a lazy gurgling way of talking—as if the whole world were a huge joke—and dimples appeared whenever she laughed.

The house, delightfully untidy, was noisy with dogs, littered with papers and books, gay with flowers, and from everywhere one caught glimpses of the sea. It seemed to me the perfect house. My aunt's lovely house looked like an advertisement for one of our largest furnishing firms and Cynthia, in our rather grim fortress-like villa built into the granite cliffs, had a mania for what she called tidiness. Thalia had to fold her clothes in the most ridiculous fashion and I had to fold Claude's jerseys and knickers in a similar way. In this white rambling villa it was evident that nobody ever dreamed of hanging anything up.

An elderly plump lady known as Aunt Phoebe appeared to control the household. She gave us tea at which five dogs were present, then took me up to Catherine.

She held out a slim hand to me. 'Come and let me see you. Clodagh says you're an artist. That you're going to be a painter. Go away, you two—and play with the dogs or eat fruit or something. Leave Rachel with me. I like her.'

I sat down in a low chair. The two girls, Clodagh and Thalia, went away happily enough.

'Come and sit near me where I can see you. Clodagh has taken a liking to Thalia. It's splendid. She hasn't many friends.'

'Thalia has none.'

'Poor child. She looks so awkward. I hear she has a very beautiful mother.'

'Cynthia *is* beautiful.'

'She's your friend?'

'No. I wouldn't call her my friend. I'm really here doing a job for her although I'm not paid. I'm here for Thalia, to go about with her; and I help with the little boy.'

'But she could still be your friend.'

'I don't think she likes me,' I said firmly.

Catherine Tracey began to laugh—a rich, infectious gurgle. 'It's not surprising if she prizes her beauty. You're much younger. Beauty doesn't last, Rachel. There are always younger ones coming up.'

'Does it matter so much—age?' I asked.

'Not if you have the things which are ageless.'

'Such as?'

'The inner knowledge that nothing dies.'

'But it *does*,' I insisted.

'No. Only the obvious dies. Age won't matter at all to you if you're going to be a painter.'

'Cynthia minds very much.'

'Perhaps she's not sure of what she's got.'

'She's unhappy. I don't know why—except that her husband's in India. She doesn't care much for Dinard.'

'We're mostly grass widows or real widows here. Haven't you noticed the surplus women?'

I hadn't but then I hadn't been looking for them.

'Most of the husbands are in India or Egypt or abroad somewhere. It's cheap here, you know, and much warmer than England for those who're accustomed to the East.'

Clodagh had told Thalia that her parents were separated. Her father was in Ireland and she spent her summer holidays with him. I hadn't passed this information on to Cynthia. She had funny ideas on separations.

Catherine asked me a little about myself. She wasn't inquisitive, but she wanted to know why I was in Dinard. I told her about the disastrous portrait of the Reverend Cookson-Cander. She went into gurgles of laughter . . . 'Clodagh told me you want to be a portrait painter. Would you like to try and do one of me? A friend of mine very much wants a portrait of me.'

I was excited at the idea—but reminded her of the failure of the only commission I had attempted.

'I know you're very young—still studying . . . but I shan't mind if you make an egg of me as long as it isn't a disagreeable egg.' She gurgled again. 'Will you try?'

Aunt Phoebe came in. 'Philippe's here, Catherine. Can he come up?'

'Of course. Rachel, this is the friend who wants the portrait. His brother, Xavier Tréfours, is a famous painter. You've heard of him, haven't you? Philippe loathes his work. I shall call you Tintoretta. Rachel's too dull for such a piece of quicksilver. Ah, Philippe!'

Two men had come into the room. Both were tall for Frenchmen. The elder man was dark, heavily built with unexpectedly blue eyes, the young man fair and slender.

'This is Philippe Tréfours, and this is his rascal of a son, Armand. This child's name is Rachel, Philippe, but as she's going to paint my portrait I'm going to call her Tintoretta.'

Philippe Tréfours took my hand, then bent and kissed Catherine's. Armand kissed Catherine's hand.

The impact of Catherine on me was still so great that I scarcely noticed the two men. She was very much at ease with both of them, and there was a resemblance between them in spite of their different colouring.

'Well, and how do you find our little town?' Philippe Tréfours asked me. He was sitting very close to Catherine and still held one of her hands. She was regarding him with the delightful teasing air of one who humours a little boy. And there was something of the eternal boy in this great heavy man. The eyes themselves were those of an astonished child —a child delighted at his own luck . . . afraid to believe that that luck will hold. I think I knew instinctively that they were in love—and that she was the sort of woman I would never meet in my aunt's drawing-room.

Before I could answer the question about Dinard, Thalia came running in to say that we must go and I saw her eyes narrow as she took in the group round Catherine.

'Armand will run you back to Dinard. Take Clodagh with you.'

The young man, Armand, escorted me downstairs and outside to his white sports car. I sat next to him, and Thalia behind with Clodagh.

We didn't talk at all—the engine was too noisy, but I noticed his beautiful hands on the steering-wheel and the curious pleasure that close proximity to him gave me.

He dropped us at the gate of the villa, declining to come in, turned the car deftly, if noisily, in the narrow street, and was gone.

Cynthia was in the *salon* with Terence Mourne. She was standing by the window looking out at the sea and he was in the only comfortable chair, smoking. When she turned at our entrance she had a lovely rose colour in her face but her eyes were hard and very, very blue. Whenever Cynthia was angry or about to be disagreeable her eyes were of the most wonderful forget-me-not blue.

'Rachel . . . so here you are. It's late. Claude's in bed so you needn't rush up to him.'

'I promised to tell him a story because he had to stay behind.'

'Sit down, please. I have something to say to you.'

I sat down. Thalia was fidgeting uncomfortably and looking in disgust at Terence Mourne.

'Sit down. *Do*. Thalia, you'd better hear this too.'

'Rachel. D'you happen to remember the address of old Yves' sister Marie?'

'No. But it's somewhere near the station. I can easily ask—their name is Duro.'

'To-morrow morning I want you to go and find her and ask her to come and see me immediately.'

I looked at Terence. He looked away. Thalia and I exchanged glances. I got up. 'All right. I'll go up to Claude now.'

'Wait. There's something else. Madeleine has gone. Her things will be collected to-morrow. You and Thalia will have to get the evening meal. And see to the breakfast to-morrow.'

Thalia turned furiously on her mother. 'Why? Why? Only at lunch to-day you were praising her. What's she done?'

'That's enough, Thalia. Madeleine has chosen to go off and leave me of her own accord. Of course I had paid her yesterday. The French were always an ungrateful people. It's too bad of her after my having taught her English ways.'

I looked at Terence Mourne smoking nonchalantly. He wouldn't look at me. I was hurt. Madeleine might have told me she was going. We had been good friends. Or so I had thought. Thalia and I went into the kitchen. 'What shall we eat?' I asked helplessly. The larder was strangely bare. Madeleine shopped from day to day.

'Omelette,' said Thalia, 'with lots of garlic in it. Mother hates it—it isn't genteel!'

We collapsed on the kitchen chairs giggling. 'What else?'

'The most smelly cheese we can find—I'll go out and get it now—she hates that too . . . and bitter endive.'

'She's made the soup,' I said, lifting the lid from the pot on the stove.

'Oh, joy! Brown onion soup!' cried Thalia gleefully. 'Mother hates it. Give me some money, Rachel. I don't want to go in the *salon* and breathe the same air as that poodle!'

I looked at her. The venom in her voice was unmistakable.

'Why d'you call Captain Mourne a poodle?—he's not at all like one.'

'Not to look at. But he likes ladies' drawing-rooms.'

She took the money I handed her and raced off down the path. She was singing 'Excelsior' loudly and looking astonishingly happy.

When I went up to my room after cooking the highly flavoured meal I found a note on my dressing-table. It was written in violet ink on paper which came from the lavatory off the hall.

CHÈRE MADEMOISELLE RACHEL,

It is better that I go. *Le beau Capitaine Mourne* has said that if I don't he will tell Madame. In any case the fleet comes to St. Malo next week. Dear Mademoiselle Rachel, I like you very much, and for this reason I give you this advice. Do not marry an Englishman. I speak from much experience. May Ste. Thérèse protect you.

MADELEINE

Terence Mourne was leaving as I reached the hall.

'Rachel,' he called. 'You're coming to the Casino with me on Saturday. It's all arranged. I'll call for you at eight. Wear a pretty dress. It's a gala night.'

I ran after him. 'What did you say to Madeleine?'

He looked whimsically at me. 'There was no need to say anything. *La belle Madeleine* and I understand each other very well.'

I wanted furiously to tell him that I wouldn't go with him on Saturday, but there was something so disarming in his smile, so attractive in his amused bantering glance, that my words died away unuttered.

CHAPTER V

MARIE DURO presented herself at the back door the next morning. She was dressed in black with a woollen shawl and a small white coif. She had a white frill at her neck and her whole person exuded an aseptic cleanliness which Madeleine had lacked. She was dark, her hair drawn uncompromisingly back from a fine forehead. There was something of the hard granite of the coast in the ruggedness of her face as she stood there with a straight dignity which compelled admiration and respect.

'You are Mademoiselle Rachel? My brother Yves has spoken about you. Don't believe a word he says—he's a good for nothing—an *ivrogne*.... Is the Madame in?'

'She's upstairs in bed. Come in.'

She entered slowly, looking carefully and suspiciously round the kitchen.

'It's untidy—I've tried to clean it up but there hasn't been much time,' I apologized.

'It'll need a thorough cleaning after *that one* has been in it,' was all she answered. We ascended the stairs and I asked Cynthia if I should bring her in.

'Yes—and stay and interpret for us, Rachel....'

Marie contemplated Cynthia in the bed. Then she said to me: 'Is she ill?'

'No.'

'Then why is she in bed?'

'Madame stays in bed until eleven.'

'It's strange,' she said. 'But all Englishwomen without husbands stay in bed a lot, while those *with* husbands can't get up fast enough.'

'Are the French so different then?'

'The French women stay in bed *with* their husbands—those without husbands get up....'

I translated this for Cynthia, who went very red and didn't smile.

'Ask her how many households she's worked in and read me her references....' was her only comment.

Marie had a sheaf of letters all testifying to her cooking ability and her cleanliness. Two of them, however, stated that she was inclined to be difficult. I didn't translate these to Cynthia. I had taken an immediate liking to Marie—and I didn't want to clean out the kitchen or do the cooking. It took half an hour to settle the wages and conditions. One of Marie's was that she did all the marketing herself, and that she was free to attend Mass every Sunday and feast day. Finally all was amicably arranged and she departed to arrange her affairs and pack her box, which Yves would bring for her. She would arrive with him in the afternoon.

'She's pig-headed—like all the Bretons,' said Cynthia after I had made her some coffee and brought it up to her room. She was sitting at her dressing-table brushing her golden hair, and the sun streamed in on it and caught its brilliant lights as she brushed. Few women had long hair now, but Cynthia's was so beautiful that I understood her not having cut it.

'I think I'll go back to bed,' she said. 'I'm not feeling too well this morning.'

She climbed back under the cupids and as I handed her the tray I thought suddenly that she and Catherine Tracey ought to change beds. For Cynthia, in spite of her golden hair, and apple-blossom skin, had an almost Victorian primness, a consciously false modesty which made a mockery of the emblems of love holding the heart above her head. Catherine in the iron bed had pulled me warmly to her and kissed me, I had hugged her unrestrainedly—and yet I had never seen her before that day.

Cynthia sipped her coffee now, and looked sideways at me. I knew suddenly that Terence had told her about Madeleine, and that she knew that I had known about her. She looked at me with a studied intentness and said meaningly: 'I don't want you to become as familiar with Marie as you were with Madeleine.'

Again it could have been my aunt speaking. So she had spoken when I had gone for two long walks with Janet, her parlourmaid.

'Madeleine's young,' I said. 'With all this interpreting there's bound to be familiarity—I make mistakes—very funny ones sometimes. Besides—I like her.'

'You're not the only one who makes mistakes,' she said with a rueful smile. 'It seems I made one over her. You should have told me, Rachel. . . .'

'Thalia tumbled to it before I did,' I said. 'It's really very funny!' And in spite of myself I began laughing helplessly again.

But Cynthia was angry now.

'It was your duty to tell me immediately you suspected. It's disgraceful of you.'

'Why?' I retorted rudely. 'I'm not accustomed to having to suspect those around me of immorality. Besides, I've told you. I like Madeleine.'

When I used the word immorality she looked searchingly at me as if to try and fathom my meaning. Then, changing the subject, she said: 'Enough of Madeleine. It's about Thalia I really want to speak to you. She's of an extremely jealous nature—and she's becoming very attached to you.'

There was resentment in her voice.

'But isn't that what you wanted? What I'm here for? To help her. She's lonely—like I am.'

'I'm sorry there are so few young people here for you, Rachel. I can understand that you're missing the young students at the Slade. In the Christmas holidays it'll be better. I'm told it's very gay then. Lots of families have young sons at the universities in England who come over for the vacations. And, anyhow, you're going out with Terence Mourne on Saturday.'

'He's old,' I said resentfully, remembering what the stewardess had said on the boat. 'And I didn't mean that sort of loneliness.'

'Old?' she said sharply. 'He's not more than thirty-eight or so. What is this absurd resentment against age?'

I didn't know. It was more a resentment that I was young than that he was old, but it was useless to try and explain this to anyone.

'If you're lonely you'd better work hard at your languages. Mademoiselle Caron wants to exchange French for English conversation with you. It would be good for you both. She could come here one evening and the following week you could go to her.'

'It's not that kind of loneliness . . .' I said again. 'It's something I can't explain. Madeleine had it too—and she had plenty of men—'

'Don't mention Madeleine again. That incident is closed. To come back to Thalia. I ought to warn you, Rachel. Thalia can be unpredictable when she's jealous. She plays very unpleasant practical jokes. You've noticed that? I don't want it encouraged. I've suffered too much from her already.'

I couldn't answer her, such a wave of distaste came over me. That she could speak so of her own daughter disgusted me. I excused myself as the bell rang and went downstairs.

Thalia watched me dress for the Casino. My aunt had given me a pale yellow tulle dress before I came away. It was a mass of billowing frills, and although the effect was pretty enough I didn't know how to manage the skirt. I sensed that Thalia was annoyed that I was going. It was the first invitation I had received in which she wasn't included.

Cynthia, although she and Captain Mourne had made the arrangement themselves, also seemed to resent it. When we were having tea that afternoon she said: 'It's a pity you're going out tonight. I've just been asked to Colonel Simpson's.'

'What short notice!' I said.

'Someone's let him down,' said Thalia slyly.

'Nothing of the sort. He's getting up an impromptu party.'

'He's such a bore,' said Thalia, 'that I wonder anyone goes!'

Cynthia reproved her sharply.

'Well, it's true,' said Thalia. 'Father said so. He tells the story of his shooting a rogue elephant every time we see him!'

'I haven't heard it,' I said mildly. 'And I've met him here several times.'

'You will,' said Thalia grimly.

'Do you want me to telephone Captain Mourne and tell him that I can't come?' I asked Cynthia.

'No. Of course not. Terence wouldn't appreciate that at all.'

'Do you know him *very* well, Cynthia?' I asked.

She looked put out by my question, then she said swiftly: 'I've known him for several years now.'

'Since Meerut!' said Thalia. 'He came to the Regiment at Meerut. He transferred from another one to ours.'

When I had put on the dress, some whim made me pile my hair on top of my head with a Spanish comb. Thalia said nothing as she watched me do it. I asked her how it looked.

'All right,' she said. But Cynthia thought it absurd, and said so.

'It's too short for that,' she said. 'All the ends will come down with the sea breeze, and when you dance you'll look a sight.'

I decided not to change the style.

'If he's left the Army do I call him Mr. or Captain or what?' I asked Cynthia.

'His name is Terence as you know—but as he's so old, you'd better address him as you think fit.'

I looked at her. Was she serious? I decided she was.

'He's a very good dancer,' she said. 'That's how I first became so fond of dancing. Tom doesn't dance.'

I had an evening cloak which my godmother had given me. Cynthia had already borrowed it twice. It was rather nice to wear it myself.

'Are you sure you're warm enough? It's cold on the Promenade.'

I thought that if she didn't want to be thought old she shouldn't keep on fussing about rain or cold or wind. Their loveliness and variety make life interesting. But then she had been living in India where she had become accustomed to warmth.

'Don't keep her out too late, Terence,' she said as we left. She looked rather forlorn and wistful as she watched us get into a taxi.

'Why didn't you invite her too?' I asked, but he didn't answer me. In a dinner jacket, with the hair I didn't admire darkened with some kind of brilliantine, he looked very distinguished, but the hairs on the back of his hands were just as red as before. He looked like a very handsome fox. I am very fond of foxes—but only as animals.

The Grand Casino is right on the Promenade of the Plage de l'Ecluse, with its huge windows looking on to the sea. We had dinner in between the dancing; a space had been cleared on the floor and the great room was crowded. Among the faces which I had encountered constantly in the streets were only one or two which I knew. Cynthia had invited me to accompany her to cocktail parties on several occasions but I had stayed with Thalia. She knew I didn't play bridge, and except for a reception at the British Consul's to which we had all gone, I hadn't as yet been anywhere. As soon as Terence and I entered I saw heads turning and asides being exchanged at the tables nearest us, and Terence had to pause several times on our way to a table, to introduce me to people. They were all inquiring after his health. He knew everyone, it seemed, and was in great demand.

'I spent last winter here,' he explained to me. 'I went to London for a couple of months while this place was crowded for the season. I was coming back when we met on the boat.'

Cynthia was right when she had said that he was a good dancer. He was a skilled partner, and accustomed as I was to indifferent performers among the students at the Slade, to dance with someone like Terence was a pleasure I hadn't experienced. We danced without talking much for the sheer enjoyment of perfect timing and perfect partnership. He complimented me on my dancing as we sat down.

'Why d'you *really* live here?' I asked him later, when we were drinking some very light white wine.

'For the reason I told you. It's cheap, and I can get more out of life here than I could for the same money at home—besides, I play.'

'Play what?'

'Baccarat. Would you like to have a look at it? I'm afraid you're too young to play that, but you can have a try at boule if you like.'

I said I'd like to try. The group round the table fascinated me. My aunt was very fond of telling me that my father liked gambling. He had explained boule to me. I read the various combinations allowed in this casino, and said I'd start with a single number. If it won I would get eight times my stake.

I chose seven. The ball stopped at seven. I left the winnings on; the ball stopped again at seven. I had put on 100 francs and now had 6,400 francs.

'I'll leave it on,' I said.

'You can't leave all that on a single number—you are only allowed 5,000 francs on a single number,' said Terence. I left 5,000 on number seven. It came up again. I had won 40,000 francs.

'Try Passe et Manque now,' suggested Terence. I put 5,000 on Manque. It won. No matter what I chose it won.

'Beginner's luck,' said everyone round the table, looking at the great pile of chips in front of me. How Father would have loved to have seen my extraordinary luck!

Just as I was going to put another 5,000 francs on seven, something compelled me to look up. Behind the croupier, smiling at me, were Philippe Tréfours and his son. He shook his head deliberately. 'Leave off now. You'll lose it all,' he said, laughing.

'He's right,' said Terence. 'The trouble with me is that I simply can't leave off. But that's enough for one night. I'll be accused of corrupting the young!'

He changed the chips for me. My gold evening bag was stuffed with notes. I'd never had so much money in my hands.

'This is all on a very small scale here. You'll see real gambling at baccarat,' said Terence as we danced again.

When we were watching the cabaret later, I saw that Philippe Tréfours and his son were with Catherine Tracey. She waved to me as soon as the number was over.

'Who is she?' asked Terence.

'Catherine Tracey. I'm going to paint her portrait—or try to.'

A change passed quickly over his face at the mention of her name.

'So that's the lovely Mrs. Tracey!' he said in a peculiar way, 'and how did you meet *her*? You seem to have a positive genius for meeting the wrong people.'

'Wrong people!' I said indignantly. 'I suppose you mean Madeleine. Cynthia chose her. And thanks to you she's gone! As to Catherine, Thalia and I went there to tea the day you turned Madeleine out. The daughter Clodagh is at school with Thalia.'

I was angry with Terence, and he began laughing. 'You knew perfectly well what Madeleine was—and you deliberately kept it from Cynthia,' he accused me.

'Thalia knew—I didn't know for some time.'

He frowned. 'Thalia! She's precocious, she knows far too much. Take care, Rachel. She's deep.'

I wanted to go over and talk to Catherine, but Terence swept me on to the floor again. We were dancing a waltz, and the lights kept changing colour. I found it fun to have a different coloured dress every minute and to have a partner with a green, then violet face. Every time we passed the Tréfours table, Armand's eyes were on me.

'Who's the fair admirer?' asked Terence, who missed nothing.

I was annoyed. 'He's not an admirer. I met him at Catherine Tracey's—just once. That's his father with him.'

'And he, if I'm not mistaken, is Monsieur Philippe Tréfours, the great man of the district.'

When the waltz ended he said: 'Come along, let's go and look at the sea.'

I put my cloak round my shoulders and we went out on to the deserted Promenade. It was as light and tranquil as the night on which we had crossed. The sea was smooth and each wave as it rolled lazily on the pale sand was caught in an unearthly phosphorescent light. About the entire place was the strange hushed peace which moonlight carries. We walked towards the great bend to the right where the cliffs tower above the narrow path round the rocks to the Pointe. I knew that Terence was going to kiss me and I didn't mind.

I didn't exactly like him—but something in him attracted me, and he was a wonderful dancing partner. At home, if a man took you out to dinner and dance he expected to kiss you, or so my friends said. Having never been out alone with one I didn't know.

When he took me in his arms I looked at the moon—not him. And when he kissed my mouth I shut it very tightly.

'You're a cold little fish,' he said. 'Kiss me, don't just behave like a passive martyr.'

This made me laugh and I opened my mouth. Immediately he kissed me again savagely, hurting me, and at the same time bending me back against the rock. My cloak fell off, and I felt such a revulsion and fury that I struggled wildly. But he held me, laughing down at me; and I thought of Madeleine's words, 'He is cruel, that one. Life has hurt him and he wants to hurt.'

'Let me go! Let me go!' I hit wildly at him.

He released me contemptuously. 'I'm disappointed in you, Rachel. You look passionate—you've all the signs. But you're about as responsive as cold porridge.'

'Try Cynthia! Perhaps she's the reverse,' I said angrily, wiping my mouth with my handkerchief. He had bruised my lips and my chin felt sore.

For a moment I thought he was going to strike me. He was furious.

'I'm sorry,' I said quickly. What had I said to bring such a look of fury to his face?

'Don't say that again. There are things little girls don't understand—and never will.'

His accent on the *little girls* was contemptuous.

'I'm sorry I'm so disappointing,' I said meekly. 'I've not had much experience. Let's go back and dance. You dance divinely.'

He was pleased. 'You're not so bad yourself. Better than you are at kissing.' And then he caught my hands and we both began to laugh and I kissed him lightly on the cheek. He showered little kisses on my neck and I liked this better than when he had kissed my mouth.

It was Thalia, not Cynthia, who had waited up for me. I let myself in with the key entrusted to me and crept upstairs, but when I reached my room, Thalia was crouching by the window.

'I saw you come back,' she said, and then she stared. 'He's been kissing you,' she said accusingly.

I wondered how she knew, and glanced in the dressing-table mirror. There were red marks round my chin, and my lipstick had smeared badly, and Cynthia had been dead right about the hair. It looked appalling, hanging down in wisps round my neck. There was an ugly stain on the back of my frock where Terence had pressed me against the damp rock, and I had caught my foot in one of the frills of my skirt and it hung in a forlorn hoop!

Thalia continued to stare. She was bunched up now on my bed in an all-enveloping childish nightgown. 'How can you let him? How *can* you?' Her voice was hysterical.

'Go to bed,' I said crossly. I was mortified at what the mirror revealed. 'It's none of your business what I do. Get that clear.'

She got up without a word, then as she reached the door she said: 'That's how Mother came home when he took *her* out.'

I flung off the frock, and scrubbed my face with soap and water, and then my neck, and everywhere his mouth had touched me. I hated myself so much that I felt physically ill.

Marie woke me the next morning. She wore a stiffly starched white apron over a grey stuff gown and a tiny white coif on the crown of her head. Her hair in its severe knot was perfectly dressed and her face had that look of soap-and-water cleanliness which was rapidly becoming rare.

'*Bonjour*, Mademoiselle Rachel. May God guard you to-day!'

'Did you sleep well?' I asked politely.

'Yes, after I'd disinfected the room after *her*! I haven't brought you that water and leaves they call tea. I've brought you a bowl of *café au lait*—like I drink myself.'

I appreciated this way of being awakened. She stood there by the window looking out at the sea: 'There'll be a storm to-day. The wind's already high. More for the Cimetières des Naufrages!' and she sighed deeply. 'Where's the crucifix which was in this room?' she asked sharply.

'I don't know,' I said. 'There was none here when I came.'

'Every room in this villa has a crucifix. Have you looked in the *armoire*?'

She went over to the huge carved Breton cupboard and pulled open the doors. On the top shelf on which I had placed my hats she thrust her arm right to the back and held up a crucifix in triumph. '*Là voilà!*'

'How d'you know there is a crucifix in every room here?' I was curious.

'I used to work here,' she said quietly.

'With an English family?'

'No. With the owner.'

'Where is she now?'

'In Paris. She's married again—a Frenchman.'

'Wasn't she French then?'

'She's a Breton.'

'That *is* French.'

'Yes. It's French—but only after Breton. *Française, oui! mais Breton surtout!*'

'Was her first husband Breton?'

'Of course. A God-fearing man. This new one is from Paris.'

She spoke the word Paris as if it were Hell.

'Where's the first husband then?'

'Where should he be but in his grave?' She crossed herself and murmured something.

'Drink your *café*, Mademoiselle.' She took the small crucifix tenderly in her hand and dusted it carefully on the immaculate apron.

'It belongs over the bed. See, the hook is still there.' She reached over me and hung up the cross. 'You are a Catholic?'

'No.'

'But you're a Christian?' She peered at me anxiously.

'Yes . . .' I said doubtfully. I was thinking of the Amarna theory and my rather agnostic views.

'You attend the Anglo-American church with the Madame?'

'Yes.'

She seemed satisfied with this. 'It's a good church,' she said grudgingly, and looking approvingly again at the crucifix above my bed she rustled out.

Thalia came in. 'You've got coffee,' she said enviously, 'and a great bowl! Marie brought me a cup of tea—all water and milk.'

The bowl was of thick Breton china from Quimper with two little handles. The *café au lait* was delicious.

'Have some,' I offered. 'You can drink from the other side.'

I turned the bowl round. But she turned it back, and looking at me with her strangely opaque dark eyes she deliberately put her lips to the place from which I had drunk. But when she returned the bowl to me I couldn't bring myself to do the same. I dressed quickly and went down to awaken Claude. He lay in an enormous bed like a tiny flaxen doll, his arms flung out, and his face so beautiful in sleep that I hated to wake him. I decided to get up early the next day and to creep in and draw him while he slept. He awoke instantly when I shook him lightly. 'Hello,' he said. 'Silly old Rachel! I dreamed a crocodile had bitten you up,' but his warm little hands were stroking my face as I sat on his bed and his eyes were full of mischief.

Marie came in with a parcel. 'For Monsieur Claude. . . .'

'Ooh! Ooh! It's a football. It's the football Daddy promised me from London!'

I signed the paper for it and together we fell upon the wrappings. The football was deflated, the bladder and an extra one enclosed. Claude was disappointed.

'I want it blown up. Now! Immediately, Rachel. Blow it up for me. At once!'

'I can't,' I said. 'We'll have to get a pump—I can't.'

'Do it at once. At once!' he screamed in a fury, kicking me as I sat on the bed.

Marie was scandalized. '*Il est gâté, ce petit!*' she said. 'Yves will blow it up for him presently—but tell him not unless he stops this noise.'

Claude went on screaming, so I shut the door of his room and left him. I heard Cynthia's voice calling me.

'What's the matter with Claude?' She was sipping her tea and reading a letter.

'His football has come—and it isn't blown up. He wants it done at once.'

'Can't you do it? A child always wants things done at once. . . .'

'No,' I said. 'It needs a pump. Marie says her brother will do it after breakfast....'

'Hurry with yours, then, Rachel, and take it along. Claude has been looking forward for so long to the football.'

'I don't think he ought to have it done as soon as he wants it,' I said. 'He's been screaming and kicking—he's too old for that ... he must learn that he must wait sometimes.'

Her face was suddenly thin and hard. 'It's bad for him to scream.... What do you know about children? You've not had any....'

'There hasn't been much time ...' I retorted. 'I'm only eighteen.... But I wouldn't let a child of mine kick and scream as much as he liked—I would let him wait.'

Her eyes had narrowed. 'Eighteen! I thought you were twenty.'

'No,' I said. 'You may as well know now—you'd know anyhow when my passport has to go to the police for my residence permit ... I'm eighteen....'

'You deceived me.'

'Yes. I don't see what difference it makes. It's better for Thalia that I'm young.'

'But it's not better for *me*. It explains why you're still in this silly giggling stage, I suppose.'

'I'm sorry,' I said lamely.

She got up and, throwing on a négligée went into Claude's room. 'My darling, don't cry. *Don't*. Rachel will get it done for you as soon as you've had your breakfast. I promise you.' She held him close to her, rocking his head to her breast. He turned a baleful eye towards me.

'She didn't want to do it. She only likes doing things for Thalia,' he shouted.

Cynthia hushed him. 'I don't want Rachel to dress me. I want *you* to. I want *you* to.'

'He ought to dress himself,' I said angrily. 'He's almost seven.'

'When I want your advice, Rachel, I'll ask for it.'

'Little beast!' said Thalia, who had been listening from the landing above. 'Ali always dressed him, he used to throw his toys about just to make Ali pick them up....'

'Your mother's just discovered that I'm eighteen, not twenty —and she's a bit peeved.'

'You're only eighteen! Oh, Rachel, how lovely. I'll be sixteen soon. Funny, I always think of you as younger than me.'

She was standing in a pair of striped knickers pulling at the straps of a white brassiere.

'How does one manage these things?—they are either squashed together into one mound in the centre—or one falls out and the other stays in . . . I liked it much better when I was flat like a boy. . . .'

I agreed with her. Life had been much simpler before one grew a figure. She was angular and at the same time fat in bits— just as I had been—the only thing was that she was doing it all at the proper age whereas I had done it very late.

'Come here,' I said. 'I'll adjust those straps for you, they're too tight.'

We faced the small mirror at her dressing-table, and as I was bending over her to fix the shoulder strap she suddenly seized my hand and covered it with kisses. I snatched it away as if she had bitten me.

'Don't! Don't!' I was unpleasantly reminded of last night's kisses by the Pointe du Moulinet.

CHAPTER VI

My aunt had spent a great deal of money on clothes and never looked smart. Cynthia had very little money to spend and invariably looked elegant. She would stand in front of her mirror studying a hat from every angle before she would buy it. Dresses would come from the couturier's in exciting striped boxes and she would try them on, walking about, sitting down, bending and stretching in them before choosing one. She always called me in to ask me my opinion.

I admired her slender elegance but I did not envy it. I found Catherine a type which appealed to me far more. I began the portrait of her the following week.

'What shall you wear?' I asked her.

'Nothing. I want it in the nude—three-quarter length.'

The nudes I had hitherto painted had been professional models, ugly and uninspiring, so that when Catherine said this I was upset. But when she let the wrap drop off her shoulders I was startled. Her flesh was of a warm creamy whiteness and she was very lovely. The clean canvas waiting and the beauty of my subject intoxicated me. I could not paint fast enough. I worked furiously at white heat, the afternoon going by in a flash. What can I say of Catherine sitting there against the white wall except that for me it was a new concept of the human body?

She talked lightly and gaily and I felt completely at ease with her. When the sitting was over and I stepped back from my easel to look at my work I could have wept. The colour was there—fresh and clean, and I had caught her look—but the drawing and the whole form of the thing were so far from what I intended that all my exhilaration was swept away. Too late I remembered the advice of the Slade professor that for me the drawing was far more important than the colour.

But Catherine was excited with it.

'I like it, Rachel. It's so fresh! I like it. The colour's lovely.'

I sat down. As always, after working hard and furiously, I felt as if I were dying. A complete lassitude came over me and I could not move. Catherine was concerned, and Aunt Phoebe brought some tea, which revived me. Thalia, who had accompanied me, came in with Clodagh, a tall girl with a mass of chestnut hair and hazel eyes. Clodagh exclaimed in pleasure when she saw the painting, but Thalia looked from Catherine with the wrap thrown round her shoulders to the canvas.

'Where will you hang it?' she asked disapprovingly.

Catherine was delighted at this.

'That's my business,' she said laughing and pulling a jersey over her head. 'Do you know, Tintoretta, one day when you're very famous I shall point to this and say: "Yes, she did that when she was very young in my villa by the sea."'

'If you would wait a little I could do a much better one,' I said. 'I'm still a student.'

'But you're very, *very* charming, Tintoretta, and you'll get married very quickly—that's why I want it done now.'

She had taken my face between her hands and was looking searchingly at me. 'It would never be better than it is now,' she said. 'A painter should know either nothing or a great deal about his sitter. You know nothing about me. But you're in love with painting, in love with life—a little in love with your sitter. Aren't I right?'

Thalia had listened to this banter with a wooden face. Now she said to me: 'I don't like it, Rachel. It's too fantastic. It's full of colours I can't see.'

'How could you see them?' I said. 'I'm only just beginning to see them myself and I study them all day.'

'I shall never see them,' said Thalia obstinately, 'because they *aren't there.*'

I was annoyed at her vehemence. Catherine was amused. 'You don't like me, do you, Thalia?' she teased her. Thalia was suddenly red-faced. She began blinking nervously and muttering something about not being able to explain what she meant. Catherine hugged me ostentatiously. 'I do believe she's jealous. She wants Tintoretta all to herself. Come now, Thalia, be honest. Confess that you really like the painting but dislike the subject!'

But Thalia had rushed out of the room without answering, and after a moment, Clodagh ran after her. I was scraping my palette and wiping my brushes.

'What a thistly young thing!' said Catherine. 'I'm not at all sure that I like her. How'd you put up with her, Rachel? I hear she's quite uncivilized at school.'

'She's all right,' I said shortly. I felt a violent aversion to discussing Thalia with anyone—even Catherine.

'And I hope that you are doing all you can for Cynthia and the children.' So ran the letter from my aunt which I was reading on the rocks below the steps of the villa. Was I? It seemed to me that I was doing a great deal more than I had ever expected to do.

Cynthia was now caught up in a whirl of social life in the Colony. She was always out. I saw her every morning to take the day's orders, and these were becoming daily heavier as she left more and more to me.

'It's just like India,' Thalia said contemptuously. 'Golf, bridge, gossip and tea. Cocktails and dancing with other people's husbands!'

'I thought you liked India.'

'I like *India.* Not what people like Mother *think* is India.'

She had, I found, a kind of Kipling love for the ordinary poor man and woman in India. She had no use for the attitude of memsahibs in the army circles in which she lived. Her father encouraged her in learning their language and interesting herself in the troubles and miseries of the poor. She told me that she went every week to visit the wives of the men in the regiment, and that she knew all the complicated names of the families and children. Cynthia, on the other hand, was always terrified of the diseases among them, and she didn't like Indian smells.

'It was her duty as the Colonel's wife to visit the women in the lines,' said Thalia. 'But she's never learned anything but how to order in Hindustani from the servants, so she can't talk to the men's wives.'

It was the same here in France. Cynthia wouldn't learn French. It fell to me to see to everything.

My aunt was on her way to Egypt now, this letter had been posted from Port Said. I had written her at length and complained of the amount of chores Cynthia expected me to do.

'You are extremely lucky to be in such a lovely place and to be able to continue your study of languages. You will very soon have to earn your own living and learn to take responsibilities. This is the best time of your life. Make the most of it.'

I screwed up the letter into a ball and flung it into the sea. The gulls thought it was food, and cascaded down to it.

My aunt had never known what it was to have to do chores for other people. She, like Cynthia, employed others to do them for her. Cynthia didn't even employ me, but the amount she expected me to do in return for the doubtful privilege of living with her seemed to be increasing daily.

I had come here for Thalia. Tom Pemberton had told me that. The girl interested me enormously. She was unlike anyone I had ever met. When one considered that she was Cynthia's daughter it was even more extraordinary. There seemed to be no bond of any kind between them.

By the time I had carried out all Cynthia's commissions and attended to all Claude's wants there wasn't so much time left for Thalia. As to my own studies there was even less. I would draw on the kitchen slate while Cynthia was trying to make up her mind what we should eat for the day. I never listened, because she invariably gave up the struggle, saying: 'You think of something, Rachel—but it must be cheap. I've no money this week.'

She never had any money for anything except bridge and she was losing heavily.

'Why d'you play for money?' I would ask her when she would tell me ruefully how much she had lost.

'Everyone does,' was her reply. 'I must do as others do.'

I thought this very stupid—as Thalia did. We both wanted to do something which other people didn't do. Cynthia, like my aunt, drew a pattern into which they and those surrounding them must be fitted. I preferred to draw the pattern round myself—as did Thalia. Life was too short to be bothered with doing the dull things that everyone else did. Didn't the sundial in my aunt's rose garden say: 'It is later than you think'? And the roses' death-stained petals strewn over it confirm it?

Cynthia was wrong when she thought that Thalia and I looked down on older people, that we despised them. We envied them their experience, their advantages over youth. But how blind they all were to our needs. Couldn't they see that we were thirsting to live? Longing to taste life for ourselves. But did they ever discuss with us the burning questions which beset our minds and stirred our bodies?

'You're too young . . . you wouldn't understand!' they said. Thalia and I discussed the stupidity of *Them* endlessly.

At night, after Thalia had reluctantly gone to her room, I would stand at the window and look out at the sea. The mimosa was still flowering—the kind here in Dinard bloomed twice a year and its scent was intoxicatingly sweet. Sometimes the sea was so beautiful that I couldn't bear it—and I would almost weep. But I didn't know why except that, as Marie said, to-morrow the storm might change its face to one of savage fury.

My cousin had died when he was sixteen. He and I had loved poetry. When he lay on that balcony in Davos he would ask me to read to him—and it was always poetry he wanted. I turned to it now again for comfort in the months which lay ahead. I went to Thalia's school and asked to borrow books of poetry. The English mistress there did more than just lend them. She suggested that as I was in France I should read only French poetry and introduced me to the Renaissance poets—and I fell in love with Pierre de Ronsard.

Perhaps it was that his exquisite lines about the brevity of beauty reminded me immediately and vividly of the sundial.

Comme on void sur la branche au mois de May la rose
En sa belle jeunesse, en sa premiere fleur,
Rendre le ciel jaloux de sa vive couleur,
Quand l'aube de ses pleurs au poinct du jour l'arrose

seemed to me as exquisitely sad as his lovely one about old age.

Quand vous serez bien vieille, au soir, à la chandelle,
Assise auprès du feu, devidant et filant,
Direz chantant mes vers, en vous esmerveillant:
Ronsard me celebroit du temps que j'estois belle.

I was enchanted with him, and tried to make Thalia as enthusiastic as I was. She would listen while I translated as well as I could the lovely sonnets and odes, and she would say: 'I don't like them. Some of it is silly. I like Kipling—but some of him is silly too.'

But if I stopped, she would beg me to go on. 'I like listening to you, Rachel.'

And I would go on, thinking that surely something of its beauty would touch her, something of the words themselves would remain with her. I persevered not because of this only — but because I was in love with Pierre de Ronsard.

As to her French, she wasn't getting on at all according to Julie Caron. Julie was constantly coming to me in tears. 'She won't try. She won't say a word, and yet I know she understands a great deal of what I say to her.'

And she did understand. I discovered this from Marie. Marie knew no English, in spite of having worked with both English and Americans.

'Why should I speak English?' she demanded. 'Breton and French are sufficient for anyone.'

But Marie carried on some kind of conversation with Thalia because I heard them in the mornings when Marie was waking her.

'Mademoiselle Thalia is clever. She says nothing—but she sees a lot!' was Marie's comment on her.

'What d'you talk about to Marie?' I asked Thalia one morning.

'She was hanging up the crucifix which was in the top drawer of my chest,' said Thalia. 'She won't be happy until she's done the whole house.'

'She's done the top floor,' I said. 'I wonder who put them all away?'

'Mother, of course. She hates anything like that.'

'But she goes to church!' I said in astonishment. Cynthia seldom missed the Sunday morning service in the Anglo-American church.

'Her brother went over to Rome and she says it's because he had a crucifix hanging in his room as a child.'

'We all had them at school,' I said, 'but we didn't go over to Rome.'

'If you ask Mother, she'll tell you that you'll be converted to Rome if you leave that crucifix in your room.'

'Marie says it keeps the Devil out.'

'It's the same as the charms they put round the children's necks in India to keep away the evil spirits.'

'So you *do* understand what Marie says!'

'Some of it.'

'Then why don't you speak French more? Why won't you do as Mademoiselle Caron wants? She says you won't say a word.'

'Because Mother wants that very much. I'm not pretty. And I'm not clever. She'd like it if I could chatter French as Claude is beginning to do. She doesn't count Hindi and Urdu and Marathi as languages.'

'But surely you *want* to learn French. It'll make your whole stay here much more interesting.'

'I don't like it here. I'm just waiting to get back to India and look after Father. I know all the French I shall ever need.'

Letters were coming from Tom Pemberton. Thalia had received several and he had written a long one to me. He was now up on the North-West Frontier.

'This is a wild place, and the people are wild,' he wrote. 'There is a lot of trouble again with the tribes. They can be so quickly stirred up by religious factors and their leaders use them shamefully for their own political ends. The Government made a big mistake in their retrenchment of the Army policy last year. The tribes get to know these things very quickly, and its effect on them has been most exhilarating. They are splendid fighters, in spite of their poor weapons—they have the courage of lions; and emerging from the rocks in the narrow passes in the mountains will swoop wildly down. We lost thirty men in an ambush in the Nahakki Pass recently, and two of my officers. Some of the prisoners we took, fine men with wild elf locks and the look of eagles, hadn't the least idea of what they were fighting against. They'd just been promised food if they fought and killed some of the British. Here, under the blazing sun, with the vultures above us, one realizes vividly the shortness of life. Any of those bodies we buried so quickly to save them from these foul birds might have been mine. I haven't told Cynthia of this affray. She would worry—and that's bad for her heart. But Thalia, she's of another calibre. I'm writing her an account of the whole exciting incident—although I'm afraid that Cynthia will probably see it in the papers.'

'Of another calibre.' Was she? I didn't know what went on under those freckles and the nervous eyes.

She had brought her letter to me and the hands holding it were shaking. 'Read it. *Read* it. He might have been killed. He might have been killed. I can't bear it. I can't. He oughtn't to be out there all alone.'

'A soldier's always alone,' I said. 'No one can go with him on these expeditions. You wouldn't be allowed near the Frontier.'

'I hate the whole thing. The whole beastly stupid Army and the stupider Government. I wish he'd come out—like Terence.'

'It's his life, he's a fine soldier!' I said mechanically. But I felt like Thalia did. It was a wicked waste of men.

'He may be killed by now!' she cried dramatically. 'This letter has taken over two weeks.'

'We can all die at any minute,' I said, thinking of my cousin. But I was wondering how it would feel to go out on an exciting expedition such as Tom Pemberton's letter described. To know that at any moment death could come to you from behind those great boulders in the Pass. The tribesmen lying immobile, their bodies melting into the heat of the rocks, waiting with their out-of-date Enfields or their 'long, lean, Northern knives', as Tom described them in the words of Kipling, to fall upon the narrow file of soldiers as they entered the Pass. How would one feel?

I tried to reassure Thalia, who was pinched with anxiety and misery. It was no use telling her not to worry. I made up my mind to write to Tom Pemberton and tell him that Thalia should not be told these things. Although disconcertingly adult in some things, she was only a child. She might be of a different calibre from Cynthia, but it seemed to me that perhaps he had made a mistake as to which of them could take such horrors lightly.

'Robin Thorne was killed. *Robin!* He was the only one I liked,' she cried passionately.

'Don't tell your mother. Your father expressly says not to.'

'She wouldn't care. He couldn't dance or play bridge.'

I was shocked at the cynical way she said this.

'Next to father I love *you*, Rachel,' she said, rubbing her face along my arm like a cat does.

I pulled the arm away. Since my cousin's death I had shied away from human affection. It hurt too much when it was taken away—and yet I longed for it as much as I sensed Thalia did.

Claude, rushing up to ask us to play football, chased away our gloom. We kicked the ball over the sands, sending it as near the waves as possible. Claude cried with rage and frustration when he couldn't get it every time. Thalia laughed and laughed. She could kick splendidly, and sent the ball far up the beach. We collided racing to get it before the sea did, and lay laughing helplessly at poor Claude, who was hopping mad with impatient fury.

'The sea'll get you. It'll get you both and drown you for taking my football.' He screamed as a wave came right up, splashing our heads as we lay giggling in the sand.

Thalia tore away suddenly and rushed up the steps. Halfway up she leaped dramatically down on to the sand crying wildly: 'I am Tristram leaping from the castle. Look, here I go!' and she hurled herself on to the one sandy patch, where she lay laughing. I had to drag her to her feet before a really huge wave caught her.

Claude looked contemptuously from me to Thalia. 'You're not a bit like Tristram. He was a knight. A fighter in armour. You're silly. Silly, stupid pigs! Girls can't be knights.'

And snatching his football from me he stood there glowering at us—but we only went on laughing.

Madame Anastasia gave her ballet classes in a room built right out over the sea. She was old, with a face like a small fierce eagle. She stood in the centre of the class with a stick which she used on the legs of the pupils. We did our exercises at the *barre* with the sea before our eyes and its reflection behind ours in the great mirror. We wore short black tunics for the practice classes.

When one afternoon Cynthia insisted on coming to watch us, Thalia, always acutely nervous, became so utterly miserable and self-conscious that it was agony to watch her. With Cynthia sitting there looking beautiful and Claude watching every movement, she couldn't perform the simplest step.

She was directly behind me at the *barre*, and I kept encouraging her with instructions and turning as much as I could to help her until Madame's stick came down on my legs, and Madame's hands seized my head as if it were screwed on and turned it relentlessly away from Thalia.

'Attend to yourself! Are you so good that you needn't attend to *me*?' And a storm of words was hurled at me.

Most of the pupils were young French girls, all much younger than I was, but there were one or two who were much older and amongst these was Judy van Klaveren. She was a small, slim American woman with short curly hair cut like a boy's. Her face was like a mischievous monkey's, her eyes so intelligent and alert that she held my attention at once. She was chewing gum all the time she went through the routine at the *barre*, where she was immediately in front of me.

'Don't take any notice of the old girl. She's on one of her show-offs to-day,' she said over her shoulder to me.

My leg was still smarting from the stick. 'Does she often use that stick?' I asked.

'She wouldn't use it twice on me. I'd like to see her try!'

'I don't mind if she doesn't use it on Thalia,' I said.

'You mean Cynthia's daughter? The one behind you?'

'Yes.'

'Why has Cynthia come? Madame doesn't allow onlookers in the classes. It makes us nervous.'

'She insisted.'

'*Madame Klaveren! En troisième position! La TROISIEME!*'

Judy subsided and dutifully corrected her position. She looked delightful in her short tunic, like a naughty little girl. There were little laughter lines all round the eyes and mouth.

When we rested, Cynthia called me over. 'You can help Thalia practise at home,' she said. 'I see that you have done a lot of this before.'

'They are the routine exercises.'

'Your aunt told me that when you grew so fat last year the ballet classes were your salvation. She said that you were always graceful because of your training. That's why I'm insisting on Thalia learning ballet.'

'I didn't feel graceful,' I said shortly. 'I felt as Thalia does now. It's wretched for her.'

I remembered the misery of not being able to get my bursting figure into my practice dress—and the even greater embarrassment of keeping it there when it was on. Thalia wasn't exactly fat. She was lumpy in places, angular in others, and she seemed to have lost co-ordination of her limbs. She came over to me now. Her face was dreadful. Drops of sweat were still on her forehead. 'I hate it. I'm going,' she said.

Judy heard her. She was standing chatting to Cynthia.

'Don't give up!' she said laughingly. 'You should have seen me when I began. Of course I'm too old. All the little French girls laugh at me—but I don't care at all. I do it for the exercise. It's wonderful. You just keep on—you'll be fine.'

'No,' said Thalia. 'It's silly. I think all the positions are ridiculous.'

'Have you ever seen any ballet?' asked Judy.

'No. I like Indian dancing. They don't stand on one toe and stick the other leg in the air.'

'You've seen a lot of Indian dancing?' asked Judy.

'Yes. A lot,' said Thalia.

'*Au centre, Mademoiselles! Au centre, s'il vous plaît.*'

Thalia sat resolutely down; Madame had her up in a second. 'What's this? You're tired already? A child like you? Or are you lazy? In the centre, Mademoiselle Thalia! And when I say in the centre I mean it!'

Thalia shrugged and took her place.

Madame hadn't wanted to accept her when I had gone at Cynthia's instruction to arrange for the classes. 'If she's never done any ballet what's the use of starting now? She's almost sixteen, you say. She will have to start with the babies—right at the beginning.'

The vision of Thalia in a class of five-year-olds, a giraffe with the gazelles, was too awful. I pleaded with Madame Anastasia, explaining all I could about Thalia and how difficult she was. 'It's her mother who wishes her to attend,' I said. 'She thinks it will make her more graceful. Less awkward in her movements.'

'She should have thought of it earlier. Probably it's too late. Bad habits are difficult to correct.'

'Isn't it lovely? Doesn't it make you feel good?' asked Judy as we wiped our faces with towels. Madame was ruthless and worked us hard.

She came up to me after the class and said: 'See that Madame Pemberton doesn't come again. I don't allow visitors and the poor child is useless when she is watching. Get rid of her now. I'm going to take Thalia by herself. And you go too. You can't be nursemaid always. She's got to learn to stand on her own feet.'

'She can't speak French,' I said, feeling awful at the thought of deserting Thalia.

'And neither can I. Don't you hear my mistakes? I've been out of Russia seventeen years and I haven't learned this language yet. Go on home and leave her with me.'

'She's not supposed to walk home alone.'

'You can wait in the vestibule.'

'Come back with me and have tea,' said Judy van Klaveren when I went into the hall.

'I've got to wait for Thalia,' I said.

'I'll wait too. I've got my car outside. I live at St. Lunaire.'

'I'll have to ask Cynthia.'

'I'll ask her now.'

Judy ran off and returned grinning. 'Not very enthusiastic —but you may both come. Cynthia's gone on with Claude. He's going out with her. What a beautiful child he is.'

Cynthia liked to take Claude about with her. His angelic face and blond curls enchanted everyone—especially the French. She was very proud of his good looks and the two of them together made many heads turn in the streets.

'Why doesn't he have his hair cut off?' Thalia would ask. 'He looks like a girl.'

The child hated his curls and I often found him trying to plaster them down with water. 'Soldiers don't have curls,' he said angrily. 'I want it straight like Daddy's.'

When Thalia came out I saw that she had been crying. Madame followed her. She was smiling: 'She did very well —I shall take her alone after each class for a time.' She patted Thalia on the shoulder. 'Stand up! Head up. Never down!' and when Thalia had gone to change she said to me, 'Poor child. Poor child. But I'll improve her. She shall learn to walk so that everyone will look at her. The mother dotes on that angel boy. And he's beautiful, too,' Madame sighed. 'Why doesn't she have *him* taught ballet? He's graceful and just the age to start.'

The idea that a son of Cynthia's should learn ballet dancing made me laugh. I explained to Madame that the family were all in the army, always had been, and that Claude was destined for a military career.

'What's that got to do with it? In Russia the Cossacks danced divinely and there were no better fighters in the world.'

Judy looked at me and smiled. She understood Cynthia as well as I did.

'We're going to tea with Mrs. van Klaveren,' I said to Thalia when she appeared in her coat and beret.

'*Judy* to you both, Rachel. Come along, Thalia, you must be starving.'

Thalia brightened. 'I am,' she said simply.

Both Thalia and I had taken an immediate liking to Judy van Klaveren. There was in her that quality of youth which is ageless. Her blunt speech and easy manner appealed to both of us, as did her dislike of anything sham or superficial. Perhaps the fact that both of us had been brought up in the traditions of our families and that hers simply had none, was what we liked most.

'My father was a bricklayer—and made a pile out of his bricks!' was what she told us. 'And I just don't understand all these do's and don'ts of the colony here.'

Cynthia did not really approve of her, but Judy was witty and very good company—she was popular with all the men—a rich, attractive young widow with a small daughter, Mimi.

Her husband had been killed in a car accident three years previously. She had stayed on in the villa they had bought in St. Lunaire and had made it her home. She was about the same age as Julie Caron—perhaps a few years younger. I asked her if she knew Terence Mourne. She said that she played bridge with him often and he was not only an excellent player but a most amusing partner. She liked him.

'I want to have you meet my young brother, Buddy, Rachel,' she told me. 'He's studying to be a painter, as you are. He's studying in Paris—but comes here occasionally, usually when he's broke. Come upstairs and see the view from the windows.'

The upstairs rooms looked directly down into the clear green water. The rooms had balconies with high railings and from them it was a sheer drop down to the depths below.

'I could leap down here as Tristram did!' cried Thalia as we stood there with Judy.

'Have you been to Cap Fréhel?' she asked Thalia. 'Some people think that the castle of the legend must surely have been out on that promontory. It's lovely—there's an hotel with a terrace with a glass floor so that you can watch the fish and sea-creatures while you eat. How's the portrait of Catherine Tracey getting on?' she asked me.

It was not getting on—that was just it. I said so. It was slowly taking shape as I went through the alternate stages of hope and despair, but I was too inexperienced to have attempted such a task. 'She's so lovely,' I said, 'that I'm afraid to paint her.'

'She looks a delightful person,' said Judy.

'Don't you know her?' I asked.

'I met her once—quite three years ago—just after we came here to live. She doesn't mix much with the set I seem to have gotten myself into.'

'How did you know I was painting her?' I asked. I hadn't spoken to anyone of the painting. Judy hesitated, then said: 'Cynthia told me about it.'

'She doesn't like Catherine Tracey—although she's never spoken to her.' And now I thought about it I saw that Cynthia invariably made some excuse to prevent me from going for the sittings.

'What's wrong with Catherine?' I asked Judy now.

'She's a woman who has the courage to defy convention and live as she pleases—it takes a lot to do that in a small colony like this.'

Judy, who was usually willing to discuss anything with Thalia and me, seemed strangely loath to discuss Catherine Tracey, although it was she who had brought up the subject of the portrait.

'I don't like her—but I like Clodagh,' said Thalia. 'Mother doesn't like Clodagh because *her* mother doesn't get asked to the Consul's and doesn't belong to the Club. It's exactly like India. If you didn't get asked to Government House parties it was the end of you!'

'And you want to go back to India—to *that* sort of life?' I said.

'I want to look after Father. When I'm old enough I shall live as I like too—as Catherine Tracey does.'

'How d'you mean as *you* like?'

'I shall live as the Indians do.'

'And is that so very different?' asked Judy.

'I mean those who stay Indian. Not those who copy us,' said Thalia decidedly.

CHAPTER VII

IT WAS IN October when the days were sharply beautiful, with that heartrending quality of each one being the last perfect one, that I first became aware of the runner. I had taken to going down to the rocks on the deserted *plage* with my sketch-book every morning unless it were raining.

Cynthia seemed to be becoming obsessed with the preservation of her beauty. Handbooks on the subject and samples of all kinds of aids to it were constantly arriving from London and Paris. She would lie with them spread out on the bed, her silver hand-mirror by her side, and would gaze carefully into it as she came to each point in the treatment.

I was fascinated by this absorption—because she had no vanity as I knew it. She merely accepted her beauty as something everyone would acknowledge and which it was her duty to cherish and preserve.

Thalia told me that one of the reasons why her mother hadn't returned to India this year was that she had been afraid of the drying quality of the heat in the plains.

'She might get a wrinkle,' Thalia had said. 'All the women get lined and withered—like trees!'

Sometimes Cynthia would ask me to pat in some cream or to smack her cheeks sharply after it were removed. She said I had good sensitive fingers for this.

I usually went to the large Plage de l'Ecluse because there was more sun there than on the smaller St. Enogat one. I sketched there on a sheltered rock, longing all the time to be back at the Slade. I became aware that every morning a young man was running systematically across the sands. And then, as each day the tide came higher, he came closer to me, for he always ran along the hard edge by the incoming surf. I began to notice the beautiful rhythmic movement of his limbs against the water.

Fleeting poses always attract me more than static ones, and I began sketching the runner. He was tall, slender and blond. He could have been a Greek, and it wasn't until the tide had brought him quite close to the rock on which I sat that I recognized him as Armand Tréfours. Until he turned that morning and waved gaily to me he had been merely a subject for my pencil.

In his brief running shorts, with his bare torso and hair blown by the wind, it was no small wonder that I hadn't immediately known him as the young man I'd met at Catherine's and who had driven us home that day. He'd looked very different then—as he had that evening at the Casino with his father.

He came deliberately over to the rock on which I was sitting and greeted me. 'Mademoiselle Rachel, don't you know me?'

I said that I had only just recognized him. He was very brown, his muscles hard and clearly defined on his lean body.

'You're drawing me?' he asked delightedly, taking the sketchbook from me without preamble.

I told him that I was trying to keep up my drawing.

'Catherine told me you are painting her portrait,' he said, sitting down on the rock beside me, 'but she won't allow me to see it.'

I was annoyed that Catherine had talked about the painting but grateful that at least she hadn't been showing it to people. It would probably prove to be a failure and I was sensitive about my efforts.

'She seems delighted with the start you have made,' he said.

I took the book from him and snapped it shut.

'They're good,' he said simply. 'You must meet my uncle, Xavier Tréfours. He's often at Pont Aven and then he visits us. Just now he's in Paris, of course.'

'Your father doesn't care for his work?'

'No. But I do. He's ahead of his time—and isn't appreciated properly. He will be.'

'Like Gauguin and Van Gogh?'

'Like many painters,' he agreed. 'You like Gauguin?'

'I think he is the greatest of all painters.'

'Not Cézanne?'

'Not Cézanne.'

He stood up, he was shivering a little. 'I must go and get some clothes on. Don't go, will you? I'll only be five minutes.' I liked his voice not only because all voices sounded better to me in the French language than in my own, but because for a blond man it had all the depth and timbre I had hitherto associated with dark ones.

His eyes were very green as he smiled down at me. I studied his ears, throat and the upward sweep of the wheat-coloured hair. I stared at him and he stared at me, and something intangible passed between us.

'You won't go—will you? Promise?'

'Promise.'

He ran off with the easy gait of the trained athlete and vaulting up on to the Promenade disappeared into one of the *cabines* built into the rock.

I took the small mirror from my handbag and looked at my face in it. Compared with the almost classic beauty of his it appeared nondescript. Dark hair with chestnut in it, dark green eyes not clear emerald like his, dark brows, an oval pale face curiously transparent in quality. The only feature which satisfied me was the mouth. Full lipped and very curved, it formed a shape which was pleasing to me as an artist, and when it smiled the teeth were small, evenly formed and spaced. I put away the mirror as he came running back. His movements in the flannel trousers and yellow sweater were just as perfect as when he had been unencumbered by them. I didn't understand the strange, intense happiness I felt when he sat down again by me and said in that disturbing voice: 'Rachel—I may call you that, may I? You know my name, it's Armand—I saw you dancing at the Casino some time ago, d'you like dancing?'

I said that I adored it.

'So do I—let's go and dance, shall we? What about the tea dance on Sunday?'

I said that I would like that—if Cynthia was agreeable.

'I hope she'll be agreeable,' he said, taking my hand and spreading it palmwise in his. 'You see, I believe that you and I are going to be very great friends.'

Claude came rushing up and, flinging himself on me, cried: 'Show me the drawings, show me the drawings of the running man.'

'Here is the running man in the flesh,' said Armand laughing, but Claude, not understanding what he said and suddenly affronted in the way that children can be for reasons which we cannot plumb, cried: 'Who is he? Who is he?' I told him he was looking at the running man himself.

'No. No, it's not! You're teasing me!' He edged himself firmly between Armand and me and sat with one arm round me, glowering from under his brows at what he obviously considered was an intruder. When Mademoiselle Caron and Thalia came up and as I introduced the Frenchwoman to Armand she smiled curiously. 'We already know each other,' she said.

I thought Armand was not too pleased to see her. 'Everyone knows everyone else in this little place—and also everything one does . . .' he said.

'She's got a big son, he's a sailor. She's *Madame*, not mademoiselle really. Did you know that?' asked Claude.

'Say it in French,' said his governess.

'Shan't,' said Claude.

Thalia had adopted the same attitude as had Claude. Her tightly drawn mouth and averted eyes showed plainly her displeasure at finding me with a companion. Armand looked whimsically at me. 'I know when I'm not wanted,' he said, ruffling Claude's hair. 'Will you be here to-morrow?'

'If it doesn't rain.'

'It won't rain—and I shall be running as usual,' he said confidently. 'Au revoir then.'

He bowed ceremoniously to the sulky Thalia and to Mademoiselle Caron, leaped lightly over the rocks and ran up the beach to the Promenade.

'I don't like him. He's French. I don't like any French people. They can't talk properly.'

'Speak in French!' I said sharply. 'It's still only a quarter to eleven. Your lesson with Mademoiselle hasn't finished.'

Mademoiselle backed me up by saying that she'd let them out early as it was such a lovely morning. 'The lesson is still on,' she said.

'I don't care what time it is. I *won't* speak French,' said Thalia.

'You can't,' teased Claude. 'That's why you won't.'

'Your little brother makes much better progress than you,' reproved Julie Caron.

'I don't want to make any progress,' snapped Thalia.

'Monsieur Tréfours is champion runner for the whole of Brittany, do you know him well?' asked Mademoiselle Caron, turning her darting little eyes on me as we walked along the Promenade towards the Casino.

'I met him at Mrs. Tracey's,' I said.

She looked a little startled. 'You know *her*? You go there?'

'Yes.'

She said no more and bade us good-bye.

'I don't like Armand Tréfours,' said Thalia. 'He's too good-looking. He knows Mademoiselle Caron quite well.'

'You heard what he said. Of course he knows her.'

'That's not what I mean,' said Thalia.

I went to the tea dance with Armand the following Sunday. He danced as he ran—superbly, but I was so nervous that I couldn't follow properly. After several stumbles I could have wept with chagrin—but Armand only laughed. 'Come into the little ante-room and we'll try in private,' he suggested, and he took me slowly and patiently over each step. When we returned to the ballroom it was better, but not as good as it had been with Terence. It infuriated me that I could dance better with a man I didn't like than with one whom I did like.

'You'll soon get accustomed to my way of dancing,' said Armand, 'because we're going to dance together a great deal.'

The fact that I had seen Terence Mourne, sitting at a table with a very attractive Frenchwoman, watching my poor progress made me acutely nervous.

'Relax! Let your body relax!' said Armand. 'Forget everything except the dance itself. . . .' But how could I with the cynical, amused eyes of Terence Mourne following me round the room? When we sat down in the interval he strolled slowly over to us. I introduced Armand.

'May I have the next dance with Rachel?' he said suavely. 'Perhaps you would allow me to introduce you to my friend Madame Delcros, she's a beautiful dancer. . . .'

Armand didn't seem enthusiastic but he gave in with a charming smile and allowed himself to be introduced to Madame Delcros.

'You do better with *me* than with your blond runner,' said Terence as we danced to 'I've got you under my skin'. 'He's too intense for you. I'm a lazy, nonchalant fellow and better for your impetuous temperament!'

I was angry—but there was something in what he said. The easy grace with which he held me and piloted me had something to do with our steps matching so perfectly.

'How do you know he is a runner?' I asked.

'Seen him. Running with his blond hair against the blue sea—very romantic. Watch out, Rachel!' He laughed down at me with that cruel, foxy look. 'Does Cynthia know you're here to-day?'

'Of course.'

'She's coming here with my party to-night.'

'Don't I know it! She's at home putting a yeast pack on her face.'

'Don't be a cat. It doesn't become you. You're more like a small rabbit.'

'And you're the fox, I suppose?'

'Don't cast aspersions on my colouring. I loathe it.'

'Then don't compare me to a rabbit. My teeth don't stick out and I'm not hairy.'

'I know that,' he said laughing. 'I've seen you in a bathing suit. Don't hold yourself so aloof from me. You'll never dance well like that.'

I wanted the dance to end. I could see Armand dancing with Madame Delcros and it upset me that I couldn't do as well as she did.

'Armand,' I said, when we were trying a tango, 'I don't want to dance again with Terence Mourne.'

'And I,' he said, his arm tightening round me, 'have no wish to dance with that well-corseted widow.'

We laughed a lot and after that the tango went better.

I had to leave early to put Claude to bed as Cynthia needed several hours to dress. Armand took me back in his car but he wouldn't come in. He was going on to Catherine's. I wondered a little at the obvious intimacy which existed between Catherine and the Tréfours. I had noticed that the Anglo-American colony kept very much to themselves and mixed very little with the French residents, whereas in Catherine's house I had not only met Philippe and Armand Tréfours but several delightful Frenchwomen. There was a plaque on the rocks of the cliff walk commemorating a hundred years of British and American residents in Dinard, and it seemed to me extraordinary that they didn't associate more.

'They do—at the top and bottom levels,' Armand said. 'It's the middle ones—and the colony is mostly composed of them—who don't mix.'

'Enjoyed your dance?' asked Cynthia when I got back. She still had a yeast pack on her face and was sitting very still in case it cracked and peeled off before the correct time to remove it.

'Very much,' I said. 'Terence Mourne was there.'

'Alone?' asked Cynthia sharply.

'With Madame Delcros.'

'A Frenchwoman?'

'Of course.'

'Was he dancing with her?'

'Yes. He danced once with me.'

'What was she like, this Madame Delcros?'

'Attractive—Armand called her a well-corseted widow!'

Cynthia would normally have taken me up on this. Now all she said was: 'He must have held her pretty closely to know that.'

'Not as closely as Terence does.'

'How did your young French friend dance?'

'He's good. But I dance better with Terence Mourne. It's *sickening*.'

Cynthia laughed, then, remembering her face, stopped abruptly. 'Help me get this off, Rachel.'

I put a towel round her and took the stuff off as she told me. When we'd bathed her face with some lotion which looked like milk she held a mirror anxiously to her.

'It's lovely,' I said. 'Why d'you bother to do all this? You don't need it.'

'Do I look better than Madame Delcros?'

'There's no comparison,' I said. 'She's just a smart, well-dressed Frenchwoman. She's not beautiful like you.'

She was pleased—so pleased that I didn't add that Terence Mourne, who spoke exquisite French, had obviously been enjoying the witty repartee of his attractive companion. Somehow I doubted if beauty were enough for Terence Mourne.

'Well, how does *he* dance?' asked Thalia.

'Very well,' I said.

'And you?'

'Not so well with him. Better with Terence Mourne.'

'You can't dance with him because you like him. It makes you nervous.' She was resentful.

How did she know? She was sitting on the window-sill of the schoolroom. Claude was doing transfers. The table was covered with gaily coloured little stamps which he was transferring with the help of water into a book. 'Do some of these soldiers for me, Rachel—they just won't come off whole. All their legs stay behind.'

I took up a small square of a Guardsman. 'Where did you get these?' I asked him.

'Ali gave them to me. He got them in the bazaar. Look! All the Indian regiments as well!'

'Is your father's here?'

'I spoiled them all. Not one came off properly. I'm going into the Guards. Not an Indian Regiment like father's.'

'They won't have you. Nor will any Indian one!' taunted Thalia.

'Why d'you want to be a soldier?' I asked him as I began cautiously peeling off the transfer.

'Father's a soldier. Grandfather was a soldier. Great-grandfather was a soldier,' said Claude. 'Oh, Rachel! Goody! Goody! It's a beauty. Do another. *Please.*'

'One more, and then bed. Which will you have?'

'Wait a minute. I'll find a Guardsman. A Grenadier! That's the regiment I shall join. Here it is!'

'D'you really want to be a soldier?' I insisted.

'Yes, I do. I want to shoot and mow down the enemy. And all those tribesmen Daddy goes after. Bang! Bang! Down they go!' He had his toy gun in his hand and was firing at imaginary enemies.

'Silly! Silly little ass!' said Thalia contemptuously. 'It'd be *you* who was mown down. The army's hateful.'

'Look! Here's the Grenadier. He's very smart,' I cried.

Claude was enraptured and allowed himself to be carried off to bed clutching the page with the transfers on it.

When Cynthia was ready to go out and waiting in the *salon* for Terence to fetch her Marie came in grumbling. There was constant trouble between her and Cynthia, and I was always wretchedly involved as interpreter. 'Tell Madame that unless I can have my niece to help me I won't stay. I'm not accustomed to so much work. I'm a cook. Not a *bonne à tout faire*!'

'Tell her her niece wants too high wages. I cannot afford all that.'

'I'm quite willing to go on helping her with the bedrooms, and I'll do the children's tea,' I said.

'It's not only that. I want help with the *salon* and the *salle-à-manger* and the wash.'

'Tell her I can't discuss it now. I'm just going out. She must wait until to-morrow.'

Marie went off grumbling. She was a person who invariably got her own way. She never argued. She just got what she wanted by sheer will-power. I knew that the niece would be on the doorstep to-morrow morning and Cynthia would have to give in and agree to the wages. Every room now had its crucifix restored. Even Cynthia's. Marie simply put them back every time they were taken down. She didn't hang the one in Cynthia's room over the bed. She considered the bed 'heathen'. It was an importation from Paris of Madame's new husband.

'The honeymoon bed!' she had called it contemptuously. 'The old carved Breton one her first good man brought her to as a bride wasn't good enough for this man from Paris. No. He must have this heathenish painted horror.' She wondered Madame could sleep in it. There was a spare bed up in the attic and she had offered to change it for Cynthia. But Cynthia liked the bed. I think she rather fancied herself under the cupids holding the heart, and in any case, as she said, it was the only modern bed in the villa, and the most comfortable. Marie had brought her own feather mattress. She had arrived sitting on it in the cart drawn by Napoleon. She couldn't sleep on any other, she told me. Marie put the crucifix in a little alcove at the side of Cynthia's bed. Cynthia had removed it four times and hidden it each time in a different place, but it was no good—Marie always found it and restored it to the alcove.

'She says she can't work in a house which isn't protected from the Devil,' I told Cynthia. 'She says the Devil can get in any window and only the crucifix can keep him out.'

'These Bretons are ridiculously superstitious,' said Cynthia. 'I don't know if I'm going to be able to put up with her.'

'She's a wonderful cook,' I urged. 'And she's very economical.'

I knew this would weigh with Cynthia, who was always short of money. Her allowance came monthly to the Jules Boutin bank—but she had always spent it by the third week. And why should she mind the crucifixes? Thalia and I liked them. But I needn't have worried. Cynthia had given in. There was nothing else to do.

When she had gone and Claude was asleep, Thalia and I sat talking to Marie and Yves in the kitchen. Yves had come to borrow some money from Marie. She wouldn't give it him. 'He only wants to drink. The dirty drunkard!' she grumbled. 'I'm not throwing away my money. I have to work hard for it.'

Yves only laughed. 'She'll give it,' he said. 'She's not a bad old hen. A bit stringy now—but what can you expect?'

'Be silent, you wretch!' cried his sister.

'I was wondering,' said the old man, 'if you and Mademoiselle Thalia would care to come for a little ride. Napoleon's outside.'

'*Non!* Not unless I accompany you,' said Marie firmly. 'Don't go, Mademoiselle Rachel. He'll stop at every bistro and *boîte* and he gets so sozzled that he can't drive home. If it weren't for that clever horse who brings him home every Saturday like a sack of potatoes he'd be picked up and put in a cell.'

'I should love to go—perhaps another time,' I said.

'*Do* let's go!' cried Thalia.

'There's a Pardon in a fortnight. A special one,' said Marie. 'He could drive us all there.'

'But the cooking?' I asked.

'My niece is arriving to-morrow, she can do it,' said Marie calmly.

Thalia and I laughed. We had guessed correctly. Yves coaxed and coaxed and at last Marie went upstairs and came down with an old black leather purse. She drew a hundred francs grudgingly from it: 'Here, you good-for-nothing idle old wretch!' she scolded. 'I'll never see that back again. It'll go down the drain.'

Yves gave her a resounding kiss. 'You should be grateful to me for this kiss,' he chuckled. 'For no other man will give you one. You're nothing but an old stringy hen cooked in vinegar!'

'Be off with you. *Salaud!*' she screamed angrily, thrusting him out of the kitchen door. 'And don't show your ugly face in here again unless you bring me back that hundred francs.'

'Ah, but he's not a bad old thing,' she said, watching us laughing helplessly. 'But he's a man. They're all good for nothings—and you, Mademoiselle Rachel, meeting that Tréfours boy each day on the *plage*! Have a care. That's a wild godless family. The mother's from Paris.'

'But what's wrong with Paris?' I asked her. 'It's the capital of France.'

'It's the capital of wickedness,' said Marie lugubriously. 'And although I love my mistress, the Madame who owns this house, I wouldn't accompany her to that godless city. Brittany is good enough for me—as it was for her first dear husband.'

'But he's dead. She can't help her new husband being a Parisian.'

'One husband should be enough for any woman. What's she going to do in Heaven when they both turn up? Answer me that one.'

The prospect of this spectacle was so amusing that I drew a picture on the kitchen slate of the Madame with wings standing between two Monsieurs with wings. Both had their arms outstretched towards their wife and she with tears rolling down her plump face was torn by the dilemma of whose wife she now was. Marie and Thalia laughed heartily at this. 'But it's not a laughing matter,' Marie said gloomily. 'I often pray to the Virgin about it. For she's a good mistress and how she could be so foolish as to take a second husband I can't think.'

'You don't like men?' I asked curiously.

'They have their uses.'

'Without doubt!'

'But . . . no, Mademoiselle, I *don't* like them. They're all animals. It's the women who have the souls and the men the bodies.'

'What did she mean about the Tréfours?' asked Thalia when we were listening to the radio later.

'I don't know. She's a man-hater,' I said.

'But they're not liked here.'

'How d'you know?'

'At school. The girl Thérèse comes in for English lessons twice a week.'

'What girl?'

'His sister. Armand Tréfours's sister.'

'Where does she come from?'

'A convent in Dinan.'

This was news to me and for some reason it excited me. 'What's she like?'

'Very pretty . . . fair like him,' said Thalia grudgingly, 'but she's stuck up. No one likes her. They say, the other girls, that she's got no cause to put on airs. They say her father's a bad man.'

'Don't listen to such talk.' I was angry—and again I didn't know why. 'You should know better.'

'We have to talk about something,' said Thalia resentfully, 'why not the Tréfours? They are the richest people round here, it seems.'

This was also news to me—and news which I didn't like. I hadn't thought of Armand as a rich man's son. I suppose I should have known from the sports car. Not many boys in this part of France had their own expensive car.

'And Thérèse—*d'you* like her?'

'No,' said Thalia. 'I don't like her. I shouldn't like her anyway even if she weren't stuck up. She's Armand Tréfours's sister.'

'I'm going to write to your father to-night,' I said.

'Tell him Mother has gone dancing with Terence Mourne,' she said viciously.

Cynthia had gone in a party. She hadn't gone dancing with Terence Mourne. 'Why d'you distort things?' I asked.

'You don't know Mother,' said Thalia.

I was meeting Armand every day now—on the beach in the afternoons, on the wild wooded slopes of La Vicomté and sometimes even slipping out at night to meet him in a little bistro in the nearest square. Cynthia didn't allow me a key and it was Marie who let me in after these meetings. I would throw a pebble up at her window and she would come padding down in her old grey coat with a shawl thrown over her head. And she would scold and grumble at me, 'Take care. . . . Take care what you're doing. Every time you go to *him* I light a candle to Ste. Thérèse for your safety! Men are all the same. No! they won't be content until they've got what they want—and then they no longer want it.' Every time she let me in she would peer into my face and ask anxiously, '*Vous êtes encore vierge?* I lit a candle for you again. It was very expensive.' And she would scold and upbraid me soundly, but I would coax her and give her the money for the candles she burned.

Cynthia did not appear to notice my state of mind. She was immersed in herself, absorbed in some secret worry or trouble connected with her beauty. It was Thalia who intruded and forced herself into the dream in which I now lived. She would not be put off; she begged and persisted and followed us wherever she could. I couldn't refuse her often for I was after all there because of her. No matter where I was meeting Armand she invariably turned up somewhere in the offing. If he were reading to me—for he shared my love of poetry and was introducing me to his favourite poets—suddenly I would see Thalia's head bobbing up behind a bush or above a rock. It infuriated Armand. The only time when we could count on being free of her were the early mornings when she was at school or when I could slip out at night and he would be waiting for me down the road in his car.

I hadn't stopped to think what was happening to me until the day Marie came into my room when I was getting ready to go out with him. She had dressed for the afternoon in a stiff black dress with a small lace apron. She stood looking at me, her arms akimbo, her shrewd old eyes watchful as I fastened my dress.

'You meet him every day now, hein?'

I bowed my head. 'Almost.'

'In the woods above the Vicomté?'

'How d'you know?'

'Nothing is hidden in this place. Take care, take care, Mademoiselle Rachel. Youth is so impetuous—always in such a hurry. I must light a candle to Ste. Thérèse for you.'

I said nothing. I was silent.

'You are in love with him?'

Was I? I didn't know because I'd never been in love.

'His mother will not like it—and the Madame here—what will she say? She doesn't like the French.'

'It doesn't matter to me what *she* says,' I retorted. 'But *his* mother—that's different. Why won't she like me?'

'She has other ideas for her son. A rich industrialist's daughter. They live along the coast past St. Enogat. *His* mother's from Paris.'

Enough for Marie. I knew by the way she said it that she hadn't a good word for Armand's mother.

She saw the displeasure in my face and caught my arm. 'Don't think I'm interfering, Mademoiselle Rachel, but I'm a Breton—so are they. You don't know us. And your father, what will he say?'

'I don't know,' I said truthfully. I hadn't thought at all—there hadn't been time. What would he think? And my aunt? For that Armand was serious in his intentions I sensed. He hadn't kissed me as Terence always did. We danced, walked, drove and read poetry and books together, talked and exchanged ideas on everything. He spoke very little English but had taken my French in hand. 'You must read and read and listen!' he urged me. 'And you'll fall under the spell of my lovely language.' But he didn't need to urge me. I was already caught fast in its rainbow web.

That evening after I'd come in from spending the afternoon at La Vicomté with Armand, Thalia came to me. Her face was wretched. 'You never want me with you now—you never have time for me. It's Armand—Armand always. I hate him! I *hate* him!' and she burst out weeping.

I was stricken with remorse as I remembered my promise to her father.

'You were so lovely to me. So lovely—and now it's all changed.' She stood weeping bitterly. 'I thought you were different.'

'Be fair,' I said. 'We are together almost every evening and many afternoons. We go together to the ballet class and to Italian with Madame Valetta. On Sundays I'm with you all day and usually all Saturday too. The times I spend with Armand are short and squeezed in between my times with you—he has to work too.'

'He seems to have nothing to do but enjoy himself.'

'He is studying for his last examination. He's going to be a barrister—he's almost finished. He has to go to Rennes. He'll be away all the week—I'll be with you.'

'He's old. He's twenty-five!'

'How d'you know?'

'His sister told me so. She knows about *you*.'

'What did she say?'

'That Armand was mad about an English girl—and was it the Rachel who lives with us.'

But I heard no more. Those words 'mad about an English girl' gave me such bewildering joy that I knew then that I loved Armand Tréfours. I loved him—loved him.

I couldn't look at her and turned away.

Suddenly she began reciting in Armand's voice the poem 'Les Elfes' which I particularly loved—because it seemed to fit in with the curious fairy-tale quality of the country here. Armand, although he shared my love of Pierre de Ronsard, was teaching me to appreciate Leconte de l'Isle, Paul Verlaine, François Villon, Alfred de Musset and many others. I loved Leconte de l'Isle especially.

'Couronnés de thym et de marjolaine, les Elfes joyeux danse sur la plaine . . .'

Her voice was exactly his—his intonation, his accent . . . She must have been sitting very close to us and studied it when he had been reading to me on the cliffs above the Rance. Every verse of Leconte de l'Isle's lovely poem ends with the line she was quoting now. I could have struck her, I was so angry. 'Stop it! stop it!' I cried.

She laughed. 'I do it well, don't I? Yes. I heard him reading it—not only to you—but on several *other* occasions.' Then she said simply, 'You see—I like it too. I found it in the book he gave you and learned it all—shall I say it for you? I can say it almost as well as he does.'

'Thalia,' I said, 'd'you mind getting out of my room? I'm going to prepare my Italian lesson.'

She flung herself on me crying again. 'You're angry! You're angry! I only learned it to please you. You like it and I wanted you to be pleased.'

I thought of Mademoiselle Caron and her complaint that Thalia wouldn't speak a word of French. The way she had recited the poem had astounded me. I looked at her red-rimmed eyes and the tear-stained, blotched face, at the thin mousy hair, and I was immensely moved. I pushed away the fact that she must have been eavesdropping and spying on us even more frequently than I had suspected.

'I'm not pleased,' I said. 'How can I be? If you can learn a poem like that you can learn all that Mademoiselle Caron is trying to teach you.'

'I hate Mademoiselle Caron. She's two-faced.'

What could I say? I had disliked Mr. Cookson-Cander for no good reason at all. 'I do not like thee, Doctor Fell.' She didn't like her French governess and that was that.

'Rachel.' She put a timid hand on me. 'We don't laugh like we did. It's all changed. It was so lovely—so lovely! I was *so* happy. This Armand's spoilt it all.'

I pushed back the straggling hair and looked at her eyes. Unblinking and steady now they stared back at me. They were like the eyes of my spaniel Rags. She pressed her face against mine and her tears wetted my cheek.

'Thalia. Don't, don't,' I said, but she broke into dreadful sobs and it was ten minutes before I could comfort her.

I spent all the following week with her. Armand had gone to Rennes. He hadn't said that he would write but the day after he left Marie stumped up with a letter.

'From *him*!' she said dourly. 'Not content with telling you lies he must write them!'

I took it with my heart thumping in a sudden surge of emotion and with my hands shaking so much that I could scarcely tear open the envelope. . . .

'*Rachel, petite fleur, Ici seul dans ma chambre je t'écris . . .*'

Marie was standing there, her head on one side. '*Une lettre d'amour?*'

I read on . . . 'Yes,' I said, 'a love letter . . . my first.'

After that, knowing that his letters would come by the early post, I would run down and snatch them from Marie before Thalia woke. For they *were* love letters—the first I had ever received. Armand loved me. He loved me! I was radiantly, deliriously happy. 'When I come back, darling little English Miss,' he wrote, 'I will take you to my mother. I have told her about you, and she wants to see you.'

I had suggested to Cynthia that Thalia should go out sometimes with Marie's niece, Elise. But Thalia had other views. 'I won't go with her. I want to go out with Rachel.'

'You haven't been sketching lately,' said Cynthia languidly.

'It's not so warm now,' I said. It was never cold, but the wind could be very sharp and unless one could find a sheltered spot as Armand and I often did in the thick wooded slopes of the Rance, it wasn't possible to sit about for long.

'But you don't talk French with me,' I said.

'I think you'd better have French at the school now,' said Cynthia. 'You're not getting on at all with Mademoiselle Caron.'

Thalia said nothing. She knew that it would take her mother a long time to summon up energy enough to do anything about her French. Cynthia was strangely apathetic and seemed to have something on her mind. I asked her several times if she was well. She was often sleepy and looked dazed. She always replied that she was all right—it was just a tired heart. But she always managed to get up and look absolutely lovely for her afternoon bridge. She went out, as I often did, with Terence Mourne. I liked to dance with him, and he talked to me about all kinds of things. He was travelled and well read, and could be very good company. We never mentioned Cynthia. Since that first evening when I had made such a gaffe I knew better than to offend him again. Had it not been for this I would have asked his advice about her now—for he had known her in India. I asked Thalia if her mother was always sleepy and dazed like this. 'She's been taking her stuff,' said Thalia contemptuously.

'What stuff?'

'Some drops she gets in India. Ayah gets them for her. They cost a lot of money.'

'But what does she take them for?'

'She gets migraine . . . and she can't sleep.'

Remembering my promise to Tom Pemberton I asked Cynthia. She wouldn't look at me as she answered, 'They're quite harmless. They just make me sleep and forget things. No, they're not really for sleeping. I've got tablets for that.'

What could these drops be? My aunt took sleeping pills. It seemed extraordinary to me. I just got into bed, read a little because I wanted to—and when I wanted to sleep I slept. It was as simple as that.

Letters were coming fairly regularly from Tom Pemberton. After the incident of which he had written, which had got into the papers so that Cynthia had known about it, things seemed to be quieter on the N.W. Frontier. But there were constant skirmishes and the Fakir of Ipi was always stirring up trouble against the British. I had asked Terence to tell me about Frontier life and he had described it vividly to me. I had shown him Tom Pemberton's letter and he had told me about the Nahakki Pass and of the terrific heat there—so great that one could see it quivering and dancing on the great barren rocks.

'You were in the same regiment?' I asked him.

'For a time, yes. I left it rather suddenly.'

'Something funny happened,' Thalia had said. 'Something funny.' But Thalia's idea of fun was not everybody's. There was something cruel in it as Cynthia had warned me. What was that something funny? He didn't tell me and I couldn't ask him. Nor could I ask Cynthia. Whenever I mentioned Terence a little flicker crossed her face and she usually changed the subject. And yet she went out with him —or anyhow in his parties. He entertained a good deal both at the Casino, which was now only open at week-ends, and in the lovely Crystal. Cynthia and I could never be in his parties together because Cynthia wouldn't leave Claude in the house with Thalia and Marie. She didn't trust her beloved son to either of them. Sometimes Thalia took him on the beach or for a short walk—but Cynthia would be in a fever of anxiety until they came back.

'But Thalia will soon be sixteen!' I protested. 'She's got quite a sense of responsibility.'

'You don't know her yet. She's unpredictable. I don't trust her with Claude. She's jealous of him.'

Claude and I still sat opposite one another every morning wrestling with reading. He was getting on very slowly—but he could read a little. I had found that by drawing objects and animals he learned far more quickly. I had made some large sheets with letters and the objects they represented in bright chalks. He loved these, and really tried hard. The day he actually read a whole page of the reader I hugged him. I felt the same strange intense happiness which achieving a difficult feat in the ballet class gave me. Cynthia was delighted and praised me warmly. When she came back from the town that afternoon she gave me a pair of very fine silk stockings and some perfume I had liked when she had used it.

Every afternoon of that week, Thalia and I went for long rambles round the coast. The path wound above the steep cliffs through thick dark tunnels of bushes emerging into dazzling glimpses of sea. Sometimes we would be standing sheer above a little bay, its white virgin sand untouched as yet by a mark. The water was so green and translucent that we could lie on our stomachs and see the fish and each frond of sea-weed. I remembered legends Armand had told me, and told them to her, lying on the rocks looking up at the sky with the sea far below us. I told her about Vivian and Merlin, Gilles de Bretagne and of Tristram and Iseult. This last was her favourite. She liked to say that she hated history—but she was entranced with these legends. 'Can we get them to read?' she asked.

'Only in French.'

We went to St. Lunaire to Judy, and took Claude to play with Mimi. They fought and scratched each other, but Judy only laughed. It was good for Mimi—for them both, she said. But Claude had a long angry scratch down his left cheek and Cynthia was furious. 'American children are so ill-behaved.'

'Mimi's much better brought up than Claude,' said Thalia, who had loved Judy's fat bundle of a daughter.

'It may leave a mark,' said Cynthia.

'Good thing if it does. He looks like a girl.' Thalia was contemptuous.

'You would be lucky if you had his skin and complexion,' said her mother angrily, and at Thalia's sudden withered look I was angry too. I put some ointment on Claude's face and that night when I was bathing him, he said, 'I didn't mind her scratching me. I'd like to be covered all over with wounds and scars—like some of the Gurkhas and Pathans! They're all criss-crossed!'

'Did you like Mimi?'

'Not much. Rachel, I wish I had some boys to play with.'

I asked Cynthia if he couldn't go now to the kindergarten part of the school. They had a number of little English and American boys there. But she was dubious. 'He's so young.'

'He's getting on for seven,' I said. 'In England he'd have to go to school.'

'He's doing very well with you and Mademoiselle says his French is excellent. He has a perfect accent.'

He had. It was far better than mine.

I took Thalia to St. Malo and we visited the ramparts, the dungeons and the tower built by the Duchesse Anne, the famous Quiquengrogne Tower. I took her into the museums there and told her about the history of Brittany and of how the Duchesse Anne had united it with France. We pored over maps and engravings and portraits of Chateaubriand, and of Jacques Cartier, the discoverer of Canada.

I had been fascinated at the other side of history—the French version of famous battles and events. Cynthia, when I had commented on this, had said stiffly that she was surprised that I could even entertain their veracity. There was only one version of history—the British one—and for me to doubt its integrity was in her opinion treachery to my country.

And I don't want Claude taught such distorted facts!' she had said severely.

'Mother's just like that over anything Indian,' said Thalia scornfully. 'Anything Indian must be wrong—only the British can be right.'

But Tom Pemberton did not think that way. From the few conversations with me on the subject he had made it abundantly clear that his whole outlook was to be of service to India—even if that involved, as it undoubtedly did, considerable sacrifices. Whenever Cynthia spoke of this, and of how she could have pulled strings for her husband's promotion if he would give up some of his ideas, it was with unmistakable bitterness.

All that Armand had showed me I showed Thalia, all that he had told me I told her. We went up the steep narrow streets of St. Malo with the open drains running down each side and with people throwing slops into it from their windows, we went over the old cathedral which was more like a great fortress than a church and was used as such in the days of the constant sieges and sea battles. I bought her books and pictures to remember what I had told her, postcards and souvenirs, and then we sat in a café and ate as many *vedettes*—little cakes shaped like the boats, filled with green and white cream—as we could.

When we were going back to Dinard she said, 'I wish you taught me history and English literature. I hate it at school—and when you tell me it's so alive that I'll never, never forget it.' And that's how it was when Armand told it to me. I would never forget it. Never.

'Thalia,' I said, as we passed St. Servan and the estuary of the Rance, 'will you do something for me?'

'What?' she said suspiciously.

'Write a letter to your father and tell him a little of what we've been doing to-day and all this week.'

We were sitting over the built-in engine of the boat and foul smoke kept coming up and obliterating us from one another, but the wind was keen and it was warmer here in the centre.

Her face was hidden now in a puff of evil-smelling smoke but I heard her say, 'I'd have done that anyway. I write everything we do—you and I—to him, just as I write it in my diary.'

'He'll like all the bits of history—tell him all about the Quiquengrogne Tower and the Duchesse Anne—you liked that, didn't you?'

'Quiquengrogne! Quiquengrogne!' she repeated. 'I like it . . . did you notice that everything had been named after it? Cafés, restaurants, shops and streets?' She took my ungloved hand. 'You're cold, Rachel. Put it in my pocket.'

I put my hand in her pocket. She pressed her hand over the pocket. 'Only two more days,' she sighed.

'What d'you mean? Two more days of what?'

'Two more days of *you*. He'll be back on Monday.'

My heart leaped. I could have shouted and sung with the sudden rush of feeling. 'Yes. He's coming back . . . he's coming back—and then he'll take me to his mother.' But what I said was, 'I'll take you to the concert in the Casino on Saturday, and there's the Pardon on Sunday . . . we'll get Cynthia to let us go with Marie and Yves, after all, she's got Elise now.'

She was pressed into my side trying to keep the wind off me. 'You're so frail-looking, Rachel,' she said. 'You mustn't blow away in the wind.'

There was a colour in her cheeks from the whipping air, her hair blew all over her face and her beret had slipped over one eye. I had never been so drawn to her as at that moment. Poor lonely, unhappy child . . . what could I do about her insistent following of us? Suddenly I had an idea. I would get her a dog. She missed her pets, she said so frequently. I had seen how she loved Clodagh's dogs. She should have a dog—and perhaps she would leave Armand and me alone.

CHAPTER VIII

CYNTHIA HAD to be coaxed about our going to the Pardon. It was not the religious ceremony to which she objected most, although she didn't approve of that, it was the fact that we were going with Yves and Marie and that their relatives had invited us to midday dinner with them.

'You've been to the Mont St. Michel Pardon, and to the fishing fleet one at St. Malo—they're all the same. Why go to this particular little affair?'

It was just because it was a particular little one that we wanted to go. Anyone could go to the large Pardons—the small, special, almost private ones were difficult to hear of and more difficult to attend.

'I don't care for your going to these peasants. I'm not at all sure that I like Marie and Yves.'

'Thalia and I *do*! We like them immensely. And Marie has been with the owner of this villa for years.'

'That's exactly what I don't like. The way she's wormed her way into this house again and is gradually getting it back to how *she* likes it.'

'She didn't worm herself in. You sent Rachel to fetch her after Madeleine left,' said Thalia indignantly.

'She's very clever. She works her way like a mole—underground.'

I could not see that this was fair. It was natural that Marie should love the house where she had worked for so long. Thalia and I loved her. We would often coax her up to the little room, push her into the old basket chair and implore her to tell us some of the very old legends of the district. Sometimes she would, but not always. Sometimes she was dour and silent and wouldn't talk to us at all.

'If you both go on Sunday I'll have to take Claude to church with me and have him all the afternoon,' was Cynthia's next objection.

'Let Elise take him on the beach or the Promenade.'

'I don't know if she's trustworthy.'

Claude was a handful now that he had the football. He was for ever kicking it along the Promenade, which in the afternoons boasted quite a number of nurses and governesses with small children. The ball frequently hit some small child or Claude would send it flying through the railings on to the beach far below and then scream with fear lest the sea got it. I was quite accustomed to chasing after both the ball and him. Cynthia wouldn't dream of running; it would be bad for both her heart and complexion. If Claude went out with his mother the football stayed at home and he sulked. He loved the thing so passionately that he never went to bed without it. Cynthia objected to its presence in the bed for hygienic reasons, but often when I went in to wake him and attend to his needs at ten o'clock at night he was asleep with the football clutched in his arms.

Finally the problem of Claude's Sunday afternoon was solved by Judy inviting both Cynthia and him out to St. Lunaire.

'I'd adore to come to the Pardon with you,' said Judy, 'but your old Marie would never agree.'

'Why not?'

'She disapproves of all Americans. I wanted her to work for me—she's a wonderful cook—but when she found out that I have silk sheets on my bed she wouldn't hear of coming.'

Judy went into fits of laughter at the recollection. 'She was scandalized. Said no respectable woman would sleep in silk. That God meant good women to sleep in linen or cotton. But I think it was really the fact that they were of coloured silk that shocked her most. No, I've lost me a good cook by my sybaritism.'

'What colour are they?' I was thrilled about the silk sheets. I had never seen any but linen or cotton.

'Pink—peach really—and a lovely soft blue.'

'And are they really made of silk?'

'Crêpe de Chine.'

'How heavenly.'

You silly child! I'll give you a pair for Christmas. I always have silk ones. They are much warmer than cotton and linen.'

This story explained the extraordinary stiffness with which Marie always greeted Judy when she came to the house to see us.

'Tell me all about the Pardon, won't you? And I hope Napoleon gets you there. It'll take hours!'

'That's the attraction for Thalia. It isn't the Pardon, but the horse. Yves has promised she can drive him part of the way.'

When Sunday came, although it was one of those wet, dreary days such as only Brittany can offer, we went with Yves and Marie to the Pardon. And there, near the tiny village, in the dripping rain, I saw, to my astonishment, Armand.

He had written me that he would not be back in his home until Sunday and that he would telephone me that evening, but suddenly I saw his face amongst the crowd of rapt peasants gathered round the Calvaire. Was it him? Or was it someone like him? No. There could be no other like him. He stood between two men in dark, sombre Sunday clothes. All the men were bare-headed, their wide-brimmed black hats in their hands. Armand's hair caught the light, he was as fair as was Claude. I could see only his profile against the dark ones of the men beside him—but the absorbed devotion in it caught at my heart. Between those rugged old faces on either side of him the young lines of his nose and throat were doubly noticeable.

Thalia stood beside me, between Marie and old Yves. It had rained all night and the ground in the little wood was sodden, and drips fell like great tears on to the Christ of the Calvaire around which we were gathered. We were on the outer edge of the crowd, it was almost noon, and the High Mass was being celebrated. Many of the pilgrims had been here all night and around us were their conveyances—buses, cars, lorries, bicycles and motor cycles, horses and traps.

Marie did not know the exact reason for the Pardon. It was just a special one, she said, almost a private one without any tourists and vulgar sightseers. She stood with me, her face withdrawn, enraptured. Yves was weeping as were many of the pilgrims. The great Pardon at Mont St. Michel had failed to move me—but this one did. Devoid of any commercialism its simplicity was lovely.

We had missed the Procession because Yves hadn't started early enough and the drive had been a wet and slow one. Enveloped in mackintoshes, Thalia and I had sat in the back of the cart, in spite of Marie's shocked protests that my place at least, was in the front with Yves. As it was, it had taken all her urging and chivvying to get her brother and Napoleon here in time for the Mass. Thalia and I had clung together as the cart swayed and rocked over the bumpy roads, giggling at Marie's loud abuse of her brother's driving.

I wondered now what Thalia was thinking of the scene as we stood there in the rain. Her face was expressionless. Neither of us had actually discussed religion beyond accepting the Amarna tenet. Cynthia insisted that we accompany her to church just as my aunt had insisted that I help her decorate the church and altar each week. But did they really believe in it?

I had a shock when I saw Armand there. I was struck by the almost fanatical devotion in his face, and with another shock I realized that he was absolutely one of these people gathered here—he belonged here.

I had seen him as the runner in brief trunks, I had seen him in expensive lounge suits, in sports clothes, and in immaculate evening ones, but here, as I saw him now, was the real Armand—as if he were naked. I could not doubt this as he turned his face towards the Calvaire. He had a dedicated look—one I didn't know at all.

And then, instead of thinking of the solemn spectacle around me, I began thinking of how little any of us knows of the others. Perhaps that was why portraits fascinated me so much. Sometimes the painter sees more—sometimes less than the ordinary observer. Cynthia? What was the thing which was tearing at her? So that she could not sleep or eat? Thalia? Why did she hate her mother now when once she had adored her? And my aunt? Was she as devoted to her religion as were all these simple souls here? She went to church every Sunday and all the best flowers in the garden were saved for the altar. But if I spoke of God—and I often did—she looked faintly embarrassed and ashamed. To her He certainly was not an everyday name such as He was to these Bretons.

Cynthia had been so contemptuous of the Pardons. 'They're no better than heathen worshipping idols,' she had said. 'Carrying round their preposterous saints and treating them as if they are real.'

But what if they were right? These people were good. Really good—it was stamped indelibly on their faces and in their eyes. Their simplicity demanded that their saints were there in concrete form. An absent or symbolic Christ or saint was too difficult for their imagination. The rain trickling down my neck and making Thalia's hair into wet snakes was uppermost in my mind, but on the weather-beaten faces around us the drops simply fell off, leaving no impression but an even cleaner, more shining transparency. Immersed in their devotion, rapt, entranced, they stood apart from everything but their God.

And Armand was one of them. He was a Catholic. And I an agnostic, a worshipper of the sun. What if I were wrong? As I looked up at the Calvaire an emotion I had never experienced swept me, and tears suddenly poured down my face, mingling with the rain. I did not look at Thalia when she squeezed my arm in concern. When it was over and I raised my head again, Armand was looking at me. Above that sea of bent heads he had recognized and smiled at me; and although the rain was now deluging down it seemed that the sun was out and a rainbow stretched from him to me.

After the Mass he fought his way through the crowd to us and asked us where we were going to eat. He seemed as astonished at seeing us here as I was at seeing him.

'With Marie's relatives,' I said. 'Here in the village.'

'You've no idea how honoured you are,' he said, surprised. 'They don't care for strangers here. It's not like Dinard.'

'We've brought a contribution to the feast,' I said.

'I hope it's in liquid form,' he said laughing. 'You'll be very popular guests if it is.'

Marie had advised Calvados and Armagnac as our gift to her relatives who were to be our hosts. I hoped that Yves or Marie would invite Armand to join us, but they did not. They seemed relieved when he said good-bye, watching us climb up in the old cart with a rueful smile.

'I can drive you—it's far too wet that way. Let me take you in the car.'

But Thalia adored the cart, she said it reminded her a little of the bullock carts in India, and she was determined to drive Napoleon. I think Armand thought we were mad—but it did not worry us. We were Yves' and Marie's guests, and as such were accepted here. The villagers, as Armand said, did not much care for strangers at their special Pardons.

I watched Armand drive off alone in his white car. It looked out of place and almost vulgar amongst the humble vehicles around it. I wondered why he had come? I asked Marie. He had spent part of his childhood near here, she said indifferently.

We were very wet when we reached the small farm belonging to Marie's cousins and climbed down stiffly. Grand'mère and the very old women of the family had waited at home with the meal for us, and they welcomed us in with a simple courtesy which was lovely.

The kitchen was dark, with very small windows, and seemed crowded with people and massive furniture. Marie, who took us outside, had warned us of the primitive sanitary arrangements, but even so we were not prepared for the great pit with the two handles to which one had to cling. We laughed so much that she came banging on the door of the privy reminding us that others were waiting.

'Imagine Mother here,' shrieked Thalia. 'The tent at Dinan Market was nothing compared to this.' And we laughed helplessly at Cynthia's horror of the French lack of modesty.

The men were drying their boots round the kitchen stove, which had a long chimney, and they all hung their dripping coats over the pipe and their wet boots steamed and smelled. Everyone was cheerful and merry and we were both handed a glass of a strong spirit which caught at one's throat.

'Drink it, Mademoiselle,' urged Yves. 'It'll save you getting colds!'

It was Calvados, which I had not yet tasted. We were taken upstairs to wash in a dark, terrifying room. There was an enormous feather bed in it with a magnificent carved head-piece and massive great cupboards. We washed from a china basin and dried our hands on a towel of very fine embroidered linen.

'You know what?' said Thalia. 'That sampler ought to be in here.'

I looked round the austere, forbidding room. Extraordinary to think that many young brides had been brought home to it. Marie had told us so. Yes. Thalia was right. The sampler belonged to just such a room. The tiny windows shut out the trees and the sky. Here a child might have sat and embroidered such words as those while its eyes sought longingly for the sun.

We ate at a rough, thick oak table, polished with use and age. The hen was cooked in a kind of thick soup with garlic and vegetables in it. We all dipped hunks of bread in it and put our mouths down to the plates when they all but overflowed. The men smacked their lips noisily and Yves teased Marie constantly, saying that her cousin's cooking was better than hers. Our plates were of a thick, brown earthenware and our spoons and knives of pewter.

Thalia and I found the food wonderfully good for we were very hungry after our early start. We drank cider, and a rather weak beer made locally, and ate quantities of a soft cheese which they made at the farm, with hard, sweet, small pears.

Yves took us round the place with his cousin and we petted the animals—miserable as they were, the dogs tied to short chains in the yard and the cows and horses, thin and dejected. The place smelt of manure and wet—a steamy earthy mustiness, but it was all neat enough and much of the dreariness and dirtiness was due to the weather. There was a small terrier of a kind I had noticed in these parts with a most appealing face. Thalia couldn't tear herself away from him. She was indignant at the short chain to which he was fastened and at which he had strained so much that his neck was sore and all the hair had rubbed off.

'He's a misery—a nuisance,' said Yves' cousin. 'He's not worth looking at, Mademoiselle. A miserable dog—always howling.'

Thalia asked his name. 'Name? He has no name. He's just a dog. We never bothered to name him.'

When she had gone with Yves to harness Napoleon I asked our host if I could buy the dog. He was astounded. 'Buy him? Why, Mademoiselle, he's not worth buying! We shall drown him one of these days if he doesn't stop howling.'

I persisted and finally he agreed to accept two hundred francs for the animal.

We took him on a piece of rope, much to Marie's horror.

'Madame won't like that creature,' she grumbled.

I knew Madame wouldn't, but I didn't care. For Thalia's face when I handed her the dog, saying that I had bought him for her, was compensation enough for Cynthia's displeasure.

Thalia drove Napoleon home. She had harnessed him herself, Yves told me proudly, just as she had taken him from the shafts on our arrival and fed and watered him. I asked her how she knew how to do all this. 'The Regiment had three tongas at Dehra Dun,' she explained. 'They're little two-wheeled carriages, and the syces or grooms let me harness the ponies and groom them.'

Old Yves was greatly impressed with the deftness of her handling of Napoleon. 'The horse is no fool—he realizes that you know your job,' he told her. 'You should marry a farmer, Mademoiselle—you'd be worth your weight in gold to him.'

Did you understand?' I shouted to her as we bowled along the bumpy roads.

'Not all,' she yelled back above the howls of the dog tied in the back with Marie and me. She flushed with pride and pleasure when I told her what Yves had said.

It took a long time to get home. Yves had drunk a lot of our Armagnac and Calvados and we had to stop frequently for him to disappear into the bushes. 'It's only out of courtesy to you that he bothers to disappear—usually he doesn't trouble,' grumbled Marie. The rain had stopped and the air was soft and the smells from the countryside redolent and fresh. Marie complained at the hardness of the cart and at the dog's plaintive howls. I pulled the dirty creature on to my lap in spite of her protests that I wasn't to touch him until he'd had a bath in disinfectant. He curled gratefully into the warmth of my lap and I didn't listen to her warnings about fleas, mud, and above all, Madame's not being pleased at such an addition to the household. I was seeing again that crowd of rapt, devoted faces round the Calvaire. I wanted to paint a composition of the scene and of all those faces, that of Armand as I had seen it then was the most vivid and disturbing.

My aunt had reached Egypt now and postcards and snapshots had begun arriving from her. I couldn't look at them without thinking of the terrible fuss which was responsible for my having come to Brittany. Two months ago I had resented it—but now I almost loved the Reverend Cookson-Cander—but for him I might never have met Armand.

'I will send you all the reproductions for which you asked me,' wrote my aunt on a postcard of the Pyramids, 'and all that I can obtain of your beloved Akhenaten and Nefertiti.' She was, I knew, rather annoyed at the way in which I had taken to heart Akhenaten's 'Living in Truth' theory. Like my father, she reminded me that there were certain standards of convention in courtesy which sometimes necessitated what I unhesitatingly called lies.

'Mr. Cookson-Cander,' she had written on a snapshot, 'has been bitten by a camel. . . .'

Thalia and I examined with growing merriment the extraordinary pictures of the party on camels—with veils tied on their hats to shield them from the sand, Mr. Cookson-Cander, proud and erect, leading them on a most contemptuous-looking beast. Thalia adored this snapshot and we decided that the contemptuous mount was undoubtedly the one which had bitten the Reverend. 'Perhaps it thought he was an egg!' she giggled. She knew the story of the egg-like portrait.

'You're absolutely right, Rachel. He *is* like an egg!'

'A camel bite can be very nasty,' remarked Cynthia seriously when I showed her the snapshot. 'There were camels in the bazaar in Lahore. They came in with the merchants from the desert—some of them were quite vicious.'

'I like them. Especially this contemptuous one carrying the Cookand!' giggled Thalia unabashed. This was a nickname she had contrived for the double-barrelled name. From my descriptions of him she could and did give excruciatingly funny imitations of his pompous dissertations.

'How silly you two girls are!' said Cynthia disgustedly. We were sitting in her room the evening of the Pardon. There had been trouble because we had arrived home so late and she had been apprehensive, thinking that perhaps Yves had been drinking and there had been an accident. When we began telling her about the Pardon she cut us short. 'I don't want to hear anything about it. I saw quite enough of those religious outbursts with idols and hysteria in India—they make me tired. And so do these people here all going to Mass and coming home with a yard of bread under their arms.'

She was polishing her smallest finger-nail with a buffer. She didn't paint her nails as I did but put on some pink stuff and then polished them. The postcard and snapshots at which we were looking were scattered all over her bed. She pushed them now towards me in a heap and without looking up said: 'I'm going to Paris on Tuesday for a week or so. I'll be leaving Claude and Thalia in your charge, Rachel.'

I was so astonished that all I said was: 'By car or train?'

'Train,' she said shortly. 'Can I trust you to look after Claude properly?'

'You should know whether or not you can trust me,' I said reluctantly. It wasn't that I was afraid of the responsibility of a child but that my immediate reaction was that if she went away my time with Armand would be curtailed.

'I *do* trust you, Rachel. It's just that you're so young. When I see you giggling in this way with Thalia I realize how immature you are.'

'Then why not get somebody else to look after them?' I said stiffly.

'I've made all my arrangements to go on Tuesday. I'm sure I can safely leave the household to you for a week.'

Why didn't she tell me with whom she was going? She wasn't a person who would go anywhere alone.

'I'm going out to dinner with Armand Tréfours to-morrow,' I said. 'And I shall want to go out with him while you're away.'

She had looked at me in an odd way when Thalia had mentioned that we had met Armand at the Pardon but had made no comment. Now she said crisply: 'Go out to dinner with him to-morrow, by all means, but a week without seeing each other will be very good for you both.'

'You mean I shan't be able to go out with him while you're away?'

'I expect you to be here in the house when I'm away.'

'Every evening? But why? Marie and Elise are both here.'

'I don't care to leave Claude with French servants.'

'But you left him with Indian ones.'

She flushed angrily. 'Thalia has been talking again.'

'Can I ask Armand here then?'

'I'd rather you didn't.'

'Cynthia,' I said, 'you don't trust me. Otherwise you'd allow me to ask Armand here.'

'It's not that. It's that he's most unsuitable for you—he's a peasant—a Breton peasant. You met him at Mrs. Tracey's, didn't you? When you've finished the portrait of her, Thalia's not to go there any more, and I'd rather you didn't.'

I was very angry at what she had said about Armand—but at this last I stared at her in astonishment. 'But why ever not? What has my friendship with Armand Tréfours to do with Thalia and Clodagh's?'

'Mrs. Tracey isn't received at the Consul's or at any of the British houses here.'

Thalia, who had been staring at her mother with a white, tense face, demanded: 'D'you mean I'm not to go to Clodagh's any more?'

'I do. And she's not to come here either.'

Thalia got up from the bed. She gave her mother a look of open contempt. 'But she's at school—I see her every day—you can't stop that!'

'But why? What's the reason?' I asked, bewildered.

'It is because I like Clodagh and you like Catherine,' said Thalia angrily. 'Mother's like that. You'd better know it.'

'Be quiet,' said Cynthia. 'I'm not prepared to discuss my reasons with you at the moment, Rachel. I'll wait until you've finished the portrait. I don't want to spoil it for you.'

'It's spoilt now. I won't be able to finish it after this— you *must* tell me what's wrong.'

'I've already said that I don't care to discuss the matter with you at present. Sufficient that Thalia is not to go there and I'd rather that your friendship with Mrs. Tracey ceases when you've finished her portrait.'

'But I like Catherine immensely. I can't treat my friends like that.' I was so angry that the words were choked.

'Then ask her yourself why she isn't received anywhere.'

'I wouldn't dream of it. It's because she's separated from her husband. Because she's had the decency to be honest instead of living as a hypocrite,' I said scornfully. 'My uncle ran away with his cook years ago because he couldn't stand the hypocrisy of living with a woman he didn't love. No one receives him now except Father.'

Cynthia lay back on her pillows. 'You're so young. You make me tired. You're impossible. You tire me more than Claude did this afternoon. You'd better get to bed. It's late. I'd like some hot milk—I'm going to take a sleeping tablet. Good night, Thalia.'

But Thalia had rushed from the room and was waiting for me on the stairs. Her eyes were wretched. 'I shall go to Clodagh's. I *shall*. She's the first school friend I've ever had.'

'Don't worry. We can meet her in the town. I'll take you both to Le Bras sometimes.'

This was the large *patisserie* which Thalia and I liked to visit.

'Oh, Rachel! Will you? Will you really?'

'Yes,' I said firmly. 'Unless Cynthia gives me a good reason for your not going there I'll certainly take you both out in the town.'

'And I've got Quiquengrogne now!' she said. 'He's better than anyone—except you.'

Cynthia had made surprisingly little fuss about the dog. She had been thinking of nothing but her trip to Paris—and except for stipulating that he slept outside in a kennel she made but a feeble objection. 'It's not a bad idea to have a dog if he's a watchdog,' she said. 'We have no man in the house.'

Thalia had named the creature after the famous tower of the Duchesse Anne. It got shortened by us all to Kiki—but Thalia stuck firmly to his full name. With a bath and daily brushings he improved out of all recognition. He adored Thalia and the two were soon inseparable.

CHAPTER IX

I WORE my first black frock to dine with Armand that night. Madame Cérise had made it for me, and it was the first dress of mine which really pleased me. She had told me to strip when I went to her. 'Walk,' she said to me when I was naked. 'Walk, bend, stretch, up and down. *Allez! Allez!*'

As I paced up and down her work *salon* she studied me carefully.

'I shall design something to make the best of your figure. To flatter your good points—to eliminate your bad ones,' she said. 'By the time you are twenty there won't be any bad ones.'

Did she tell everyone this? I asked Cynthia if Madame Cérise had made her strip and walk naked up and down the work *salon*.

'She had the impertinence to suggest something of the sort, but I soon put her in her place,' said Cynthia. 'I hope you did no such thing?'

I admitted that I had. Cynthia was horrified. 'How stupid you are, Rachel—she's a divine *couturière* but she's definitely *odd*. I should have thought you'd know about such things.'

'She isn't odd,' I retorted hotly. 'If you were an artist you'd understand why she needs to study a naked figure. Everybody is different, it's she who has to camouflage the bad points, how can she do that if she hasn't actually seen them?'

'My figure has no bad points to hide,' said Cynthia shortly, 'so there's no possible excuse for it in my case.'

When the black frock arrived I thought it a dream. Thalia watched me dress in silence. I had twice asked her to get out of my room. She had been sulking ever since she'd discovered that I was dining with Armand. When I stood surveying myself in the inadequate mirror she set her lips tightly together. 'You look about forty!' she wailed. 'I think it's an awful dress.'

'You need to be blonde to wear dead black,' was Cynthia's only comment. And Armand didn't like it.

'Too sophisticated for you,' he said thoughtfully, screwing up his green eyes. 'I like you better in that silly little-girl English dress that you usually wear.'

I could have cried with disappointment for Madame Cerise wasn't cheap and I had spent all that money just to please him. He must have seen this in my face for he said: 'Little idiot, wanting to look older than you are. Most women want to look younger.' And he had laughed at me.

There was a curious embarrassment in our meeting that night. Between us lay not only the letters but the Calvaire. We had said in the letters what we hadn't spoken and it was as if the bridge which they should have made had become a gulf. The formality of his greeting had shattered me. What had I expected?

I couldn't eat, the food stuck in my throat. We sat opposite each other in the restaurant and the silence grew unbearable. Quite suddenly he took my hand and gathered my fingers into the palm of his own. 'Let's go,' he said.

There were still flowers in the ornamental gardens on the Clair-de-Lune Promenade and on the dark bushes by the sea; in the moonlight their everyday form and colour was transformed. They were strange, exotic, unknown blooms.

Warm, windless, still as glass, the sea washed with the regular pulsating beat of a heart on beach and rocks, making a little sighing swish as each successive wave broke. We walked with our arms twined, our bodies pressed closely together. I looked from his downbent head to the enchanted sea and sky behind us and I knew that for the beauty of this moment the whole of my life had been waiting. When, as his hands caressed me, there tumbled from him all the lovely endearments he had used in the letters they seemed, because they were what I wanted so much to hear, as beautiful as the poetry he had read so often to me on the banks of the Rance.

How long we stayed there in the shadows of the tamarisks and ilex I don't know but it was very late when I threw a pebble up at Marie's window. She came down grumbling and disapproving, but I flung my arms wildly round her old neck and cried that I was deliriously happy.

She put her hands on my shoulders, pushing me back a little so that she could peer into my face. 'So you're in love with him! I was worried, it's terribly late. It's a scandal!'

'But it's all right. I'm quite safe with Armand. He loves me, Marie. He loves me!'

'Dear Mother of God, just listen to her. No one who loves is safe. No one. You'll weep before this business is finished. Two candles have burned down almost to their sockets for your protection this night!'

Dear, gloomy old Marie. I pulled a handful of notes from my bag and stuffed them down the neck of her thick flannel nightgown. 'Take these for some more candles.'

She hurried me grumbling under her breath up the stairs past Cynthia's door.

'She's only just put out her light. Packing! For Paris.'

Even in the whisper there was venom in her pronunciation of the town whose name spelled magic for so many others.

I stood at the window. The last sounds of Armand's car had died away but the feel of his kisses still burned me up. I put my arms across my chest and hugged myself. 'I'm in love! I'm in love!' I told the sophisticated woman in the black dress who smiled back at me from the mirror.

Cynthia left in a taxi for the station and didn't want me to see her off. She had left me an address in Paris in case of emergency. It was an hotel in the Passy district.

'But I don't want you to bother me with letters and things. I need a complete rest for a few days,' she insisted.

Thalia came in very late from school with a smug self-satisfied look on her face. I asked her where she had been.

'Seeing Mother off.'

'She wouldn't allow me to go with her to the station,' I said, astonished that she had permitted Thalia to do so.

'She didn't know I was there,' said Thalia. 'And she wasn't alone.'

'Who was with her?'

'Two guesses,' she said in a maddeningly mysterious voice. I was giving Claude his lunch and hadn't time to waste. I offered the names of two women with whom Cynthia frequently played bridge.

'No.'

'Well, who was it then?' I was impatient.

'The person I knew she would be with—Terence Mourne.'

I stared in disbelief. Cynthia was correct in every detail of conventional social life—that she would go to Paris with Terence astounded me. I didn't believe Thalia. I was becoming accustomed to her love of telling extraordinary stories about happenings in India and then saying calmly that she had invented them.

'Alone with him?' I said sharply.

She blinked, but I stared unmercifully at her. '*Was* she alone with him?'

'There were two others,' she admitted grudgingly. 'But maybe they'd just met on the station.'

Claude finished his meal and ran off.

'What happened to Terence Mourne in India?' I asked, 'tell me—and I want the truth.'

'You're very fond of truth, aren't you, Rachel? Sometimes it's better not to know it.'

'It's always better to know it. There is nothing else that matters.'

'Well, if you must know. There was an urgent despatch which came for Terence and he should have done something at once. He should have been in the station but he was off somewhere with Mother. Ayah said a runner was sent after him but that Mother took the despatch and kept it from him because it would have spoilt their week-end.'

'And?'

'Seven men got killed in the riots because no reinforcements were sent.'

'And your father, where was he?'

'Dealing with the riots—waiting for the reinforcements which Terence never sent.'

I hated myself for asking the girl about all this—but it seemed to me essential to know the truth of it.

'And where was all this?'

'In the Cantonments. Ayah says that Terence hates Mother since that. She says that Mother ruined his career . . . he had to resign from the Regiment.'

Did this explain the rather cynical, bitter outlook which one couldn't fail to notice in Terence Mourne? Did he regret his career? 'Thank God I've finished with all that . . .' he had said lightly to Tom Pemberton when we had been standing on the quay at St. Malo. I was suddenly ashamed of having listened to this gossip—but hadn't I asked a child to tell it me? That was worse. But the story intrigued me. I *had* to know.

'Where were you at that time?'

'In the bungalow with Ayah and Ali.'

'Weren't you lonely?'

She shrugged her shoulders. 'There were the animals. We had a little tiger called Samshi. He was a darling and played with our Sealyhams. Daddy found him in the jungle as a tiny cub—and we brought him up with the dogs. And I had a mongoose—and the loveliest little fawn. . . .'

Her voice, as always when speaking of India, was full of a nostalgic longing.

'Didn't you have a pet snake too?' I shot at her. She flushed, and an alert look replaced the dreamy one. 'Yes,' she said shortly. 'Rachel, Clodagh has asked me for the week-end. I *must* go! I can—can't I?'

Cynthia had said that she wasn't to go to the Traceys' again. I looked at her eager expression. If only Thalia was given a chance she would become very friendly with Clodagh and perhaps she would leave Armand and me in peace. I was becoming sick of her unreasonable jealousy of him, of her constant spying and following of us wherever we went. I never felt alone with Armand. There was always the horrible feeling that we were being watched. If Thalia could only make a real friend of her own age surely she would leave me alone. I had thought that the dog would help her. Now I saw that he would merely provide another and more expert tracker of my footsteps.

'You can go. I'll take the responsibility,' I said.

She gave a cry of pleasure, then said: 'I'd *love* to go—but I'd rather stay with you. You'll be alone here.'

'Go on Saturday. I'll come out on Sunday to finish Catherine's portrait and bring you back.'

'And Claude?'

'He can come with me or stay with Elise and Marie.'

'You won't be able to see Armand.' Her eyes had a malicious pleasure as she said this.

'No. I won't,' I said shortly.

'Thérèse won't speak to Clodagh in the English classes.'

'Why not?'

'I don't know. But I'll find out. No one likes those Tréfours.'

'I do. I like Armand . . . and when I meet his mother and sister I know I'll like them too.'

'You don't know what he's really like.'

'I don't know what *you're* really like. But I'm beginning to think that you like to make mischief,' I said brutally.

'No. No. That isn't true! Anyhow, about you it isn't true. I only want to stop you from getting hurt.'

'I shan't get hurt,' I said impatiently. 'I can look after myself. *Do* stop interfering with my affairs.'

Julie Caron came into the room with Claude. I had asked her to stay to lunch, Cynthia never invited her. She looked, as usual, compact, cheerful and competent.

'He's been a very naughty boy to-day,' she said laughing. 'But he's a boy. They never like learning.'

'We've been talking about the Tréfours family,' I said, handing her an apéritif. 'Thalia says they're not popular here.'

Julie had a glass of Rancia in her hand—Cynthia and I often drank a little before lunch—and it dropped suddenly with a crash on to the parquet floor.

'Dirty girl! What'll Marie say?' said Claude delightedly. Thalia went at my bidding to fetch Elise to clear up the mess and in the excitement of finding all the splinters of glass my question was never answered.

With Cynthia's departure I was a prisoner to the house and children. Armand telephoned me in the evenings, and every morning I met him on the *plage* for ten minutes. I would hurry along the Promenade past the gossiping nurses and governesses and their charges, barely acknowledging the greetings of the ever-increasing number who were becoming acquainted with us. Claude played with any child who would suffer his arrogance on the beach. At last I would reach the *cabine* which belonged to Armand and in which he changed into his running things. He was always there first, and would pull me in and in the dark stuffiness of the small sandy place we would kiss and cling together. Cynthia had been away three days and except for cards of the Eiffel Tower, Notre Dame and the Arc de Triomphe to Claude she hadn't written.

Thalia said nothing when Claude's cards came, but on the fourth morning when there was nothing for anyone and Claude set up a howl, she turned on him fiercely: 'What are you howling for, you little stupid?' she said. 'You've had three—I've had none!'

She had a cold coming on and her eyes were red and watery, her face flushed and blotchy. In addition to this it was her time of the month for misery—and she was wretched. She heatedly denied feeling ill—unlike her mother she suffered in silence and with a stoic patience; and in spite of my remonstrances she insisted on going to school. She came back shortly after accompanied by one of the French teachers. 'Thalia fainted at prayers,' she told me. I put her to bed. She curled up very wretchedly, and turned her face to the wall. She was green with pain and burst out violently: 'Why do I have to have this? I hate it. I hate it. Why not Claude? It's not fair. . . .'

'Claude's a baby. You had your childhood too.'

'It's not fair,' she repeated angrily.

I didn't think it was either—but saying so couldn't help Thalia. Claude was having his French lesson with Mademoiselle Caron. It was time for me to rush down the rue de la Malouine and across the Promenade with flying feet to the haven of the *cabine*—and Armand. But I couldn't leave Thalia like this. She made no sound but her face and whole body twisted in contortions, and tears rolled down her face. Her hand clutching mine was very hot. I fetched a thermometer. She had quite a high temperature.

'I'm going to telephone Dr. Cartier,' I said.

'No; no,' she cried violently.

I bathed her face and gave her some aspirin.

The doctor was a young and up-and-coming man. I liked him, and found him refreshingly frank in contrast to the reticence of the medical world at home. He had come twice to Cynthia, and supplied her with sleeping tablets very unwillingly.

'Does she take these things often?' he asked me after I had interpreted all her symptoms for him.

'I don't know,' I said.

'She's got to stop. She's neurotic. She needs exercise—then she would sleep better.'

'Her heart's too bad for exercise.'

He had smiled. 'The heart, Mademoiselle, is a very tough organ. It has to be. She has a nervous heart—but it's not dangerous. It may frighten her—but it won't kill her—at least not before her time.'

After this Cynthia reluctantly took up some gentle golf with Colonel Simpson at St. Briac.

I telephoned the doctor now, and he promised to come later in the morning. I knew I ought to stay with Thalia but I wanted to see Armand. His name kept coming to me—even the misery of Thalia seemed a little vague because of the thrill of seeing Armand.

Marie promised to go up to Thalia. She was polishing the parquet with a felt pad on her left foot and a rope from it was attached round her waist. Her niece watched sullenly at her side.

'You lazy good-for-nothing! There's only one way to polish—like this!' She performed the forward and backward movement of the foot vigorously with a duster tied to the *polisseur* on her foot. Thalia and I had loved trying this out with Madeleine. Elise did not seem to be enjoying it. Where she had last worked, she said, the Madame had said it was old-fashioned. She should use a mop, she had said. Marie was contemptuous. She paused in her violent exercise to say that she would make Thalia a tisane. The rubbish doctors gave was useless—a tisane was much better.

It was late—Armand would be impatient. I tore up the pebbled path and out of the gate.

Alas, Claude was hanging dangerously over the balcony.

'Where's Mademoiselle?' I shouted frantically after telling him to go back into the room.

'In the lavatory!' he shrieked. 'I hope she stops there hours. Take me with you, Rachel. *Do* take me. She'll still be there when we come back.'

'No. Go back and work. I'll bring you a *sucette*!' I cried. I ran down the street, past the many acquaintances calling '*Bonjour, Mademoiselle*'.

'*Bonjour. Bonjour,*' I kept saying automatically . . . and all the time as my feet clattered on the stones I was thinking of Armand . . . Armand. . . . Will he be there? Will he be there? And I hated everyone who delayed me from him by one minute.

He was just going—and he was angry with me. Angry because he'd been kept waiting, angry because he was afraid that I might not come, angry with apprehension that something had happened to me. I knew it all because it was the same with me, a mixture of delight and anguish.

He drew me into the *cabine* roughly. 'I was just going. What kept you?'

'Thalia. She's ill. The doctor's coming . . .' I panted.

He cursed under his breath. 'That girl. It's always her. She's always trying to keep you from me. How can you stand her spying and prying on you?'

I did not have to answer because of his kisses. But for the first time since we had been meeting in these short, snatched contacts something spoiled our pleasure.

Thalia . . . Thalia. . . . Now that I was in Armand's arms the irritating vision of her blotched red face, her twisted features, her silent tears came as a reminder of my duty. I was responsible for her and I had deliberately pushed her out until I reached Armand. Now that he held me, her face refused to disappear. 'Go away. Leave me with him. I'll come back to you very soon . . . just leave me now, I begged it. But it wouldn't go; stubborn and mocking it was there, and I shivered in his arms.

'What is it? What's the matter, my darling?'

And when I stammered that I was worried because I had been left in charge of the children he said quickly: 'That girl spoils everything. Damn her!'

I was angry with myself and with him. We had barely five minutes together.

'Listen,' he said. 'It's low tide to-night. I'll come along the beach and up the steps. We can talk on the terrace. It's sheltered there—and the girl'll be in bed.'

I agreed reluctantly, still thinking of Thalia. Suppose she were worse?

But when Dr. Cartier came he said he thought it was nothing worse than a chill. She suffered his examination sullenly and reluctantly. When we went into the *salon* he said: 'Where's her mother?'

'In Paris.'

'You're alone here?'

'Oh, no. I have Marie.'

'The girl interests me,' he said, sipping his apéritif. 'It's difficult to imagine that such a beautiful woman could have such a daughter. How d'you get on with her? She's devoted to you. I can see that. How do you feel about *her*?'

How did I feel? I did not know. Anger, irritation, resentment, amusement, pity, affection—even love sometimes. He didn't press the question. She bitterly resents being a woman. Something which you don't, do you?'

'I *did*,' I said truthfully.

'And now?' He looked quizzically at me over his glass. 'Now that the handsome young Tréfours is in love with you?'

How did he know?

'Well?' he repeated.

'I am glad and sorry at the same time,' I said. 'I want to be a painter—and for that it's better to be a man.'

'And for love?'

'I don't know.' I was doubtful. He laughed at me.

That's something I don't know either. But it's a point which has been much discussed.'

He left after warning me that Thalia's temperature might rise in the evening. He would look in next morning but if I were at all worried or anxious he would come again in the evening.

'I'm at your service, Mademoiselle Rachel,' he said as we walked out to his car.

He said he missed seeing Cynthia in the town. 'She's so beautiful that it is a joy just to look at her.' And I thought how lovely it must be to be as beautiful as that.

'But for you—it's wonderful to be young and in love, isn't it? Even if it's with a *Frenchman?*' he teased me, laughing at my discomfiture. 'How do I know? A doctor has eyes—special ones.'

I went up to Thalia. 'Do you hate being a girl?' I asked her curiously.

'Yes,' she said violently. 'Mother would like me so much better if I were a boy.'

'But your father wouldn't.'

'He would. He adores Claude—just because he's a boy. Besides, men have a much better time than women.'

I looked at her flushed misery and patted her head.

'Did you see *him?*' she asked resentfully.

'Yes,' I said. 'I saw him.'

'And he kissed you?'

'Yes.'

She sat up, shaking back her straggling hair. 'It's beastly. How can you? Men always want to kiss.'

'And you want to be a man?' I teased her.

She tossed her head impatiently and would not answer. She looked very ugly, with a kind of defeated wretchedness such as a sick sporting dog shows; and as I covered her up she seized my hand and held it to her face.

'Lie down. I'll read to you,' I said. 'Mademoiselle Caron says she'll take Claude out for me.'

'What will you read?'

'Some Breton legends. They're lovely.'

'No. I want poetry. Leconte de l'Isle.'

I looked at her averted face and I hated her for deliberately choosing Armand's favourite poet.

'You're getting Alfred de Musset,' I said firmly.

But before I had read more than a few lines she was asleep.

Cynthia returned unexpectedly on the Sunday night. I was on the terrace talking to Armand. He had come up the steps and I had unlocked the iron gate with the great key, and with one of Marie's shawls flung round me was with him on the stone seat under the palms when Thalia came running down the garden path to the terrace. She was in her dressing-gown and called urgently: 'Rachel! Rachel! There's a taxi stopping at the gate . . . Mother's back . . . Come in quickly. . . .'

I was horrified at her coming out like that. She had been quite ill the previous night. 'Go in. At once! Are you mad?' I said.

'You come in, too. Mother'll be angry with you. I know she will. . . .'

'Go in! At *once*. Go back to bed.'

'I'm not running off as if I'm doing wrong in talking to you,' protested Armand. 'It's ridiculous, Rachel, next Sunday I'll take you to my mother. We must be engaged formally, this won't do.'

'Mademoiselle Rachel! Mademoiselle Rachel!' Marie's voice came down the path. 'Madame's back. Come! Madame's back.'

Armand caught me to him and kissed me passionately. 'Go now. I'll see you to-morrow? And to-night I'll speak to my mother.'

I went in slowly. Cynthia was in the hall talking to Thalia. She hadn't taken in the fact that Thalia had been out in the garden, but I said quickly: 'Thalia, go back to bed—you've had a temperature. How can you be so mad?'

'A temperature? Is Claude all right?' asked Cynthia quickly. She wore a lavender-coloured long tweed travelling coat and a little violet velvet hat. She was pale but she looked utterly lovely.

'Claude is very well—but Thalia has been quite ill,' I said. 'Doctor Cartier was here twice.'

'Then what's she doing out of bed?'

'I came down to see you—I heard your taxi,' said Thalia.

Cynthia looked at Marie's shawl round me. 'You've been out?'

'In the garden.'

'At this hour?'

'Talking to Armand.'

'I thought I asked you not to have him here.'

'He hasn't been here. He came up the steps and I talked to him on the terrace.'

'Every night?'

'Last night and to-night.'

'Go to bed,' she said sharply to Thalia. 'I'll see you presently.'

We went into the *salon* and I told Marie to bring some tea and sandwiches. Cynthia hadn't had any dinner.

'We didn't expect you until Tuesday,' I said.

'So it seems.'

'What d'you mean by that?'

'I come back late at night. I find Thalia walking about in a dressing-gown instead of being asleep—and you out in the garden with a young man.'

'And you,' I said pointedly, 'weren't in the hotel you told me you were in.'

Her eyes grew very blue and the pupils became smaller.

'What do you mean?'

'I telephoned you there. I was worried about Thalia.'

'There was a mistake. When I got there they hadn't reserved a room for me. I had to stay at another hotel.

There had been no address on the postcards. I had written twice to tell her all was well.

'Did you get my cards?'

'Of course. They sent them on.'

'They didn't know where you were when I telephoned you.'

'I don't care for your tone, Rachel.'

'And I don't care to be left in charge of your children when you don't let me know your whereabouts.'

'Don't let's quarrel, Rachel. I'm sorry if you were worried.'

'I was worried about Thalia. She's been quite ill.'

'She's very strong. There's nothing much the matter. She looked all right to me.'

'She didn't yesterday or Saturday—and she fainted at school on Friday.'

'The usual, I suppose?'

'Yes—and she had a bad chill.'

'She does such stupid things—such as coming out of bed just now.' Her tone was indifferent. It was quite changed when she said again: 'But Claude's all right?'

'He's very well. And he's been very good while you've been away.'

The tea came in and she took off her hat. Marie and Elise bore her bags away.

'Did you enjoy Paris?'

'It's a lovely city—yes, I enjoyed it.' There was not the slightest enthusiasm. It seemed to me that the visit had gone wrong somehow—it hadn't been a success.

'I brought Claude a present. And something for you.' She handed me a box. In it was a little jacket of some fluffy white stuff made as only the French can make such things.

'And Thalia?'

'I couldn't find anything for her. She's difficult. Nothing suits her.'

'Would you mind very much if I gave her this?'

'It won't suit her. But give it her by all means—I thought you'd like it.'

'I *do*. I love it. But she needs a present just now.'

'Then buy her one and keep the jacket.' She was sipping her tea. Her voice sounded bored.

'Cynthia,' I said. 'You give it her. Now, when you go upstairs. . . . Do.'

'I can't climb all those stairs—my heart's not too good.'

Her eyes met mine. She was angry with me.

'Then I'll take it up myself now.'

'Wait a minute. I want to show you the new dress I bought. It's for the big party at Colonel Simpson's next week.'

We went up to her room on the first floor and she pulled a frock from the tissue paper enfolding it. It was an ice-blue evening dress. She held it up against her. 'Like it?'

'It's lovely—and it suits you.'

When I went up the stairs to Thalia I left Cynthia standing by Claude's bed looking down at his sleeping form. I handed Thalia the jacket in its wrappings. 'From your mother,' I said. She didn't undo it. 'I heard it all,' she said bitterly. 'Keep your jacket, Rachel. I wouldn't wear it for anything.'

What was the use of telling her that she shouldn't have been listening? She was cut to the heart. I put my arms round her but she turned away to the wall again and wouldn't speak to me.

CHAPTER X

I HAD NOT finished Catherine's portrait, I no longer cared for it. It seemed that it was always so. There was the first wild fever of impatience to get it on the canvas, the terrible struggle to say what one wanted to say, the white heat of excitement when the first glimmerings of success appeared —and then the downward rush of complete disillusionment when one had to face up to failure. But Catherine liked the painting—she wanted it completed.

I had taken the drawings of Claude to a gallery in the town to have them framed. The owner, a round, shrewd-eyed little man, liked them. He asked me if I had any paintings to show him. I had only done one which in any degree pleased me. It was a small painting of two children, their arms round one another, sitting alone on a wet seat on the *vedette* in the rain. They had been returning with a funeral party from St. Malo when I had seen them. Alone, in deep black they sat, this boy and girl, while the rest of the party were crowded together gossiping. It was only an impression —the figures with neither features nor detail—but there was in them something of the quality which had so appealed to me on the *vedette*. I had called it 'The Orphans', and except for the set compositions at the Slade it was my first serious attempt at such a picture.

The gallery owner asked me to put it in a forthcoming exhibition of local work and reluctantly I agreed. The morning after Cynthia's return he telephoned me that my picture had a prospective buyer, but that I had not priced it. How much was it? I had not the vaguest idea, never having sold a painting.

'Come in and discuss it,' said the man.

'You're going to be very surprised when you hear who your prospective buyer is,' he greeted me.

I wasn't interested in the buyer, I was only madly excited that anyone actually wanted it.

'It's Xavier Tréfours, the painter,' he said. 'He's taken a fancy to it. Says it's lyrical painting. Now then, Mademoiselle, what shall we ask him for it?'

I was so thrilled that a famous painter wanted my little sketch that I said I would not dream of asking anything for it. I would like to give it him.

'Impossible,' said the owner of the gallery. Every picture in the exhibition had to be priced and from that he had to take his own commission. 'Besides,' he said, 'Monsieur Tréfours wouldn't dream of accepting it.'

I said I would leave such a delicate matter to him—but affirmed that I did not want anything for it.

'I will tell Monsieur Tréfours,' he said firmly, 'that the price is two thousand five hundred francs.'

I was shocked. The franc was worth about twopence, to ask twenty guineas for such a sketch seemed robbery. I was only a student, how could I ask such a price?

'Mademoiselle,' said the dealer laughing, 'you have a great deal to learn, and not only about painting. A picture is worth what it will fetch, what anyone will pay for it.'

'But why does he want to buy my sketch when he can paint so much better himself?'

'There is something he likes in it, Mademoiselle—and he is always glad to encourage young painters.'

Suddenly the thought came to me that he was buying the picture out of kindness—or out of curiosity. He had surely been told that I was painting Catherine Tracey's portrait. My spirits went down as in a lift, and again I was struck by the fact that these Tréfours were always cropping up somewhere.

There was the father, the son and the uncles. Madeleine had talked of this uncle, he had wanted her to pose for the nude and she had been outraged. There was Thérèse, Thalia was always talking about Armand's young sister. It seemed impossible to get away from them.

'Do you know Monsieur Philippe Tréfours?' I asked the gallery owner.

'Mademoiselle, I ought to know him, it was he who set me up in this gallery,' he said simply. He assured me that Xavier Tréfours's only reason for wanting the painting was that he liked it.

I ran home with wings on my feet. I would work and work. I would never have to ask anyone for anything again. No more reminders that my training was expensive, that my painting materials cost too much, that I had a large and healthy appetite. I would work—and sell my work. Running up the rue de la Pionnière I bumped into Judy. She was delighted at my news. 'But I'm sorry he's bought it,' she said. 'I was going to make you an offer for it. I love it. How about you doing me a sketch of my Mimi? I should so like one of her in this fat bundly stage. Will you try?'

I couldn't think of anything I would like better than to give pleasure to Judy, and said that of course I would try.

Cynthia opened her eyes when I told her about the picture being sold.

'You're lucky to be able to earn money so easily,' she said enviously. 'What are they going to pay you for Mrs. Tracey's portrait?'

I didn't know, because we had never discussed it.

'If you're painting her for nothing you might do one of me,' she said. 'Tom would love it. I shall wear my ice-blue dress, of course. The new chiffon one from Paris.'

I wondered how she had paid for it. How horrible money was! It was only now that its power was beginning to dawn on me. Somehow one took it all for granted until it concerned oneself. Cynthia was constantly borrowing money from me, and I was getting a little worried as to where it would end. Mademoiselle Caron had to be paid; and it was I who found Thalia's share of both the Italian and ballet classes, and for this reason the money for the picture would be doubly welcome.

Armand had spoken to his parents, and I was to be introduced to his mother on the following Sunday. Cynthia looked at me askance when I told her.

'He's quite unsuitable for you. His father is a common, vulgar sort of person. He grows apples and tomatoes and such things.'

'And what's the matter with apples and tomatoes?' I shouted rudely. 'You enjoy eating them.'

She reproved me, and said quietly, 'That's not all. There are other objections. Rachel, give this young man up before you're made unhappy by him.' There was real feeling in her voice, and she caught me impulsively by the arm. 'I tell you, Rachel, Armand Tréfours is not for you.'

'He's asked me to marry him,' I said. 'And I've written to Father about it.'

'It's impossible, utterly impossible. He's a Catholic, in the first place. Bretons are fanatically religious—as you've seen. His family will never accept you.'

'Cynthia,' I said desperately, 'I love Armand. I *must* marry him.'

She looked consideringly at me. I was almost in tears now. 'It's your first affair, isn't it?'

'Yes. But I'll never love anyone else. I know it.'

'There'll be others,' she said quietly. 'And what about your career? Just now you were excited about becoming a painter. Your father is set on it.'

'You're either a painter or you're not,' I retorted stubbornly. 'You can't be a painter just to please others.'

'And you're willing to throw up everything to marry this young Breton?'

Was I? I did not know. I wanted to be a painter—but I wanted Armand. I wanted him desperately, besides that everything else paled. 'I can marry him and still become a painter,' I said. 'Lots of artists are married.'

'Rachel,' she said entreatingly. 'You're making Thalia terribly unhappy. She's devoted to you and she doesn't like Armand; and after all you came here to be with her.'

So she had noticed Thalia's violent jealousy. I had not thought that she observed anything about Thalia. Since her return from Paris she had paid but the briefest visit to her daughter, who was still in bed.

'Thalia is too fond of me. . . .' I was suddenly embarrassed. 'It's not good for her. She ought to be more with younger girls—with Clodagh.'

'You know how I feel about *that* friendship, Rachel.

'If she were she wouldn't be so jealous of Armand.

'Love is always jealous—you'll discover that. Give him up, Rachel, before you're badly hurt.'

I looked at her composed beauty. What did she know of being hurt? And yet something in her vague, distrait manner since her return made me wonder. Was she really as cold and composed as she appeared?

'I can't,' I said woodenly. 'On Sunday, Armand is taking me to his mother.'

'We'll see what your father says,' she said calmly.

I had written a long letter to Father telling him all about Armand and my feelings for him, and asking permission to become engaged. His reply was prompt and typical. He hated writing letters and never did so unless compelled. He got out of his aversion by sending telegrams; and this he did now. I opened mine apprehensively, fearing bad news—a refusal.

'BRAVO STOP VIVE L'ENTENTE CORDIALE LOVE FATHER'.

Dear, unpredictable Father. How funny he was. He was always urging me to take a less serious view of myself. 'If you could only see yourself objectively you'd enjoy a good laugh!' he had told me when discussing the affair of the vicar's portrait. 'It's got its funny side.'

I took the telegram to Cynthia. She read it in the *salon*. Even against the hideous blue and red stripes of the wallpaper I could not but be fascinated by her loveliness. She read it in silence, then she said: 'Your aunt told me that your father was eccentric. I see what she means. Well! I suppose you're determined to go to the family to-morrow?'

'Armand is fetching me after church, if that is all right with you.'

'Rachel,' she said, taking both my hands, '*won't* you believe me when I tell you that the whole thing's hopeless? It can never work out.'

I really liked her at that moment but perhaps that was because I was so happy. Father did not object—and to-morrow Armand was taking me to his mother.

Thalia came into my room that night. I was reading Paul Verlaine. She stood against the door in her old darned dressing-gown and I thought how selfish Cynthia was to make her wear such shabby old garments when her own négligées were exquisite.

'I can't sleep,' Thalia began. 'There's something on my mind. It's something I must tell you, Rachel.' Her eyes were intent and steady.

'Listen,' I interrupted. 'Listen, d'you remember this? Do you remember the concert in the Casino and the song we both loved?' And I began to read the lovely lines of Verlaine's *Sagesse*.

'Le ciel est par-dessus le toit,
   Si bleu, si calme!
Un arbre, par-dessus le toit,
   Berce sa palme.'

But before I had got any further she had taken up the lines so beautifully, so perfectly, that I dropped the book and stared at her. She stood now by the window and the lovely words fell one by one into the murmur of the sea. The moon shone in on her from my open shutters as she stood there with her hands at her throat and her face stretched up to its light. She was etherealized, transformed by the witchery of the night and the words she was quoting. We had heard a *diseuse* sing them to a modern setting at the concert in the Casino. She had had one of the low husky voices coming into fashion and had recited rather than sung. It had delighted me—and because it had delighted me, Thalia, unknown to me, had learned the words, and was now reciting them in exactly the same way as the *diseuse* had done.

I stared stupidly at her. She was quite lovely as she leaned there. 'She could be a great actress,' I thought. 'Beauty is not necessary for the stage. It's enough, perhaps better, to give the illusion of beauty.' This was the second time she had astounded and stirred me to admiration. I was again captivated by the charm of her voice and some absorbed, withdrawn quality in her. And then she turned—the miracle was gone. Her face as she approached me was the old mouse-like one with nervous flitting eyes. 'I learned it by heart, because you liked it so much. Are you pleased?'

I was very moved, more than I eared to be. 'Let's try and get the piano accompaniment and see if you could sing it, I suggested. 'You have a lovely voice. Perhaps you'll become an actress, Thalia.'

'No. I shan't,' she said abruptly. 'I'm too ugly. I'd rather write things—poems and plays for others to act. Rachel, there's something I *must* tell you.'

Her face was ominous with disaster.

'What is it?' I said resignedly. 'What do you want to tell me?'

'It's Armand, Rachel . . . you're not the only one. . . .'

I stared at her again, this time horrified. Was she going to tell me that she was in love with Armand too? Had she carried her imitation of me to this extent?

'You love him too?' I asked faintly.

'Love *him*? No. I don't love him. *He* loves someone else.'

I jumped out of bed, knocking the books on to the floor, and took her by the shoulders. Forgetting that she had been ill I shook her roughly. 'How dare you? How dare you say such a wicked thing! You're jealous.'

She bore the shaking in silence and when I let her go she said unsteadily, 'No. I *was* jealous. But now I'm not. Because there's someone else. He loves someone else besides you. You'll never stand for that—you're too proud.'

'There may have been someone else,' I retorted angrily. 'But now there's only me! He's going to marry *me*. Tomorrow he's taking me to his mother. Now go to bed and leave me alone. I'm sick of you and your vile insinuation.'

She turned and went. I leaned down and picked up the books which had fallen. On the top was Alfred de Musset. I opened it. 'A Rachel, Souvenir de Vicomté—Armand.'

I put it under my pillow with Father's telegram, but now it was I who could not sleep. The lighthouse flashing across my bed irritated me to-night. I got up and pulled the curtain across the open shutters but before I did so I looked out again at the moon on the water and it seemed to me suddenly that all beauty was an effect of light. The image of Thalia as she had leaned against the window-sill was still with me. I had deliberately shut out the one of her with bowed head and shoulders as she obediently left the room. But her words wouldn't be banished. 'He loves someone else. He loves someone else.' 'No! No!' I cried violently, burying my head in the pillows. 'She's wicked. Wicked. She wants to upset it all.'

That Sunday we sat under the window donated by the British and American children with their Sunday school pennies. St. Bartholomew's, the Anglo-American church, was, as usual, crowded. Thalia and Claude were on either side of me. Cynthia, who usually came, had stayed at home. I didn't hear a word of the chaplain's sermon nor did I heed Claude's fidgeting. My mind was filled with apprehension of the coming ordeal. The sun caught the brass tablets of two names which would be famous in history—Captain Constantin Fitzgibbon who had raised the Iraq Levy and died commanding it in battle, Colonel Monteith of the famous VI Bombay Cavalry—and then on the plaque to the young nurse who had been drowned while bathing at St. Lunaire. And this last one captured my imagination. Perhaps she was in love, I thought, and hadn't been alert enough for the treacherous currents and so had drifted away until she was too far out.

And so I dreamed on and only awoke to my whereabouts when I saw Claude putting a tiddly-wink in the collection bag.

Thalia saw it too and no sooner had we stepped into the bright sunshine under the palms and the flower-filled church garden than she attacked her small brother.

'Where's the penny Mother gave you? Fancy keeping a penny given you for church. That's stealing from God. . . .'

Claude's mouth turned down, Thalia's words sounded so ominous. 'It isn't stealing,' he said stoutly. 'It was my penny before I gave it. If I didn't give it at all it couldn't be stealing, could it, Rachel?'

I didn't want to argue on this point. 'Go back and give your penny to Mr. Clarke the verger,' I said.

'Only if you come with me.'

When the penny was handed over and the tiddly-wink handed back we emerged again. Everyone was standing about chatting and greeting each other in the sun, and news of absent husbands and sons was being exchanged. Several acquaintances inquired for Cynthia. And suddenly Terence Mourne was standing by us.

'What about seeing something of me this week?' he asked. What stopped me from telling him that I was about to become engaged? I said that I was occupied by my studies in the evening.

'It's your education I'm thinking of . . .' he said laughing. 'You mustn't neglect the social graces. . . . I'll telephone you and we'll go dancing. . . .'

Judy came up then: 'Come back to lunch with me, Rachel. We'll drop the children on the way.'

'I can't,' I said. 'I'm going to the Tréfours for lunch.'

A curious, rather startled look came into her delightful monkey face. 'You mean the Philippe Tréfours?'

'Yes. Armand is going to introduce me to his mother to-day.'

'You're friendly with the son?'

Now why did I tell Judy what I didn't tell Terence?

'We're to be engaged,' I said, 'as soon as his mother has consented.'

Judy seemed taken aback. 'But, Rachel . . . have you thought this over seriously?' She seemed so curiously perturbed that I was astonished. It wasn't like her at all. She was always so gay, so impulsively kind and reassuring to me. 'Aren't you going to congratulate me?' I asked, hurt.

'No,' she said crisply. 'I'm going to congratulate him.'

She kissed me warmly and impetuously. 'Get in, all of you, and I'll drop you at the villa.'

'How strange Judy was about Armand,' I said to Thalia as we walked up the long path to the house.

'It's not surprising,' she replied with another of those secret, delighted smiles.

Armand was waiting in the *salon* with Cynthia, looking terribly ill at ease. Cynthia hadn't bothered to learn any French except the names of vegetables and a conversation consisting of these must have been difficult. He jumped up immediately we went in and said that we had a long drive and must hurry.

'You'll be back to put Claude to bed for me? I'm going to a cocktail party,' said Cynthia as we were leaving.

I was annoyed. I'd had to stay in the house the whole of last week-end because Thalia had been ill. And now she was making me be nursemaid again. 'I'll be back,' I said shortly.

We drove in silence until we were well on the St. Brieuc Road and then Armand looked at his watch and turned the car down a side track. We kissed—not once but again and again; then he said: 'Rachel, darling, be patient with my mother, won't you? So much depends on this first meeting....'

'I'm not patient—and I don't seem to be tactful,' I said ruefully. 'I'm always upsetting Cynthia and now I seem to have upset Judy.

'Judy?' he said sharply. 'Do you mean Mrs. van Klaveren?'

'Yes.'

'I used to go there with a friend. She's lived here for some time. Her husband was a friend of mine. We used to go tunny fishing together. He taught me, in fact I've bought his boat with the special revolving seat....'

'She's a darling,' I said, 'she's been so good to me but just now when I told her that you and I are to be engaged she was quite queer.'

'You told her that?'

There was faint displeasure in his voice.

'Yes. She's my best friend here.'

'Women are funny about such things,' he said soothingly. 'You probably blurted it out suddenly.'

I didn't see what difference that made but I couldn't tell Armand that Judy hadn't seemed pleased. He cut the conversation short by kissing me with passion. The leaves were late on the trees and a few brilliant coloured creepers on the high stone wall above us were shedding their last ones. They fell into the car— some of them on to my face as he kissed me.

'*Tu m'aimes?*' he asked me, stroking my hair back from my forehead and looking gravely at me.

'I am so happy that I'd like to die now—like that nurse at St. Lunaire,' I said. For the strangest foreboding had come over me that it could never be as perfect for us as it was now—before our engagement was official.

'Morbid little idiot!' said Armand, starting up the car. 'I adore your nonsense . . . but now we must hurry. Maman will be annoyed if we're late.'

The Tréfours' home lay far back from the road down a long winding drive through orchards. I was astonished to see the trees still heavily laden with apples of a curiously deep mulberry colour. They were bent down groaning under their burden and, almost stripped of their leaves, looking curiously exotic. They were of a shape unlike any other apple I'd seen and had almost a silken sheen. To the left of the drive lay the glass-houses where the tomatoes and grapes were grown.

The house itself, of the local grey stone, was pretentious indeed. It had once been a simple farmhouse but as the Tréfours had flourished so they had added to it—each one apparently in a more florid style.

'Hideous, isn't it?' said Armand, as, rounding the last bend, the full impact of the monstrosity in the pseudo-chateau manner, with turrets, spire and battlements, hit us.

'The only worth-while part of the place is the old original farmhouse—the kitchen, dining-room and one small *salon*—the rest is rubbish.' His voice sounded amused but I sensed some bitterness in it too. Was he ashamed of his pretentious home?

Madame was awaiting us in the *grand salon*, said a red-faced, fat old woman with several wobbling chins. She was dressed in black with a small lace coif, and like Marie wore a large gold cross round her neck.

'This is Rosalie,' said Armand, chucking her under one of the chins. 'My old nurse. Here she is, Nana, my little bride-to-be.'

The old woman scrutinized me keenly, as Marie did, then took both my hands in hers: 'Armand's bride will be welcome indeed.' Her round child's eyes took me in from my head to my shoes—which I was suddenly aware were very dusty—then she prodded my breasts, felt my stomach and pinched my thighs.

'She's small—but the small ones often breed the best stock,' she chuckled.

'Don't mind Rosalie, she's an old fool,' said Armand hastily, but I didn't mind at all. The farmers' wives on Dartmoor also prodded one and regarded all young women as potential breeders.

'We need children here—the place is dead,' went on the old woman, 'and this good-for-nothing here despises it. It's not smart enough for him—he must always be off to the town like they all are now.'

'Rosalie,' called a sharp voice. 'Bring them in here and stop gossiping.' Rosalie made a little bob of apology to me, Armand took my arm and drawing my hand firmly through his and proceeded by Rosalie, we entered the *grand salon*.

The impression of this great room was one of soft yellow and grey crowded with black-robed females, but after a deep breath I made out four women and the curé, whose robes had misled me into thinking him a woman—and two men, one of whom I recognized as Armand's father. A short woman with white hair and of extraordinarily commanding appearance in spite of her lack of height turned from the group at our entrance. She greeted me courteously but formally, with none of Rosalie's warmth.

'This is Rachel, *Madame ma mère*.' Armand remained at my side, his fingers pressing reassuringly on my arm, until his mother drew me away to introduce me to the others in the room. Two of the women were her sisters, the other her sister-in-law.

I had thought that since having grown slim my former agony of shyness had left me; but to have to stand there under the concentrated scrutiny of these black-clad women was an ordeal which brought waves of humiliating self-consciousness over me. Beyond them the eyes of the men were also focused on me. A burning misery swept me, leaving me shaking and cold as I sensed in their combined attention not only their curiosity but their hostility. The introductions continued as I was led round like a mare on a visit of approval. Armand kept close to me, reassuring me with his amused tolerance. It was sheer relief from the tense silence in the room which made me exclaim joyfully: 'Ah, here is someone whom I already know!' when at last Philippe Tréfours greeted me warmly with real welcome in his restless blue eyes.

'Already met? You know my husband, Mademoiselle Rachel?'

'Yes,' I cried. 'We met at Mrs. Tracey's, that's where Armand and I met too.' Too late I felt Armand's sudden warning pinch on my arm and heard his whispered '*attention*'. I looked at him—and then at the group—what was wrong? A strange, almost frightening silence had fallen on the old women—for they all seemed old to me—they had stopped their little buzz of comments on Armand's English friend and were looking with ill-hidden delight at Suzanne Tréfours, his mother. Her look, sharp and penetrating, moved from her husband to me. 'So! You met him there. Are you then a friend of Madame Tracey's?'

Another warning pinch from Armand almost made me squeal. I was angry—he hurt me—what *was* all this?

'Yes,' I said loudly. 'I like her immensely—enormously—and her daughter too. Clodagh comes to us frequently.'

'Madame Pemberton allows Madame Tracey's daughter to visit and play with her children?'

'Yes,' I said uncertainly. I was puzzled now—what could be wrong? I looked from one face to another. Armand's eyes were anxious but at the same time amused, but Philippe Tréfours was regarding me with the pleading eyes of a spaniel. The curé was gazing out of the windows.

'And you, Mademoiselle Rachel, are you a friend of Madame Tracey's?'

'I don't know her very well,' I said, becoming less and less assured by her steady, unblinking eyes, 'but I'm painting her portrait. She's very lovely.'

'Ah! Mademoiselle is a painter?' interposed the curé, who had swung round from the window, and he immediately began questioning me about my studies. His kind, wise eyes calmed and reassured me. They seemed to be saying: 'Don't worry, my child. You've just put your foot into something you don't understand. You're out of your depth. Leave it alone—don't try to extricate yourself.'

Philippe, his brother, and Armand joined us in a lively discussion about art and the respective merits of Epstein and Maillol until the folding glass doors were opened without a sound and Rosalie announced ceremoniously: '*Mesdames et Messieurs sont servis!*'

I was placed on my host's right with Armand's uncle on my left. Armand sat between his two aunts. The curé was on Suzanne Tréfours' right. I was too nervous and ill at ease after the extraordinary conversation about Catherine to enjoy the meal. It was long and served excellently by two young girls in black. Both had some beautiful lace on their coifs and minute aprons. Rosalie gave serving directions from a small table near the door and she attended to the wines.

Everything we ate was written as indelibly on my consciousness as if it were one of those violet-inked menus of a Breton *hostellerie*. Parmentier soup, lobster in *coquille* with shrimps, and lamb, which had been treated with garlic, in some sharp piquant sauce. Afterwards a great wooden board with a variety of cheeses came in and baskets filled with the local small grapes, pears, and apples. I didn't exchange one word with Armand but occasionally he gave me a commiserating roll of his eyes. The food just refused to go down—it stuck in my throat as it did when I had quinsy. The table was massively ugly with elaborately carved legs. The great sideboard which was more like a heavy Welsh dresser had some magnificent pewter on it. The walls were of a dark panelled wood and gave a sombre brooding look to the room which the hunting prints could not disperse.

There was little conversation once the serious business of eating and drinking had begun. Looking round the table it wasn't very different from the Sunday scenes at my aunt's—our relatives and the Reverend Cookson-Cander in the place of the curé, but my aunt's and Cynthia's eyebrows would have been lifted at the succulent noises of approbation expressed by Uncle Jules, who with napkin tied round his neck gave his opinion on each and every dish and wine. Both Cynthia and my aunt had the British horror of any lapse from what they had decreed as their own code of table manners, which didn't include opinions on the food and drink. But our hostess seemed pleased and even gratified at her brother-in-law's expressions of approval. Frequently he would lean across the table and ask me if I didn't find the menu to my taste—I was eating nothing, he insisted. Rosalie quietly removed the food which I couldn't eat. The plates weren't changed so that this was a problem of acute anxiety to me. We rested our knives and forks on a silver rest and the plates were wiped clean with bread. At last it was ended—and we all got up. The men were smoking cigars now and drinking Courvoisier and Armagnac. We all went back to the great *salon* and Rosalie brought coffee and liqueurs for the ladies. I was given one which was very sweet and sticky and we sat there sipping coffee in a rather awkward silence.

Philippe Tréfours offered me a cigarette.

'She doesn't smoke,' said Armand. One of the young girls brought a box of cigarettes and placed them near me, giving me a soft shy glance. I could tell that all the staff were aware of the importance of the impression I made. I looked round the *salon*— there were great french windows the whole length of one wall and through them was the sea.

'You're so near the sea?' I asked Armand, astonished. 'We seemed to have been driving inland.'

'This coast curves like a corkscrew—but that's the sea all right. Come and look at it.'

I got up and went over to the window with him. My back burned with all those pairs of eyes which followed it. I turned suddenly and they were all watching us.

'Come over here—that is the far bank of the Rance,' said Armand. 'Isn't it beautiful?' At the same time he drew me into a small recess. 'You look like a frightened deer,' he said concernedly. 'Is it so terrible? Don't mind them. They're all old and jealous of us. Kiss me quickly.'

I kissed him but perfunctorily. He was piqued and tilting my head back he kissed me deliberately. 'Don't. Don't,' I pleaded— and at that moment a great roar of delighted laughter from Uncle Jules made us spring apart.

'Ha! Ha! The love birds, the turtle doves are busy already … bless them,' he shouted to the group round the coffee table. He was flushed with wine and food, his eyes wickedly alert and alive but his glance so benign that I couldn't be angry, although I was upset at the gale of laughter his remark provoked.

'Come over here, we see little enough of you … your mother wants to speak to Mademoiselle Rachel,' said Philippe.

Suzanne Tréfours had the glittering restless eyes of a small lizard. Her husband's were darting too—but beside hers, his seemed still. There was something reptilian about the heavy lids and the ageless mask of her face. Her hair was white—that beautiful bluish white, not the dirty grey kind—and it was elaborately dressed in a piled mass of curls. Her black dress looked as if it had been sewn on her. 'Come and sit down,' she commanded us.

The chairs in this *salon* were of gilt cane—as were those in the *salon* of our villa. Armand sat down on one then shifted to a small *bergère*. 'Come here,' he said. 'You look unhappy on that gilded horror.'

'How old are you, Mademoiselle Rachel?'

'Eighteen and five months.'

'Only eighteen—then you will need your parents' consent to an engagement. What do they say?'

I didn't think she was the sort of person who would appreciate Father's telegram so I said Father would be agreeable.

'Your father. What does he do?'

What did Father do? I didn't know. He went fishing whenever he could—he made casts of minnows and his own flies. He drew exquisite plans for viaducts and bridges.

'He doesn't do anything,' I said.

'He doesn't work?'

'No.'

'He is old then?'

'Not at all,' I said sharply. 'He's much younger than *your* husband.'

'Then why doesn't he work?'

This was too much. 'I've never asked him,' I said. 'But if you write to him you could inquire the reason.'

A sudden look of acute displeasure warned me to be careful. I was already sorry that I had answered so rudely.

'You live in Devonshire, Armand tells me?'

'We live on Dartmoor near the prison,' I said.

'What prison?'

'The one built for the French prisoners.'

Armand gave me a sharp nudge. What had I said now? Just in time I remembered that she couldn't possibly know that Napoleon was my hero. I had been about to explain that the prison had been built for the French prisoners from Canada.

'What are you doing in France? Are you a guest of Madame Pemberton?'

I explained that I was companion to Thalia and that I helped with Claude.

'So. You are a kind of governess. Madame Pemberton pays you?'

'Pays me? What for?' I asked.

'Then you are "*au pair*", aren't you?'

I was getting tired of this inquisition and assented that she could call it that. I saw where it was leading, after several more delicately put questions. She wanted to know that all-important thing—far more important here than at home—had Father any money? Had I?

Money was a subject seldom mentioned at home except in moments of crisis for the simple reason that we never had any. Father's tastes in fishing rods and his habit of renting expensive stretches of water to indulge his love of the sport left very little for his large family.

Nevertheless I knew that I'd have a small income of my own when I came of age. It had been left me by my grandmother.

'Rachel is studying art. She lives with her aunt,' said Armand, trying to divert his mother from financial paths. He had been fidgeting and shifting during my ordeal.

'Your aunt lives in London?'

'No. She lives about thirty miles out.'

'She is there now?'

'No. She's in Egypt.'

'What is she doing in Egypt?'

'Looking for the Sphinx,' I said impatiently.

'But what is it—*qu'est-ce que ce Sphinx?*'

'It's one of the wonders of the world,' interposed the curé, who had been listening intently. 'One of the miracles made by man.'

'She has gone to Egypt on holiday?'

'Yes.'

'And you live with her?'

'Yes.'

'She has children?'

'No. Her son died.'

'Has she adopted you?'

'No. My father didn't wish it.'

'What will she say about this idea of yours and my son's?'

'I don't know,' I said truthfully. 'But I don't think she likes foreigners.'

'In that respect, Mademoiselle Rachel, I resemble her.'

There was a little smile of satisfaction on her face and the heavy lids were lowered. Once again the curé came to my rescue, by commenting on my fluent French. 'Where have you learned it?' he asked me. I explained that we'd had French governesses and that I'd been to a finishing school in Switzerland.

'You speak very well—but you have an accent, of course. I should say your governess was an Alsatian and that your French teachers in Switzerland came from the German-speaking part.'

'They didn't,' I retorted. 'But that I have an accent I can now hear.'

'For heaven's sake don't take your accent from these parts—the French here isn't pure by any means.' Armand sounded impatient and bored and his mother looked at him just as Cynthia looked at Claude when she wanted to placate him.

'You'll have to teach Armand English—he's lazy,' she said, smiling at me.

'Armand's very lazy at learning anything except how to charm women,' said Philippe Tréfours. 'He's an expert at that—isn't he, Mademoiselle Rachel?'

'Perhaps I take my cue from you,' replied Armand lightly. 'My father speaks a little English,' he said to me. And then I remembered that when I had met him at Catherine's they had been conversing in English. I was about to say so when Philippe said quickly: 'Take her round the place—it's a lovely afternoon. No one would think that it was November.'

Armand wasn't enthusiastic but we all went out and stood with our feet planted in the soil looking down the long irregular lines of trees through which one glimpsed flashes of the sea—blue, cerulean blue to-day. The soil smelt fetid with dung and the scent of the late apples and tang of the sea came sharply to me. I looked from Philippe to his son—and each of them had something of this strange but savage land in them —Philippe dark, intensely alive and aware of life with the peasant's shrewdness in that love of its fruits and rewards, and in Armand was the strange unreal dream-like quality which this whole land possessed.

And then I thought about the woman who had just been questioning me. Suzanne? What had she? I didn't know as yet because I didn't know the land. Only what I had seen. A land has to be lived in to be known; like people it only shows the aspect conveyed by its mood and by one's own mood. I was so happy standing between these two men that I didn't want to think about Suzanne Tréfours.

When, after seeing all the glass-houses and all the complicated system of packing and storing the apples and the despised tomatoes, we had tea made especially in my honour, I bade her good-bye, she said: 'We will wait a month or so. At Christmas if you are both of the same mind we can discuss the question of an engagement. There are serious things to consider.'

She looked at me through those heavy lids and smiled. She even kissed me on either cheek now that I was going. But I wasn't deceived—she didn't like me. And as for me—I had taken the same violent, unreasonable dislike to her as I had taken to the Reverend Cookson-Cander.

CHAPTER XI

THALIA AND I returned from the ballet class one afternoon in December to find Cynthia angry and baffled because Mademoiselle Caron had given notice.

'Why?' I asked.

'That's what is so absurd. She won't give any reason. Of course her English is limited—but it's good enough for me to have understood that she wants to leave. She doesn't want to return after the Christmas holidays.'

I knew that Julie Caron found Claude very tiring, but after all she did not have nearly so much of his company as I did. I had thought that I loved all children—as indeed I always had—but this one I just could not love. I thought that perhaps Julie Caron felt the same way and didn't like to say so.

'Did she complain of Claude?'

'No. She just insists that she would prefer not to come back after Christmas. It's too bad—just as she's got into our ways.'

'He *is* very difficult,' I said. 'I don't seem to be able to teach him anything.'

When Julie Caron came next day I asked her why she was leaving us. She was picking up some sheets of children's pictures which she used in teaching Claude and she didn't reply for a moment, then she said: 'I find it no longer possible to come here.'

'Is it Claude?'

'No. He's difficult—but I expect him to be so, what else could one expect? He's never punished.'

'Shall I speak to him? He's fairly obedient with me. I won't read to him or tell him stories if he isn't. It's the only way I can manage him.'

'No. It's useless. I am leaving.'

I had grown quite fond of Julie. We exchanged English and French conversation in the evenings. She came to the villa one week and I went to her flat in the town the following one. She lived above a small grocer's shop with her mother, a sour, grumbling old woman who disliked the British. She had a fixed idea that it was they who had started the war which had taken her husband from her. It was, as Julie said, useless arguing with her.

I asked her now whether or not she wanted to continue the exchange of conversation. She went on packing up the sheets of coloured pictures and didn't answer for a moment. When she did, she said, without looking at me: 'It would be better that they cease.'

I was very upset. I had enjoyed the evenings with her. Apart from the conversation we both loved music and had devoted a lot of our time to playing records of our favourite composers. She must have seen that I was both surprised and hurt, for taking my hand she said quickly: 'You'll understand later why it's impossible. But just now—don't ask me.'

'Are you taking another job?'

'Possibly. At Rennes, not here.'

'But your mother?'

She shrugged her shoulders and said nothing. She had smooth black hair, small liquid black eyes and an olive skin. She was short and rather dumpy, but she moved with the quick grace of the Frenchwoman and dressed with care and taste.

I was as puzzled as Cynthia; she had given me no good reason for leaving.

'Are you in any sort of trouble—I mean is there anything I can do about it?' I asked, trying to make her look at me. It was this strange unwillingness to face me which forced this question from me. She did look directly at me then.

'No. There is nothing that you can do. Nothing. *C'est la vie*,' and she shrugged again, but there were tears in her eyes. I was disturbed, for in spite of the tears her look had been intent and calculating—as if she would sum me up.

I confessed my failure to discover the reason for her determination to leave. Cynthia was indignant. 'I suppose it's Claude. I know he's naughty. Everyone says that he's spoiled. All boys are naughty—I suppose her own was a paragon.'

'She says it isn't Claude.'

'Then what *is* it? Does she want more money—like all these French?'

'She never mentioned money. She isn't a mercenary person at all.'

'Oh well, let her go. I'm not going down on my knees to any Frenchwoman to stay on with me. There are plenty of others to be had. She must remain until Christmas—she has to give me proper notice.'

I asked Marie if she knew what was the matter. She was diffident and evasive. I could understand her unwillingness to discuss her own compatriots with a foreigner—but she had always implied that she disliked Julie Caron and paid her but scant courtesy whenever she encountered her in the house.

'She's jealous,' she said, shaking her head.

'Jealous? But of whom?' I asked astonished.

'Use your head a little—or have you "*les araignées au plafond*"?'

This was one of Marie's favourite expressions. She used it whenever she came upon Thalia and me giggling or frolicking about laughing at nothing. We were enchanted with it until the day Claude accused Cynthia of having the equivalent of 'bats in the belfry' and I was obliged to translate it under her withering look. Just now I could not understand what Marie meant.

'Wait. Wait. You'll soon find out,' was her cryptic reply.

She and Cynthia were not getting on at all. There were frequent scenes. Cynthia had a way of putting a command into her voice—which Thalia called her 'memsahib' one—which Marie resented. She would toss her apron in temper and scream that she was not accustomed to working as a slave or of being spoken to as an animal, that she came of as proud a race as the Madame. That if the Madame thought that she was one of her Indian slave servants she was mistaken ... she was a Breton! And Madame had better remember it.

Cynthia would listen in contemptuous silence—not understanding much of it—a little smile on her beautiful mouth. 'Poor old thing. She doesn't know any better.'

Then, if Marie persisted, she would say angrily: 'But she had better keep in her place. I won't stand insolence. I don't believe you translate all that she is saying, Rachel.'

I did not; had I done so Marie would have been out with her boxes and I knew that it would be me who would have to cook and clean—for if Marie went Elise would go with her. The niece was completely under her aunt's domination. Marie, when really roused, was magnificent. Her face would become a brilliant rose—then a darker red—then a deep purplish flush would envelop her; not just her face but her neck and hands too, and one sensed that if she were stripped her entire body would be brick red with indignation. She would scream in a harsh, savage way which reminded me of the seagulls, and her blue eyes would flash and wither with scorn.

There had been many of these scenes since Cynthia's return from Paris. I hated being dragged into them. I loved old Marie and felt that much of her resentment was justified—but on the other hand I was there to help Cynthia and certainly to uphold her before her children. If I remained silent and refused to translate she would order me to do so in the same voice which had so upset Marie.

There were days when neither Thalia nor Marie seemed to be able to do anything right for Cynthia, and on one of these the climax came after a series of small annoyances when Cynthia began complaining as usual about Marie's cooking. If there was the smallest quantity of butter in any of the food she would be furious. Elise was out, and Marie was handing round the plates at lunch. They were in a pile in her left hand. It was the third time Cynthia had complained during the meal, forcing me to translate for her. At the third complaint Marie's patience snapped. 'Do it yourself then! Cook your own vegetables. Drown them in water and enjoy them if you can! But I, I am a cook! I don't just fill my stomach. I eat. Yes. I have respect for my stomach. And respect for other people's!' And she hurled the top plate across the *salle-à-manger*, following it with a second and a third.

I watched, in fascinated glee, the plates crash on the parquet floor. Thalia sat smiling. Claude, delighted and excited, jumped from his chair and rushing round the table seized a plate from the pile and flung it through the window. The glass splintered in thousands of pieces and came flying into the room. Marie suddenly came to her senses. She had been shouting some of the unpleasant words which Madeleine had taught me. But at Claude's action she stopped as if appalled at what she had done, and dropping the last plate in her confusion, fled from the room.

Cynthia's eyes were very fixed. Thalia's glance darted here and there in sheer delight, her face had an expression of almost gloating joy, but I suddenly felt sick . . . sick of it all. Sick of people's tempers and grumbles and of having to try and be the go-between. I longed to be back in my aunt's well-ordered dining-room with the prim Janet handing the plates in deft and perfect service. I got up and closed the door after Marie.

'Thalia, help me sweep up these pieces—go and fetch a brush and pan, will you? Sit still, Claude . . . don't touch anything. You'll get cut.'

'Wait!' commanded Cynthia. The icy calm in her tone struck us all. Claude, who was laughing immoderately at the mess and confusion, stopped at once.

'Claude! Didn't your father tell you to behave properly to me, to do all you could for me while he was away?' I had never heard her use this tone to him before.

'Yes,' he said, frightened now.

'And didn't you promise to do so?'

'Yes.' His eyes were scared, it was the first time I had seen any sign of fear in him.

'And do you think that what you have just done is keeping that promise?'

'No.'

'Thalia! Fetch me your riding whip from the hall.'

I stared at her in disbelief. Was she actually intending to punish Claude? When Thalia returned with the whip she handed it to me: 'You will give Claude two sharp cuts, please, Rachel. Bend down, Claude.'

'No. No,' I protested in dismay. 'I couldn't. I've never hit anyone. I don't think corporal punishment is right.'

But Claude had dashed away at Cynthia's words to me and I heard him running down the passage to the garden door. Thalia, at her mother's insistence, went in pursuit.

'Claude has never been thrashed. But he must learn that he can't behave like that, especially in front of a servant. He's going to be a soldier. He must learn discipline. You know how weak my heart is, Rachel. You must do it.'

'No. No. I can't,' I cried, and to my horror I burst into tears.

Thalia returned, dragging Claude after her. She did not appear as elated as I had expected her to be at being allowed to lay hands on her small brother.

'Come here,' said Cynthia sternly. But Claude remained gazing at her in fascinated horror—as if he were unable to move.

'Come here,' she repeated. And then there ensued a sickening battle between mother and son. Unable to force him to bend over, she hit him anywhere she could reach him. I could not endure the sight of that small, terrified boy who had never been chastised being treated in such a way, and after several sharp cuts I interposed my body between them, receiving the whip full on my neck.

Cynthia, at this, dropped it as if it were red-hot. Claude, who had not uttered one cry, now ran to me, and burying his head in my groin began sobbing in the high, hysterical way of the very highly strung. Great shudders ran through his small body and he began shaking all over and breathing in uneven, gasping, choking gulps. I held him tightly but he couldn't stop, and went on in a terrible monotonous panting as if he were wound up.

Finally I carried him upstairs with Thalia's help and put him to bed. His sobbing was absolutely mechanical but it still went on. We covered him up and left him to sob himself to sleep.

Cynthia called me when I came down. She put up a hand and touched my neck where the whip had caught it.

'I'm sorry, but it had to be done. It has upset me horribly. Get me some aspirins, Rachel, and some eau-de-Cologne.'

I said nothing. I still felt sick with disgust at the whole scene. Cynthia's face, when she had been beating Claude, had been so intent, so calm. Even that degrading business of hitting a small child had not broken the beautiful mask, and somehow it made the whole affair more revolting than if she had exhibited some loss of temper.

'I'm sorry about this,' she said, fingering my neck again when I took her the aspirin. 'Put something on it.'

She felt my silence and said: 'You think I'm a monster. There *is* a limit. Marie was the last straw. She must go.'

I was going to the Club with Terence that evening and I determined to ask him about Cynthia. She had been utterly unpredictable and impossible since her return from Paris. Unless there were some good explanation for her behaviour I felt I could not stay any longer with her.

Marie was locked in her room and I heard her moving about packing her boxes. I knocked and after a time was admitted. Her trunks were almost filled, the dressing-table swept bare of her possessions and the *armoire* open and empty.

'Don't go. *Please*, Marie, don't go. If you go I can't stay.'

For almost an hour I pleaded with her. I had none of Cynthia's pride and I begged and implored her not to leave me. I loved the old woman. She was good, hard-working and simple. To me she was Brittany with her store of folklore and legends, her superstitions and fears. I felt completely in tune with her. I loved the things she loved, the soil, the sea, the fruits of the earth and of the sea—the wonder of life and the inevitability of death. The one thing I could not share with her was her unshakable, unswerving faith.

At last she said: 'And the Madame? Is she willing for me to stay after my behaviour?'

I said that she would be. Cynthia had intimated that she would accept an apology after having said that Marie must go. She was really quite fond of her, too.

'I am willing to apologize for throwing the plates. That was inexcusable of me. The plates belong to *my* Madame in Paris, and I will have to replace them. I realize that. But this is the last time. If she isn't satisfied with my cooking let her get someone else. I can't stand grumbling and complaints. I'm a good cook—let no one deny it!'

Cynthia put a chiffon scarf round my neck before I went to the Club to meet Terence. It didn't suit me, and did not match the dress. Terence told me to take it off. I wanted to see his reactions to the weal across my neck, knowing that Armand would surely notice it immediately.

'It was an accident. I got in the way of a whip,' I explained.

'Cynthia's very fond of the whip. Discipline—and all that. Thalia's had it often.'

'She actually beat Thalia?' I asked, horrified.

'Frequently in India,' he said indifferently, 'but I should have thought she was beyond that now.'

'It was Claude.'

'Good! The little brat's insufferable. I've seen him kicking and hitting his bearer times enough.'

'If he has seen Cynthia beating Thalia it's small wonder,' I said disgustedly.

'You know nothing about the life there. The climate can be insufferable—it makes people do things they wouldn't dream of doing in their own country—

'Terence,' I said. 'You *must* tell me about Cynthia. I can't make her out. Since she came back from Paris she's impossible. She's restless, always brooding. She's irritable and unhappy. What happened in Paris? *What?*'

'Why should you think that I can tell you?'

'Because you went with her.'

'How d'you know that?' He sounded annoyed.

'Thalia saw you on the station.'

'That peeping Tom! I wonder if you've any idea of the trouble she's caused already? D'you know she put a snake in Cynthia's hat-box knowing that her mother would thrust her hand in to get out a hat?'

'But it was harmless.'

'It may have been. But she knew Cynthia has this weak heart and that she's terrified of snakes. She is convinced it was a krait.'

'She loves her mother. She adores her. I can't believe it's Thalia's fault that they don't get on,' I said, bewildered.

'She's got a strangely distorted way of showing love,' he said shortly.

'But what's the matter with Cynthia *now*?' I insisted.

'There's no *now*. It was and is always the same with Cynthia.'

'But what?'

'Oh, for God's sake use your head. If you can't see, then I can't tell you. Come on. Wrap up that neck and we'll dance.

'Have you seen her since you came back from Paris?'

'Rachel, I'm not going to talk about Cynthia to you.'

'Terence,' I said desperately, 'you *must* tell me. I'm going to marry Armand Tréfours and it's going to cause a lot of trouble with both Thalia and Cynthia.'

We were dancing, and he stopped dead. The band was a noisy one and it made hearing difficult.

'Good God! Are you mad?' was what I thought he was saying, and from his angry, disconcerted face I knew that I was right.

'No. Not mad. Sane—and terribly happy,' I said in his ear.

When the rhythm was somewhat less noisily thumped out and we were a little further away from the band, he said, his hands pressing my shoulders and his body closer to mine than I cared for: 'D'you mean to tell me you're seriously in love with that blond runner?'

I was so angry that I trod heavily on his toe. The music stopped and he pulled me to our table. He drank some wine, then said abruptly: 'You can't be serious?'

'I am very serious.'

He looked intently at me and said: 'My God! I believe you are. It's preposterous! You're totally unsuited for each other. You're in love with his legs. With his Adonis looks . . . his blond curls. You know nothing about him. *Nothing.*'

'Terence,' I pleaded. 'Don't. Oh, don't. I love him. I love him. Terribly . . . terribly.'

He smoked in silence. 'It's your first affair? You needn't deny it. I know. Damn it all I've kissed you—and I knew.'

'Cold porridge,' I said laughing, but there was no hilarity in it. I felt like crying. No one understood that I loved Armand. That I was quite sick with love for him.

'Well,' he said at last. 'I promised that if you wanted a friend I'd be here. But Armand Tréfours! It's impossible. They'll never accept you.'

'They have,' I said curtly.

'Are you sure? I doubt it.'

'And now tell me about Cynthia. You *must*.'

'No,' he said curtly. 'But don't run away with the idea that she's not tried to find a solution to Thalia. She has. She realizes her responsibility there.'

So that was all he was going to tell me. But surely there was more—much more that he knew.

'Was she *never* in love with Tom?' I persisted.

'I've told you I am not going to discuss Cynthia with you.' His voice was icy. I dared not ask any more.

Some friends came up to our table and began talking of the burning topic in the French newspapers—King Edward VIII and Mrs. Simpson. Terence was cool, reluctant to discuss his monarch. I was thrilled and asked several questions when they had gone. Was it true that he was going to marry her?

'No,' said Terence curtly. 'And it's an impertinence to discuss it.'

'The King can do no wrong,' I said. 'Aren't you going to congratulate *me*?'

'No,' he said deliberately. 'And if you're doing this just because you want to get married you might just as well have me.'

'You don't love me,' I said irritatedly. He was always teasing and annoying me.

'Neither does Armand Tréfours.'

I was so angry that I got up. 'I'd like to go home.'

He followed me out of the Club and down the rue du Casino. It was cold, with a whipping, biting wind and an exciting tang of iodine in the air. He took my arm and drew me close. 'Rachel . . you're such a silly sweet. You can't throw yourself away on this young Greek god. You're too young. What *is* your father thinking of to allow it?'

But I was too angry to answer him. Pulling myself away from him I walked as far away as I could on the pavement. It was too cold to linger and we said good night abruptly and uncomfortably.

Christmas, in spite of the influx of young men from the universities, was not a very gay season. The colony had been shaken by the abdication of the King which had taken place on the 11th December. The French, discussing it far more avidly than the British did, considered it highly romantic, if unnecessary, to give up a throne for love of a woman. Opinion in the colony—largely voiced in the Club—was sharply divided; on the whole it was shocked and outraged.

Thalia and I thought it wonderful that our own views about the hypocrisy of the social world should be shown up so nakedly. We admired the King for his courage and honesty—the latter in particular, and we said so. Cynthia listened to our comments in silence, then she said coldly: 'Your opinions are of no value. Neither of you has had any experience of the world. If you had you wouldn't talk as you do.'

She was adamant on the subject. Duty came first—and that duty was to one's country; love was left far behind. The large photograph of the King was removed from her writing desk, but two larger ones purchased in the town adorned both Thalia's and my dressing-table. The King was our hero.

I thought I detected a certain reluctant envy in Cynthia's dismissal of the whole affair. I remembered my aunt's words: 'She is a woman who would never fail in her duty', and I wondered.

Did she love anyone except her beautiful little son? Wasn't even that love a kind of self-love? Claude was made in her image. Thalia was not. And yet there had been sadness in her face when we were discussing the Abdication; a look which had belied her stern words. She held for me the fascination of a deep, still pool. I simply could not fathom her. Among a crowd of women she stood out not only for her flawless beauty but also for a rare, strange stillness. What went on beneath that calm inscrutability? What?

When I asked her if she disapproved of divorce simply as divorce and didn't she think it more honest for couples who were not suited to separate, she looked at me as if I were a fool and said: 'If only it were as simple as that.'

I began to see that some of her undoubted attraction for men must lie in this detached, enigmatic silence. They must wonder and wonder as I did what she was thinking, feeling, under that beautiful mask. Her young niece Deirdre came to stay with us and it was impossible not to see Cynthia's preference for this child of her only surviving brother to her own unsatisfactory daughter. Deirdre had the same calm beauty as her aunt, the same poise and assurance even at the age of seventeen; but to me she was insipid. She lacked the remote and at the same time beckoning charm of Cynthia. But Thalia thought her wonderful and adored the cousin who had scant time for the hobbledehoy younger girl. The visit was not an unqualified success and it left Thalia discontented and jealous.

Official sanction was more or less given to our engagement at Christmas. Philippe Tréfours announced it at the end of a family dinner party even more stiff and formal than that first lunch. There were flowers on the table—white and red—and flowers everywhere with the candles, but no real gaiety, rather a cold, deliberately put-on show. I sensed under all the champagne toasts and kisses that there was something very wrong in this family—some skeleton not too well hidden. All the relatives who had been present at that first lunch were again there with several more added—including Xavier. He was a large man with a reddish beard and round eyes like Claude's marbles. He had a malicious wit and a glib, clever tongue and it was evident to me that Suzanne Tréfours loathed him.

The only warmth in my welcome came from him. When I went into the *salon* with Armand—late because the car had broken down on the way—he had taken me in a great bear-like embrace and kissed me impulsively on both cheeks. I noticed Armand's displeasure at this affectionate greeting, and Xavier's malicious delight as he deliberately kept an arm round me. 'Well chosen, Armand my boy. You resemble your uncle in your good taste. And she's a painter, too. You couldn't have pleased me more. D'you know I've acquired one of your paintings, young woman?'

I liked him instinctively but I loved him for his warm welcome. I didn't move from the shelter of his arm and I saw Suzanne's displeasure with indifference.

I said that I was flattered—terribly flattered by his having liked my painting. It was my first attempt at composition. He questioned me about my studies and my masters. He didn't think much of the Slade. 'You must come to Paris . . . there you can find more freedom and more stimulation. I'll see that you go to the right masters.'

'If Rachel is contemplating marriage she will have to think carefully about painting,' came the silvery voice of Suzanne.

'And why should she? No woman can paint unless she's had sexual experience. How could she? It's much better that she gets this marriage business over young and settles down to work.'

There was an unpleasant silence.

'Well, don't you agree with me, Mademoiselle Rachel?' boomed Xavier, whose voice was strong and forceful, and at the same time his arm moved lower down my back.

'Freedom for a woman can never be the same as for a man— especially the freedom you practise in *your* world,' said Suzanne swiftly.

'I'm asking Mademoiselle Rachel—Armand's and her generation have very pronounced views on the subject.'

'Oh, yes. I want to be absolutely free—I'm sick of being tied and bound by conventions. . . .'

Suzanne's eyebrows went up and Armand looked anxiously at me.

'You are referring to conventions in work, aren't you, Rachel?' It was the first time Suzanne had omitted the Mademoiselle—and I knew then that she had, anyhow on the surface, accepted me. I saw Armand's eyes on me and I said very quietly: 'Of course.'

The cool appraising stare of Armand's sister, Thérèse, disturbed me. I felt that she, like her mother, was hostile—the others merely interested or amused. For Philippe was amused—that was evident in the way he announced our engagement.

When all the toasts had been drunk, Rosalie came in with a small white leather box in which was the ring left by Armand's grandmother for his bride.

As he took it from the silken nest and handed it to his son, Philippe Tréfours' eyes rested maliciously on his wife. 'For Armand's English bride!' he said and it seemed to me that there was an accent on the English. Suzanne Tréfours was impassive as she watched Armand take my hand and place the ring on my finger. It was set with three sapphires and clusters of small diamonds. I thought it pretty but I do not care for jewellery. As to its value I hadn't the slightest idea. My aunt had a great deal of valuable jewellery and was always piqued at my indifference to it.

We stood there at the top of the ugly, heavy old table with its trailing ferns and white and red flowers in our honour. Armand had drawn my arm through his and gave it a little squeeze. Philippe Tréfours kissed me, and then gravely and deliberately his wife added her kiss and then all the aunts and uncles, so that I felt quite sick from their mouths not all properly wiped and still smelling of the last food they had eaten. Xavier's lips were hard and agreeable after the wet, sloppy ones. The last to congratulate me with condescending casualness was Thérèse, blonde, heavy-lidded and as pretty as Thalia had said. She didn't kiss me. She took my hand—the one on which Armand had placed the ring—and examined it carefully.

'You must be a very difficult person if you're not pleased with this ring—it's beautiful,' she said. There was envy in her tone.

'But I do like it. I think it's lovely,' I retorted quickly. But I didn't really like it. Was it that the family from whom it came frightened me? What was there here which chilled my natural gaiety and impetuousness? I looked at Armand and was reassured. He was laughing with Xavier but his eyes were on me, and there was in them that which flooded me with a joy so intense that my doubts vanished in a wave of love for him.

The day of the formal announcement of my engagement coincided with Julie Caron's last day with us. She was redeyed when I saw her saying good-bye to Cynthia.

'I don't know what the tears were for,' remarked Cynthia dryly. 'She isn't fond of any of us and she's leaving to please herself—they're an emotional race!'

I was so happy that I scarcely took in her departure. Thalia's remark on the subject came back to me later and made me wonder. 'I know why she's leaving—it's because of you, Rachel,' she had said. What could my engagement possibly have to do with Julie Caron's leaving?

Catherine had gone to the Midi with Clodagh after Christmas and in some ways I was glad. She had been odd about Armand and me and I had been puzzled and hurt. I couldn't think why she was so strange about it. I had met Armand in her house, I thought she would be pleased—but she wasn't. The portrait wasn't finished either—and somehow I knew now that it never would be. For I already saw her differently. Whether or not it was wrong to see things through my emotions I didn't know—but I couldn't help it. Xavier Tréfours, who had taken me to Pont Aven and shown me all the famous places where Gauguin had lived and painted, had told me that I was right.

'Paint and paint only through your emotions—nothing else is painting,' he had said, telling me his reasons for liking my picture of the orphans.

'In this your strong lyrical feeling has surmounted your lack of technical skill and knowledge—and the result is a small work of art,' he had said. 'That's what attracted me so strongly to it. Technically it's bad—but the feeling conveyed in it is so moving that nothing else matters.'

And so it was with the portrait of Catherine. I had loved her on sight—and tried with passionate vehemence to show that love on the canvas. Now that my feeling was mixed with Catherine's own displeasure with me I knew that I could never finish it. When she returned in January I went for the last sitting. She wanted it finished.

'It is for Philippe Tréfours,' she said, looking straight at me when, already in my overall, I was squeezing paints on to my palette.

'Yes. I know,' I said, busy with the arrangement of the colours.

'Rachel!' I looked up at her insistence.

'Doesn't that convey anything to you?'

'Doesn't *what* convey anything?'

'The fact that this picture is for Philippe Tréfours.'

'No. Why shouldn't it be?'

She looked again at me, then she said: 'And this house belongs to him. The car which I drive was given me by him. Clodagh's school fees are paid by him. Now do you see?'

The peculiar insistence in her usually laughing, gurgling voice made me look at her. And from her I looked at the picture I was painting. Naked to the waist. A half-length nude. And for another woman's husband.

'But Suzanne . . . Philippe's wife . . .' I faltered.

'This is France,' she said curtly. 'And if you're going to marry a Frenchman you'll have to remember that.'

A thousand hints . . . remarks . . . veiled references came flooding over me.

'You're shocked?' she asked in a mocking, laughing way but at the same time rather anxiously.

'No. Oh, no. I believe in freedom for love—we all do at the Slade.'

'Well, if by that you mean promiscuity I *don't*. I believe in *love*. And I love Philippe Tréfours—just as you believe yourself to be in love with his son, Armand.'

And now I already found that I couldn't paint. My hand shook a little. Not because I was shocked—although I was—but because this was an issue which must affect me through her. I was to marry Armand—and his father was Catherine's lover. I put down the brush.

'Darling . . . Tintoretta darling . . .' She came over to me, pulling the wrap round her body. 'Darling . . . don't look like that. How could I guess that things would turn out this way?'

'It doesn't make any difference . . . I'm fond of you too . . .' I said.

But it had already made a difference, for I could not finish the portrait. She had assumed for me another aspect than that one she had shown me when I had first seen her. A more interesting and exciting one perhaps—but not the one I had first loved and tried to paint.

It was too difficult for me to digest. I had known somehow that she and Philippe were in love—there was that certain something between them which is unmistakable. Why, then, was I so shaken now?

'Darling . . .' Catherine was saying again. 'How much do you know about love?'

How much did I know? Nothing . . . I knew nothing except that I was already doomed, lost, irrevocably lost in it.

'Put down your paint brushes. I am going to talk to you about love. You'll be grateful to me all your life . . . come here and sit by me. . . .'

Her voice, low and entreating, went on and on, and through it all was the murmur of the sea. Love . . . love . . . she spoke only of love; and although I knew that ostensibly she was doing it to help me, she was inevitably trying to justify herself. But she needed no justification for me. I had never thought honestly about the moral aspects of love. I had discussed them, oh yes, bravely and openly at the Slade. But what does anything mean to one when it remains purely objective? My views had never been put to the test. I had never loved—never fallen in love—and now that I had, its aspect changed for me just as Catherine's had for the portrait.

When I next saw Armand I felt a constraint. Not only because he must know about Catherine and his father—hadn't I met him there? But because of the things of which Catherine had spoken to me. He noticed it and he was awkward, too. When he became too intimate in his caresses I pushed him away. He was hurt. On the other hand he was surprised and shocked at my blunt question as to why he hadn't told me that Catherine was his father's mistress.

'How could I? You're a young girl. Such things are better left unsaid.'

'I may be a young girl but I'm going to marry you—and your father is Catherine's lover.'

He was upset and angry at my openly mentioning it.

'Who's been talking?' he asked angrily.

'Catherine herself.'

'Catherine! How could she? It's too bad of her.'

'I like honesty. I like truth. I hate lies and deceit of all kinds,' I said vehemently.

'And you think that as soon as I fell in love with you I should have said to you, "My father is Catherine Tracey's lover." Is that what you think? Or should I perhaps go round with a label on my coat, "My father has a mistress—her name is Catherine Tracey"?'

I had never seen him so angry. His eyes were dark and the pupils small as if they would withdraw from the light.

'No . . . but you knew I was painting her. You knew how fond of her I am. . . .'

'Well? Is that any reason to disclose what is solely his and her affair?'

I couldn't understand myself why this matter had assumed such importance for me. Was it because I suddenly understood Suzanne Tréfours and her impossible position? Was it that with the prospect of being a wife myself I was unconsciously taking the wife's part? It wasn't my business, but yet it was. I remembered Father's words about not giving my opinions. Armand looked wretched. How could I have brought up the subject at all? It must be horrible both for him and for Thérèse.

'Darling . . . I'm sorry. Kiss me and don't let's talk of it again.'

We were happy together and the matter blew over—but it was there—just as the Calvaire scene was.

Cynthia had begun smoking. It was good for her nerves, she said. She had given it up in India when her heart gave trouble. Now she always had a cigarette in her mouth in a long holder. She took it out when I brought up the subject of Catherine.

'So you know,' she said quietly. 'I'm sorry, Rachel—but it's amazing that you haven't been told before. It's common knowledge. It was the scandal of the place—but it's dead news now—it's an accepted fact.'

'Why don't they divorce?'

'There's no divorce for Catholics—something *you'd* better think about.'

'Why didn't you tell me?' I said passionately. 'Am I such a child or such a fool?'

'You're neither—but you're wilfully blind. And very obstinate,' she said carefully. 'What good would it have done if I'd blurted it out when I was told? It was too late. You were already in love with the son. I did try to warn you —everyone did. Do you still want to go on with this engagement?'

I looked at her in astonishment. 'What has it got to do with Armand and me?'

'It is bound to affect you.'

'Cynthia,' I said. 'What do *you* think about it? They love each other—they really do. Catherine has told me about it. It's something they can't fight against, any more than I can fight this feeling I have for Armand. I love him—and that's that.'

'You've come to the wrong person on that point,' she said bitterly. 'There is duty. One is brought up to duty. One gives hostages . . . and the price is high . . . but let me tell you something, Rachel. Unless you love and really love . . . the act which marriage involves—the act of so-called love—is revolting and vile. . . .'

She lay in that carved bed and the cupids above her, holding up the heart, seemed to be laughing. She had borne two children . . . and Tom Pemberton worshipped her. She lay down with her face buried in the pillows and I left her.

CHAPTER XII

ARMAND HAD GONE to Rennes again—he was to be there for some weeks so that I would see him only at the week-ends. Thalia was overjoyed and made no bones about it. For me life lost half of its delight without those stolen meetings in the *cabine* on the *plage*. We wrote daily—and he telephoned. I didn't go to his home unless he took me. His mother had paid a stiff, formal call on Cynthia, but the visit was not a success. I had to be present to interpret and I found it an ordeal to sit between two women, neither of whom I liked, and to translate their remarks to each other, endeavouring either to leave out or to emphasize the veiled spite in some of them. I realized then what integrity is expected and required of interpreters and what power lies in their tongues.

The conversation was confined to the usual subjects of household, servants and food. In none of these was Cynthia really interested. Claude was a subject which never failed to absorb her and I led the talk on to their respective sons. Claude himself came in and delighted Suzanne with his perfect French accent and his beauty. 'Armand was just such a lovely child,' she sighed, stroking Claude's curls, 'and he's such a handsome man now.' It amused me that the very questions which she was longing to ask—those which concerned the financial status and position of my father—were ones which she couldn't with any decency ask me to interpret. And so they were forced to sit there eyeing each other's clothes and conversing of trivial things. Suzanne asked to see Thalia. 'Thérèse has told me about her. We would be pleased if she came for a day with Thérèse during the holidays . . . it would be good for her English.'

Thalia, when she reluctantly entered the *salon* to meet Armand's mother, was abrupt to the point of rudeness. No, she wouldn't care to come out. Yes, she did like horses—she loved riding but she wouldn't care to ride with Thérèse. Suzanne's eyes began to flash, her lids to drop over them at this veiled insolence. Cynthia couldn't understand what was being said but she was astonished and pleased at Thalia's French. 'She's got on so much better since Mademoiselle left,' she observed. I couldn't reprove Thalia in English, because Cynthia would have been furious with her. When Suzanne had left I tackled her.

'I don't like her,' she said, 'I don't like any of that family.'

'There's no need to show it,' I said angrily.

'Isn't that what you believe in,' she said simply, '"Living in Truth"? You told me yourself that it's deceitful to pretend to like someone when you don't. Are you going back on your word like the Cookand?'

What was there to say? The post had brought a whole collection of reproductions and pamphlets from my aunt—and amongst them my beloved Nefertiti.

'There have been exciting new discoveries,' wrote my aunt, 'which may well prove that your favourite Akhenaten may have been a hypocrite indeed.' We had been told of the discoveries of the 1922 British expedition that in several places the name of Akhenaten's lovely queen had been erased, thus suggesting her fall from grace.

Now some years later they were trying to blacken the name of a great king—the lover of the Amarna 'Living in Truth' concept, the builder of a city of dreams. I was very angry at her letter. I felt that she was glad to be able to send me this news. 'I am sending you a book on the subject,' she finished.

There were several reproductions of Akhenaten, Nefertiti and their daughters—and of the two exquisite heads found by the German expedition at Tell-el-Amarna. I looked again and again at one of these. It showed only the profile. It reminded me of someone—but I couldn't think of whom. The other was a full-face reproduction and this was not like anyone whom I had seen. Both were so absolutely beautiful that I was entranced with them.

In the middle of the night I awoke—I had remembered of whom the profile reminded me. It was Thalia as she had leaned in the window reciting Verlaine's *Sagesse*. She had a long slim neck and her profile was strangely like the one of Nefertiti—and yet Thalia was ugly. Or was she? Hadn't I myself decided that beauty was largely a trick of light? I was terribly excited at the discovery that it was Thalia of whom the sculpture reminded me. It seemed absurd—even fantastic—but it was true. Next morning I called her in. 'Stand over there leaning out of the window with your neck stretched out,' I said. She was surprised—but she never questioned my whims. She went and stood there. And I was right. The modelling of her nose and upper lip which I had always thought quite her best feature was strangely like the Nefertiti—especially the brown sandstone one which was not as well-known as the painted limestone one.

An idea was slowly revolving in my head. She wanted to be beautiful. More than anything in the world she wanted to be beautiful. I would make her beautiful—for one evening she should be the most beautiful girl at the children's fancy-dress ball which the Casino was holding at the end of the holidays. I had been racking my brains to find a suitable costume for her. She should be Nefertiti—'the Beautiful One who has Come'.

She stared at me in disbelief when I told her. Then she turned away. 'Don't make fun of me, Rachel. You know I'm ugly—Nefertiti was one of the most beautiful women in the world, wasn't she?'

'She was. That's exactly why you're going to be her at the ball.'

'No, no. I can't. I don't want to go.'

'Thalia,' I said, fired now with my idea, 'I *want* you to. I'll make you beautiful—so that everyone will look at you and admire you. I *can*, you know. I'm an artist. I can do it.'

I got to work at once copying the dresses in the reproductions of the paintings on the tombs of Akhenaten and Nefertiti. When I had drawn the dress I wanted I went with it to Madame Cerise. 'Yes. I can do it . . . but bring her here so that I can look at her.'

I decided to make the great crown myself from papier mâché and then paint it.

At the ballet class I asked Madame Anastasia to help me. She was teaching Thalia to walk beautifully, balancing something heavy on her head. Already she was far less awkward in her movements. The ballet class was doing wonders for her although she hated it. And she was slimmer and less angular. She was taller than me—but still not too tall for a girl—and the freckles would all be covered with paint.

I worked with enthusiasm at the crown and with Madame at the dress. We spared no pains. I sat up night after night and when it was ready and the crown was finished I began rehearsing Thalia in wearing it. From the first moment when she put it on I saw that I had been right. With the straggly hair ruthlessly pulled back and plastered down under the crown, her face made up to a warm golden tint and her eyes painted and outlined heavily in kohl, her weak eyebrows sharply outlined and her mouth painted out and beyond its normal shape, she was astonishingly like the head of Nefertiti; and with the lovely dress she assumed an unconscious dignity.

I wouldn't let her look until her face was painted and the crown on. Then I said, 'You are Nefertiti, Queen of Egypt. Great of Favour, Lady of Grace, charming in loving kindness, Mistress of South and North, the Great Wife of the King whom he loves, the Lady of Two Lands living for ever and ever! Repeat it after me.' She did so and unconsciously her whole demeanour took on the spirit, feeling and grandeur of the lovely words. Her head held high, bearing proudly the great crown of the South and North, she stood there. I turned her round to face the full-length mirror in my room. 'Look at Nefertiti, Great Queen of Egypt,' I said.

She looked and looked. She couldn't speak. Her tongue went nervously over her painted lips—then she turned, and as she smiled with incredulous delight I noticed the evenness and whiteness of her teeth. She held out both her hands to me, then with a little cry, flinging herself at my feet, pressed her crowned head against my thighs. I could feel the shuddering sobs of her frame. 'Get up. The Queen must never kneel. She is the Great One-Beloved of the King. Get up!'

I pulled her to her feet and repaired the ravages the tears had made on her make-up. She was lovely. And as I looked at her I knew that here was my best work of art. Better than any portrait I had painted or would ever paint was this living, moving image of Nefertiti the lovely one. And I had created her. She was my living work of art. Just as the toy-maker must have felt when he created Coppelia and Pygmalion when he had fashioned Galatea, so I felt now. Exhilaration, excitement and that incomparable thrill of satisfaction which creation and nothing else—not even Armand's caresses—could give me.

I called Cynthia and Claude, Marie and Elise. They stood and stared as Thalia walked slowly and with great dignity down the stairs to the *salon*. Cynthia caught her breath, then she said to me, 'Rachel, you have many faults . . . but you are an artist. . . .' And Claude stood there speechless at his Egyptian sister.

'If we were really Egyptian you would have to marry me, Claude,' said Thalia shakily. 'Nefertiti was married to her brother.'

Claude was dressed in a replica of an early grenadier guardsman's uniform. I had sent to London for an old print and drawn the design for Madame Cérise, whose assistants had made it up. She herself made Thalia's.

'Why don't you take up dress designing?' she asked me when she was examining my drawings for Thalia's dress. 'You could study in Paris and go into partnership with me. We'd do very well together.'

I told her about Armand and my engagement to him. She was contemptuous. 'You want to get married with talent like that? You are very stupid. Anyone can marry and have children—but not all can draw like this.' But how could I tell her that I wanted Armand? That I was suffocated with my love for him?

Cynthia and I went to the parade of the fancy dresses at the end of the children's ball. Chairs were put all round the great *salon* where the sea and the twinkling lighthouses flashed through the windows. The children, over two hundred of them, were lined up and paraded slowly round the room. There was never the slightest doubt as to the winner. A terrific burst of applause greeted Thalia, as, walking erect with the great crown perfectly balanced on her head, and with the slow, graceful glide taught her by Madame Anastasia, she came slowly round the room. Exclamations of surprise and pleasure burst out all round us. She took no notice, as, looking straight ahead as if in a trance, she completed the round of the huge room. Knowing the weight of the crown I didn't breathe freely until she was safely back at the starting point. Armand came up to me afterwards. He was excited. Xavier had been one of the judges and all four had unanimously awarded the first prize to Thalia. She received a beautiful enamel and silver toilet set. I don't think she had ever had such a present in her life.

'You worked a miracle! When I think of that girl and how she looks—and then see this transformation. Why, she's beautiful—quite beautiful! You must be fond of her to have taken all that trouble.' He didn't sound too pleased—and neither did Cynthia.

But Xavier called me over to him at the table where he was still sitting chatting to some of the children. 'You designed her costume, I hear. Let me congratulate you. It's a real work of art. Lovely. And she was in perfect keeping with the role. Proud, dignified and aloof!'

'She's really ugly—quite ugly,' said Armand contemptuously. 'You'd never recognize her. Rachel has re-created her.'

'There is no such thing as an ugly woman,' said Xavier sternly. 'And Rachel has proved it. She can't be ugly with that line of the nose and upper lip—Rachel couldn't have altered that.'

'She has,' insisted Armand. 'The girl has thin, unattractive lips. Rachel painted them.' And now I was angry.

'You seem to have studied her very carefully that you know so much about her,' I said.

'I can't avoid it—she's always trailing us,' he retorted.

When I had taken all the thick make-up off her face and washed the stiff lacquer out of her hair there once again was the plain, mousy Thalia. But it no longer mattered to me, any more than it did to her. She would remember all her life, as I would too, that flashing moment of beauty when, as Egypt's Queen, she had enchanted everyone.

'Was I really beautiful?' she asked wistfully as I laid the dress and crown away in the *armoire*.

'So beautiful that I'm going to immortalize you in that costume—I'm going to paint your portrait like that,' I said. 'Now go and have your bath and get the rest of that grease-paint off your arms and legs.'

And then I saw laid out on my dressing-table the toilet set she had won as her prize. Under one of the hand mirrors was a note. 'For Rachel—whom I love more than anyone in the world— even more than Father.'

I stood there stupidly with the note in my hand and into my mind came some disturbing lines in the last letter Tom Pemberton had written me. 'All her letters are full of you . . . what you do . . . what you say . . . what you think. She adores you . . . is almost obsessed with you . . . she's in love with you, Rachel. For God's sake try to understand and be good to her. I'm so afraid for her. She will go to any lengths for those she loves. . . .'

Girls at school had these crushes on older girls or teachers. But never me—and it had never happened to me. And I loved Armand. Only Armand. I wanted him now as never before. I *didn't* understand as Tom Pemberton hoped I would. A sickness came over me as I looked at the toilet set. Late as it was I went to the telephone. His mother answered me. No, Armand wasn't in. He'd gone to a party. I was surprised. He had told me he was going to work all the evening. Her voice sounded curiously pleased to give me the information.

CHAPTER XIII

SUZANNE TREFOURS got her way and Thalia and I had no choice but to accept her invitation to spend a day with her and Thérèse. It was Cynthia who insisted. 'If she's going to be your mother-in-law the sooner you get to know her the better. You'll find that she may be somewhat different to you when your fiancé isn't there.'

There was an intentional accent on the way she spoke the word mother-in-law and on an impulse I said, 'Did you get on with your mother-in-law, Cynthia?'

'I made it my business to get on with her,' she said coolly, 'and that's exactly what you're going to find difficult. You'd better get to know her now.'

Thalia didn't want to come. She didn't like Thérèse whom she considered to be stuck up and vain. But Cynthia was adamant. She was to go—behave herself and use her French.

'I'm being asked so that Thérèse can use her English,' said Thalia. 'Her mother wants to see if the lessons at our school are worth while.'

'How d'you know that?' asked Cynthia.

'Thérèse told me so. She said that was the reason why I have been invited.'

Thalia looked at me and I at her—and we began to giggle. We were both amused at the idea of two mothers and their respective daughters.

'I shan't talk any English with her at all, and she won't speak any French, so there'll be silence,' said Thalia triumphantly.

'You're ridiculous!' said Cynthia dispiritedly.

'Bring your riding things,' they had said on the telephone.

'Are you going to ride?' asked Thalia.

'Yes. I suppose so,' I said doubtfully.

'I am,' said Thalia decidedly. 'That's one thing I can do better than Thérèse Tréfours—she looks like a dressed-up doll balancing on her horse.'

A smart young chauffeur came to fetch us on the morning arranged for the visit. Armand was in Rennes. I was terrified at having to face Suzanne Tréfours without him. We hadn't been encouraged to take Claude with us. I had wanted him as a buffer between Suzanne and me. It was a cold, grey day—cheerless and heavy. Thalia looked sulky and untidy in her old jodhpurs which were rapidly becoming too small. She had no riding coat and wore a thick, Fair Isle jersey. My riding coat was much too large, for I was still rapidly shedding the unwelcome fat which had so upset my aunt last year, my breeches were equally loose now—but neither the coat nor breeches fitted Thalia when we had tried to exchange.

'I must say,' remarked Cynthia as we stood waiting in the hall, 'that you both look a poor advertisement for your country.'

She had generously brought out all her own riding wardrobe for us in an attempt to help put up a better show. But perfectly cut as her things were, they were useless for us. She was much taller than I and much slimmer than Thalia.

We didn't mind in the least that we were anything but smart. Our things were old and comfortable and we loved them.

'What an awful house!' exclaimed Thalia as the car wound round the last bend of the drive. 'It looks like tomatoes.'

'Now you sound exactly like your mother.'

'Well, no one could call it beautiful,' she said. 'It's frightening, Rachel. It's not a friendly house, is it?'

It wasn't. It had a forbidding conventional air of self-complacency and a stiffness which was strange for a country house. My aunt's house had the same air of stiffness inside—but its exterior was a charming, welcoming one.

Suzanne and Thérèse stood by the windows in the great *salon* and came over at our entrance. Thérèse was as cool and at ease as her mother. Her fair, naturally curling hair was drawn back into a loose knot and tied with a ribbon. She was slim, graceful and very much mistress of herself.

We all sat down and stared surreptitiously at one another. The cold morning light streamed through the windows and on to the pale yellow carpet and the yellow and grey curtains. Suzanne Tréfours was in grey; she seemed to melt into the walls and only the white hair and face stood out sharply. Thérèse, immaculate in smart black riding clothes and white shirt, had a little smile on her pretty mouth as she looked from Thalia's old jodhpurs to my worn breeches. Suzanne inquired after Cynthia, my father and my aunt.

'She is still in Egypt?'

'Yes. She's sending me lovely photographs and books.'

'When is she returning?'

'I don't know,' I said truthfully.

'As you have no mother it would be a good thing for her to have a little talk with me. Perhaps she would come and stay with us here when she returns?'

'I'm sure she will be delighted,' I said suavely.

'I thought that while the girls ride you and I could have a little talk, Rachel.'

Thalia looked at me in dismay. 'Oh, but Rachel's coming riding, too. She's changed purposely.'

The thought of sitting here with Suzanne's sharp little eyes probing me as she questioned was alarming.

'Of course I'm coming—that is if there is a mount for me,' I said firmly. 'I love riding.'

'Of course there is a mount,' said Suzanne stiffly. 'We have several horses. She can have Crépuscule, Thérèse. Go and tell François to saddle her.'

Thérèse looked astonished but said nothing but 'Coming?' to Thalia.

'Yes. Go with her,' said Suzanne. 'Rachel will follow you.'

Thalia went reluctantly. 'They'll soon talk when they get to the stables. Girls of that age are self-conscious.'

I couldn't see any signs of it in Thérèse. She already had the poise and assurance of her mother.

'You have heard from Armand?'

'This morning.'

'He's coining this week-end. He told you?'

'Yes.'

'He wants a date settled for the marriage. I have told him it's impossible.'

'Impossible?' I asked, amazed.

'There are very important things to be decided before any date can be settled. *Very* important matters.'

'Such as?' I asked, bewildered.

'It takes some time for you to be received into the Catholic faith. Armand doesn't seem to realize that.'

'The Catholic faith?' I repeated stupidly. 'You mean I must become a Catholic? But Armand doesn't mind. He said so. He says it doesn't matter.'

'As your children will have to be brought up as Catholics it would be much better if you embrace the faith yourself. You won't like it later on if your children look on their mother as a heretic.'

'Armand and I have discussed all this. He says it doesn't matter. We agreed on each of us going our own way in religious matters.'

'If you're going to become a Tréfours you will have to become a Catholic.'

'If you're going to become a Tréfours.' If. If. So that was how it was. There was a price for entering this family.

'Have you any objection? Would your father mind?'

'Not at all,' I said automatically. When I had told Father that I was following the Ankh-en-Maat—the 'Living in Truth' —he had been unperturbed. 'There is Buddhism, Mohammedanism,

Confucianism and Hinduism,' he had said gravely. 'It's as well to try all those before you decide on Atheism.'

'You're teasing me,' I had said, provoked by his lack of surprise, and he had said, 'Not at all. You're following the normal development of a daughter of mine.'

'Then that's all right. I'll speak to Father Ignace,' said Suzanne with satisfaction, ' . . . and he can call on you in Dinard.'

'Rachel . . . Rachel . . .' called Thalia. 'Come on, *do!*'

'Yes. They're ready. Enjoy your ride. I'll come and see you go off.' She put an arm through mine as I got up and drew me into the wide hall. Outside by the prim hedges and the rockery, Thalia and Thérèse were mounted. A groom stood with Crépuscule waiting for me. She was a lovely little Arab mare.

'Oh, what a beauty!' I cried, delighted.

'She's spirited. She needs a firm rein. She's my own—my special pet,' said Suzanne. 'D'you think you can manage her, Rachel?'

'Mother never lets *anyone* ride her,' said Thérèse.

'I appreciate the honour very much,' I said. She watched me mount. Crépuscule wouldn't stand still a moment. She stood on her hind legs and flung up her head. I set my teeth and after a struggle mastered her.

'*Bien! Bien!*' said the groom François, mounting his own horse. 'But take care, Mademoiselle. She's a little devil. She always gives trouble.'

We went out of the drive with Suzanne watching us from the steps of the house. It took me all my time to manage my mount. There was no trick she didn't resort to in her efforts to unseat me. I had ridden twice with Armand—but not on Crépuscule.

'Give her the whip, Mademoiselle!' said François. 'She understands that. You're too patient with her.' But after a time when we got into the woods she quieted down a little. Thalia and Thérèse had no trouble. Thérèse, despite Thalia's remarks, was an excellent horsewoman.

'Shall I take Crépuscule?' she suggested. 'I've never ridden her and I'd love to try.'

'*Non*,' said François immediately. 'Madame has given strict orders that you are not to ride Crépuscule, Mademoiselle Thérèse. She's too unreliable!'

So, I thought. The mare's not safe enough for the daughter —but she's all right for the future daughter-in-law. I was angry and unconsciously gave her a flick with my whip. She was off like a rocket, dashing through the woods like a mad thing. The low overhanging branches tore my hair and grazed my face, although I crouched low. I couldn't stop her although I tightened the reins and exerted all my strength and will-power. There was no room to take her round in circles—there was only the narrow path cut for riders through the undergrowth. Behind me I heard Thalia's horse thundering. She was chasing me, calling wildly, 'I'm coming. I'm coming. Hang on, Rachel. Hang on!'

But the hooves of the pursuer merely excited the mare to further efforts. She fairly raced now and it was all I could do to keep my seat. At last we came to a clearing where the trees had been cut down and here I pulled on one rein and forced her into a circle, then into smaller and smaller ones until at last she stopped and began grazing calmly as if she'd never thought of anything else. I dismounted.

'I'll take her. You're tired,' said Thalia.

'Can you manage her?' I asked. I was exhausted. Thérèse and François came up.

'She's a devil. Didn't I tell you, Mademoiselle? Madame never lets up for a moment on her. She keeps her on a tight, hard rein.'

'You'd better ride her home. She's your mother's horse,' said Thalia to Thérèse.

'Not me,' said Thérèse quietly.

'You're afraid of her?'

'Yes, I am.'

'I'll ride her,' said Thalia decidedly.

The groom demurred. The mare had a bad streak. She gave a beautiful ride once you'd mastered her—but she was up to all the tricks. He could never groom her without the little wretch trying to corner him and kick and bite.

'Why does your mother keep her?' I asked Thérèse.

'She's a beautiful creature—and Mother enjoys a fight,' said Thérèse indifferently. 'I like a well-behaved mount—so that I can enjoy the exercise. I don't want to fight all the way.'

Suzanne hadn't intended me to ride at all—that had been clear. When I'd insisted she'd given me Crépuscule. Papillon was lame—she'd hurt a foot. That was the horse usually given to guests.

'I can manage her easily. I'm used to difficult horses,' Thalia insisted. She was patting and fondling the now indifferent mare, and suddenly sprang on her back. Immediately the creature began the same unpleasant tricks she had tried on me. Thalia took the whip, administered three sharp blows, tightened the reins and brought her under control.

'You'll do,' I said. 'Keep her well in. Don't slacken.'

Crépuscule gave no more trouble. Thalia handled her firmly and with skill. Both François and I praised her horsemanship. Thérèse said nothing. The woods thinned out into open fields and coarse, rough ground and we were able to give our mounts their heads. 'Take care with that one, Mademoiselle!' warned François. 'She'll go off again if you don't hold her in.'

But although the speed which Crépuscule attained alarmed me it didn't appear to upset Thalia. With her hair flying and her face brilliant with colour she was enjoying herself. 'She rides like a boy! Like a jockey!' said the groom delightedly.

'Where did you learn to ride like that?' I asked Thalia when she came up from several mad gallops round the great sweep of ground.

'On the racecourse at Meerut,' she said. 'We rode every morning and every evening. We exercised the polo ponies.'

'You rode with Cynthia, or your father?'

'With *them*? No. I rode with the grooms and the stable boys. They taught me to jump, too.'

What a strange life this girl had had. I couldn't visualize it at all. 'Didn't Cynthia mind your riding with them?' I asked.

'She didn't know. She was asleep in the early mornings—and dressing for parties in the evenings. You can't ride during the day, it's too hot.'

'Well, how was Crépuscule?' asked Suzanne as we sat at lunch. There were only the four of us to-day, and we were separated by great spaces at the huge table.

'Disgusting, as usual,' said Thérèse.

'She was too much for you?' Suzanne turned to me.

'She was as much as I could manage—she tired me. I was glad to give her to Thalia.'

'Thalia rode her?'

'Yes. She was splendid with her.'

'I hadn't expected you to ride—I'd hoped you would have stayed with me. There were things I wanted to discuss—Papillon is lame. I'm sorry that my mare behaved so badly.'

'She didn't,' I said warmly, 'she was just lively. I couldn't manage her. Thalia can.'

Suzanne looked at Thalia, who had relapsed into her usual indifferent apathy. 'She's much stronger than you,' she said resentfully. 'You don't appear to be very strong, Rachel.'

'She's been ill,' said Thalia quickly, 'that's why she's here.'

'I'm perfectly well now,' I said, irritated at Suzanne's air of annoyed concern.

'Armand is never ill. He enjoys perfect health.'

'He's lucky,' I said.

'He's a wonderful athlete—and a wonderful horseman,' said Thérèse.

The girls began talking of school. They used mixed English and French and were discussing the various teachers. The lunch was simple—but perfectly cooked and served.

'You'll have to learn to make some of our dishes,' observed Suzanne as I praised one of the ones we were eating. I said that Marie was teaching me some Breton dishes.

'She's an excellent cook,' said Suzanne. 'And a cousin of Rosalie's.'

This was news to me—and not such pleasant news. It explained how Marie had known about Armand and me long before anyone else had.

'Everyone's related to everyone else round this piece of the coast. I mean those of us who reside here—not those who come for a time. What d'you think of Thérèse's English, Rachel?'

'It's excellent,' I said politely.

'I'll arrange with Father Ignace to call on you, Rachel—when would suit you?'

'Father Ignace?' said Thalia.

'Our family priest,' said Thérèse. 'You've seen him. He came to the school last week.'

'But what has Rachel to do with him?'

She's going to be a Catholic,' said Thérèse.

'But she can't. She's an agnostic like me—we believe in a sort of universal God but we're not Christians.' Thalia said this in English.

'Be quiet,' I said quickly.

'What did Thalia say? Translate for me please, Rachel.'

I saw Thérèse's amused eyes on me and I dared not translate anything but what Thalia had actually said. Under Suzanne's astonished, incredulous stare I grew hot and uncomfortable.

'Do I understand rightly that you and Thalia are not Christians—that you believe in some sort of Egyptian cult?'

'I believe in God—but . . . we follow the Ankh-en-Maat—"Living in Truth".'

'But what is this Ankh-en-Maat?'

'It's a theory—a way of life. It means that we live as we believe—that we don't lie to make things look better.' I trailed off . . . it wasn't easy to explain at all. It no longer sounded as strong and simple as it did.

'Your aunt—does she follow this too?'

'No!'

'But she's in Egypt.'

'We attended lectures on Amarna Art and she's gone to the Nile Valley.'

'But you—have you told Armand of this extraordinary belief?'

'Yes.'

'And what did he say?'

'That I would think differently later.'

'But you attend the Anglo-American church here.'

'Yes.'

'Why?'

I was about to say that Cynthia insisted, when I saw Thalia's amused eyes. She was delighted at my predicament.

I gave it up and remained silent.

'I don't know what Father Ignace will have to say to this. It puts a very different light on what I've already told him.' Her voice was frosty—her face outraged. I was angry with Thalia for putting me into this position. After lunch when we were packing up our riding things, for we had changed for lunch, I told her so.

'You wouldn't become a Catholic just to please *her*?' she demanded incredulously. 'Rachel ... how *could* you?'

'It'll be all over your school to-morrow,' I said angrily.

'What'll be all over the school?'

'That we're agnostics and follow the "Living in Truth".'

'The Christians were persecuted,' said Thalia staunchly. 'I don't care what they say at school.'

I looked at her in astonishment. Only a few months ago she had been too nervous to go into the school building.

I was angry at having the religious aspect of my marriage forced to an early issue. Armand had made it quite clear that he did not want me harried or bothered over it. I felt that Suzanne had taken an unfair advantage—and Thalia had deliberately played into her hands. Even now she wouldn't leave it alone. 'But you wouldn't become a Catholic, would you, Rachel?' she insisted.

'I don't want to discuss it,' I said firmly.

When I saw Father Ignace a few days later he wasn't in the least perturbed.

'If you don't believe in anything except that, it makes my task easier,' he said smilingly. 'It means that we start right from scratch.'

CHAPTER XIV

THE PAINTING of Thalia as Nefertiti went easily from the very start and the sittings in the attic at the top of the villa were some of the happiest memories I have of that fateful year in France.

Armand was away a great deal in the weeks immediately after the New Year; and as Claude no longer had the services of Julie Caron, Cynthia was persuaded to send him to school. Here he was happy when after some stormy fights and many tears he found his own level. He was mastering French so fast that he found it no trouble to learn everything in that language.

Thalia was now attending school every day and I had more time to myself. I made a drawing of Cynthia. It was cold and expressionless and pleased neither her nor me. She had been delighted with the drawings of Claude which I had given her as a surprise for Christmas. I don't think I had ever seen her face so alight with pleasure as when she untied the parcel and saw the drawings of her sleeping son. She had thanked me warmly and spontaneously, but then she had spoilt it all by remarking that they would have been so much nicer had he been awake. Nothing was ever quite right for Cynthia. She simply hadn't the capacity for enjoyment—at least not as I knew it.

Thalia sat for me with a patience which I found astonishing. She had that power her mother had—rare in English people—of being able to be perfectly motionless and still. Immobile, quiet, as if in a dream she sat there in the window so that she was in shadow against the light and only her forehead and the sensitive line from the nose and upper lip were lit up. There was from the beginning something mysterious and compelling in the portrait.

I worked in an excitement as intense as that when I had begun the one of Catherine, as fast and as passionately, and this time it seemed to me that something of the quality of what I was wanting so urgently to say was appearing on the canvas. There was the sea, dark and stormy behind her, as I saw it from the window where she sat, and the almost green sky in the winter light. The problems of tone, colour and line were maddeningly difficult but I battled with them in a frenzy—and it was apparent to me that whether good or bad I was getting nearer to that which I wanted.

And the whole sittings as well as the painting had an enchantment and delight which bewitched us both. I couldn't have explained what it was—but it was something far beyond the usual passionate desire to create beauty, to catch its fleeting magic. As I worked I talked to Thalia about Nefertiti. The book which my aunt had sent me had added a good deal to my knowledge of her. We talked of her and Akhenaten and of their daughters ... of the Ankh-en-Maat—the 'Living in Truth' concept which he loved—and of the new city he built, Akhetaton. Whether it was partly the magic of the place itself which had gripped me from the moment I landed, or whether it was sheer delight in the realization of a dream, I don't know, but when at last the portrait was finished and I laid down my brushes I felt that all that was best in me had gone into the picture and there was nothing left but the shell.

Xavier was staying with friends at Pont Aven. I wanted to show him the painting and Armand took me there. Armand had not said one word about it himself. I knew he didn't like Thalia but I was hurt at his silence. Cynthia had looked at it for a long time; then she said, 'It's your conception of Thalia—it's not her as she really is.' Couldn't she see that a painting must always be an artist's conception? And that this was how I *did* see her then?

The first time I had seen Pont Aven I had been bitterly disappointed in the place. I don't know what I expected—from the lives of Van Gogh and Gauguin certainly far, far more—but on this second visit it seemed to me that there was some quality in the air of the place which emanated from all those men who had striven and battled there with the problems of the painter. Xavier was staying in a studio down by the bridge when we visited him, and he had a handsome buxom model with him. I showed him the painting of Thalia, asking him for his honest opinion. He said nothing for a long time, looking at it with his head on one side and an arm round the woman whom he had been painting. Suddenly he swung round to me. 'You are an artist, child. You'll have to give up this idea of marrying Armand and get to work. Work, work. That's what the future means for you. Work and more work—all your life—it never ends—you'll never be happy until you've achieved something of what you're after! Perhaps you never *will* achieve it—but you'll have to try. Go to Paris and get down to it. This is good —*very* good.'

I was so happy that I flung my arms round his neck—he wore a velvet painting coat—and hugged him. His beard was wiry and scratchy but I liked his hard, rough face. He was delighted. 'Ah, she's got the impulsive temperament and the passion of the painter, Armand my boy. But don't try this on the masters I'm going to send you to—not all of them will be content to remain her future uncle!' And looking maliciously at Armand he put the other arm round me.

Armand didn't find this as funny as his uncle appeared to. He was very angry with Xavier. He didn't really approve of my wanting to be a painter any more than his mother did. To her it was a hobby which must be given up when the more serious matters of household and children would arise. She had made that clear to me, and because I was so much in love I had said nothing.

When we were leaving Pont Aven Armand said, 'You will be able to study in Paris the year I am there.'

I didn't answer because I knew that I would need many years, not just the one which would fit in with his movements.

'My uncle lives in some ways a very disreputable life,' he said as he started up the car, 'and I'd rather you didn't become too intimate with him.'

'He's a great painter—and I adore him!' I said.

'And don't use such extravagant terms . . . people are apt to misunderstand you. For instance, some men wouldn't like you flinging yourself on him as you did just now.'

I shrank back into my coat. It was as if he had struck me.

'I'm sorry,' I said stiffly.

He was going back to Rennes again and I wouldn't see him until the following week-end, he said. He wouldn't be able to get over. I said nothing but once when he had told me he would be away all the week I had been astonished to see his car out on the Vicomté road. I knew it was his by the colour and the number. It had been parked near the lovely little Chapelle de la Divine Bergère in the Franciscan Monastery on the Rond Point there. The brothers ran a school which was attached to the monastery. Armand had at one time attended the school—and he was very fond of some of the brothers. Seeing his car I had gone timidly into the chapel to look for him but it had been quite empty except for a monk in his marron robe. When he had asked me whether he could help me I said I was looking for Armand Tréfours. 'I haven't seen him. He hasn't been here to-day. I expect he's on the cliffs or walking on the beach . . . he's fond of coming to the Vicomté.'

I knew he was—didn't he bring me here? This place was to me our special dedicated paradise. I loved it. Even now in February it was sheltered and warm if one went lower down on to the banks of the estuary, where below the thick pines, the tamarisks, rosemary and myrtle and mimosa bushes mingling with the gorse made a thick screen from the winds. Thalia had seen his car there on two occasions. But I didn't say anything—his affairs were his own business—and if he went to see the Brothers he would prefer to go alone. Since that first small difference over the matter of his father and Catherine there had sprung up between us the very faintest coolness. I had been right when I'd said that it could never remain as perfect as it had been before our engagement had been made known to others.

One afternoon in March, Thalia and I went walking round the coast beyond the Vicomté. Claude had gone to a party with Cynthia. Kiki had hurt his foot and we had left him unhappy at home. It was one of those sudden warm days which flash out after a cold spell and nature seems to awaken and force one to notice her. 'Look at me, look at my wonders . . . look at me for I am life . . .' and every cell in one's body is aware of that life.

It was really spring. The sea, the emerald after which the coast is named, was smooth as shining glass and as mystic. The trees were full of gossiping noisy birds, under our feet violets and small white star-like flowers thrust up everywhere. There seemed to be a burst of life . . . a throbbing of insects and small creatures awaking.

We raced each other, clambered up and down the steep, rocky descents to the beaches below for sheer love of being alive. It was still—and a strange, misty, unreal quality which marked the entire coast was over it as a living cobweb. It was very warm, and we pulled off first one garment and then another. All around us the gorse in great golden masses wafted the scent of almonds, below us the dark, sinister rocks gleamed wet from the receding tide and their savage agelessness never failed to awe me.

Suddenly Thalia raced madly away from me and when she was almost on the edge of the steep cliff she screamed wildly, threw up her arms and disappeared from view. Terrified and stricken with horror, I raced to the place where she had disappeared. Hardly daring to look I peered over the edge of the ravine-like cleft in the cliffs calling 'Thalia . . . Thalia . . . Thalia . . .' but there was no answer. I screamed again and again and the echoes answered up from the depth. Shaking and unable to realize what had happened I prepared to descend the frightening granite cliff face. And then I heard her laughing . . . laughing wildly . . . 'Rachel . . . Rachel. Don't go down. Look nearer. . . .' And there flat in the long grass she lay laughing at me.

I was so angry that I couldn't speak. My stomach was full of quivering terror and my heart beat in uneven tearing breaths and suddenly my knees gave way and I sat down in the grass on the edge of the cleft.

'You're not angry . . . don't be angry, Rachel. I was pretending to be Tristram. I can't help teasing you to-day. It's that sort of a day. You really thought I'd gone over. Why, you're quite pale. Did you mind *so* much?'

She was obviously pleased at my fright and distress, and came and sat with her arm round me. I was so thankful that she was safe that as she sat close to me in her plaid skirt and schoolgirl's blouse for once I didn't push her away as I usually did.

'Thalia,' I said suddenly, 'd'you know your freckles are disappearing?'

Her face literally glowed with joy. 'Really? You're not saying it to please me?'

'Look for yourself.' I handed her the small mirror from my handbag. She peered anxiously in it, then turned to me. 'It's true, it's true!' she cried as if she couldn't believe it.

'D'you mind them so much?' I asked as she squeezed herself to me in impulsive delight.

'You *know*. You know I do. I want more than anything in the world to be beautiful—like when I was Nefertiti. I know I'm ugly—and Mother hates it. She should have had Deirdre for her daughter. Deirdre's lovely, isn't she?'

'Deirdre's not lovely. She's just pretty.'

'Mother thinks she's lovely. She said so. She's going to be presented in the spring. She's having a white tulle frock with bunches of rosebuds on it. . . .'

I could sense the wistfulness of Thalia for something similar, although she would have looked ridiculous in it.

'It's all very silly . . . and meaningless. I hated it,' I said.

It was so hot in the sun that we lay there in the sweet thick grass full of little flowers. She put out a freckled hand and timidly touched my arm. 'Rachel . . . there's something I want to tell you.

Oh God, I thought, if she's going to tell me that she loves me I shall be sick.

'Don't,' I said urgently.

'I must. I've tried to tell you so many times—but you won't let me. . . .'

I sat up angrily, 'And I tell you again—I don't want to hear it.'

She sighed and her face was suddenly old. She set her lips tightly together and, her eyes blinking and her hands twisting in an agony of nervousness, she began again . . . 'But this time, Rachel, I've *got* to tell you . . . it's common knowledge. It's about Armand . . .' her voice rushed on, gathering speed and strength before I could interrupt. 'It's Armand . . . there's another woman. I've seen his car . . . here . . . he brings her here—up there. . . .' She pointed higher up the slope. 'He reads her the same poems as he reads you, that's how I learned "Les Elfes". . . .'

I stared at her and then I laughed. 'You're making it up,' I said. 'You're jealous! You're always making trouble. Your mother has warned me about you. . . .' And now I was angry.

'But this time it's true, it's true! You must believe me. I'll show you the exact spot where I've seen him. . . . He was here two days ago when you had gone to Dinan with Judy.'

The thought that Armand took another woman to the spot which I had thought was sacred to us alone infuriated me. But it wasn't true—and as I thrust it from me my anger with her increased. 'I don't want to see it. I don't believe you. Let's go home. You've done enough for one afternoon.' I was still upset from that horrible trick she had played on me.

We began climbing up the steep slope to the open, even ground above. . . . When we reached the top and paused for breath she said musingly . . . 'You know what the matron at school tells you about sex and all that . . . well, it just isn't true. When I asked her where one did all the things she was telling me about, she told me to use my common sense and did I suppose one would choose the open air?'

I started walking quickly along the path past the monastery which Armand loved; she came behind lumbering and panting a little. . . . 'It isn't true . . .' she repeated. 'They *do* choose the open air. Armand does.'

'Shut up!' I cried violently. 'You make me sick . . .' We walked back in complete silence.

This was the evening I used to spend with Julie when I would go to her flat and we would play records and talk. Since she had left I had met her several times in the town—she hadn't yet obtained the post in Rennes. I still had a number of books she had lent me and two of her gramophone records. After dinner I felt restless and told Cynthia I would go for a walk. I longed for

Armand—but he was in Rennes. 'Then take Thalia. . . . Don't go alone . . .' she said.

I didn't want Thalia. I could hardly bring myself to speak to her since the afternoon. But she went at once and fetched a coat and scarf.

'We'll take these books and records back to Julie Caron,' I said.

'No!' said Thalia violently. 'Don't let's go there.'

'Yes. *Do* go. And ask her if she would consider taking Claude out for two afternoons a week until she goes to Rennes,' said Cynthia. 'I can't think why she left like that. She wrote me a charming letter in English telling me she was so sorry to leave me.'

The flat was over the little grocer's shop in the Square and as we were turning the corner we met Julie's old mother. She greeted me with a strange malevolent stare. 'Is Julie at home?' I asked. 'I'm returning these books and records to her.'

'Oh, yes. She's in! She's in all right. Go up. The door's open. I don't think the bell rings. If she doesn't answer—go right up.'

I thanked her, and regarding me with a studied intent she said insolently, 'I must congratulate you, Mademoiselle Rachel. Since you came here last you have become the fiancée of Armand Tréfours!'

I was too taken aback at her tone to answer, and before I could—'Felicitations! You've done well for yourself!' she called and turned the corner.

'How queer she was!' I said to Thalia.

'I don't like her—and I hate Julie Caron. Don't let's go up, Rachel. Let's leave the things on the doorstep.'

The Square was quite deserted except for a starved cat. Behind the brightly lit, steamy windows of the bistros the men sat arguing, and from one came the tinkle of mechanical music. The door at the side of the grocer's shop was painted yellow and it was very dirty. We rang the bell and waited. There was no answer.

I pushed the door open. The small narrow passage inside smelt of garlic and of drains; it was dark, but a light burned on the landing above.

'I'm not coming up. I'll wait for you here,' said Thalia.

I went up. The stairs led on to a small landing where the Carons had three rooms. The paint was peeling off the walls and the banisters were scratched and shabby.

'Julie! Julie!' I called softly, pushing open the door of the sitting-room.

The room was in darkness except for a small rose-pink table lamp by the couch. The first thing I saw was a skirt on the floor—Julie's new pleated blue one—then a pair of bare legs. But I saw no more ... for I would have known those legs anywhere in the world. Hadn't I observed and sketched them a hundred times when Armand was running across the beach?

I turned, and stumbled down the stairs, and the gramophone records fell, clattering to the hall below, and smashed into small pieces.

I pushed Thalia roughly before me through the door into the street, ignoring the broken records, closing it behind me as if I would shut out for ever the vision of what I had just seen.

'Take these,' I said, leaning against the wall outside.

She took the books without a word and I leaned there. The Square was no longer there—it was an empty space as was everything. A space in which like a meaningless object I was suspended. Suddenly I felt her dragging me away from the house. She pulled me across the Square and I recovered myself sufficiently to notice Armand's white car parked outside one of the bistros.

'He's coming out,' she whispered, dragging me urgently round the corner until we were in the shadow of the trees. 'I saw his car when the old woman was talking to us. *She* knew he was up there.'

I thought of Madame Caron's malicious smile and her insolence. Yes, she had known all right. And then I turned on Thalia. And *you*! You knew too! You saw the car.'

'I tried to stop you,' she said sullenly, but there was no conviction in her voice, and I knew that it was what she had wanted—that I should see for myself what she had seen on the slopes of the Rance.

'I didn't *know*. How could I have known? I saw the car—that's all. I tried to stop you. You never listen to me.'

There was in her voice that pleased satisfaction which maddened me. I walked on, not feeling the solid ground, not seeing anything which we passed.

She said desperately, 'Rachel . . . Rachel . . . Don't look like that. *Don't.* He's not worth it. It's been going on for months. That's why she left us—because of you. He can't love you. He *doesn't.*'

'Go away. Go quickly . . . or I think I shall kill you,' I said passionately.

I don't remember anything of the walk back to the villa but suddenly I was back. I felt stricken . . . withered . . . I wanted to hide myself from the bright light at the remembrance of what I had seen. Hot waves of shame came over me at the thought of my having been such an unwitting fool. But even as I fought the tumult in me, unable to weep, in a dry searing anguish I wondered why it was that I hated not Armand and Julie Caron for what they were doing but Thalia for having always known it.

I was with Claude the following afternoon when Marie came to tell me that Armand was downstairs. Cynthia was playing bridge in the *salon*.

'Where is he?' I asked her. She was peering at me with her sharp old eyes. 'I've put him in the kitchen—that's the best place for him.'

'Tell him to go down on the terrace—I'll come down.

'But it's cold to-day,' she protested.

'Where else can we talk?' I demanded.

'Claude can come in the kitchen and he can come up here,' she suggested.

'No,' I said, 'Thalia will be coming in at any minute now. I'll come down—you stay here and give Claude his tea—will you, Marie?'

I rubbed my cheeks until they were red, and brushed my hair violently, put on a jacket and went down the white pebbled path in the garden to the terrace. Armand was pacing up and down and hurried to me at once.

'Rachel . . .' he began, and then I suppose he saw in my face how I was feeling. He stopped, and tried to take me in his arms. I pushed him violently away. 'Don't touch me—if you do I'll vomit.'

And now he looked angry. His face was white, two red spots appeared below his high cheekbones.

'So that's how you feel about me—I make you sick?'

'Yes,' I said, 'you do.'

'All you English are prigs!' he said bitterly. 'I suppose you are shocked. How could I imagine that you would come into someone's flat without knocking?'

'Madame Caron told me to go straight up. She knew the bell didn't ring.'

'You could have knocked.'

'So that you and she could have arranged yourselves in time?' I retorted. 'What difference would that have made? I'd have known just the same.'

'I'm sorry you had to see that. . . . For a young girl it must have been a shock . . .'

'It's not that. It's the lies. Lies! How can you lie to me? I can't stand deceit. I hate it and I hate liars.'

'But what would you have me do? Would you have me tell you every time I went to my mistress? Would you prefer that?'

'Your mistress? You admit that she's that?'

'Of course,' he said impatiently.

'No . . . no . . .' I cried. I couldn't bear it. A wave of some new, violent feeling assailed me. Was it jealousy?

'But you accepted the fact that my father had a mistress—why can't you accept the same of me?' he asked, genuinely bewildered.

But I couldn't. 'It's quite different. Quite!' I cried.

'But what has it to do with *you*?' he insisted.

What had it to do with me? Was he mad?

'Tell me,' I said coldly, 'do you intend to keep a mistress after our marriage—as your father has apparently done?'

'Rachel!' He was furious now. 'What are you saying? Think! What *are* you saying?'

'I am asking you a question—that's all. Are you going to continue this after our marriage?'

'I won't answer such an infamous question,' he said, his eyes hard and his voice unlike I had ever heard it before.

'Then take back your ring,' I cried, taking it from my finger and holding it out to him.

'No! No!'

'Take it!' I shouted, furious now.

But he wouldn't—and, darting to the low terrace wall, I hurled the ring violently over into the sea below. 'That's what your promise is worth! That!'

He caught me by the shoulders. 'You had no right to do that. It's a family ring! It belonged to my grandmother. You had no right to throw it away.' He was so angry that he shook me violently back and forth. I struggled to free myself and when I couldn't, I struck him across the face. He released me abruptly. We stood staring at each other. And then I heard footsteps, and there was Thalia coming out. Armand cursed viciously. 'That limpet . . . that lovesick limpet. She's the cause of everything. We've never had a chance with her trailing us everywhere. Rachel, darling . . . darling. . . . Can't you understand and forgive me?'

'No,' I said furiously, 'I can't. If you had to do that—why not with me?'

'Are you mad?' He stared incredulously at me. 'With the woman who is to be my wife?'

'No. No . . . I see. It's all a filthy lie! On the surface everything must be *comme il faut*, while underneath there's all *this*.'

Thalia was approaching now and Armand turned roughly to me. I could not bear the misery on his usually debonair face, the wretchedness in his eyes. I loved him so . . . I longed to be in his arms again—no matter if Julie Caron had been in them last night. But I could not get over his treachery—his deceit. I could not. It wasn't what he had done with her, it was what he had not asked me to do. His life was his own—his body was his own—according to *his* code. But I loved him. My body was his according to my code, and of that he had taken no thought at all; and I let him walk away up the path and out of the gate without moving from the wall on the terrace.

I collected Claude's milk and biscuits from Marie. She looked hard at me.

'*Eh bien!* You know now. You've found out for yourself. You wouldn't have believed anyone had they told you. All men are the same. *Salauds!*'

'Don't, please, Marie. Don't!'

'He's not worth your tears! Didn't I warn you? Didn't I?'

There was no need to ask her how she knew. It was a small place—especially in winter—and Madame Caron was known as a gossip. 'Am I crying?' I asked fiercely.

'*Non*. It would be better if you did,' she said sharply.

I hadn't wept—not one tear. Something in me was shattered—as a vase holding roses so that the water and blooms lie indecently exposed. And so I felt. Indecent—naked—exposed to all and everyone's interested stares and comments. The whole Colony must know the story of last night's horror —at least I felt so.

Cynthia said very little, but she at least refrained from saying, 'I told you so.' When I was saying good night to her she had said, 'Rachel . . . if it would help you, tell me about this. . . . Thalia has told me the bare details. . . . You realize, of course, that she isn't blameless in the matter. . . . She's terribly jealous.'

'She may be jealous—but she couldn't possibly have had anything to do with last night.'

'I'm not so sure,' said Cynthia. 'I'm going to tell you something. Sit down there. Where *is* Thalia, by the way?'

'Writing poems in her room.'

Listen. She must have told you why Terence Mourne had to resign? She hates him—and she is responsible for his having had to resign. Yes . . . a girl of fourteen. You wouldn't think it possible, would you?'

She told me something about a despatch,' I said unwillingly. Couldn't she see that I was bruised, crushed, flattened? That all I wanted to do was to hide from myself?

She told you that it was found in the pocket of my négligée?'

'Yes.'

'And I tell you that *she* put it there.'

'No, no,' I said, sickened. I couldn't bear any more.

'And the snake? You heard about that?'

'Yes,' I said wearily, 'even Claude told me about the snake.'

'That was bad enough—although I accepted her explanation that it was meant as a joke, one of the silly pranks she's so fond of playing. She knew I would put my hand in the hat-box and that I had a weak heart. But the other—that was deliberate. It was malicious, to put it mildly. Do you think I like having to tell you these things about my own daughter? I'm doing it to warn you. I'm not at all sure that Thalia had not a hand in last night's happenings.'

Tom Pemberton's words in the letter, in spite of myself, came back to me. 'She will go to any lengths for those she loves.'

'She *couldn't* have!' I cried angrily. 'She begged me not to go up to the flat.'

'And why? What reason had she for not wanting you to go there? It's obvious that she knew what you would find.'

'No, no,' I insisted. 'She couldn't have known. It's monstrous to think such a thing.'

'It's the effects of her pranks which are monstrous!' said Cynthia wearily.

'She'll grow out of them. They're all part of her unhappiness. I know how she feels. I know what it is to feel like that . . . uncertain . . . fumbling, groping . . . being hurt. . . .'

But this feeling I had now . . . of death . . . of complete nothingness. This I didn't know. It engulfed and suffocated me with emptiness while still allowing me the anguish of pain.

And now I felt again as I had a year ago. As if I were a human elephant that everyone must notice—on which every glance must rest in amusement. They all knew! They must. I gathered from Marie that the story was all over the market. From Cynthia's set white face that the Colony were revelling in it. They knew about Suzanne coming in a fury because I had thrown away the ring and telling me that I would have to make good its value to them. They knew that she had called me badly brought up, badly behaved, and most unsuitable for her son. They knew because Marie and Elise must have heard us shouting at each other in the *salon* while they had been laying the table most conveniently in the *salle-à-manger*. I had seen them through the glass doors and was too proud to ask them to go away.

And Madame Caron? According to Marie her tongue ran away with her all too often. When I went with Claude on the Promenade where the children were roller skating outside the great Casino while their governesses and nurses huddled gossiping on the seats in the sheltered corners, I could feel their lascivious delight in the details of the denouement of the silly English girl and the handsome French Adonis—as they had called the runner on the beach. The wind rushing round the corners and hurling its blinding spray in my eyes couldn't erase for me the picture which was imprinted as a wood-cut on my mind ... and it wasn't only its violence which made me shrink into the shelter of my coat.

When Thalia came back from school and said that all the girls were talking about it and that Thérèse hadn't come in for her English lesson I remained silent. She shouldn't have the satisfaction of knowing how I felt.

'You're not engaged any more, are you, Rachel?' she said, and she couldn't hide the delight in her voice.

'No,' I said evenly, 'I'm not engaged.'

All the time I was listening ... waiting ... hoping. Armand would write. He would telephone. He would come. But he didn't. All the evening Thalia kept on rubbing her head against my arm—as my aunt's spaniels did when they were wanting food. She kept looking at me with fixed vague eyes all the time she was doing her Italian homework for Madame Valetta. I ached in some place where I had never ached before—but I couldn't have said where it was. And nothing mattered ... nothing ... this, I thought, is what death must be like ... extinction ... nothingness ... only in death the ache would be gone and now it was an agony not to be borne.

At midnight I was still awake and as if in a trance I got up. I knew what I had to do. I put a few things into a small suitcase, packed up my paint-box, took my sketch books and strapped them on to the case. I dressed in the suit my aunt had had made for me and which I hated, and crept downstairs. It was quiet, a sleeping house which was now hostile and alien to me. I could hear the faint ticking of a clock—Marie's alarm clock ... the sigh of Claude as he turned in his sleep as I passed his room ... and knew the strange, unreal feeling of being the one soul alive in a sleeping-beauty world. I unlatched the heavy door and closed it noiselessly so as not to wake Kiki, picked up my cases and went silently down the pebbled path.

At the station I found that there was no train until five o'clock—the market one to Dol. It was bitterly cold. There was a light in the window of the little house where Yves lived. I knocked. Yves came to the door. He peered at me uncertainly just as Marie did. 'I have to wait for a train—it's too cold in the station,' I said.

'Come in,' he said, 'come in,' drawing me into the malodorous little room and taking my cases from me. 'You'll be catching the five o'clock train to Dol?'

He stated it as a simple fact, showing no surprise, and I was grateful now for the curious pity with which we English were regarded here—as if we were semi-idiots to be tolerated and petted. I was English. If I wanted to get up at midnight and go to Paris on the five o'clock train there need be no other reason except that I belonged to a nation which chose to be ridiculous.

He pulled a large turnip-type watch from the pocket of his rough blue trousers. 'You'd better get to sleep for a few hours. . . . I'm getting up at half-past four to harness Napoleon. I'll wake you. You can sleep in Marie's bed.'

He showed me to a cell-like little room with a small palliasse bed with a white, starched counterpane. A jug and basin were on a rickety table—and over the bed a large crucifix.

'If you hear thuds . . . it'll be Napoleon. He kicks in his sleep . . . and his stable is on the other side of this wall . . . we built it on. It's only wood—thin wood. Sleep well, Mademoiselle. Sleep safely. I'll wake you and take you to the station in good time for the train.'

I lay down on Marie's hard bed and covered myself with my coat. It was cold. . . . Yves didn't go to bed, he told me. In winter he slept in his clothes by the stove.

It wasn't Napoleon's constant kicking which kept me awake. It was an agonized longing for Armand.

Dol was crowded with peasant women, their great baskets full of clucking hens and angry ducks . . . with workmen in their blue overalls and berets. The little train disgorged us all on the small junction platform. My things were handed out to me by cheerful, appraising men who remarked on my legs and body in the same breath as they commented on the livestock in the baskets. One of them offered me some coffee from his flask—another a piece of fresh bread. It was still dark—but the sky had those eerie streaks of uncanny light already and the darkness wasn't thick as velvet but like chiffon. The train was almost empty—it was a slow one.

I was cold—not with the cold of the body, although my feet and hands were numb, but with the deadly cold of fatigue. Since Armand and I had had that terrible scene on the terrace I hadn't slept at all nor had I been able to eat.

My stomach rumbled now and I clutched it firmly and held my hands tightly over it. There were ten minutes to wait. I went into the *salle* and got a cognac. I drank it down very quickly, bought a roll with some ham in it and huddled back in a corner with my coat pulled round my ears. I dozed a little ... Rennes! ... Rennes! ...

Armand had a room here ... a room where he studied. He had brought me to it ... kissed me there ... shown me his books, his desk. And she? Had he brought her here too? I couldn't think of her any more as Julie. She was the other woman—the one who had caused all this. She was old ... thirty-five or more ... horrible, revolting, to love such an old person. I looked out of the window at Rennes. I hated it—hated it. Armand had used this town as his excuse to be away from me and with her. 'I shall never love Rennes ... I shall never love Rennes ...' the words went round with the wheels ... and then I slept again. I had left a letter for Marie. Yves had promised to deliver it to her. And two lines for Cynthia. 'I have gone to Paris—Forgive me. Rachel.' Eugénie lived in Paris. Eugénie who had been at the Slade ... she was old, too. Older than Julie—but with the charm and insouciance of a child—an ugly child. I would find Eugénie. She had a little *pavilion* in Montparnasse. My ticket said Gare Montparnasse; the train would take me there. And the street—what was it? In my haste I had left the piece of paper with her address on my dressing-table. Edgar something ... Edgar Quinet, that was it. Presently when I felt better I would remember the number.

And now it was light—mournful grey light—not like that of the coast. The coast was gone ... tall poplars lined the roads ... and there were hills and rivers and beautiful fields. The track was terribly bumpy, the carriage swayed from side to side. The old woman opposite me grumbled and put a handkerchief smelling of naphthaline to her nose. Coal dust came in the window and covered the seats. The old woman shut it angrily. I slept again. Le Mans ... Le Mans ... more poplars ... and heath like England ... like the country round my aunt's home. The sun began to flicker timidly through the steel sky. My head ached . . . I felt sick . . . I couldn't move. Suddenly I smelt eau de Cologne . . . the old woman opposite was holding it under my nose. I sniffed it gratefully. The rocking of the train was appalling and the noise '*formidable*' as she said angrily. She had to shout at me to make me hear and I felt too sick to answer. Chartres . . . Chartres! a name drummed into my ears by the history mistress at school. The cathedral . . . the rose windows. I staggered up and let the fresh air in with a rush.

It revived me a little—and apologizing to the kind old woman I stood there breathing it in deeply in spite of her warnings that I was swallowing coal dust. Suddenly to my astonishment she pulled out a packet of Gauloises and offered me one. Who could have imagined that she smoked? But she sat there contentedly puffing at cigarettes until the fields and poplars gave way to houses . . . to the familiar and hideous back views of dwellings flanking the railway line, giving quick cinematic glimpses of humans eating—cooking—washing, through the dingy windows with their soiled sordid curtains.

Then the hoardings with great shrieking advertisements—Eau Javel . . . Eau Javel, beloved of Marie. La vache qui rit! La vache qui rit! . . . Thalia's favourite cheese in a round box with the laughing cow on it . . . Thalia . . . Thalia . . . I thrust her remorselessly away as I had Armand. The old woman was busying herself with her packages. 'On *arrive*, Mademoiselle. *On arrive!*' 'PARIS . . . PARIS . . .' With a shriek like that of a soul entering the Hell which Marie considered it to be, we stopped with a violent jerk. Doors opened, voices in a babel of excited argument . . . porters eager for baggage and tips.

'*Au revoir, Mademoiselle,*' my travelling companion was saying. Montparnasse, stated the huge notices on the station. . . . I was there.

PART II

CHAPTER XV

WORK, WORK, and more work. That was what Xavier had said. I would work. Eugénie had taken me to a friend of hers, an elderly woman with a large *appartement* in the Place Delambre. She took four women students as paying guests.... 'You can't possibly stay in a hotel, it's expensive as well as asking for trouble. You must get a fixed price for the month out of Madame Robert—leave it to me,' she had said.

Madame Robert lived on the fifth floor in one of the tall grey houses with grey shutters. It was over-furnished, prim and hideous, with no air of comfort or repose in it. She fed us extremely well but she was very strict about the hours we kept. If we came in after eleven the chain was up on the door and not for anything would she open it. The other three guests were all French. One was a sculptress with the largest goitre I had ever seen. She was studying at the Beaux Arts and was fanatical about Maillot. The others were both studying philosophy at the Sorbonne. Eugénie, when I had found her little *pavillon* off the rue Edgar Quinet, had been upset that she couldn't take me in herself. She had a lodger, she explained—a painter like herself. He was a sad-faced Swiss whom she called Théodore.

After a week of working at the hard routine of the Chaumière, as they called the *académie* in the street of the same name, I began to settle down. Eugénie and Théodore worked here, and it was due to them that I was so quickly accepted and given a place in the painting room under Monsieur Prinet. He was an exacting master and one who would accept no compromises. Everyone worked in deadly earnest with an enthusiasm unknown in my former fellow-students. But although I put all that I could, everything of which I was capable, into my efforts, it seemed it was not enough. Monsieur Prinet was never satisfied. Never.

I was fascinated with Théodore's painting. He had been a hairdresser in Switzerland. He had left a wife and four children to come to Paris and express himself in painting.

'Like Gauguin,' said Eugénie proudly. And he painted in the style of that genius. I couldn't work for the fascination of watching Théodore's canvas. He was a curiously honest person and yet he could stand all day in front of our blonde, pink-and-white model and on his canvas would appear a dark-skinned, slit-eyed squat girl with a banana tree behind her and scarlet blossoms in her hair. Monsieur Prinet would stand scratching his chin thoughtfully as if wondering how to take this phenomenon. The whole room was divided into violent controversy over Théodore's paintings. The Americans would defend fiercely his right to paint as he pleased and his right to respect. The young French students would bring in their friends at the mid-day break and take them round the easels, giggling and shrieking with mirth when they came to the determined follower of Gauguin. Théodore remained completely unmoved and went on producing more and more exotic canvases.

The magic of Paris, with its exhilarating exciting air of expectancy, was a lovely background to my melancholy. The plane trees in the rue Edgar Quinet were in new tender leaf, in the Jardins du Luxembourg the lilacs were out; everywhere there were lovers, in the restaurants, cafés, in the Bois, in the streets. Everywhere arms entwined, tender glances, eyes meeting in some inner understanding; in the evenings open love—heads on shoulders and mouths savouring the impact of one on the other. I couldn't bear to see them—but could not avoid looking. Every time I saw a pair of lovers a vision of Armand and the enchanted hours with him swept away all concentration on my work. From every window, in every *boîte* there drifted the strains of the dusky voice of Lucienne Boyer ' . . . *Parlez-moi d'amour* . . .' And all the time I somehow imagined that with the extraordinary feeling in this city anything could happen—that nothing was impossible—that one day I would see Armand. That he would walk into the Dôme—or La Palette, where all the students gathered, or even into the Chaumière itself. He came to Paris sometimes . . . his mother's relatives were all here.

And then I would shake myself in anger. I had finished with Armand. It was finished. Even if he wanted to come after me, Suzanne would take good care that he did no such thing. The triumph and satisfaction on her face when we had faced each other across the hideous *salon* had been unmistakable. At night I couldn't sleep and it was not only because of the traffic and the stuffiness of my over-furnished, heavily curtained room after the wide-flung shutters and seaweed smell of my room in the villa. The faces of Cynthia and Thalia intruded. Thalia especially . . . Thalia laughing, mocking, imitating someone . . . imitating me . . . teasing me triumphantly about the sordid end of my love affair. 'Go away. . . . Go away . . . let me forget you . . . just for tonight,' I would beg. But the face remained . . . mocking . . . intent . . . purposeful. And Cynthia's was sad, reproachful, wretched. I tossed and in vain flung myself from one side to the other in the bed but the endless record revolved . . . Cynthia . . . Thalia . . . Cynthia . . . Thalia. . . .

And there were other worries. What was going to happen to me when the fifty pounds my aunt had given me for emergencies had gone? I had rushed away in such a wild impetuous hurry that I had left behind my gold bag still stuffed with the francs I had won at the Casino. My father sent me odd sums of money at rare intervals. I had lent a good deal of it to Cynthia, What should I do? Write to Thalia and ask her to send the bag?

Eugénie told me not to worry so much. Why didn't I write to my father and ask him to send me money direct to Montparnasse? I wrote that same evening, sitting with our usual crowd in the Dôme. I told him of the broken engagement, of the reason for my flight. I explained that I was heartbroken and could never go back to the scene of my former happiness.

His reply was an unpleasant shock. Just a telegram. 'ADVISE YOU RETURN DINARD IMMEDIATELY STOP FATHER'. No mention of money at all.

I wrote again, repeating that I couldn't return. I took a long time composing what I thought was a heart-rending letter. His reply angered me. 'HEART RESEMBLES THE CAT STOP REMEMBER CONTRACT STOP REMEMBER CONTRACT STOP RETURN DINARD IMMEDIATELY STOP FATHER'. I had been so certain that he would understand. But this nonsense about a cat. What did he mean? In some ways he was like Thalia. He loved jokes and riddles. He was always urging me to develop a sense of humour which would stand me in better stead than talent or beauty. Every day the pile of notes in my purse grew less—and with their dwindling my hopes dwindled too.

I had been working in the Chaumière for almost a month when Judy's brother found me there. She had written him as soon as she had returned to Dinard from her tour of the Loire and urged him to look for me in Montparnasse. I had told her about Eugénie, and she was sure that I would make for Montparnasse.

I would have known him anywhere as Judy's brother. A large edition of her with the same unruly hair, irregular features and laughing eyes, the same overwhelming generosity. 'Know who I am?' he asked, planting himself in front of my easel one morning.

I looked up from my canvas—Monsieur Prinet had just left me.

'Buddy,' I said.

'Didn't take me long to oblige Judy,' he said, looking appraisingly at my painting. 'Heard the old boy praising you just now. That's very strong! Shouldn't have thought you had it in you. Where you staying?' abruptly.

He saw my hesitation. 'All right. Don't tell me. I only want to help. I know the ropes here. How're you making out?'

'Fine,' I said shortly. Was he a spy sent to find out my whereabouts and get me sent back? But Judy had sent him. That was different. She would approve what I had done. She saw things as I did. I had wanted to rush out to St. Lunaire to her when I'd discovered Armand's treachery but she had been away touring the Loire valley.

'Judy's worried about how you're getting on. She'd appreciate a few lines to reassure her.' He looked directly at me as if to see what kind of mood I was in. 'How about coming for some lunch—we'll talk this out.'

We went to a small restaurant on the Boulevard and ate. In twenty minutes we were talking like old friends. He was working at Julien's but came sometimes to the Chaumière for short poses. 'I saw you in the vestibule there last week,' he said, 'with the lugubrious disciple of Gauguin. When I got Judy's letter I felt sure it was you talking to him.'

'The blonde model objected to his making her so dark-skinned.' I began laughing at the recollection. 'She made an impassioned speech from the model throne saying that she hadn't a drop of native blood in her and that none of her forbears had ever been to the South Sea Islands. What d'you think of him? I'd give anything to know if he has hypnotized himself into seeing the world as Gauguin did—I'd love to be able to do the same.'

'I don't know,' said Buddy slowly. 'Some of Gauguin's Brittany paintings are pretty dreary. Has the ex-hairdresser ever been to the Pacific?'

'This is the first time he's left his native Basle,' I said. He had shown me photographs of his plump, pleasant-looking wife and his four stolid children; even one of his shop which the wife was now running for him. When I asked him how she had taken his desertion of his business he said simply, 'She understood. I am an artist—whether with the hair or paint-brushes.'

I promised I'd write to Judy and he agreed not to reveal my address in Paris. Letters sent to me at the Chaumière would find me—or even to the Café Dôme. I was reluctant to write, even to think of Dinard. Surely Cynthia would ask Judy for my address. And Thalia? Had she found that slip of paper on my dressing-table with Eugénie's address on it? Of Armand I wouldn't allow myself to think at all. Armand was dead as far as I was concerned.

With Buddy I fell at once—perhaps because he reminded me so much of Judy—into an easy friendship. We could and did talk about anything and everything. He took me to all the art galleries and museums, showed me the sights of Paris which I hadn't even thought of visiting. With him I felt none of the inferiority and inadequacy which my love for Armand had given me, and none of the tantalizing attraction which Terence Mourne aroused in me. His steady, sensible attitude to life was something I'd not as yet encountered.

'It's all right to be enthusiastic about things—but don't for Christ's sake get drowned and submerged in them,' he kept telling me. 'You're too passionate, too impulsive. Try and take things as they come. Don't rush out to meet them. You'll never come to satisfactory terms with life like that—what's more, you won't develop your talent that way. Talent wants nursing. Steady nursing.'

We would sit every night outside or inside the Dome or the Rotonde or some smaller, cheaper café with our fellow students; and I would soon be involved in some exciting, stimulating squabble. 'Don't take it so hard . . . take it easy . . .' Buddy would urge me when I got excited over the Abdication.

'I can't be any other way.'

'You will. You're still green. Wet behind the ears,' he said undisturbedly. About the 'Living in Truth' he was cautious. 'Could be a very dangerous theory,' he said finally, 'and hurt a lot of people.'

I was angry. 'There you are,' he said. 'It was an intolerant concept—and it's making *you* intolerant—you're angry because I say it's a dangerous theory. It doesn't fit in with human relationships and the necessity to live with other people harmoniously.'

We talked about Thalia.

'That girl interests me,' he insisted. 'Have you any younger sisters?'

'No,' I said.

'Did you never have some older girl or teacher you thought perfection? That you were nuts about?'

'No.'

'You had only boy-and-girl affairs?'

'There was only Armand,' I said angrily. 'He was the first. I shall never love anyone again.'

'You'll get over it.'

It was only on these two points that I fell out with Buddy. The Living in Truth'—and Armand. He laughed at both of them.

'No. I'm not sorry for you. You're only suffering from growing up. Now Thalia—that's the child I'm sorry for.'

And then there came a letter from Judy. 'I don't know that I have any right to advise you, Rachel, but I think you ought to come back. Cynthia looks ill—she's getting very worrying news from her husband. Thalia looks like a ghost. I am worried about them both. I expect you have got over the worst of your unhappiness. Don't you feel that you ought to come back?'

This letter made me angry, too. How could she think that I'd ever get over a thing like that just to please her because she was worried about the Pembertons? I didn't answer it—nor did I tell Buddy about it. And then one evening when I returned tired and dirty after a long day's work, Madame Robert handed me a telegram. '*Enfin!* Something for you!' she said with satisfaction.

She was always suspicious because I never got letters and parcels as the other three girls did.

I opened the telegram slowly. 'INSIST YOU RETURN DINARD IMMEDIATELY STOP FATHER'.

'Bad news?' Her voice was hopeful.

'No. Excellent news,' I said, tearing the telegram into pieces and throwing them in the stove in the kitchen. That night I dreamed of Thalia. She was chasing me over the cliffs towards St. Briac. I ran and ran on the soft, peaty turf and couldn't stop when I came to the edge of the cliffs. I began to fall. Down, down, down. I woke with a terrible start and lay sweating in bed. I slept again and a similar nightmare woke me. Again I was falling, falling. . . . There was a sharp pain in my left shoulder-blade. Just like the one I'd had when I'd been ill with pleurisy. I was shivering and wretched. I went and knocked at Madame's door. She hustled me back to bed, asked me to show her where the pain was, and came back with a box. From it she took a lot of little glass bottles with methylated spirit and a wick in them. She lit them all.

'Lie on your back and take off your night-dress,' she commanded. I was too frightened of her to disobey. She put the bottles on the place where I felt the pain and let them burn until I screamed.

'A little longer . . . a little longer . . .' she insisted.

My screams brought the others from their rooms.

'Hold her down. She'll be ill with pneumonia unless I burn it out now,' said Madame Robert firmly. They willingly—especially Mademoiselle with the goitre—held me; and the atrocious counter-irritant of the scorching of my flesh went on mercilessly.

When at last it was over, and pieces of skin had come off, the new pain was much worse than the old one.

'But this isn't a dangerous pain,' insisted Madame. 'The first one was. I'll put some ointment on you and you'll sleep it off.' She gave me aspirins and a tisane and presently I slept; and although sore and irritable when I woke the next day the frightening pain in my left side had completely gone. But in the afternoon there came another telegram—this time from my aunt, now back in England. 'INSIST YOU RETURN CYNTHIA IMMEDIATELY'.

And now I couldn't paint at all. Everything went wrong. Monsieur Prinet was exasperated and disappointed. Where my former approach had been vigorous and strong it was now weak and feeble. The colours were all squeezed out on my palette but they didn't register on the canvas. He was impatient and urged me to concentrate, to discipline myself to a method of work.

'Discipline ... that's what you need, Mademoiselle. Discipline ... not this unconsidered mess!'

And only a few weeks ago he had urged me to let myself go ... to be freer....

'Too tight ... too tight ...' he had said. What *did* he mean?

I was in despair, and found the hot rooms, the heavy air, the long hours unendurable. I had very little money left. Father had remained resolutely silent about it. Madame Robert didn't supply a mid-day meal on the pension rates, we had to find that ourselves. If I didn't pay promptly at the end of the month I would be out, that was obvious.

Should I write to Thalia and ask her to send my gold bag with the francs? It looked as if I would have to.

On the day when I was at my lowest ebb Terence Mourne appeared at the Chaumière. Immaculately dressed and groomed, he looked out of place in the atelier. He was on his way to London, he said. My one suit which I had brought with me was now much the worse for wear. I had taken to a pair of the workman's blue trousers with bib and brace which were at present much favoured at the Chaumière. I was fetched out of the painting room by Madame Rose. Terence was waiting in the hall. He looked me up and down. I wiped the paint on my trousers as did everyone else.

'Christ! You're a sight, Rachel!' he exclaimed. 'Go and put on some decent clothes and I'll take you out to lunch.'

'How did you know I was here?'

'Judy,' he said briefly.

My first instinct was to refuse rudely—but I was very hungry and could no longer spare the money for a mid-day meal. We went back to the Place Delambre and he waited while I changed. The suit was impossible. I put on the black dress and Cynthia's fluffy white jacket.

'I like the dress,' he said approvingly. 'Haven't you got a hat? Or gloves?'

I hadn't either.

'We'll get you some,' he said resignedly.

'If you can't take me like this I won't come at all.'

Madame Robert, who had been hovering round, came eagerly, proffering a pair of her gloves. I accepted them. Her hat—a toque—was clearly impossible.

'Brush your hair if you're coming hatless.'

Angrily I brushed it, hating myself for this stupid obedience which Terence always invoked in me. 'You'll do,' he said, grinning. 'Come on. I'm hungry.'

I saw Madame Robert's inquisitive eyes watching our taxi from her window. My side was still horribly sore from her ministerings. I winced when Terence put his arm round me.

'Well, you've made a nice mess of things,' he said half an hour later, when we sat opposite each other under lilacs at a restaurant in the Bois attended by half a dozen eager waiters. I hadn't said anything much until now—I'd been too busy eating.

'What d'you mean by a mess?'

'You've behaved abominably to Cynthia—not that I hold any brief for her—but you've broken your word. Because you found that the world isn't quite what you imagined in your half-baked adolescent way you rush off to Paris and generally behave like an idiot.'

'You know nothing about me,' I said hotly. 'I'm working very hard.'

'But look at you! Untidy, pale, half-starved, and all for what? Pique over a worthless young man.'

'You don't understand. That's all finished. I'm going to be a painter. Nothing else matters.'

'You don't have to go about advertising the fact by displaying your trademark on your clothes.'

I said coldly, 'Why have you come to see me?'

'Because I have a weakness for you—silly as you are—and to ask you to go back to Cynthia. She needs you.'

'She has *you*,' I said spitefully.

He ignored this. 'D'you know that Marie has left her—and taken Elise with her? Cynthia can't manage things. She isn't strong enough. You agreed to stay a year with her. Go back. If you need money I'll give it you. I'll buy your ticket and settle up with your landlady.'

'Cynthia hasn't asked me to go back.'

'She's proud.'

'So am I,' I retorted. 'And I'm staying here. I want to paint.'

'Rachel, can't you ever think of anyone but yourself?'

'Art is selfish. It has to be.'

Now you're quoting something you've read. D'you know that Cynthia's so worried about you that she's written to your aunt and to your father?'

So that explained the telegrams. I was furious. The only person Cynthia ever worried about was herself—and Claude. It seemed to me that she was the selfish one. I wouldn't go back. I said so vehemently.

'I see it's hopeless. Well, I've kept my promise.'

'Let's forget it and enjoy our lunch. You're a darling to bring me here.' I looked round the place, which enchanted me. I was lunching in the Bois! It was incredible. I adored everything about it.

'What I love about you are your mad enthusiasms,' said Terence. 'You amuse me enormously. If I were twenty years younger I might be tempted to marry you—just so that I would never be bored.'

'But you *are* twenty years older, and you're not in love with me,' I said crossly. It isn't funny to be told that a man might marry you in order to avoid boredom.

'It's time I got married,' he said seriously. 'I've come into quite a bit of money and property. That's why I'm going to London. I'm thinking of settling down.'

'But not with cold porridge,' I reminded him.

'It's a little warmer than it *was*,' he said laughing. I liked him much better here than I had in Dinard. He was catching the afternoon plane to London and pressed money on me before he took me back to Montparnasse in a taxi. I wouldn't accept it. I thought that in some way it would influence me in the decision I had taken about Cynthia.

CHAPTER XVI

Quite suddenly the painting began to improve. The fog of uncertainty in which I had been wandering cleared, and a definite meaning and form began to show itself in my work. Monsieur Prinet was pleased and urged me not to relax my efforts but to persevere now that I had found a glimmering of what I wanted to say. He actually praised me several times, and even called the other students in the room over to look at my painting. All the despair and wretchedness of the last weeks fell away as if by a miracle. I was thrilled, excited, in a transport of delight. Xavier had perhaps not been so wrong. I *would* become a painter. I no longer minded the severe warning and harsh criticism which followed on my next piece of work. The memory of the praise made that bearable.

One morning when we had a particularly interesting model, a negress whose skin was almost blue, and I was working in a fever of excitement, Buddy came into the room. He had left Julien's and was working downstairs in the other painting room. He beckoned me mysteriously, but I went on painting, annoyed at the interruption. He came over to my easel. 'You're wanted urgently outside,' he said. 'You've a visitor from Dinard.'

For one dazzling moment I thought it must be Armand. My heart gave a bound. Then I felt cold and frightened. I didn't want to see him. I *couldn't*. That the very thought of him could still upset me like this infuriated me. I put down my paint-brushes and wiped my hands on my trousers and followed him out. In the passage outside, sitting on the wooden bench where the models waited to be interviewed, was Thalia. On her lap, looking acutely miserable, was Kiki.

She looked up apprehensively at me as I came out with Buddy—then, letting the dog slither to the floor, she stood up, clasping her hands nervously. She was dirty and untidy, her clothes pulled on anyhow and her coat covered with dog hairs, but at the sight of her dejected figure a wave of tremendous feeling swept me. I was overjoyed to see her!

She must have seen this, for her face lighted up and dropping the dog's lead she took a step towards me. 'Rachel . . . Rachel . . .

I had to come. I *had* to. I couldn't stay there any longer. Don't be angry.... Please ... please.'

But I didn't answer her. I caught her to me, and kissed her warmly. She clung wildly to me in a paroxysm of weeping, and conscious of the interested stares of the models and students, I pulled her away up the passage. 'Come into the cloak-room,' I said. She picked up the dog's lead and all three of us went into the wash-up.

For several minutes she couldn't stop crying. Great choking, gulping sobs enveloped her. She looked dreadful with the tears making water channels down her dirty face. 'I want to stay with you. I won't go back. I *can't*. I *can't*,' she kept repeating. 'Let me stay with you, Rachel.'

'Does Cynthia know you are here?' I said at last. She shook her head. She had run away—as I had.

It was about eleven o'clock. Cynthia would surely be frantic with anxiety. 'We must telegraph her that you're here.'

'I don't think she'll be worrying about me,' she said cryptically.

'What d'you mean?'

'She has other things to worry about.' And she burst into tears again.

'Thalia, what *is* it? Is your father all right?'

'He was all right in his last letter. There's one for you in my satchel. It came with mine.' She was still crying hopelessly.

'Have you quarrelled with your mother?'

'No. Oh, no.'

'Is there some trouble at school?'

'No. I haven't been lately. Marie and Elise left, and no one would come and help. I've been doing all the cleaning and the cooking.'

She gave a thin smile and made a determined effort to stop crying.

'Wash your face, here, use my handkerchief.'

We cleaned and tidied her up somewhat. When she was calmer she said, 'How thin you've grown! And how lovely! Can I have some of those trousers? They're all wearing them here.'

'Yes.' I was absently washing the paint off my hands. What was I to do with her? What? Should I send a telegram to Cynthia?

What a complication to my own worries ... and yet I was glad to see her. There was no denying the joy I'd felt at the sight of her.

Buddy was waiting for us in the passage-way.

'Well, what now?' he asked, patting Kiki.

'We must take him out on to some grass. The journey was over five hours,' said Thalia.

We went into the Luxembourg Gardens and walked Kiki there. Then I sent a telegram to Cynthia. Thalia was suspicious and sulky at my insistence. She begged me not to send it. She implored me. I showed her the bare words on the form: 'THALIA IS HERE WITH ME' with the address added. 'You'll be sorry. You'll be sorry, Rachel,' she kept saying.

'You must take her back to Dinard at once,' said Buddy, firmly.

'No.'

'Yes. You *must*, Rachel. Don't you see that it's impossible? She's a child. You both are. You need a nurse!'

'It's none of your business,' I said angrily.

'It's somebody's business to see that you don't make a worse fool of yourself than you have. That girl must go back to her mother.'

'She can't go back to-night. I'll ask Madame Robert if she can stay with me. I've just paid her so she won't object. Thalia, come along. We'll go and see Madame Robert.' Madame was willing that Thalia should share my room for a time, but adamant about the dog. Dogs were not allowed in the flats. Thalia refused to be separated from him. What to do now?

'Oh well, I guess it'll be me who has the little brute. He can sleep at my place,' said Buddy resignedly. Thalia was humbly grateful. She looked terribly tired—as if she hadn't slept at all. In the afternoon I took her to a hairdresser. She emerged minus the straggly tails, her hair cut as short as a boy's.

'I want some blue cotton trousers like yours,' she begged.

It was then that I wondered where she had got the money for the journey. I asked her. She looked confused and evaded the answer.

'You never wrote,' she said resentfully. 'Not even a good-bye note—nothing.'

I could not answer this. I had deliberately not written to her.

'I saw Armand,' she went on, looking at me out of half-closed, speculative eyes. 'He brought Quiquengrogne back to me. He was lost for a whole day. Armand wanted your address; he wouldn't believe that you hadn't written to us. Do you still love him, Rachel?'

I would not answer her. The very mention of Armand's name caused such a tumult of feeling in me. Her own arrival, after that first joy at seeing her, brought back vividly those last painful scenes.

'He was terribly upset—quite pale and his mouth all straight and queer—and I was glad,' she went on, still watching my face. 'I told him that you had gone back to England.'

When I still said nothing she said defiantly, 'And so you might have done for all I knew—you never wrote me one line.'

'You did right to tell him that,' I said at last. 'But listen to me, Thalia. If you want to stay here with me never mention Armand again. It's as if he is dead as far as I am concerned.'

'But we talk about the dead—Robin Thome and your cousin Lawrence—both dead so young. We talk about *them*. You don't love Armand any more?'

'No,' I said, thrusting down the clamour of my heart and the urging of the 'Living in Truth'. 'No, I don't love him any more.'

We bought the trousers. She was much slimmer and they suited her admirably. When we got back, Madame Robert had put a folding bed in my room. Thalia had dinner with the rest of us. She was extraordinarily gay—almost hysterically so, keeping us all laughing. But when I asked suddenly after Claude a change came over her. She mumbled that he was all right and became silent. Each time I asked about Dinard, the villa, or her mother a mutinous silence was my answer, and if I persisted she would reluctantly mumble something. I couldn't blame her. She had run away from it all—as I had. I hadn't wanted to think of it either.

In the morning she accompanied me to the Chaumière. Madame Rose allowed Kiki to lie at her feet under the table at which she sat checking the students and taking their admission tickets. Thalia was allowed to work in the *croquis* or quick sketch room. Here she made friends with a charming French boy, Guy, who wasn't much older than she was. Her drawing was quite as good as that of many of the adults there. The students liked her. They found her amusing, eccentric—refreshing. She had quite a success. When we went back to the Place Delambre in the evening after leaving Kiki with Buddy, she looked happier than I had seen her since the day she'd been dressed as Nefertiti.

In the evening we went to Eugénie's little *pavilion*, where she made even Théodore laugh. He was unusually melancholy that evening, having had a letter from his wife saying that she couldn't manage the hairdresser's business and would he please come back. But Thalia made him laugh with her imitation of Monsieur Prinet giving a criticism to a spoilt young student, and with a brilliant impersonation of an American lady who told the astonished master that she reckoned it would take her just one year to paint as Cézanne did.

'She's clever. Very clever. She's a born mimic. She must study languages and elocution and singing too. Then if she studied deportment and went to a school of drama she would be wonderful. . . .'

He said all this with the air of the business man who always has an eye on a possible investment.

'D'you hear that, Thalia?' I said delightedly. 'It's exactly what I'm always telling you.'

'I'm too ugly,' she said, dejectedly.

'Mademoiselle, you have a face of india-rubber! It can become anything! *Anything* or *anyone* you wish. You have something much more valuable than beauty. Pretty girls are two a penny. What you have is as rare as an albino! You mustn't waste this talent. You must train it!' Then, looking sharply at her, he said, 'What imbecile has cut your hair?' We said meekly that we'd been to a hairdresser on the Boulevard.

'Wasting your money on unskilled fools. Eugénie, bring my sharp scissors.'

He cut not only Thalia's shorn hair to a far more attractive line, but trimmed mine to a neater, more shapely length.

'I'd better get into training again,' he said sadly. 'My poor Annemarie can't manage—and without money from the shop they can't eat and I can't stay here.'

'Oh, Rachel, I'm so happy. I love it here. I'd like to stay here always with you,' Thalia cried as we walked back along the streets full of people as in the day, the cafés packed with gay throngs, music drifting from some, the sound of dancing and pleasure from others. I reflected as we wandered slowly, taking in all the vivid pulsating night life round us, that until now I hadn't really laughed the whole time I'd been in Paris. I'd found the Hell of which Marie had such a horror a singularly sad place. Since Thalia's arrival I had scarcely stopped laughing. She seemed hysterically gay, and her eyes were brighter than I'd ever seen them. 'Tell me,' I said as we climbed, giggling, up the five flights of stairs to Madame Robert's, 'can you think of any resemblance between the heart and a cat?'

She began giggling more violently. 'What is it—a riddle?'

'No. Someone said that the heart resembled a cat—how?'

She thought a while, climbing slowly and stumblingly behind me. 'Some people say that the cat has nine lives,' she said, thoughtfully.

'And you? What do you think?'

'I don't know about cats—but as to the heart—mine has only one life—and so, I'm afraid, has yours.'

In the night I was awakened by the sound of her weeping. I sat up. 'What is it? What's the matter?'

'Nothing. Nothing. I had a bad dream. That's all.'

But she wept again the next night—and in the morning she was pale and puffy-eyed.

No answer came to my telegram to Cynthia and I was puzzled and worried. For now my conscience was making itself doubly felt. Buddy and Eugénie kept urging me to take Thalia back. 'You'll get into serious trouble if the mother likes to lodge a complaint,' said Eugénie. 'I like the child. She's an original—an unusual type—but you can't keep her here indefinitely. How are you going to manage for money?'

In the intervals in the painting room Buddy argued vehemently with me. 'You must take her back—she's not sixteen yet, is she?'

'She will be very soon.'

'Rachel, you can't possibly keep her here. You've no money for yourself, let alone her. Do be sensible.'

'I can't go back to that place. Everyone there knows about Armand and me.'

'Would it make it any easier if I came back with you?'

I stared at him uncertainly. 'Meaning what?'

'Meaning just that. Would it make you feel any better?'

'Yes, I think it would. But I can't go back even to please you, Buddy darling.'

Later we sat sipping an apéritif. Thalia and her friend Guy had taken Kiki for a walk.

'Listen, Rachel. You ought to go back to that woman in Dinard. You don't want to—but you *must*. You gave your promise to that girl's father, didn't you?'

'Yes,' I agreed resentfully.

'If you don't go back you're going to feel pretty mean later on. Your own father'll be upset. He's upset now, isn't he? So's your aunt.'

'They don't understand.'

'Rachel, I've got to go back, too—and I hate leaving Paris as much as you do. I'm twenty-five. You're eighteen—all right, eighteen and a half. You've got talent. I haven't. No, don't contradict. It's been a hard pill to swallow, but I've swallowed it at last. I'll never be a painter. *Never*. So I'm going back to the States. If I can do that—couldn't you go back to that woman? It's only for a few months more and you'll be in London at the Slade.'

I hesitated. He was such a darling person. I liked him more than anyone I'd met. Why, oh why couldn't I fall in love with someone like him?

'Well—is it a deal?' he said, grinning just as Judy did.

'You'll come with us?'

'Yes. I want to see Judy and my young niece. I'll take you both back—and it had better be at once.'

'To-morrow,' I said drearily.

We drank to it very sadly and sat there looking at the plane trees on the Boulevard. At the grey houses with their grey shutters, at the gay awnings of the cafés, at the flower sellers and the vendors of snails, postcards, newspapers. At the five rows of wicker chairs in the Dôme, at the tall iron plant stands with their cascading greenery, at the brazier still burning although it was May. They were suddenly, inexpressibly dear to us both.

'We'll come back,' said Buddy.

'We'll come back,' I said. But when, when? I thought wretchedly. And if we come back it'll never be like this again, never as enticing, as exciting, as lovely. Next time it'll all be different—because we'll be different people.

When Thalia joined us with Guy we told her of our decision. She stared at me unbelievingly, sat down at the table, pushing the dog under her legs, then she said passionately, 'I can't go back. You don't understand. I can't. I can't. Never. *Never*. I didn't think you'd give in, Rachel.'

'It's not a question of giving in,' I said wretchedly. 'I just haven't the money to keep myself here—let alone you.'

'We can work. I've had to scrub and polish and cook since you left. I've done the whole villa. Let's work.'

'We can't get a work permit,' I said bluntly, 'I've tried—Eugénie has been into all that for me already.'

'So you're going back to *her*. You'll be working there all right.'

'There's no alternative. We're going to-morrow.'

I was going with Buddy to a party that night. We debated what to do with Thalia. I was for taking her with us. I felt that she shouldn't be left alone.

'She's too young for such a party. She must stay with the old Frenchwoman.'

'She's not young at all,' I said. 'She was born knowing more than most people ever find out.'

'Listen, honey. We can't take her. It's out of the question.' He was adamant.

Madame took the news of our intending departure very calmly. She had been afraid something was wrong because of all the telegrams. She had another young woman waiting for my room. 'Your little sister can stay and talk to me this evening,' she said. 'And the dog can stay too, if your American friend will remove him for the night.'

I was sorry I had given Thalia Kiki. Instead of easing matters he was an added complication. She wouldn't go anywhere without him. I had told Madame Robert that Thalia was my sister. I didn't know why, except that it would have been difficult for her to refuse a sister where she might have refused a friend.

I felt dreadful at leaving Thalia there. I had seldom met a more funereal companion than our landlady. Her conversation tended to run on two topics—cemeteries and unfaithful men. Her husband had run off with his young secretary and she had been obliged to divorce him.

Thalia, whose face was bleak and old since I'd told her we were going back, wouldn't look at me when I said good-bye. She assured me stiffly that she'd be all right. 'If she gets on to cemeteries I shall tell her about the burning ghats in India and how they haven't always enough fuel and bits of the corpse float down the Ganges,' she said with satisfaction. I hoped her French wouldn't be adequate, but it had improved out of all recognition since she'd come to Paris. I heard her talking fluently and very intelligently to Guy, who knew no English.

'And as for unfaithful men—I can tell her about Armand!' she called spitefully after Buddy and me. We left her sitting there in Madame's *salon* with its crimson satin chairs and the huge photograph of Monsieur with flowing moustaches which had been taken before he'd been unfaithful.

The party ended at midnight because our host had passed out on his own divan and there wasn't any more food or drink left. We stopped at a bistro to have some coffee and take a last look at a corner we both knew well. It was almost one o'clock when Buddy came with me to collect Kiki. Madame had agreed to leave the door unchained. I put the key in the lock. Kiki was a wonderful house dog. The slightest sound roused him. But now he neither growled nor barked. Leaving Buddy in the hall I went into my room. Although it was dark I knew at once that it was empty. I switched on the light. The folding bed alongside mine had not been slept in.

Alarmed, I awoke Madame. She was in one of those boudoir caps one sees in chemists' shops in England but which I never imagined people really wore. Thalia, she said, had taken the dog round the square. She had promised to go no farther, but she hadn't returned. Madame had waited up for some time and had naturally concluded that she had gone to the studio of the American where the dog was to sleep.

'She can't be there. She couldn't get in,' said Buddy.

'Let's go there. She may be on the doorstep,' I urged.

But she wasn't. We went to Eugenie's—she hadn't been there. We went back to the Place Delambre. I was frightened and angry with Buddy. I hadn't wanted to leave her. *He* had insisted. Madame was up and had made some coffee. She was worried about the girl, too. Such a strange girl and not at all like me! Madame was convinced that she would become *somebody*. Oh, yes. Mademoiselle Thalia could write very well. She had written a poem that very evening. She had told Madame so—and the stories she'd told of India, of snakes and wild animals. It was better than the cinema. Oh, yes, Madame had enjoyed it enormously. Thalia, in spite of her broken French, had entertained her hostess very well.

I went back to the bedroom. On my pillow was a piece of paper.

> I've gone to Father. I took the money in your gold bag. If I hadn't, Mother would have used it all. I can't go back. *Never.* You'll soon know why. You won't miss me. You've got that American now.
>
> THALIA

On the back of this paper was the poem of which Madame had spoken.

TO RACHEL ON SEEING HER AGAIN
> Could I but hold this breathless moment sweet in my two hands
> And bear it to my breast to lock it in my heart
> That it would be forever there enshrined ...

But I read no more. I tore the paper violently across.

'What are you at?' cried Buddy, picking up a piece from the floor. '"Could I but hold this breathless moment sweet in my two hands . . ."' he read aloud. 'Did she write this? *Did* she?'

'Yes,' I said shortly. 'To me.'

'And you tear it up. Rachel, how could you? The poor kid. The poor, *poor* kid.'

'It makes me sick,' I said.

'It's a wonder if she hasn't done something desperate,' he said reproachfully. 'You were everything to her. You taught her, helped her, encouraged her, even made her beautiful just to gratify some whim of yours. And then you took it all away. Don't you see? Don't you see what you've done, Rachel?'

'No,' I said angrily, 'it just sickens me. There's something behind all this. There's been something wrong ever since she came. I *know her*. You don't. And now? What's she done now? Where *is* she?'

I was picking up the pieces of paper and trying to fit them together. 'She says she's gone to her father.'

'But he's in India. D'you think she's gone to Marseilles?'

'She's quite capable of it. She's plenty of money,' I said grimly, thinking of my gold bag full of francs. 'But not enough to get her to India—unless, of course, she's helped herself to other money besides mine.'

We took a taxi to the Gare de Lyon. A train had left for Marseilles only two hours ago. We went to the booking office. Had a young girl with a dog taken a ticket on that train? We described her. There were several ticket *guichets* and the man at the far end had sold a single ticket to Marseilles, also a dog ticket. Thank heavens for Kiki, I thought, at least he provided a clue which would help to trace her.

'What's to be done?' I asked Buddy.

'We must go after her, of course. If she's trying to get to India she'll be at the shipping agents.'

There was a fast train to Marseilles which would get us there only an hour and a half after the one she had apparently taken. We hadn't enough money for the return fare and I was still in my party dress.

'It's the young girl? She has run away?' asked the man at the *guichet* who thought he had sold Thalia a ticket. 'How old is she?'

'Fifteen—almost sixteen.'

'*Alors* . . . she's under age—she's a foreign girl, too—you can ask the police to meet the train and hold her. They can identify her by the dog.'

'We can't do that,' I protested. Thalia, feeling as she did when she wrote that letter, being met and held by a gendarme? No. No. It was unthinkable.

'Mademoiselle, believe me, it's better so. Anything can happen to her. Marseilles is no place for a child alone.'

But Thalia wasn't a child—that was it. She was swung in that painful, uncharted place between two worlds. 'There's a policeman here in the station,' urged the man.

I couldn't bear the idea. But Buddy was adamant.

'Suppose she gets off that train and finds she hasn't enough money for a passage. What's she going to do in a place like Marseilles?'

'Thalia isn't like other girls. She's travelled a lot. Backwards and forwards to India several times. She's used to ports.'

'Let's go and talk to the police.'

'We don't even know that it *was* her on the train,' I said. 'There could be other girls with dogs.'

'It can do no harm to ask the police to look out for her. She must have her passport with her if she plans to get to India.'

We argued excitedly and I got angry with Buddy. We counted our money again and the interested ticket-collector said that if we went third class we could just do it.

We sat on the deserted, dreary station and waited for the train. I pulled my jacket tightly round me—it was cold. Buddy kept urging me to go back and get some sleep—but I couldn't rest from anxiety. I felt somehow that *everything* was my fault, that if only I could get to Marseilles I would be able to find Thalia when no one else might be successful. The station, dead, empty and impersonal, devoid at this hour of the excited crowds of passengers jostling each other to reach the trains, was like a nightmare. As we sat there we could have been anywhere in the fourth unknown dimension, so phantom-like did it appear in this grey loneliness, so detached from all reality. Only the smell was real—of stale, wet humanity, although it wasn't raining. I think I slept most of the way on the long journey in spite of the hard wooden seats. I know I woke up once to find my head on the shoulder of a very fat business man. Later when it began to grow light I began looking at the landscape.

By mid-day it was quite hot. We were due at Marseilles soon after three in the afternoon. Buddy knew it all—he'd been often in the Midi. He wasn't interested in the country through which we were passing, but I was fascinated by the changing vegetation with its gradual and subtle emergence to the sub-tropical. Vines, peaches and figs! And the colour was different—even the earth was warmer, if less lush and soft. But the gnawing anxiety over Thalia never left me. I would doze, wake, notice some new and interesting aspect of nature, doze again and wake with but one thought ... Thalia.

The poem she had written me had been a shock. And all that weeping in the night after laughing all day? What was the truth behind it all? It was something more than a desire to leave her mother and be with me. She had, when off guard, almost a desperate, trapped look.

Why hadn't Cynthia answered the telegram? 'You'll soon know why,' Thalia had said in the note. Suddenly I couldn't wait to get back to that villa—so impatient was I to find out what was going on there. And for the first time I began to doubt the wisdom of what I had done. Thalia had taken *me* as a pattern—how could I blame her? The train crawled ... slower and slower. The dust came in at the windows. People began eating from bundles and the smell of garlic filled the compartment. We had had breakfast on the train but if our money was to last we couldn't contemplate lunch. The fat man offered me a roll. It was filled with garlic and butter. I accepted it gratefully and although Buddy loathed garlic he ate half of it with relish.

And here was the sea ... smooth, lazy ... lapping the white rocks. Marseilles ... Marseilles ... we crawled into the great station and were pushed with the crowd down the steps into brilliant sunshine. Thalia here alone! The thought frightened me.

'We'd better make a round of the shipping agents,' said Buddy, 'I got a list at the Gare de Lyon.'

'No,' I said. 'No, let's go to Thomas Cook's. They'll be able to give us a list of the sailings.'

Cynthia always dealt with Thomas Cook's. What more likely than that Thalia would go to them?

We dared not take any more taxis, our money had reached a level where every sou counted. Buddy knew Marseilles a little and we set out to walk. After several incorrect directions and a long, devious walk we reached the right street. We were hot, tired and hungry—and both of us somewhat short-tempered. 'Thomas Cook's,' I read, 'Wagon-Lits.' Outside, tied to a railing, was Kiki!

He set up a terrific barking and leaping at the sight of me. He was extremely dirty and woebegone.

'Well. What d'you say? The very first place.' Buddy was astonished.

'Stay here,' I said. 'She must be inside.'

I walked into the place and up to the part marked 'Voyages Étrangères'. Sitting on a tall chair studying a number of illustrated brochures was Thalia.

I stood there for several seconds before she looked up. There were smudges under her eyes and her face was as dirty as the dog's. There was a huge hole in the knee of one of her stockings as if she had fallen as a child does—and stains on her tweed skirt.

'Thalia!' I said gently.

When she saw me her face blanched. She began blinking nervously and rapidly, and her tongue passed over her lips.

'What on earth are you doing here?'

'They won't give me a passage to Bombay,' she said sullenly. 'They say they haven't got one—but I don't believe it.'

'Mademoiselle wants to go to Bombay immediately,' said the suave young man attending to her. 'I regret that we cannot offer her a passage for two weeks. We are very busy and all the tourist is full up until then.'

'Come outside,' I said sharply to her. I told the young man we'd let him know about the S.S. *Strathnaver*.

I took her by the arm and piloted her through the door. Outside she came face to face with Buddy. Her face hardened and she set her mouth in a tight line. The dog jumped madly round her feet.

'Where's the money you took from my bag?' I asked mildly.

'You're not angry? I thought you wouldn't mind—you don't care much about money or you'd never have left it lying in your cupboard.'

'I don't mind your having taken it. I was going to write and ask you to send it on to me. I had to pawn my bracelet,' I said. 'But you can just hand it over now. We're extremely hungry and we want a meal.'

'I can't get it out here. It's pinned to my knickers.'

We went to a restaurant which didn't object to the dog and, in the 'Ladies', Thalia produced a cotton bag which she had pinned to the top of her knickers with a safety-pin. I stared at the bag. I had seen it before. Where? She handed it over to me without a word. Then I realized that it was one of the cotton bags in which Cynthia wrapped all her small things during the monsoon in India.

'Thalia,' I said, 'you didn't take anything of your mother's, did you?'

She saw me handling the cotton bag. 'No—I had to go to her drawer to get my passport—I saw the bag and thought it'd do to hide the notes in.'

'Some people would call it stealing,' I said meaningly.

'But the passport's mine. It says so on it.'

'I mean the money.'

'But you said yourself that the money was no one's—that you'd made it out of nothing. That it came from nowhere.'

'True,' I agreed. I didn't count the notes—there seemed to be a lot of money there.

'You were actually trying to get to India?'

'Yes. You'll be sorry you've stopped me.' Her face was tragic.

'Let's go and eat,' I said. 'You must be starving.'

'So's Quiquengrogne. He's had nothing since yesterday afternoon and that was only scraps.'

We had lunch looking out at the port. I was determined that Thalia should have anything she wanted. She would have to realize as quickly as possible that her dream of getting to India was ended. I wanted to soften the blow. 'I want bouillabaisse,' she kept saying. 'A man in the train told me it was a special dish of Marseilles.'

She had it—also chicken, asparagus, strawberries and cream—and we fed Kiki. None of us mentioned her flight from Paris or her plan to go to India. She seemed to accept her capture passively. It wasn't like Thalia—I didn't like it. There were several hours to put in before the night train to Paris. We bought some English papers, they were full of nothing but the forthcoming Coronation, with photographs of the little princesses, and we went exploring in the old part of the port. The sun was glorious and it was when we were leaning over the old harbour wall looking at a negro asleep on a narrow ledge high above the water that she said, 'Rachel, I can't go back. You're bound to know soon. I've killed Claude. That's why I ran away. I pushed him over that steep bit round by the Pointe.'

At first I thought that she was trying one of her jokes on me. But to my horror she soon convinced me. The story came out gradually between sobs and gulps and long silences.

She had been sent out with Claude one afternoon and he had been kicking his football along the Promenade. He was in one of his tiresome moods and when they reached the dangerous unguarded walk round the cliffs to the Pointe she ordered him to give her the football. But he wouldn't give it up and kept on kicking it near the edge of the path and running after it, giving her a shock each time he almost lost his balance.

I knew very well how he loved to do this; unless I held his hand very tightly he would tease me by standing on the extreme edge with that sheer drop below him. He wouldn't give up the ball to Thalia but ran away with it tucked under his arm. She had chased him, shouting threats and warnings to him, and he had continued to taunt and tease her—eluding her grasp each time she caught up with him. At last, exasperated, she made a sudden lunge at him. The impetus had given him a shove which sent him clean over the edge.

'He fell right on to those rocks below and lay quite still—he was dead,' she said, hopelessly.

Cynthia had been, as usual, playing bridge. Thalia had stood there petrified, watching Claude—but he didn't move. 'Not even a leg or an arm,' she said, sobbing.

There had been no one about. She went home—running like a mad thing. There was no one in the villa, Marie and Elise both having left. No one saw her enter or leave the place. She had found the piece of paper with Eugénie's address and taking the gold bag from my cupboard and her passport from Cynthia's drawer, she had packed a few garments in her school satchel and, with Kiki, had caught the train to Paris.

We were still standing there in the sun, the masts and sails of the ships in the harbour spread out before us.

'But why did you rush away? *Why?*' I insisted.

'You see, I thought I hated Claude—he's always been so spoiled and always came first with everyone—but when I saw him lying there dead, I knew that I loved him. I was *terrified*, I ran away.'

'Thalia,' I said shakily, 'is this true? Will you swear to me that it's true?'

She turned so that she faced me. The wretchedness in her eyes was her answer.

'Mother only lives for him. She adores him. He's dead—I killed him. I can't go back. *Never.*'

'But you were trying to get to your father. Didn't he love Claude, too?'

'Yes. But Father would have understood.'

I wondered. My father hadn't understood me. 'You didn't climb down and see if he were really dead?' I asked gently.

'I started to—but I was too frightened. I *knew* he must be dead.'

Did this explain the silence after I'd sent the telegram? But if the child were dead, surely Cynthia would have made efforts to get Thalia back? I was too shocked to think clearly. But I could understand her action. Hadn't my brother run away and left me knocked unconscious by his cricket ball? He had thought I was dead and rushed off in sheer panic.

Thalia had put her hands over her face and was sobbing unrestrainedly. I felt an aching, anguished pity for her. When she had expressed her love for me I had been disgusted. But now, when she was in trouble, it was I who wanted to comfort and reassure her. I put my arms round her and we stood there by the sun-warmed wall. The negro woke up and smiled happily, stretched his arms above his head lazily as a cat does, and jumped down.

'Why didn't you tell me this as soon as you arrived?' I asked at length.

'I tried to. I did, really. But you were so glad to see me. I didn't expect that. It was so lovely with you—and they were all kind and liked me. I just couldn't break it all up. I knew that you would rush back to Mother as soon as I told you.'

So she had decided to try and get to her father. She was sure that the police would be looking for her. When I had insisted on our returning to Dinard she knew that she must get away.

'But there wasn't enough money for a passage to Bombay and they were funny about my booking a passage for myself,' she finished.

Buddy hadn't said anything. He had been listening carefully but looking away over the harbour. Now he said simply, 'I'd better get Judy on the telephone. She'll be able to tell us about all this.'

'You don't believe me. It's true! It's all true!'

'We have to know,' I said gently.

We went to the Post Office. It took a long time but at last Buddy got St. Lunaire. Judy wasn't at home and they didn't know when she'd be back.

As soon as we reached Paris and had reassured Madame Robert, I telephoned Dinard. The journey had been a nightmare with Thalia and the dog. After a long wait and then an even longer continuous ringing, a voice answered. A French voice and one that was vaguely familiar. I asked for Madame Pemberton.

'*Elle n'est pas ici!*' said the voice flatly. 'She's at the hospital with the little boy. . . .'

'With the little boy . . . with the little boy.' He was alive! Claude wasn't dead! I could have shouted with relief. '*Qui est là à l'apparat?*' I asked. I thought the voice said, 'Madeleine', but I couldn't catch it. I shouted into the instrument, '*Comment va-t-il, le petit?*' trying to steady myself.

'*Assez bien. La jambe est cassée, vous savez, mais ça marche.*' Her voice went on and I couldn't hear what she was saying when suddenly we were cut off. His leg was broken. His leg was broken. . . .

I slammed down the receiver, leaving Madame Robert, who was hovering by to know the cost of the call, to inquire for herself. 'Thalia, Thalia,' I cried. 'He isn't dead. Claude isn't dead. He's in hospital—his leg's broken.'

She stood there as if she hadn't heard me. 'It makes no difference,' she said stonily. 'I can't go back. She'll know that I pushed him.'

'But you didn't push him! You didn't mean him to go over the edge. It was an accident.'

'I was so furious with him that I *meant* to push him over at that moment. It's the same thing.'

'No. *No.* You didn't.' I took her and shook her violently. 'Don't go dramatizing again. Listen to me. You didn't mean to hurt him. You were just exasperated with him—as anyone would be. You lost your balance as you caught up with him so that the impetus sent him over.'

'It's my fault that he fell over. If he had died *I* would have killed him.'

She was determined to have it that way. She had lived with the idea of having caused her little brother's death for several days. She had visualized the trial, the prison—even the execution. The only thing of which she hadn't been sure was whether she would be hanged or guillotined. Whether she would have been tried by a French or British court. She was vehement as she told me how she had turned it over and over in her mind.

'I've told you the truth. Everything,' she said desperately.

'Tell me now, Thalia, what was the truth about that snake and the despatch affair in India?' She was silent, looking at me as if to sum up my reasons. 'Tell me. I *must* know,' I urged her.

'The snake was my pet grass snake. He couldn't have hurt anyone. He loved to curl up in Mother's hats. *They* said it was a krait.' Her voice was contemptuous.

'But you put the snake in your mother's hat-box? Why?'

'She always looks so calm and dignified. Everyone else gets heated and excited in India. I wanted to see what she'd do when she felt the snake.'

And Cynthia had had a heart attack.

'And the despatch?'

'That was up in Mussoorie—in the hills. Claude and I had gone there with Mother. There was trouble and Father couldn't leave the station. Terence came up to see Mother. While he was with us a runner came with the despatch. There were riots. Terence never got the despatch. I found it in the pocket of Mother's negligee when I was sorting the clothes for the *dhobi* to wash. It wasn't my job to sort the clothes—it was Ayah's,' she said resentfully.

'And?'

'I kept it and gave it to Father when we got back to Dehra Dun.'

'You ruined Terence Mourne's career.'

'No. It was ruined anyway.'

'But what made you give it to your father?'

She looked at me in astonishment. 'Father could have had *his* career ruined if I hadn't. Father sent the despatch. Terence swore he hadn't. Terence had to resign from the Regiment when it all came out about the week-end.'

And Thalia had been only thirteen at the time. 'You're very clever. Take care you're not too clever,' I said. 'For a girl of thirteen you took a lot on yourself.'

'I was almost fourteen,' she corrected me. 'You can't imagine what the life is like there. There's nothing to talk about except Army matters. I heard everything which went on. If I didn't hear it myself the servants told me. *They* never thought that I took anything in. But I *did*!'

'You're much cleverer than I am,' I said slowly.

'Yes,' she agreed seriously. 'I think I am. You're like those people in mythology—the Cyclops—with only one eye and that one in the middle.'

I paid Madame for the telephone call.

'Get your things together. We're going back to Dinard,' I said firmly.

'No. *No*,' she cried, throwing herself upon me frantically.

I had to force her into the taxi, and without Buddy to help me I doubt if we would have got her to the station. I was full of pity for her muddled, childish and yet unchildish way of thinking, but at the same time I was furious with her. But for her I could have stayed on in Paris a little longer. I was getting on at last with my painting.

'It's no use putting it off. You've got to face it some time. You can't run away from things,' I said.

'*You* ran away. You couldn't face it. Why should I?'

'Listen, Thalia. I don't want to go back either. I have no choice. Buddy's persuaded me to return.'

I wondered how Cynthia would receive me. It was only just beginning to dawn on me that I'd behaved in a way which she could only see as abominable.

If it hadn't been for Buddy, for his patience and sense of humour, the journey back would have been another nightmare. Thalia, either from nerves or from a chill caught on her flight to Marseilles, developed sickness and diarrhoea almost as soon as we left Paris. The train was full of early holiday-makers taking advantage of the sun. She passed more and more frequently up and down the corridor, returning each time greener than the last. She looked ghastly. I didn't know how to help her in her misery.

At Laval an old priest got in. His only baggage was a roll of blanket. He took in the situation rapidly. '*Tiens,*' he said, producing a flask from under his robe. 'She needs this. Come now, Mademoiselle. Drink deeply ... more ... more. Come, my poor child.' He put an arm round her, encouraging her to swallow the brandy. Then, unrolling the blanket, he wrapped it tightly round her like a cocoon, soothing her with the manner of a firm trained nurse.

When next I looked at her she was asleep, her head on his chest. He looked sharply at her tear-stained, exhausted face. 'She's had something to upset her?' he said, accusingly.

'Yes,' I said uncertainly.

'Poor child ... let her sleep. No, Mademoiselle, leave her with me. The dog can come here too. Look, he wants to creep under her legs. He knows she's unhappy.' He glared suspiciously at me and at Buddy. Everybody in the crowded compartment made room for the priest and his patient. She slept like that until we had to change at Dol.

CHAPTER XVII

THE HONEYSUCKLE was out—great hedges of it in the garden, the jasmine, a thousand white stars, draped my window-sill. Oleanders, petunias and banks of fuchsias and hydrangeas were everywhere. It was May. At the bottom of the garden on the terrace the yuccas had strange buds on them, and the palms were a fresher, more tender green.

In his great bed propped up by pillows, Claude lay with his leg in a cradle and I read *Babar* to him. He was much quieter and sweeter since the accident. On the balcony Kiki was curled in the sun; Thalia darned a stocking in the old basket chair by the windows. Madeleine came in with a tray. '*Le thé pour Monsieur Claude.*'

'I don't like *Babar* any more, Rachel. It's too babyish. I want *Jungle Book!*'

'Yes. Yes, let's have *Jungle Book!*' said Thalia. Her father had brought her up on Kipling and I was beginning to understand a little more of her through re-reading him.

I put down *Babar*. It seemed sad to me that Claude had outgrown him. Jean de Brunhoff's adorable creation enchanted me still. It was true that Claude looked older—thinner and less cherubic. He had suffered a lot of pain and still had more ahead of him. I looked around the room, at him, at Thalia and at Madeleine standing turning the pages of the book I'd put down. It was all as before. But was it?

Our return had been almost unobserved. Judy had told Cynthia of our coming and had met us and driven us to the villa. The whole place was gay with Union Jacks—in our last heavily filled days we had completely forgotten that May 14th was Coronation Day. When we exclaimed at them, Judy said that everyone was at the Consul's party in honour of the occasion.

When the door was opened by Madeleine we were surprised and delighted to see her again. The voice on the telephone had said 'Madeleine', but it is a very common name in France. Cynthia was at the hospital; yes, Monsieur Claude was progressing very well. Judy had told us that. The doctors, said Madeleine, were delighted with him. She welcomed us in as if it were *her* house. Thalia and I were mystified.

'How long have you been here?' I asked her.

'Since the day of the accident,' she replied calmly. When I asked her how she had come to return and if Cynthia had asked her to do so, her answer put me to shame.

Claude had been found lying as if dead on the rocks below the Pointe. He was still clutching his football, on which his name and address were written with indelible ink. The fisherman who found him soon spread the news everywhere. When Madeleine heard of it, she had gone at once to the villa to offer her condolences, for she had been very fond of Claude. She had found Cynthia completely alone, without help of any kind, and had simply stayed there doing what she could for her.

'But I thought you didn't like Madame?' I said.

'What has that to do with it?' she asked in astonishment. 'Madame was in trouble. That self-righteous old woman had packed up long ago and taken her niece with her. You and Mademoiselle

Thalia were in Paris. She had no one. She is very beautiful. A great lady—not used to housework. How can she scrub floors and peel potatoes?'

Business, she explained, had been poor, and because of it she had again fallen out with her proprietress. 'But now that you're back, Mademoiselle Rachel, I'll go back to her. After all, the season is almost here. I must look to myself.'

Cynthia's cool reception of us had been disconcerting. What had I expected? Tears, recriminations, anger? We got none of these. She was so calm, so matter-of-fact, so utterly detached that any kind of emotion or remorse faded. As to Thalia, she greeted her coldly, cut short her stammered inquiries about Claude and her father to comment on her shorn hair. When I tried to help Thalia's dumb despair by trying to explain that we were both terribly sorry for all that had happened she stopped me. 'I don't want to hear *anything* about it. You're both back now—and Claude is recovering. No, Thalia, I don't want you to say anything. Go and give that mutilated hair a good shampoo and brushing. It has certainly not improved you—it will take me time to become accustomed to it.'

And beyond this she had persistently ignored any reference to our flight or to Claude's accident.

I thought of this extraordinary situation now as I waited for Thalia to fetch *The Jungle Book* for Claude. I had heard Cynthia thanking Madeleine more sincerely than I had ever known her thank anyone. Had Cynthia changed? Or was it I who had been blind?

'I thought you sent Madeleine away because you were told that she's a prostitute?' I challenged her.

'And?' she said coolly, flinching a little at my blunt word.

'She's back . . .' I said lamely.

'Terence sent her away because of you and Thalia. She may be what you have just called her—but she's *kind*.'

The accent she put on this word brought a great burning flush over me. It crept up from my neck all over my face. I hadn't known such an insufferable feeling for years. I felt as I had on that day in the club in London when it was as if she had held up a mirror to me. But then it had only been the outward ugliness of untidiness which the reflection had shown. Now it was the inner spiritual one—and it was just as ugly.

And Buddy, who had brought us back and helped me on that intolerable journey, had been astounded when he'd seen Cynthia.

'But she's exquisite! She's a beautiful person,' he had said. 'I just don't understand how you and the girl can't get on with her. A woman with eyes like that must be a lovely person.' And he had looked at me with a new doubtful interest. 'What she must have suffered with that child lying unconscious so long—and no one here to help her,' he said indignantly.

'She had Madeleine,' I said shortly.

'Rachel,' he said quietly, 'there's no deception like self-deception. Get that clear. I've been practising it for years.'

The villa had been in a frightful mess, for while Claude had been in the little Bénéfice hospital with his life in the balance, Cynthia hadn't the time or heart to bother about anything else. Madeleine was no great cleaner, but she had prepared some kind of meals for Cynthia when she had returned each night from her vigil at the hospital, had seen that there was warmth and that her bed was ready for her.

Thalia and I set to work to clean the place. We scrubbed, swept, polished and dusted madly, putting all our misery at leaving Paris into the exercise as if it were part of our penance. So far there had been no mention of the accident. It had been thrust aside as something disgraceful. Thalia was very quiet. She went about silent and intent. I knew that this was but the lull—and that at any minute the storm would break. Claude was definitely turning the corner, Dr. Cartier was delighted with him. The spoilt child had shown great courage, he said. Cynthia had merely said that Claude had behaved as a soldier's son should.

Local opinion was weighted heavily against Thalia and me. We had deserted the Madame, as had Marie. Cynthia had come in for a tremendous amount of sympathy and attention for the few days when Claude's life was despaired of. We had come in for much criticism. True, we were all back now—but the damage was done.

Marie had simply turned up in the cart, on top of her bedding, a week after our return. Madeleine had left the following day, begging Thalia and me to visit her in St. Malo. She would give us *thé à l'anglais*, and it would all be very correct, she assured us. There was a little *salon* in the 'hotel' where they could receive their friends and she would see that it was at our disposal.

Marie walked in stiffly without a word, and asked me unemotionally if Madame wanted her back. She was unbending with me—then suddenly relented and embraced me warmly. I was overjoyed to see her and hugged her again and again.

'So you're back from that Hell of Wickedness!' she remarked tartly, examining me curiously. She didn't, I noticed, ask me her usual question as to my virginity. Having been a resident in a city ranking in her mind with the abode of the Devil himself, what would have been the use?

I asked Cynthia if she could come back.

'Oh, let her come if she wants to,' she replied indifferently. 'I don't know why she left—I couldn't understand a word of her explanation. Let her come. But tell her she must stay now until the lease of the villa is up. I don't want any more upsets or changes.' She looked meaningly at me as she said this.

The only reference Cynthia made to the whole episode of Thalia and the accident was to insist that she accompany her mother to church on the Sunday after her return.

'It's essential that we are seen together. All kinds of malicious rumours have been circulating. I should have preferred Rachel to have been with us too—but she must stay with Claude.'

Thalia was sullen and unwilling. She had been aloof and distant to me since our return. She resented bitterly my having forced her to return with me.

'Church to Mother is a kind of Union Jack. The family of the great Empire and all that. She uses it as a shield. I don't believe a word of it. Why should I go?'

'It's not a great deal to ask of you. It must have been pretty awful for your mother while we were both away and Claude so ill.'

She mimicked my last words—but in Cynthia's voice—cold, clipped and colourless.

'Yes,' she said when I stared at her, 'it could have been *her* speaking.'

Marie settled in again and took some of the burden of the house off my shoulders. Outwardly life went on much as it had been before I had gone to Paris. Inwardly the tension was worse. There was now a subtle difference in all our relationships. Claude, because he clung in his weakness, had become closer to me—and Cynthia too. It was impossible not to be moved by the look of fragility, the little lines of fatigue and anxiety now beginning to show in her face. To me she was infinitely more beautiful now. But between Thalia and me a gulf was widening.

I asked Marie why she had left. She looked gloomy. Hadn't the Madame explained? She'd told her all about it but had been afraid that she hadn't understood. It was the niece—Elise. She'd got herself into trouble. Yes, with a good-for-nothing type like that young Tréfours. She didn't know what the girls were coming to. They seemed to have no discrimination. There was a good, steady young farmer wanted Elise and would she look at him? No. She'd had to behave like that with the electrician from the Midi. Now he'd vanished and Elise was going to have his child. She'd had to take her out to the farm and see that she was out of harm's way. I thought of Elise out at that dreary place from where we'd rescued Kiki.

'You're very good to her,' I said mechanically.

'She has no mother,' said Marie simply. 'And neither have you. That's why I was so upset about that young Tréfours. He's tumbled many decent girls in the woods here!'

I didn't want to hear about Armand and I silenced her. I hadn't seen or heard of any of the Tréfours family since our return, but Thalia was suffering from Thérèse. Cynthia had insisted on her returning to school. One morning when she came in at mid-day, Cynthia said, 'Where have you been for the last three days?'

Thalia started, flushed and began mumbling something about school.

'Don't bother to lie to me. You haven't been to school for three days. They telephoned this morning to ask if you were ill. Where were you?'

'I went out with Yves in the cart,' she said sullenly. 'It's time I left school.'

Next day I walked with her there. Through the railings of the garden I could see the girls playing in groups. On the path several of the older girls were talking with Thérèse. She stared insolently at me, then, deliberately averting her gaze, said something to the girls with her which caused a spurt of laughter. As Thalia and I walked up the path they drew aside ostentatiously.

The headmistress told me she had ordered that the accident was not to be mentioned to Thalia. 'But what can one do?' she said, hopelessly. 'Children are very cruel.'

'They say that she pushed her little brother over the cliffs and then ran away,' I said. 'None of them will speak to her. She's been sent to Coventry. That's why she stayed away.'

'What exactly *did* happen? Do you know?'

'She doesn't seem clear. She's so mixed up that she imagines that the shove she gave him when she caught up with him was deliberate. She ran away from sheer panic.'

'It's the greatest pity,' the headmistress said. 'She was improving so much. And she's very clever in some ways. It's true that she's backward if you judge her by the usual things learned at school by girls of her age. But her mind is original and very quick. She writes amazingly well—but only if it's on a subject she likes.'

I wondered how much she knew of my relationship with the Tréfours family—and of its effect on Thalia. No doubt all of it—the place was so small and she must have heard the gossip from the satellites of Thérèse. I resented Cynthia putting me into the position of watch-dog over Thalia, but at the same time I reflected with amusement that the roles had now been reversed; but whereas she had been the willing watch-dog over Armand and me, I was an unwilling one over her.

With Claude recovering so rapidly, Cynthia began going out again. There was a spate of festivities for the Coronation. She resumed some of her bridge afternoons, and went to a number of the parties. I wondered what she was using as an explanation of Thalia's flight and of our joint return for she had not discussed either subject with us. I asked Judy. Cynthia, she said, simply evaded the whole thing by saying that she didn't feel she could discuss it, she had suffered too much; and her fragile look, her air of delicacy which had increased, gained her more sympathy and attention. Topics for gossip were sometimes scarce in the Colony, Judy told me, and Cynthia as the centre of two recent excitements was in great demand.

Terence returned from London. He had written twice to me from there and in his last letter he had suggested our getting married. I didn't take it seriously. I told him about Thalia's arrival in Paris, and of the accident to Claude and of my impending return to Dinard, but I made no reference to his suggestion. He came to call soon after his return, with flowers for Cynthia and toys for Claude. I couldn't help noticing the return of colour to Cynthia's pale face and of brightness to her eyes. She immediately went to Madame Cérise and ordered some summer frocks. She and Terence were in the same parties frequently and Claude was left more and more to Marie and me.

One evening Terence asked me to dine with him.

'Go,' said Cynthia. 'You've been in so much with Claude you're quite pale. Go and dance.'

I hadn't been alone with him since that lunch in the Bois in Paris. At dinner he asked me why I hadn't answered his question about marrying him. I said that I supposed he had asked me out of pity. He said angrily that he had no such altruistic motives— but purely selfish ones.

'But you're in love with Cynthia,' I said.

'I was,' he said shortly. 'But that's something I'm not willing to discuss now.'

'She's still in love with you.'

'Rachel,' he said irritatedly, 'can't you keep to the point? We're not talking of Cynthia—we're talking of *you*.'

'I shall only marry for love,' I said firmly. 'And I'll never be in love again. I want to paint.'

'We could live in Paris and you could go on studying at the Académie. You'd be much happier with an older man. No young one will be willing to put up with your art.'

I was tempted. There was truth in what he said. Armand had regarded my talent as something to be turned into a pleasant hobby. If I married Terence there would be no more doing what my aunt wanted. No more wearing the clothes she chose for me. But I'd have to do what *he* wanted. And I could have found men in Paris who would have done a lot for me without marriage.

'No,' I said at last. 'I'm *very*, very flattered, Terence, but I can't.'

'I suppose you're still hankering after that blond Don Juan?' he said contemptuously. 'Well, you can put him out of your mind. He's getting married—to the girl his mother always intended him to marry.'

The news was a blow. I realized that in my heart I had still been hoping that one day I would meet Armand and somehow it would all come right. I think Terence saw this, for he put his hand across the table and taking one of mine he kissed it rather sadly. Then he began talking about Thalia.

'The girl's a problem. I tell Cynthia she ought to see a psychiatrist. Cynthia simply doesn't know what to do with her.'

'She can save her money. A psychiatrist would tell her that she could try loving her daughter!'

'Could *you*?' he asked, cocking one eyebrow quizzically at me.

'I'm very fond of her—but now Cynthia's putting her against me by making me her gaoler.'

'Cynthia's had a great deal to put up with. The girl's unpredictable!'

'So's Cynthia!' I said meaningly.

> 'Brume, disparais de la mé
> Ou tu seras coupée par la moitié
> Avec un grand couteau d'acier.'

sang Claude in a melancholy chant, again and again. There was an early morning mist blotting out the sea. From his window there was whiteness and silence.

'Sing it again,' I said.

> 'Brume, disparais de la mé.'

'*Mer*,' I corrected him. 'Not *mé*.'

'That's where you're wrong! It's *mé*! Marie said it's the old form of *mer*. D'you know the story of that song?'

I did, but I wanted to hear him tell it me.

'Well, Saint Lunaire came from Great Britain—Marie says so, probably from Wales. He had to leave his monastery because of barbarians who wouldn't let him be a Christian. So he packed up with sixty-two monks and left his monastery and came in a boat to Brittany—only it was Armorica then and he wasn't a saint. He wanted to land at St. Malo—and that wasn't St. Malo then, it was Cite d'Aleth. When he was ready to drop anchor a great thick fog like this one came up and hid everything. But of course Marie says it was the Devil who sent the fog so that they couldn't land. But Saint Lunaire got into a saintly anger! And whipping out his great sword, he cut swish through the air and *vlan!* he cut that curtain of fog into ribbons and it all went away into nothing! And that's why the sailors all sing "*Brume, disparais de la mé*" when there's a fog!'

Marie had told it him in French but he told it me in English. She was tireless in amusing him.

'There's a lot more about Saint Lunaire,' I said. 'You know the place where Mimi lives is called St. Lunaire because he landed there? Well, all the birds helped him. The tit brought him an ear of corn to show him there was food, the doves found a golden statue so that he could sell it and have money for his work. And two seagulls brought him the great stone he'd had to throw overboard in a storm. He'd been using that stone as an altar.'

'I've seen the little goats killed on altars. They cut their throats. What did they kill on Saint Lunaire's altar?'

'Silly,' said Thalia. 'That was Kali's altar. This was a Christian one.'

'Look, the mist's lifting! I can see a ship and a lighthouse,' cried Claude. 'Rachel, d'you think it's because I sang that song?' His eyes were brilliant with excitement.

'No, stupid,' said Thalia. 'The mist's going because the sun's coming out.'

'Of course it's because you sang that song,' said Marie, coming in. 'It won't always happen—but to-day you've been so good that Saint Lunaire heard the song!'

'You see?' said Claude triumphantly. He believed everything Marie told him, perhaps because she was so positive of its truth herself.

It was June and the hotels and pensions were hives of activity. Bedding and curtains were hung out in the sun, chairs and tables out on the terraces. Young girls, both dark and blonde, with aprons pinching in their pretty waists, sang as they bustled about calling gaily to the passers-by. Through the winter they had slept and rested their tired feet after the summer season, and now, fresh and full of vigour and anticipation, they were getting ready for the new season's visitors.

Flags flew, flowers were planted in the tubs and beds, the *cabines* and the terrace tables got a new coat of paint. New striped umbrellas appeared everywhere and fresh gay awnings were hung over the shops. The great sweep of hotels on the Promenade was no longer eyeless. Shutters were flung back, windows cleaned and curtains hung. The market was a buzz of hotel-and pension-keepers getting ready for their incoming guests.

The plaster had been removed from Claude's leg and he began to walk again. He limped. The compound fracture had been skilfully set by a French surgeon but it was feared that the leg might prove a little shorter than the uninjured one. Dr. Cartier asked me not to say anything about this to Cynthia. Further operation could possibly correct this. But she wasn't deceived. I saw her looking at Claude when he spoke of becoming a soldier and her glance rested on Thalia in a puzzled, hopeless way.

'But why did she do it? *Why?*' she had demanded of me when I had told her of Thalia's flight to Marseilles.

'It was an accident. She was so infuriated with him for taunting her that afternoon, she imagines that she's to blame. She even thinks that she pushed him—that the impetus of grabbing at him sent him over.'

'I wonder,' said Cynthia. 'Claude remembers nothing at all of that afternoon. He remembers going for a walk round the Pointe—that's all.'

'He overbalanced trying to elude her—and fell.'

'Then why did she run away without even seeing whether he were dead? Without even trying to get help. *Why*, unless it was deliberate?'

'It was panic. Sheer panic.'

'She's been brought up to have control. To behave in the right way. Surely I've set her an example of duty.' Her voice was bitter.

'Cynthia,' I said, 'she's a very unusual girl. She's very clever. Everyone in Paris thought so. Perhaps she needs some other way. Yours seems to have failed.'

'She's clever in an *unpleasant* way. She still likes these impossible practical jokes. She's critical and sceptical of everything. That I've failed somewhere I admit.... But there's more to it than you can understand.'

'Have you discussed the accident with her?'

'No. And I don't intend to. And I don't want either you or she to mention it to Tom when you write.'

'You haven't told him?' I was astonished.

'No,' she said deliberately. 'He's having a very rough time up on the Frontier. He always tries to stick up for those wretched tribes who're giving so much trouble. It infuriates me. They're just murderers. They don't come out into the open and fight decently. They shoot from behind and often after offering the white flag of surrender. What with all this news—skirmishes every few days and casualties too—and this worry over Thalia and Claude...' She sighed heavily and put her head in her hands.

'Try and forget the accident. *Do*.'

'How can I? Every time I see him walk ... dragging that pathetic little leg, I can think of nothing else. I ought never to have trusted him to her,' and she burst into tears. It was the first time I had seen Cynthia cry.

I was alarmed for her health, and felt that it was I who was to blame. If I'd been there Thalia wouldn't have been alone with Claude. Hadn't Tom Pemberton asked me to look after his wife? She was terribly thin, eating almost nothing and smoking incessantly. She was taking more and more sleeping tablets.

'What shall you do next cold weather?' I asked her. 'Are you thinking of staying on here?'

'No,' she said violently. 'No. I've had all I want of this place already.'

'Did you come here because of Terence?' I asked her, but she would not answer me.

I told her Terence had asked me to marry him. She went very white, caught her breath and said calmly, 'And?'

'I said no. I don't love him—and he doesn't love me.'

'You've grown up quite a lot since you went away,' was her comment. But it wasn't the going away which had made me older. 'Poor child. You had a bad shock,' she said quietly.

'I've got over it,' I said. 'And it was nothing to the shock you must have had when Claude was found on those rocks.'

She looked at me with those forget-me-not blue eyes and I felt for the first time that I might one day like her very much.

Except for a telegram acknowledging the one in which I'd informed him of my return to Dinard, my father hadn't written to me. All he had said in that was: 'NOTE YOUR RETURN STOP BETTER LATE THAN NEVER STOP FATHER'.

Since my aunt had sent the telegram to Paris ordering me to return, there had been silence from her. I felt horribly lonely. I hated going to the market. Julie Caron's old mother was often there gossiping with the stall-holders. She would greet me with deliberate cordiality, then I would see her whispering to whoever she was with. I was no longer greeted with chaff and smiles there, and if Thalia was with me we came in for a lot of interested whispering, heads were put together and we knew that we were being pointed out as unfeeling monsters.

We were glad of the influx of visitors. None of them knew anything about either of us—or indeed of any of the residents' affairs. Our isolation drew us together again. Everywhere I heard that Armand was engaged to a rich industrialist's daughter. Marie confirmed this.

'The one I told you about, Marie-Laure. She isn't pretty like you, Mademoiselle Rachel, but she's rich, very rich!'

She was small, plump, and had, according to Thalia who had seen her, a little moustache and not enough neck. I closed my mind to all this. Armand seemed as far away as did the Slade. I was indifferent, depressed and somehow deflated after the strenuous life in Paris. Monsieur Prinet had been very upset when I'd left so abruptly. 'But you'll come back. If you like I will write to your father. He shall know that you have talent and must allow you to return.' There had been no time for thinking of painting since I came back, but now with Claude so much better and Cynthia out frequently again, I began to think of work once more.

I went up to the attic to see the portrait of Thalia as Nefertiti. I wanted to see it in the light of what I had learned in Paris. I hadn't finished the portrait of Catherine, and the heads I'd done in Paris were studies only. This was the only completed, planned picture which I had done.

I found the canvas in a corner. It had been slashed all over, just as I had slashed the one of the Reverend Cookson-Cander after those angry criticisms.

I couldn't believe it and stood there with it in my hands. Who had done this? Claude? No, he wouldn't have access to a knife. Thalia? I remembered what she had said: 'It was all lies ... a trick ... a trick of light and shadow if you like—but still a trick. I'm *ugly*!'

She had destroyed it. And even with those cuts across it, I knew that it was by far the best thing that I'd done.

I was still standing there with the slashed canvas when she came in. When she saw the picture in my hands a closed, furtive look came into her face.

'Why did you do it? Why?' I asked her. 'Is it because I made you come back?'

'Can't you see?' she cried passionately. 'You're changing. It was the same over Claude. You want to cover it up nicely—people don't push other people over cliffs. Not in families like ours! You want to make it all pretty and charming—like this picture!'

And then, seeing my chagrin, she caught my arm and said wretchedly, 'I'm sorry I did it. I'm sorry. Can you forgive me?'

But how could she understand what she had done? It wasn't the destruction of the painting which so shattered me but something which she had revealed by that destruction. I was bewildered, my world was upside down.

'I'll sit again. The dress is here—and the crown. I'll sit as much as you like. . . .' She was ingratiating herself with me as Kiki did when he'd been disobedient.

'I shall never paint you again,' I said bitterly.

CHAPTER XVIII

AND NOW Thalia's darts were focused on me. I could do nothing right—nothing of which she didn't make fun. I bore it in silence because I was so terribly sorry for her—and I knew that she was, underneath it all, horribly unhappy. But now it seemed that there was no bridge over which I could reach her. If I asked her how she was getting on at school, she would say briefly, 'All right.' When I said I was going to write to Catherine and ask when they were coming back, she said roughly, 'She won't come back until the wedding's over. She's been got out of the way for that. It isn't the thing to have a mistress about when one's son's getting married to a rich man's daughter.'

The cynicism of her tone was horrible. I hadn't thought of the reason for Catherine's prolonged absence. But Thalia had—or she had overheard gossip on the subject. Only when we were running on the beach or wandering in the woods would she sometimes resume her old merry companionship—as if in spite of herself she had forgotten her resentment against me.

Cynthia had relapsed again into that strange silence I had known before I went to Paris. She spent a lot of time in bed and this I understood, for she'd tired herself with Claude. I would look at her lying there and long to know what was going on under that lovely calm mask. I understood Thalia having wanted to shake her mother's composure, to break that distant, tantalizing composure. Hadn't I often wanted to throw a stone into a still pool? Only Thalia had done it with a snake, and Cynthia had suffered a heart attack and still believed it had been a krait.

Sometimes when I stood there with the kitchen slate, waiting for her to make up her mind or answer a question, I longed to shake her or throw the slate at her. And yet I admired her. What control she must have to be able to hide every emotion, thought, hope and fear under such flawless beauty. Terence Mourne was by no means her only escort. Cynthia was the favourite of a whole host of retired Army men and indeed of most of the men in the Colony. As I never accompanied her to her social engagements I never saw this. But they would call for her, sometimes she would talk afterwards; and what she didn't tell me, Judy did.

One Saturday, Thalia said she would like to go sketching with me. I was delighted and went to ask Cynthia if she had any plans for the day.

'None,' she said languidly. 'I think I'll stay in bed this morning. Claude can have his lunch with me and you and Thalia could take yours out with you.'

I asked her if there were any news from Tom. She shook her head. 'Nothing. It's over three weeks since I heard from him.'

The papers had been full of the trouble on the Frontier. The elusive Fakir had been using his religious fanaticism for political purposes. I had asked Terence about it and he had explained some of the difficulties under which the Army laboured there. The delicacy of religious corns, on which treading was forbidden, prevented any drastic action being taken. Everything had to be done tactfully—and there was now a movement to choose and retain only officers well versed in the political and religious factors in the country. Men who were both sympathetic and objective. Such a man was Tom Pemberton, who was liked and trusted by many of the tribes. To him were entrusted some of the most delicate and dangerous operations on the Frontier.

'He knows the languages and the men. He was born and brought up in India. His family have been there for three generations. His son is destined for India, too,' said Terence.

But Claude was lame now. Might be lame permanently. Terence saw me looking doubtful.

'There are other ways of serving than in the Army. There's the I.C.S. and the Political.'

'You liked Tom Pemberton.'

'Liked! Liked! Why the past tense?'

'Well.... You didn't seem at ease with one another when you met on the Quay.'

'No.' He frowned. 'I hadn't seen him since I resigned the Regiment.'

'Are you sorry?'

'When I read these accounts of the Frontier trouble in the paper, yes. Like hell I am!'

We went to the Vicomté. I didn't really want to go there, but wishing to placate Thalia and to make a serious attempt to recover some ground in our deteriorating relationship, I agreed. It was painful to me to revisit those places where I'd been so intensely happy with Armand. And I now knew from other sources that what Thalia had said about his being there frequently with other women had been true.

We sketched the far banks of the Rance in the wide estuary from the Rond Point. My painting was dull—lacking either design or life. Thalia, on the contrary, did a very quick, highly original conception of the whole panorama laid out before us from this angle. It was very good—and I told her so. She was pleased and said offhandedly, 'Have it, please. You don't like my poems—perhaps you'll like this better.'

We ate our sandwiches sitting amongst the gorse looking out on the water. As the sun's strength grew so the scent of the gorse increased. There were wild flowers in profusion and I found a small bush of broom. I showed it excitedly to Thalia. 'You remember Marie's story of why broom is so rare in Brittany?'

She nodded. 'Of course. I've made a play out of it. A comedy.'

'A play. A comedy? D'you know how?'

'Of course. I wrote two plays for the children in the Cantonments. They did them at Christmas. They were all right.'

'How could you make a comedy out of a legend of a saint and his mother and broom?'

Melaine was a small boy who looked after sheep. His mother couldn't find him when he wandered away. She was so angry when she found him that, in her relief, she seized the nearest thing with which to beat him. It happened to be a bush of broom. When the flowers discovered that they had beaten a saint their shame was so great that they produced a shower of tears and tried to hide themselves under the earth. From that day, broom has been very rare in Brittany. How could she make a comedy out of this?

But it *is* a comedy. I've made the boy an ordinary naughty little boy, the mother a nagging, tiresome woman and the broom flowers and the sheep are the Chorus, the commentators.'

'I should like to read it,' I said eagerly.

'You can,' she said indifferently.

I thought it strange that Cynthia hadn't told me of Thalia's plays. She must surely have been proud of a daughter who'd had two plays produced, if only by children, when she was only thirteen.

'She wasn't there,' said Thalia. 'She was up in Kashmir.'

'But your father?'

'Oh yes, he was pleased. There was a man—Robin Thorne—in the Regiment, the one who was killed. He helped me a lot and produced them for me. He said I was to go on writing them. I like funny things best. When I feel most unhappy I write something funny.'

'Have you those plays here?'

'Yes,' she said nonchalantly. 'But they're no good really. One day I may write a good one. I should like to act in it myself. The chief comic part!' and she began to laugh quite horribly.

'Thalia,' I said, hurt and upset. 'What *is* the matter lately? I know you're angry because we had to come back, but what else could we have done?'

'Worked!' She spat the word out. 'Washed dishes in the cafés. Oh, I know you're supposed to have a permit. But they'd have taken us on somewhere.'

'There's something else,' I insisted. 'It's not only that.

'It's Father. He hasn't written to me for a long time. And I haven't written to him. Marie saw the *Ankou* [Breton harbinger of death, usually an old man with a cart] last night.' She shivered a little.

'Why haven't you written?' I said, ignoring determinedly Marie's superstitions.

'*You* know. Mother says I'm not to tell him about Claude. The only person who will understand about the whole thing *is* Father. And she says I'm not to tell him.'

'She doesn't want him worried just now.'

'He ought to know. I'm his daughter.'

'And Claude's his son.'

'That's why he ought to know I almost killed him. I *did* push him, you know.'

'Thalia, for goodness' sake try and forget it. Come on, let's race to the top. It's time we started back.'

On the way home she said, 'Let's go round by the St. Enogat road. There's probably a wedding in the church. They always have them on Saturdays.'

We both loved watching the fishermen's weddings, in which there was often a bridal procession to the quay.

'What about Kiki?'

'We can tie him to the railings.'

'He'll howl.'

'It won't matter—they'll have music.'

The church was cool and inviting. We tied Kiki to a post and went into the white stone building. It wasn't very old but the dome pleased me, and although the altar was over-ornate, the side chapels were beautiful. There was a lovely St. Thérèse with a cerulean blue silk background. As we went in I saw that to-day for the wedding she had masses of pink lilies at her feet.

The church was very full and at first I didn't realize that this was no ordinary wedding. The guests weren't fisher-folk or peasants or local townsfolk. They were smart, well-dressed, sophisticated people.

I shut my eyes and began dreaming a little, when something unusually alert and tense in Thalia's interest in the proceedings made me look sharply at the group in front of the altar. At that very moment the bridesmaids stepped back, leaving the bride and groom kneeling there alone.

The arches of the dome began to spin strangely, the whole vaulted space was closing in on me. I bit my lips until they hurt and put my head down between my legs. When the faintness had passed I looked at Thalia. She was gazing straight ahead at the altar, but something in her awareness told me that she had observed the shock I had sustained. We were near the side door. Had she suggested our entering by the main door in the square, I couldn't have failed to have been forewarned by the Tréfours cars. For the groom was Armand!

The girl kneeling at his side was small—shorter than I. She was very dark, as far as I could make out under the bridal veil merging into a cascade of lace flowing down the altar steps. She turned in the ceremony to her groom, so that their two profiles were clear cut against the grey stone. And when I saw Armand there with her—his head bent down to her—a stab of anguish such as I'd never experienced shot through me. I hated her! hated her! This Marie-Laure, this girl who to-night would share his bed, would bear his children—I hated her.

I couldn't stay in the place. Getting up, I began pushing past the guests in the pew. They were astonished and outraged at the commotion, but I didn't care. All that mattered was that I got out—away from a scene which was torture to me. When I reached the fresh air I sat down on the stone wall round the church.

Thalia followed me out. She stood looking curiously at me, as if she were surprised and irritated at my feelings.

'Come on. They'll all be coming out soon.' She pulled me up.

'Don't touch me!' I cried furiously. 'You *knew*. You knew it was his wedding. You brought me here on purpose.'

'But you said you didn't care any more. You said so in Paris,' she said, using the maddeningly patient voice which some adults use to children.

I had a furious desire to hurt her . . . to hurt her terribly.

'Go away,' I cried. 'I never want to see you again.'

Without a word she untied the dog and walked quickly away up the rue St. Enogat, her footsteps ringing on the cobbled square. From the church came the sound of boys' clear voices singing the anthem. I must get away. I must. At last, with a tremendous effort, I got up and walked in the opposite direction to the one she'd taken.

It was as if all the bones in my legs had bent—as if they were the legs of a very old woman. I couldn't bear the thought of facing any human. It felt as if my face was old, too—fixed and set into lines of crumpled distress. I walked along the beach without seeing the surf-line, or the gulls swooping over some dead fish. The tide was going down, leaving the sands hard, white and inviting. So they had been when Armand had run on them. I didn't see the children playing in the pools. I saw only Armand running again. Armand in his shorts, his hair blown in the wind. And he was *married*. Married to that girl whom Thalia said had a little moustache and whose neck was too short.

What a fool I'd been. What an utter fool. And Julie Caron? Would she hate that Marie-Laure as I did? Or would it make no difference to her? Would they go on making love in that rose-lit flat when the old woman was out, or, as Thalia had said, on the flower-covered banks of the Rance?

How *could* he? How *could* he? When I had asked him how he could do that with Julie when he professed to love me, he had looked astonished and said it had nothing to do with love. But Cynthia had called it the act of love ... the act of love. What then had she meant? And Catherine? She had said extraordinary things about love—but she had meant *that*. I longed for her—but she was in the Midi and in the church they had whispered that the bridal couple were going to the Midi for the honeymoon.

I walked and walked until the turmoil in me had died down— and then returned slowly by the rue de la Malouine.

As I went through the gate of the villa, a boy from the Post Office was waiting with a telegram. I took it from him and saw that it was for Cynthia. I think I knew before I took it. Tom Pemberton had been in our thoughts for the last weeks; to-day we had all been talking of the absence of news from him. Cynthia exclaimed at my pallor as soon as I entered the *salon*. Then she saw the telegram. She blanched too.

'Open it. Read it out to me, Rachel,' she said faintly.

'REGRET INFORM YOU COLONEL THOMAS PEMBERTON MISSING BELIEVED KILLED IN ACTION NHAKKI PASS'. There didn't appear to be a date on it and several words were wrongly spelt. The telegram had been sent from London.

'Read it!' she repeated. I couldn't. I handed it to her in silence. She read it and let it flutter to the floor.

'Missing! They mean dead. You can't be missing there on that barren, treeless place. He's dead! Tom's dead! Killed by those vile, treacherous tribesmen! And he *loved* them. He was always trying to learn more of their beastly languages, always trying to make excuses for their treachery. And this is what he gets for it. They murder him. The brutes!'

I picked the telegram up again, staring at the words. 'Missing . . . believed killed . . .'

'Bring Claude down here.' Cynthia's voice was harsh. Her face, although calm, frightened me.

'He'll be asleep,' I protested.

'Bring him!' she said imperiously, in what Thalia called her Kohi-hai voice. Her face was so peculiar that I was even more frightened and went up to the child's room. He was asleep and scarcely stirred when I lifted him in my arms and carried him downstairs wrapped in a blanket.

She was standing by the writing table before a large photograph of Tom Pemberton in uniform.

'Put him down.'

He stood there swaying, more than half-asleep, and I had to support his warm little body.

'Claude,' she said sharply. 'Wake up. Wake up!'

'Cynthia!' I was shocked. 'He's only a baby—and he's been so ill. Don't tell him. *Don't.*' But I needn't have worried for the boy was already asleep on his feet, his head lolling forward on his chest.

She shook him. 'Claude! Claude! Your father has been killed.'

He opened his eyes and began to cry. His mother had a voice and face which were strange to him. He stumbled piteously to me, clutching at me. I picked him up, thinking how frail he had grown.

'He shall grow up to hate those tribes. Treacherous turncoats! They've killed the one man who worked for them. I always told him they weren't worth his worry and trouble.'

'Cynthia,' I said gently, 'we don't know yet that Tom's dead. It says missing.'

'It always means dead. It's a way the War Office have of breaking it. As if it made any difference. It's worse—some poor fools might hope!'

She looked so queer now that I moved towards the door with Claude in my arms.

'I'll call Thalia,' I said.

'No,' she said harshly. 'I don't *want* her.'

As I reached the door I saw Thalia in the hall. She had heard Cynthia's words.

'What's the matter?' she asked, looking in surprise at Claude in my arms.

I deliberately handed her the telegram. 'Go in to your mother. I'll be down in a minute. I must take Claude to bed.'

She read the telegram slowly, looked at me with eyes opaque and wide, then ran past me up the stairs. I heard her door slam and the key turn in the lock as I laid the child back in his bed. I was trembling as if I were cold, and there was a strange sick feeling in the pit of my stomach.

I went down and looked through the glass doors of the *salon*. Cynthia was still there sitting on the couch. She didn't move when I touched her arm. She seemed oblivious of everything.

Marie stood twisting her apron at the kitchen door.

'Help me get her to bed. She's had a bad shock,' I said.

'*Le Colonel—il est mort?*'

'*Il paraît qu'il est mort!*'

'I knew it. I knew it. Twice this week I've seen the *Ankou*. What else can you expect after that bone was brought into the house?'

'Don't be silly,' I said impatiently.

We had visited an Ossuary with Judy a few days before. Claude, unobserved, had taken a little bone from the shelf. On his return he had shown it proudly to Marie. She had been outraged and terrified. 'It must go back. It must go back at once!' she had insisted. 'It will bring terrible things on this house if it isn't returned at once.'

Judy and I had driven back to the Ossuary. It was late and the place was shut. The old caretaker whom we knocked up had taken a poor view of our worrying about it. He had looked at the little finger bone and said crossly, 'All that fuss for that. No one would have missed it.'

But Marie had been somewhat appeased. Claude had told me that he'd seen plenty of bones and skulls in India. He'd taken the finger bone because he'd decided to become a doctor not a soldier. He had an immense admiration for Dr. Cartier who had mended his leg.

'Cynthia,' I said gently. 'You must come to bed.'

She stood up as if she were a sleepwalker and, brushing aside my arm, went slowly and stiffly up the stairs. She sat down on the painted bed. Marie had followed us and stood hesitating in the doorway.

'Some tea? Some wine? Better, some brandy?'

'Some hot-water bottles,' I said, feeling Cynthia's hands and feet. They were icy cold.

Suddenly she began talking as if she were addressing a meeting. In a hard, clear, ringing tone.

'Duty. Always the same. Nothing else matters. That comes first. If you've made a mistake you must stick to it. It's your duty. Oh, God, how funny it all is. How funny!' And she began laughing—and springing up, snatched the small black crucifix from the nail on which Marie had hung it in the alcove and flung it wildly across the room. I heard it crash as it hit the floor. Her face was contorted now—broken like a lovely mask can be—so that I scarcely recognized her. In the throes of some emotion which I didn't understand—certainly not grief as I knew it—but an emotion which racked and ravaged her, she was no longer beautiful. She was ugly.

I took her box of sleeping pills from the drawer by the bed and went out, pocketing the key. She took not the slightest notice of me. Her paroxysm over, she sat down on the bed again, staring unseeingly into space.

I went into the kitchen to find Marie, badly needing some human contact to steady me. She peered questioningly at me as I stood against the dresser shaking. I couldn't stop. Without a word she bent down to a cupboard under the sink and drew out the bottle she kept for Yves' visits. '*Il est mort.*' She crossed herself. 'How pale you are, Mademoiselle Rachel! I listened to her cries. I saw her throw the crucifix.' She crossed herself again. 'She didn't know what she was doing. She's a good woman. She goes to church. God help the poor soul! Drink this. You're shaking like Claude's jellies.'

The raw spirit pulled me together. I telephoned Judy. She'd gone out to a dinner party and was not expected back until late.

'Watch her door, Marie. See that she doesn't go out. I'm going to fetch Captain Mourne.'

I had to go to Terence. It was always hopeless to try and get him on the telephone. The hotel had a number of annexes and they were some distance apart from the main building.

'Don't leave me alone for long with a woman who throws crucifixes,' she said, fearfully.

I pulled her black shawl round my shoulders and ran out of the house. I ran again up the rue de la Malouine and into Terence's hotel. He was exactly where I expected him to be—sitting on the terrace over the sea, drinking with some retired Army officers.

He wasn't at all pleased to see me—he had been drinking a good deal—but something in my face brought him quickly to his feet and away from the group.

'What's the matter?'

Cynthia,' I panted. 'Tom's missing—believed killed in action. She's so strange. I'm frightened, Terence. You must come. You *must*.'

He took my arm and hurried me away. When we were in the shadow of the tamarisks, he said angrily, 'Why d'you come to me? What can I do?'

'You're her friend. Tom Pemberton was your friend—your fellow-officer. You must come. She needs you.'

'You little fool! Are you blind? Don't you see that I'm the last person to go to her now?'

I couldn't understand him and as angrily as he, I said, 'You always talk in riddles. This is no time for it. You *must* come to her.'

He hurried me up the avenues, already dusty from a long drought, through one tree-lined street to another. There were puffs of white cotton stuff from some tree whose name I didn't know blowing all over the place. They settled like snow on Marie's shawl round my shoulders and all over his immaculate dinner jacket.

Cynthia's window was lighted as we went into the hall. Marie met us there.

'She's still sitting there. She hasn't moved.' She took out her rosary and began telling her beads.

'Go up to her,' said Terence fiercely.

'She doesn't like me . . . I think she hates me,' I said helplessly. 'What can I say? What can I do?'

'In God's name, girl, are you completely inhuman? Go in to her as you would to anyone in trouble. Help her . . . comfort her somehow . . . God, do I have to tell you what to do? Aren't you a woman? You've known what it is to love. You're not a child now. *Go in.*'

His whisper was so fierce, so insistent that I went up the stairs. He not only had the power of making me obey but of withholding the retort that it was he who should be going.

She sat on the tumbled bed looking out across the sea.

'Cynthia . . . Cynthia,' I said softly, and very gently I put my arms round her and pulled her head down to me. She didn't move at first when she felt my arms, then suddenly she broke free and flung herself face downwards on the bed. Incoherent, agonized words came from her and harsh, tearing sobs.

I stroked her hair, fallen in a golden cascade over her shoulders and so we sat for a long, long time. Marie looked in twice. I put my finger to my lips and she went noiselessly out again.

At last Cynthia sat up and buried her ravaged face on me. I held her close, longing to weep with her, but not a single tear would come—my anguish was too deep.

I felt an aching, limitless pity now, not only for her, but for all my sex. It seemed to me suddenly that I was now completely at one with her in that I had loved—perhaps as hopelessly—certainly as unhappily—as she had. And in that moment, I knew that I was as ageless as are all women in that they must inevitably know sorrow. 'No longer a child,' Terence had said. 'You know what it is to have loved.'

'Cynthia, darling . . . don't cry any more . . . don't. Perhaps he isn't dead. Perhaps he's having to hide out somewhere. Don't give up hope.'

'He's dead. I know he is,' she said stonily and the low sobbing began again.

A sudden feeling that we were being watched made me look up above her bowed head. I thought Marie was in the room again and was going to ask her for a hot drink for Cynthia. But it wasn't Marie. At first I couldn't see anyone; and then in the triple mirror of the dressing-table I saw three faces. Not Marie's. Thalia's. Thalia full face, Thalia left profile, Thalia right profile; and in all three I read an incredulous, contemptuous acceptance of this betrayal.

All those eyes, dark, hostile and watchful were taking in the impact of this scene of Cynthia and me sitting there with our arms round each other; and then, as I moved, the mirror was suddenly empty—she had gone!

When Cynthia had fallen into a heavy, drugged sleep I went quickly and remorsefully upstairs to Thalia. I was vaguely uneasy. Those eyes! Had I imagined it? It was the contempt and incredulity which stung me—the realization in them of the inevitable thing which had happened to me. I had passed that no-man's-land between childhood and womanhood.

But she had locked her door against me and there wasn't a sound from behind it. She didn't answer to her name when I called her again and again. I reminded her that she'd had no supper, using all the endearments which she usually couldn't resist. But the silence persisted. I couldn't risk waking Cynthia or Claude by making a scene. I went away. I had removed Cynthia's key—but Thalia's I had forgotten.

CHAPTER XIX

IT WAS three o'clock when I awoke with the insistent knowledge that Thalia was calling me. I awoke to a distinct cry—repeated twice. I pulled on a dressing-gown and went on to the landing. The door of her room was wide open—the room itself empty.

I ran downstairs to the garden and then I knew what had awakened me. Kiki was barking madly. I went out to the dog in his kennel and tried to soothe him, but he wouldn't be quiet. He was quivering and excited. As I went back through the hall I saw that there was a chair standing under the great hook on which we kept the key of the gate. I looked up—the key was gone. And suddenly there flashed back to me those words of Thalia's to her father as she had stood on the steps: 'I'll give it to you and to nobody else.'

It was dark, there was no moon, and a strong wind was whipping the palms. The iron gate was swinging, the steps below, dark and forbidding. They were slippery as I descended, and twice I lost my footing. The tide was almost at full height and half-way down the waves were dashing up on to them. It was as I reached the last unwashed step that I saw the slipper. A buff, woolly, shabby bedroom slipper—and I knew that she was here. And now I began to cry frantically, 'Thalia . . . Thalia . . . Thalia. . . .' The wind carried my voice away in an empty senseless echo as I stood there clutching her shoe. She was playing one of her tricks on me . . . I was waiting to hear her laughing and calling, 'Here I am . . . Rachel, here I am!' as she had done when she pretended to leap over the cliffs.

But no laugh and no voice came. Was she hiding up on the terrace under the palms? I ran up the steps again and looked on the seat in the deep shadow there. I called her again, but only the wind answered me. And then, out on the water I thought I saw her head—far out on the waves. I screamed wildly again, 'Thalia . . . Thalia. . . .' I ran down the steps, flinging off my dressing-gown and kicking off my shoes.

The water was black and deep—the rocks jagged and cruel. I was terrified . . . terrified. A cramp of sick horrible fear clutched me in the stomach so that I couldn't bring myself to dive in, although I knew that if it were indeed she out there, every second counted.

I have always been a coward in some respects . . . about leaping into the unknown especially. Once, at school, when we had a fire, they had been obliged to push me down the chute. 'Oh, God . . . oh, God, *make* me go in! *Make* me go in!' I prayed, forgetting my agnostic avowals, and raising my arms above my head, I plunged into the black water.

It was so cold that the shock of its impact all but sent me under again when I came to the surface. I was clear of the rocks and struck out in the direction of the object I thought I had seen, calling again and again. But now the tiling had gone. Fear made my limbs heavy and my strokes weak, and as my pyjamas hindered me so I thought with dismay of Thalia's voluminous night-gown. I hadn't stopped to look if her dressing-gown was missing. The blackness of the water filled me with an agony of apprehension—what monsters lurked beneath its depths? Again and again I imagined I caught sight of an arm, or a movement as a wave broke made me imagine that some portion of her body was coming above the surface. It was as if I were chasing a mirage and I began to grow weaker and weaker.

The tide was pulling me out all the time and swimming against it, trying now to get back, was an appalling body-racking battle. Suddenly a searing, shooting pain gripped me, leaving me helpless. A huge wave dashed me against the rocks below the steps. I tried to grab something solid, but before I could do so, the strong undercurrent sucked me back into the sea and once more the terrible pain seized me. I floated a little until it lessened and, making a tremendous effort, when the next wave flung me against the rocks I clutched on to them wildly, my arms and legs bruised and cut through the thin silk of my pyjamas. Again and again I grabbed some sharp edge of rock, only to be sucked back by the fierce, savage force of the ebb tide.

And then I heard a cry. Thalia? Was she on the steps after all? I looked up. Marie was there. She shouted something to me, but I couldn't hear it. Then she disappeared.

My strength was almost gone, my fingers unable to sustain their hold. I began sliding, slipping back into that black whirlpool; but now it seemed to be beckoning me, no longer icy and repellent but warm, inviting. 'I am drowning . . . drowning . . .' I thought. 'They always say it's warm and peaceful once you stop struggling.' And then Marie's shrill harsh cry aroused me. '*Courage! Courage! Tenez! Tenez!*' And there was a rope flung to me. I grabbed it—there was a loop on the end and after what seemed an endless, agonizing struggle, during which she shouted, admonished and encouraged me in rough, fierce commands, I managed to get it under my armpits. Holding the rope against the violence of the waves, she hauled me in bumping, agonizing, sprawling jerks over the rocks and on to the submerged steps, where her strong old hands, accustomed to pulling in the boats, dragged me to safety. I lay there collapsed, a dead thing. Then the warm, drifting feeling came over me again and all was blackness.

I came to myself in agonized, violent pain. I was face downwards on the step and Marie was working on my back. I was vomiting up sea water and half my inside with it. Each spasm was a fresh agony.... Marie turned me over suddenly and, supporting my head, looked at me.... '*Dieu remercie! Elle vive encore!*'

I struggled up. 'Thalia...Thalia...' I tried to say, but my voice was so weak that no sound was audible. I tried again. 'Thalia. She's gone. She's in the sea. We must find her. We *must*.' But only a cracked whisper came from me.

'Don't talk... he still.' She began massaging me, kneading my back and chest, rubbing my hands and wrists, my ankles and my stomach. Every touch hurt as if she were using a knife. I clung to her in great gulping, sobbing breaths as she worked. She must understand and get help. She *must*.

'Thalia...Thalia.... We *must* find her....'

'Mademoiselle Rachel,' she said gently, 'if she is in that sea she is dead. No one, unable to swim, could live in it for this long....'

'Her shoe. It was on the steps. You saw it?'

'I have it here. I heard the dog barking and found you both gone from your rooms. I saw her shoe. Come, do you think you could get up the steps now? Lean on me... I'm strong... don't be afraid to put all your weight on me.'

And so, in what seemed an interminable journey, we ascended the steps, halting at each new one, and at last reaching the terrace, where I collapsed again on the seat. But I wouldn't rest longer than enabled me to get my breath, which was still painful and still coming in great, audible sighs.

'Thalia.... Marie, we must get help. She may be drifting somewhere out there. I'm sure I saw her arm in the water....'

'It was a *mouette*—a seagull!' said Marie firmly. 'I saw it too. In the dark it looked like a white arm... but it was only a gull. Come now... lean on me and we'll get to the house.'

And soon she had me before the stove in the kitchen, had pulled off my pyjamas, wrapped me in warm blankets and forced some hot brandy and sugar down me, for now fresh shivering and vomiting had seized me. But I had to get to the telephone somehow. Kiki was still barking loudly and I could hear him jumping wildly against the wall of his kennel. 'Loose him!' I said to Marie. 'He must have seen her. He'll show us where she went!'

She loosed him, and without a moment's hesitation he tore down to the gate and raced down the steps barking more and more excitedly.

'You see? He knows. He saw her go. She probably spoke to him.'

It was almost four o'clock, but I picked up the telephone receiver and asked the operator for Judy's number. She answered immediately and her voice showed no surprise at being awakened at such an hour.

'Give me half an hour and I'll be with you,' she said, without asking any of those aimless and time-wasting questions which most people do.

Sit down! I'll telephone the police,' said Marie. 'They will give the coastguards the alarm.'

It was Judy who helped me through the horror of the police inquiries. Judy who staunchly denied that I could be held in any way responsible for the tragedy. Judy who insisted that Thalia had rushed out, completely unbalanced by the realization of her father's possible death, and in her wild grief had slipped on those steps. But the key? No one asked about the key. We had hung it back on the hook afterwards. When I wanted to explain about it, Marie had checked me fiercely. 'Leave well alone,' she had hissed.

It was Judy who sent for Miss Pemberton, Tom's unmarried sister. She was so like Thalia that her appearance had startled me. She was capable and practical—and she was kind.

'It's no use crying; it's done! And she probably did it all for nothing. Tom'll turn up yet. I know my brother. Poor unbalanced child. Always imagining that she was being wrongly treated! What else can you expect from the child of a woman like Cynthia, who allowed her to be brought up with a tiger, snakes and heathens?'

And she swept up the whole mass of papers I had found in Thalia's room. Poems, pages of them, some short stories and the plays of which she had spoken. These last were curious in that the characters in them were all animals commenting on the stupidities of humans. I wanted to keep them.

'A lot of morbid drivel! Outpourings of adolescence. Better burned. Into the kitchen stove with the lot!'

But I had found Thalia's diary and this I hid from Miss Pemberton, for it was full of entries about me. My name was on every page. Rachel . . . Rachel. From the time of my meeting with Armand until the final break with him, there was a complete record. The only time the diary had not been kept had been during the Paris period. She had resumed it as soon as she returned.

I noted the change in her comments on me; from the first wild, extravagant praise to gradual bitter disappointment.

All these caused me anguish—but it was that last page, the day of Armand's wedding, the day of the telegram, which burned into me as if it would never disappear.

'She's angry with me—furious.'

Then later, added in a different ink: 'I've just read the telegram. She gave it me without a word.' There was a smudge of tears here and some dirt on the place. And then the last entry—that final one which I could not forget:

'I went to tell Rachel I am sorry. I wanted comfort because of Father. I saw them together. Her arms round *Mother*!' And after a blank line, she had begun again: 'I'll get her back. I *must*. I must . . .' and here it broke off.

Did she try? Did she intend to frighten me as she had so often done? And indeed as I had thought she was doing then? Did she rush down the steps calling my name loudly, intending to hide from me? Or did the long nightgown cause her to slip, so that calling my name in real terror she fell to her death in the swirling waters?

On the day of the inquest, Xavier Tréfours came to see me. Shocked at the news of the tragedy he had hastened to offer his help in my ordeal. Cynthia was too ill to be subjected to any of it and it fell on me to answer all the searching questions about Thalia's last hours. Xavier was known in the district—known to all the authorities—and his warm, sympathetic handling of me, and his tactful help to the police, was as balm on the agitation of the whole affair. He made it all as easy for me as he could, so that there was nothing expressed but sympathy for the young English girl whose friend had met with this terrible accident after hearing the news of the probable death of her father. Almost demented with grief she had clearly fallen down the steps. Great sympathy was expressed for the beautiful mother who was the victim of this double tragedy.

Cynthia returned to England with her sister-in-law and Claude, dazed and incapable of really taking in the whole thing. 'We might have been friends, Rachel,' she had said, taking my face between her hands as Catherine had once done. 'I could have grown very fond of you—if you had let me.'

'If you had let me.' That had startled me. Surely it was Cynthia who had not wanted to be friends. But was it? And yet it seemed to me that her grief over Thalia was something deeper and more impenetrable than the noisier, impotent anger over Tom. And she had shown real feeling for me in my terrible distress.

I was staying with Judy at St. Lunaire until the villa had been set to rights and everything finished and settled up here in Dinard. This, I thought, was the least I could do for Cynthia.

Marie and I had gone through the inventory after cleaning the villa. Shining with beeswax, in stiff and hideous order, it now awaited new tenants. While the agents completed their minute examination for damage of every piece of furniture, Marie had stood with me as a kind of impartial avenging angel.

'*Non.* They did not do that. It was already there. Those Americans tore that sheet last summer. Yes, Monsieur Claude broke that chair tying the dog to it, pretending it was a sledge. Yes, Mademoiselle Thalia broke the coffee pot balancing it on her head when she was an Egyptian.'

'Mademoiselle Thalia . . . Mademoiselle Thalia.'

When the agents had gone, Marie asked me to go out with her. She had put on her best clothes—the ones she wore to Mass—and I was curious. We went along the Clair-de-Lune Promenade, past the little white boats—the dories—and the sailing ones below the yacht club, until we came to the image of Notre Dame de Lourdes set in the grotto facing the sea. Surrounded with ferns and flowers, the Virgin, serene and benign, looks out over the water; and all around her are those touching little stone tablets set in the grotto, each with a date and the simple word '*Merci*' on them.

Armand had never passed this grotto without pausing to say a prayer, so that I knew the lovely words of the Abbé Perreye almost by heart. I had always looked at them there on the wall of the grotto while I waited for him. I looked at them now. '*Ayez pitié de ceux qui s'aimaient et sont séparés. . . . Ayez pitié de ceux qui pleurent. . . .*' Have pity on those who loved and are separated. . . . Have pity on those who weep. But I could not weep. I was still scorched by a dry anguish too deep for tears.

'Up there—in that space, you see,' Marie was saying. 'The tablet will go there. The stone mason is inscribing it now,' and she named the date of that terrible night when Thalia had disappeared.

'But she wasn't saved. She was drowned. You can't put *Merci*. She was drowned!' I cried, passionately.

'And you, Mademoiselle Rachel? Didn't I drag you back from the sea that night? D'you think I could have pulled you out without help from Her? You were as heavy as an elephant, and I am an old woman!'

She went on to tell me that although the tablets were possibly intended for those who had been to Lourdes and received miraculous cures there, the curé had approved her desire to place her thanks on record. What better miracle was there than giving to an old woman the superhuman strength she needed to save a life?

'The tablet is to give thanks for *me*?' I asked incredulously.

'Who else?' she said imperturbably. 'Yves has paid half of the money. He hasn't been drunk for over a month.'

I looked at Marie's calm old face, at its rough nobility, and I was ashamed. I had not even thanked her for saving my life. I hadn't even thought of it. I took her hard, worn hands and kissed them both. 'What must you think of me? How can I ever thank you?'

She pushed me roughly round until I faced the statue.

'Give your thanks in the proper quarter,' she said sharply. 'I don't need them.'

Thalia and I had often stood there reading the dates on the tablets and even now I imagined that I heard her laughing. It was so clear that, startled, I turned away from the grotto. She seemed suddenly physically close—as if she stood there with us. I thought of that day when we had first gone to Catherine's, and of how we had laughed and laughed. Of the old peasant who had told us that soon we would weep. Well, the last laugh was on me . . . and I had heard it clearly as I stood there.

It was my last evening in Dinard. To-morrow, Judy would see me off on the boat from St. Malo. The season was well on its way.

Already the Promenade was filled with chattering visitors, the blessed peace of the empty *plage* was gone. We went back to the villa through streets crowded with holiday-makers.

'I hate it when it's so crowded—it's not the real Dinard now!' I said sadly.

'The holiday-makers are our living. We couldn't exist on the Colony alone,' reproved Marie.

For the last time we went the round of the villa. The jasmine and honeysuckle climbed in at the windows of my room, as they did at Thalia's. I could not enter either room without seeing her there, leaning at the window in her childish nightgown. In Cynthia's room the bed with the cupids and the heart looked forlorn with its little curtains removed for cleaning and its silken covers gone. The mirror on the dressing-table still reflected for me that last accusing, contemptuous vision of Thalia. I felt the strangest reluctance to leave the place which held these poignant memories.

'The sooner you get away the better,' Miss Pemberton had said briskly. 'You look like a ghost. Cynthia had no right to make such use of you. I could have dealt with a neurotic woman—but you couldn't be expected to. A woman's place is with her husband—or as near as the Army will allow her. Put all remembrance of this disastrous year out of your head. As to Thalia—fate is fate! If she was meant to go young, she would have gone anyway. The boy'll be all right. He scarcely limps at all. In a year he'll be absolutely normal.'

'Come,' called Marie to me now. 'Come, it's all finished . . . there's nothing more to be done.'

'Nothing more to be done.' That was what the police had said when I had frantically implored them to continue the search for Thalia.

I clattered down the stairs. Marie was standing in the hall with the bunch of keys in her hand, her shawl round her, waiting for me. 'Nothing good has happened in this house since she married that man from Paris. And nothing good *will* happen in it until that heathen bed is removed.'

Outside, Judy was waiting with Kiki in her car. I was taking the dog back with me. No one wanted him. My aunt would grumble, her spaniels would despise the French mongrel; but she preferred dogs to humans too—and she would not be able to resist his appealing face. We dropped Marie off at her cottage by the station and drove out to St. Lunaire.

The gangway was up. On the quay excited groups were waving to their departing friends. Marie, Yves, Judy and Terence stood together in a little group waving to me. Judy, cupping her hands, was shouting something in farewell, but the strong wind carried her voice away. I saw Terence bend protectively over her and something in that movement gave me a momentary pleasure. It seemed to confirm an intuition I had had when I had last seen them together.

My hair blew over my face and made it difficult to see them as I waved and waved before I turned to look for the last time at the coast of Brittany. The ship's siren gave three mournful sharp wails as we veered round from St. Malo towards Dinard and, as in Judy's cry, I could hear in their sound but one name . . . Thalia, Thalia.

The sky was a fierce, angry purple and little whisked tongues of flame flicked in and out of the livid clouds piling up in one solid, terrifying bank.

'In for a nice storm, the Captain says,' offered a red-faced young man who had been following me around. I didn't answer. I was still staring at the now rapidly receding coast. No longer the beckoning fairy one tinged with the promised gold as when I had arrived: it was now dark, sinister and repellent.

'On this coast I have left my youth,' I thought. Here, in this land of irresistible myth and fantasy which overlies its stark reality, I had lost that glorious certainty with which I had come to it. The world loomed ahead of me—and I was as conscious now of its terrors as I was of that huge, frightening bank of cloud above our small ship.

'You are fortunate that your aunt is a truly Christian woman and is willing to take you back,' the Reverend Cookson-Cander had written to me at the end of a long sermon which left me unmoved. How much more human and warm had been the few words of comfort given me by Father Ignace—although I was still a heretic.

'Your behaviour to Cynthia, to say the least of it, has been abominable. Miss Pemberton, however, has been to see me and in her opinion there are extenuating circumstances. I am therefore

willing to have you back until your Slade training is completed.'
So wrote my aunt.

And Father? I pulled his latest telegram from my pocket. 'MEET ME TO-MORROW TEN AM PADDINGTON PLATFORM ONE UNDER CLOCK HAVE BOUGHT YOU NEW FISHING ROD FATHER'.

He would only be able to tell me what he thought about it all while we were fishing. He had wasted money on a new rod for me although he knew I hated fishing.

Inside me now there was a continuous weeping, but outwardly not one tear had relieved that inner anguish.

> Qu'as-tu fait, ô que voilà
> Pleurant sans cesse,
> Dis, qu'as-tu fait, toi que voilà,
> De ta jeunesse?

But it was no longer Armand's voice I heard repeating the lines I had loved. It was Thalia's. Just as at night now that last incredulous, contemptuous reflection of her haunted my dreams. 'Punish me not for my sins for I know not myself,' said the words of the Amarna prayer. What had I done? What?

And now the wind began to get up in earnest. The gulls wheeled away from its unleashed fury; and in each shriek of its anger, as in their every harsh cry I heard but one name ... Thalia ... Thalia ... Thalia....

'All passengers below deck!' shouted the sailors in a sudden flurry of activity. 'All passengers below!'

'Come on,' urged the red-faced young man, appearing again at my side. 'Didn't you hear? We've got to go below.' And now the coast was blotted out in a veil of sweeping rain. I turned, and followed him down.

September 1955 — June 1956.
Dinard — Paris — Dinard.

The following newspaper story by Frances Faviell was originally published in 1956, in the London Evening Standard. *It was part of a series of articles, by various authors, published under the heading: 'Fact or Fiction? The Answer will be given tomorrow'. Unfortunately we do not now know the answer to the* Standard's *question, though the Indian setting was certainly well-known to the author in her youth. Memories of India are also a prominent feature of the novel* Thalia.

THE UNINVITED GUEST

While an art student I was lucky enough to be invited to spend several months as the guest of Rabindranath Tagore, the poet, philosopher and teacher, in the ashram or college which he founded in Bolpur, Bengal.

The Guru Devi, as the students called Tagore, provided me with a little two-roomed house of mud with a thatched roof in the compound of the ashram.

In the afternoons, instead of having a siesta, I used to bake chocolate cakes, for which Tagore had acquired a great liking in England.

One afternoon when Krishna, my bearer, had placed the tea on the veranda table, I looked up and was astonished to see a very large, ugly monkey sitting on the railing, looking intently at me as I sat in my rocking chair.

He was as large as a ten-year-old child and I was a little alarmed at his proximity, but as he was staring at the rocking chair and then at the bowl of fruit on the table I took a small reddish banana from it and cautiously offered it to him.

"Take care ... some monkeys bad ... biting very hard," warned Krishna who was just as excited at our invited guest as I was. The big ape approached closer and accepted the banana very gently from me.

"This monkey is Hanuman ape—very sacred special monkey. Living far away in jungle, not coming here," Krishna said excitedly as our visitor peeled the banana very carefully and ate it with obvious relish. I offered him a second one, and this he accepted and ate, but he refused a third, simply ignoring it in my outstretched hand, and after watching me handle the tea-pot and cup intently, he suddenly dropped down from the rail and loped away on all fours, stopping once or twice to look back at the little house before he disappeared into the jungle.

Imagine my surprise when at about the same time the next day he appeared again on the veranda and stretched out his hand towards the bowl of fruit. Refusing an orange which I offered, he made it plain that he wanted bananas, of which he again ate two. Rejecting a third, he gibbered a little at me, and then leaped with a great bound down from the railing and was gone.

And so it went on for several weeks.

The fame of my strange visitor soon spread all over the ashram and both the students and the local natives were most impressed by the favour shown me by this sacred monkey. They began hiding themselves in the bushes round the compound to see with their own eyes the English guest and the strange visitor having tea together on the veranda. Rajat was conservative in his tastes, for he would accept no other fruit than the small pinkish-red bananas which grew locally. To obtain these delicacies and wait there for Rajat became almost an obsession with me.

Alas, the summer had been a scorching one, and the rains, due then, were late. Fruit became more and more difficult to obtain, and the special bananas beloved of Rajat almost impossible to find. At first for a high price we managed to obtain a few, but there came a day when not one banana could be found in the neighbourhood although the whole community was helping me.

It was while the chocolate cakes were baking and I was putting my paints ready for my sitting at five o'clock that Krishna had one of his frequent brainwaves. I should, of course, have mistrusted him and been guided by my own judgment, but I reminded myself that Krishna was a Hindu and should know all about sacred monkeys. As he helped me pack the tubes of paint in my box he said: "Why not paint a cucumber pink and red like the banana? Rajat will be deceived, and before he has discovered that it is not a banana he will have eaten it."

"No," I demurred. "The paint might harm him—and in any case the smell would not deceive him."

Krishna said nothing but went off to the cupboard in which I kept the ingredients for the cakes. He returned grinning triumphantly with two little bottles. One was cochineal and the other bore the label "Banana essence." Both had been found by him in the bazaar.

Reluctantly I did as he suggested. The pale green cucumbers were not unlike bananas in shape and they soon became pinkish red and Krishna anointed them when dry with the banana essence.

When four o'clock came I waited as usual with the camouflaged cucumbers in the bowl with the oranges, and I had to admit that they looked delectable and smelled delicious. But at the same time I had distinct qualms as to the success of this deception. At a few minutes past four Rajat suddenly appeared. One of the most extraordinary things about this large wild creature was his capacity for appearing as if by magic from nowhere. Krishna said that was not to be wondered at—had not Hanuman, the king of the monkeys, leaped from India to Ceylon in one bound?

I looked at him sitting so close on the railing and with trepidation offered him one of the camouflaged cucumbers. He took it, sniffed it suspiciously and seemed pleased at the strong scent. But when he licked it his expression changed.

He began trying to peel it as he did the bananas, and when it would not peel a look of fury came over his face and he bit it viciously, spat the morsel out furiously and flung the remainder straight in my face, leaping at the same time on to the table.

"Run! Run! Quick! Rajat angry . . . he will harm you. Run! Into the bungalow!" urged Krishna excitedly as Rajat began hurling the fruit in the bowl at me, then the bowl itself, then the teapot, cup and saucer and plates. "Run! Quick!" shouted Krishna, calling wildly for the gardener and the cook.

I needed no warning to run, but I was so terrified at the rage of my visitor that for a moment I couldn't move: then, as he had no more missiles left, still uttering harsh, strange cries which so frightened me, and beating his breast in fury, he prepared to leap from the now empty table right at me.

I fled into the house and slammed the door. But in a flash Rajat had leaped on to the window ledge. The windows had no glass, only wooden shutters so warped by the heat that they would not close. He pushed them open and sprang through the opening into the room. I tore through the house and out at the back door, slamming it shut after me. "Hold the shutters, Krishna!" I screamed. "Keep him inside." "No. Let him out. He will tear up all your clothes and break all the furniture!" cried Krishna, who had a stout stick in his hand. I knew he would not harm Rajat for all monkeys are sacred in India.

The cook and the gardener had now joined Krishna and cornered thus by the three men, Rajat, with a wonderful leap, gained the roof, and in a veritable fury began tearing up the straw thatch and throwing armfuls down at us, almost blinding us. The three men shouted in unison, waving sticks and throwing stones to frighten him. but not until the cook, an agile intrepid little man, began clambering up himself did Rajat desist, and then with strange terrible cries and one breathtaking leap he reached the ground again, and with a last resentful look at me he loped away across the compound and over the fields to the jungle, leaving me shaken and trembling in the rocking chair.

When at five o'clock I went as usual to visit Tagore to paint his portrait, I apologised for the chocolate cakes which had burned during the excitement. He had already heard about the happenings of the afternoon and laughed heartily. "You are lucky you were not hurt," he said, with a twinkle in his wonderful old eyes. "The roof will be repaired and the tea service replaced, but I doubt if the outrage to your monkey friend can be repaired. Did you look up Hanuman in the library?" I said that I had.

"Then," said Tagore, "you will have read that the king of the monkeys tore up trees, carried away the Himalayas, and seized the clouds. The Ramayana says that the chief of the monkeys is perfect and that no one equals him in learning. How then should he be deceived by a painted cucumber?" And he began laughing at me again.

Next day offerings of fruit appeared as if by magic. My prestige had fallen distinctly low. I had offended Rajat and unless he were appeased he might bring bad luck on us all I was told.

At four o'clock I sat as usual on the veranda with a bowl of real bananas in readiness—but Rajat did not come—and although for several weeks I waited remorsefully for him he never came again.

AFTERWORD

I THINK I was about 11 when I realised my mother was becoming a writer as well as being a painter. I was home from my English boarding school for the summer holidays when my father suggested that I should not disturb my mother in the mornings as she would be working. ... At the time I was upset as my mother had never seemed to worry if I disturbed her.

My mother was born and grew up in Plymouth, Devon. She was the fourth of five surviving children born to Anglo Scottish parents. Named Olive, she showed her innate independence at an early age by insisting she be called Olivia. She showed early talent as an artist and in her late teens won a scholarship to the Slade School of Art, then still under the direction of Henry Tonks. Her tutor, and later good friend, at the school was the painter Leon Underwood.

In 1930 she married her first husband, a Hungarian academic, whose work took him to first Holland and then India. But they separated while there (and later divorced). She then stayed on for three months in the Ashram of the great Indian thinker and writer Rabindranath Tagore. Travelling on her own, painting and sketching, she visited other parts of India including Assam and for a few weeks lived with the Nagas, a primitive indigenous people in northeast India. On her way back to England she travelled via Japan and then China – still painting and sketching – until she had to flee Shanghai when the Japanese invaded.

On her return to England she lived in Chelsea, then a haven for artists, and earned her living as a portrait painter. She met my father, who had recently resigned from the Indian Civil Service, in 1939, and they were married in 1940 after he had joined the Ministry of Information. Bombed out during the Blitz, as portrayed in her last book, *A Chelsea Concerto*, they spent the rest of the war, after I was born, in the Home Counties before returning to Chelsea in 1945.

When the war ended my father was recruited to the Control Commission of Germany and became a high ranking official in the British administration, first in Berlin, negotiating with the others of the four powers on the organisation of the city, later in the British zone of West Germany.

We joined him in Berlin in early 1946 and it was here that my mother encountered the Altmann family. It was her experiences with them that inspired her to start writing her first book, *The Dancing Bear*, which movingly describes Berlin in defeat through the eyes of the defeated as well as the victors.

Each of her books, whether non-fiction or fiction, were inspired by an episode in her own life. By 1951 we had moved to Cologne and it was here that her second book, the novel *A House on the Rhine,* was conceived, based around migrant families (from the east of Germany) she had met and helped.

Subsequently, she published another novel, *Thalia*, based on her own experience in France before the War when she was acting as a chaperone to a young teenager for the summer. Her final novel *The Fledgeling*, about a National Service deserter, was also based on an actual incident.

My mother was diagnosed with breast cancer in 1956 though I did not know at the time. At first radiotherapy seemed to have arrested the disease. But then two years later, it reappeared. She fought the disease with courage and humour, exhibiting the same clear sightedness with which she had viewed life around her as a painter and a writer. She died just after *A Chelsea Concerto* was published, in 1959.

In her books as in her life, my mother had an openness to and compassion for others and, when she saw an injustice or need, would not be thwarted by authority of any kind in getting something done. But as she always pursued her causes with charm as well as firmness, few could deny her requests for long.

John Richard Parker, 2016

FURROWED MIDDLEBROW

FM1. *A Footman for the Peacock* (1940) . . . . RACHEL FERGUSON
FM2. *Evenfield* (1942) . . . . RACHEL FERGUSON
FM3. *A Harp in Lowndes Square* (1936) . . . . RACHEL FERGUSON
FM4. *A Chelsea Concerto* (1959) . . . . FRANCES FAVIELL
FM5. *The Dancing Bear* (1954) . . . . FRANCES FAVIELL
FM6. *A House on the Rhine* (1955) . . . . FRANCES FAVIELL
FM7. *Thalia* (1957) . . . . FRANCES FAVIELL
FM8. *The Fledgeling* (1958) . . . . FRANCES FAVIELL
FM9. *Bewildering Cares* (1940) . . . . WINIFRED PECK

Printed in Great Britain
by Amazon